MW00893199

Also by Wilmont R. Kreis

The Allards Historical Series:
The New World
The Hunter
Peace and War
The Voyageur
The City in the Wilderness
The Medallion
The Witch
The Chief

Contemporary Medical Thrillers
The Corridor
The Pain Doc
The Labyrinth

Available in print and e-books from
Amazon.com

Visit the Author at
www.wilmontkreis.co
And on Facebook

FEARFUL PASSAGE NORTH

Wilmont R. Kreis

Port Huron, Michigan
2015

Copyright © 2015
By Wilmont R. Kreis
ISBN: 1505678927
EAN-13: 978-1505678925

Library of Congress control number: 2014922761

All rights reserved

PREFACE

When work on *The Allards Series* began several years ago, the goal was to see the history of a people through their eyes from their beginning in a new world and to tell their story as they might have told it through each new generation. This book of historical fiction is related to early events that occurred in Puritan New England and is centered on what is possibly the largest and most violent raid of the turbulent French and Indian Wars. Following the method used in *The Allards Series*, the events are seen through the eyes of a young girl living in a village then on the edge of civilization.

How would she react to an exotic outside suitor or to being violently torn from her simple, sedate life and forcibly marched to a strange place a world apart? Her experiences and perceptions of this change are shown as she is transported through the three great cultures of that period of time: New England Puritan, Native American, and French-Canadian Catholic—fearful passages all.

A cornucopia of academic work exists on this era, and a number of sources are listed at the end. In developing this novel, I have tried to remain faithful to commonly accepted "facts." But as with *The Allards Series,* my imagination has filled in the blanks. Again, this is a work of *historical fiction,* and its contents should not be cited without checking the facts.

As with the Allards Series, I will discuss and answer any questions on my blog, both at www.wilmontkreis.com, and on Facebook. Enjoy.

For those who study the past

Hoping only to repeat the good

Acknowledgements

It takes more than an author to create a book, and since beginning several years ago, I have relied heavily on the support and encouragement of others, who bring their own individual skills and knowledge to the project. Susanna Defever has been my teacher, editor, critic and cheerleader, always urging me to do it again, but this time better. Carrie Mclean's technical talent with her computer skills, website creation and networking are valued along with her map and cover design.

Finally, I am forever indebted to my wonderful and patient wife, Susan, nurse turned healthcare attorney and voracious reader of books, for her encouragement and honest advice without which I would never have written a book, and for all the evenings she has quietly returned to her reading, understanding when I disappear up the stairs to answer the call of the muse.

www.wilmontkreis.com

Spanish civilization crushed the Indian; English civilization scorned and neglected him; French civilization embraced and cherished him.
—Francis Parkman

The fearful passage of their death-mark'd love…
—William Shakespeare*: Romeo and Juliet*

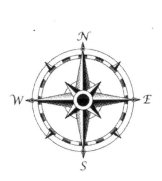

X

Fearful Passage North

March 2, 1704: Connecticut River Valley—Day 3

Cold—all she knew was cold. The horrific events of the past three days had faded into the maze of her memory. The only thing remaining was the unbearable chill. The first day had been equally frigid, but that had been masked by terror. Savage yelps answered by screams from the village, fires, shooting, utter chaos had numbed her to the icy air. Vaguely recalling her *master* placing the strap around her neck and pulling her along, she struggled to keep up as Andrew had once told her she must, stumbling occasionally, sometimes over a body, often a child. In her panic she could not even recognize them. She had seen her mother stumble, and the *master* who held her mother's leash struck her with his ax causing her to sink quietly to her knees as blood poured forth. Forbidden even to react, Lizzie was forced to step over her body.

That day the snow had been deep and hard. Had a path not been formed by the savages in the lead, walking would have been impossible, still it was so demanding that she maintained some warmth. That afternoon they had crossed the river where the Indians made camp. Her master threw her into a small tent where she cowed in a ball. Although she realized she had soiled herself, there was nothing to be done. When morning finally came, she could neither recall sleeping nor being awake.

Her master gave her a piece of dried meat to chew as he replaced her strap and yanked her along to the path. The day was warmer, turning the snow to deep slush, making it even more difficult to navigate. The freezing rain that began to fall increased her misery. That night she was given another morsel and roughly pushed into the makeshift tent.

On the third morning, she was assigned a new master, older than the first savage. He, too, put the strap around her neck but merely led her, tugging only if she wasn't keeping up. The pace was greater that day, the distance longer, so by early afternoon, she was actually drenched in sweat, but as the sun disappeared beneath the clouds, the temperature dropped dramatically. Soon her clothes grew stiff from ice as the cold became intolerable. When they stopped, her new master gave her a morsel of food before he began to assemble the simple tent. As she chewed the leathery substance, shivering out of control, he turned to her and began to remove his clothes. She was too frozen to think of averting her eyes. Soon he was naked but for a curious medallion which hung about his neck on a leather cord. He motioned and pulled on her dress, obviously suggesting she

2

disrobe as well. Realizing she had no choice, she began to shed her ice-covered garments. When she, too, was naked, she was too cold to care as he uttered the first words spoken all day, *"Agnauiañn keserañdé,"* he said softly, pointing to her, then to himself. He had no way of knowing Andrew had taught her some Abenaki words. She thought they might mean, *share warm.*

Pointing to a deerskin he had opened in the small shelter, he indicated that she lie down on it. She fell curling into a naked fetal ball facing the wall. After he entered the tent and closed the opening, he lay beside her. Cuddling like spoons, he embraced her, putting his calloused hand on her left breast. She knew she could not protest, but when she felt his heat, she understood his statement. She could also feel his member against her back. Suddenly the cold subsided and she began to wonder what atrocity awaited her until she heard the rumble. Gunfire in the distance? Thunder? It couldn't be. Finally she realized it was loud snoring. Closing her eyes, she soon joined him in sleep.

Deerfield

A - Deerfield River
B - Green River
C - Common Fence
D - Town Road
E - House Lots
F - Planting Fields
G - North Meadow
H - Stockade

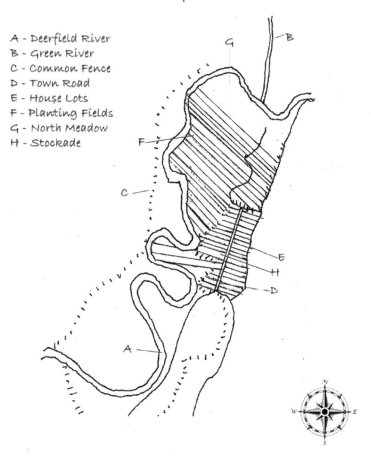

PART ONE—DEERFIELD

Chapter One

April, 1696: Northampton to Deerfield Road

Let's go, girl," she encouraged softly as she hastened her pace while loosely holding the rope. "We can't let the boys pass you with those silly pigs." Bianca would follow Lizzie anywhere. The rope around the cow's neck was only to make Lizzie's father happy.

Spring always emerged slowly in New England, like a sleeping giant slowly escaping his slumber. It was only on rare days such as today that the giant quickened his pace as the bright sunshine warmed the earth and the gentle breezes did not force him to pull his cloak against the chill. Lizzie loved springtime, but then she loved the outdoors at all times, greatly preferring it to indoor activities such as sewing, spinning, cleaning, and cooking that women were expected to do.

As she coaxed Bianca to keep up with the wagon, her eyes penetrated the leafless forest allowing a splendid view of small woodland animals scurrying about, while birds labored frantically to ready their nests in anticipation of families soon to arrive. Only bright buds clung to the tree branches while early spring blooms of wildflowers crept out to cover the forest floor. To Lizzie's right flowed the peaceful Connecticut River. High, muddy and swifter than usual due to the snowmelt, it still remained relatively calm, only becoming turbulent as they approached the bend at the falls.

Here was the small town of Hatfield near the equally small mill where three local farmers had gathered and waved as her family passed on a journey to their new home. Once they were clear of the falls, her father brought the wagon to a stop. Standing to stretch, he announced, "Lizzie, you and the boys take the stock down for a drink. Sammy and I will bring the horse." Lizzie had little difficulty convincing Bianca to go to the river bank. She enjoyed caring for the cows, but now there was only Bianca. Although she had produced two calves in the past three years, Lizzie's father, Robert, had been forced to sell them to settle some of his mounting debt. Lizzie's two older stepbrothers soon caught up. The four sheep were no problem. Hamlet, the family hound, was in charge of them. The two brothers, however, were greatly burdened by the three recalcitrant pigs they led reluctantly on ropes. The boys would have much preferred to transport the porkers in the cart, but Robert had decreed they could not waste the cart on a second 15 mile traverse from their old farm in Northampton to the new home in Deerfield.

Once Bianca was settled, Lizzie went to help her father and five-year-old brother with the reluctant horse. Taking the reins from Robert, she said softly, "Come on, Gilgamesh," as the horse followed obediently. Her father had as much success with animals as he had with crops and money. Her mother, Sarah, sat in the cart's back seat with Lizzie's sixteen-year old sister, Mary, quietly doing simple needlework while trying to ignore the complaints of the caged chickens behind them. With wonderful curly blonde hair which occasionally escaped from her bonnet, Lizzie was as attractive and animated, as her older sister was plain and stern with straight brown locks that remained dutifully beneath her headpiece. Once the stock was hydrated, Lizzie simply slapped Bianca on the rump and the cow moved back onto the trail, while she helped her father return the horse to its harness.

Eventually the wide Connecticut River made an easterly bend to disappear along with the main road to the east of a hilly range known as Pocumtuck Ridge where a poorly painted sign pointed out a smaller path to the northwest labeled *Pocumtuck.* Someone had drawn a line through this word, printing below it, *Deerfield.* Soon they arrived at the straight, mile-long town road running north and south along the top of a similarly long, narrow plateau. Both sides of the road were divided into ribbon-like farm lots, many holding a small log house facing the street with a barn in back. Near the center of the road was a stockade of cedar posts forming an enclosure for at least ten of the homes. Lizzie had seen this type of structure in Northampton, built as protection against Indian raids. As the road passed through the stockade, they entered through the south gate only to exit through the north gate a few moments later. Lizzie followed the cart with Bianca in lock-step. Occasionally she turned to smile and wave, taunting her red-faced stepbrothers as they struggled to get the uncooperative three pigs to their new home.

Approaching the north end of the road, Robert came to a halt. "This one is ours," he announced. The single-story log house was very much like those of the neighbors and set on the western side of the road, gently angled to face more sunny southern exposure. Robert gave the order, "First, let us bring our belongings inside. Then, Sarah, you, Mary and Sammy can settle the pigs and chickens in back. Lizzie, the boys and I will take the cart and the rest of the stock out to the meadow to graze." Robert was pleased they had left Northampton early, arriving with enough remaining sunlight to get settled, but then he had other motives for leaving their former home before sunrise.

As she entered the house, Sarah was overwhelmed by phantoms. When the cart pulled away, she told Mary, "Take Sammy out to the barn, I'll join you soon." After all this time, little had changed since Zeke and the neighbors had built her dream—a dream that crashed as suddenly as it had begun. Two years after their marriage in 1668, she and Zechariah Field—always called *Zeke,* decided to leave Northampton for the farthest reaches of New England Frontier—Deerfield. Here her hard-working spouse prospered, while her two boys, Ebenezer, called Ben, and John, called Johnny, were born. Life was fine until that fateful day in 1674 when neighbors brought Zeke's lifeless body home. No one had witnessed it, but they theorized he had been murdered in a small, random Indian raid.

Faced with no husband and two babies—Ben was two and Johnny six-months, she had no option but to return to her late father's Northampton Inn now run by her stepmother. The old Deerfield house, which Sarah still owned, had been rented out, but her renters had given up and left in the fall. So Sarah Webb-Field-Price was back where she had been 22 years before—the end of the earth. But now she was older and weary—and no longer in love.

Chapter Two

When the men and Lizzie returned from the field, the home crew had managed to secure the pigs in their pen and the chickens in their coop, while Sarah had a pot of porridge boiling on the fire. As she called them to the table, she confessed, "I did not make the porridge. Our young neighbor, Mrs. Hawks, brought it over." She had decided not to share that it was young Thankful Hawks' father-in-law who had brought Sarah's young husband's body home from the field more than twenty years before.

They sat, said the blessing, and began to dine. Ben claimed through his first mouthful, "Not as good as yours, Ma."

Sarah smiled, "Thank you, Son, but it was a kind gesture, and Mrs. Hawks *is* quite young."

Lizzie, who knew enough to swallow before speaking, added, "The fields are wonderful, Mother, they go all the way back…"

Sarah silenced her talkative daughter with a stare and declared, "Let the men speak, child."

Ben continued. "We met our neighbor, Mr. Stebbins. He said we can use his plow if we plow some of his land. So me and Johnny," referring to his younger brother, "will start tomorrow, and as soon as I finish our plot, I'll start on plowing Mr. Stebbins' and Johnny will start to prepare our field to be ready for corn as soon as the weather permits." Fortunately among the items Robert had managed to salvage from the Northampton farm were a few sacks of seed.

This time Ben swallowed before adding, "Mr. Stebbins, he's a Ben, like me, but Benoni. He has this great bull. Mr. Stebbins says he's well-hung, and the cows can't get enough of him…"

His mother interrupted with a maternal frown, "Ben!"

"Well, Ma, that's what he said. Anyway, he says he allows the bull to mount whoever. It keeps the village in calves and the bull satisfied."

"Ebenezer Field!"

Ben knew the use of his proper name signaled time to change the subject. "Our field is large and looks ready to plow. Right, Johnny?"

Two years his brother's junior, John Field, who was equally strong and attractive, and the more thoughtful of the two, added simply, "We'll be up and plowing at first light."

* * *

Just before dawn, the Price's psychic rooster crowed and was answered by his local comrades. Lizzie was the first up

11

and dressed, ready to go to the barn and milk Bianca before breakfast. Larger than the barn they had rented in Northampton, this structure would accommodate growth. Finishing the milking, she heard commotion in a corner. On inspection she found an unusually large mother cat nursing a new litter. "I guess we needn't fear mice," she said, stooping to pet the mother's head without interrupting her meal service. "I think I shall call you Gwendolyn."

Taking the milking bucket, she returned to the house where her mother and Mary were preparing breakfast. Like the barn, Zeke Field's house was larger than their quarters in Northampton, although it had changed little from the log structure with mud caulking that Zeke and the neighbors had built. Its floor had been replaced with new boards and it boasted two windows in front with a small one in back to provide a view of the barn. All had shutters and the south-facing front window had the home's sole luxury, a glass pane added and left in place by the previous tenant. The main room held a fireplace that served to heat the home and do the cooking. There were a few rudimentary chairs and a table with benches that could hold all seven members of Sarah's brood. A bedroom was in back and two small lofts in the corner rafters had been added by Zeke, one for his boys and one for the girls he had hoped to produce but never did.

The boys appeared along with the food and settled in to a quick breakfast. Robert was still in bed, but the children knew better than to comment. Once they were finished, Johnny rose. "We said we'd meet Mr. Stebbins first thing." He and Ben took their hats along with the lunch their mother had prepared and headed out to take Gilgamesh to plow, while Lizzie left to take Bianca to graze. As she headed north on the town road, the sun was just clearing the horizon where a small strip of cloud caused a majestic red sky in the east. Lizzie loved the outdoors as much as her sister detested it, making division of duties simple.

The walk to the meadow gave her an opportunity to get the lay of the land of her new home. Their farm lot ran west from the house toward the Deerfield River which curved like a serpent from the mountains to the west, turning north to run parallel to the town road before turning east again to join the larger Connecticut River and its journey south to the sea. A common-field fence enclosed all the lots used for larger crops such as corn and wheat. It was among these lots the boys had gone to plow. The unfenced meadow to the north was used for grazing, while the fence kept wildlife as well as grazing domestic animals out of the crops during the growing season yet would be used to enclose the grazing stock in the winter.

Once Bianca was settled in the meadow, Lizzie decided to investigate the Deerfield River. Banks on both sides were crowded by deciduous trees as the waterway snaked its way along. Both banks were low, making it simple to walk down to the river. Lizzie removed her shoes and tucked up her gray smock to wade in. The current was not strong and the water not as cold as she anticipated. Best of all, the river bed was sandy and easy to walk along. As the water cooled her feet, she wished she could submerge for a few seconds but realized that may be too risky. New England villages hardly approved of such activity. She returned to her shoes, and after reassuring Bianca she would return in the afternoon to take her back for milking, she left for home.

When she reached the house, Lizzie joined her mother and siblings turning the soil of the kitchen garden behind the home. After a brief lunch, she and Sammy returned to dig while Mary and her mother stayed to attend to more domestic tasks. Robert appeared at dinner to hear the boys extol the wonders of plowing. When he was seated, Ben said, "Pa, Mr. Stebbins said he was with you at Turner's Falls. He said two other men from here were there as well. I think a Mr. Nims and a Captain Wells."

Robert's interest peaked. "Yes, they were." Then he assured the boys he would be ready to work in the morning.

As the sun set, the girls crawled up to their loft. Lizzie jumped playfully onto her mattress, a homespun sack stuffed with straw. "Ouch! Something's hard."

Unsympathetic, Mary commented, "Serves you right for jumping."

Lizzie felt the mattress carefully, discovering the offending object, but simply replied. "Yes, you're right." She was certain she knew what it was but also knew she should wait until her prudish sister was not around before she investigated further.

Chapter Three

The day began as gloomy as the previous day had been beautiful when Lizzie and Bianca began their trek to the meadow below an ominous dark gray sky. They were not alone today as another girl Lizzie's age led her two cows toward the meadow. *Led* was perhaps an inaccurate term as the girl struggled constantly with the ropes around the animals' necks. Her two charges were as cantankerous as Bianca was cooperative. Lizzie soon caught up to them. "Hello."

The exasperated girl looked over, "Oh, hello. You must be with the new family."

"Yes, I'm Lizzie Price."

"Lizzie?"

"For Elizabeth."

The girl stopped tugging long enough to say, "I'm Sarah Belden. I'm glad you're not a Sarah—half the girls in town are Sarahs."

"Oh?"

Returning to her struggle, Sarah replied, "Yes, we use middle names to keep it straight, but I don't have a middle name so they call me Sarah-Bee—like honeybee." Lizzie smiled as she began to walk, followed by the obedient Bianca. "How do you get your cow to follow like that?" Sarah-Bee asked. "Can you get mine to do it?"

"Maybe." Lizzie rubbed the top of their snouts. "What are their names?"

"They don't have names."

"Oh. My cow is Bianca, maybe they'll follow her." She started ahead, with Bianca behind her and the two others followed peacefully.

"I can't believe it!" said Sarah-Bee. "But why do you call your cow, Bianca?"

"It's from a play by William Shakespeare."

"Who?"

"He was an Englishman who wrote plays—it's a long story."

"But I meant why did you name your animal?"

"I like to name all the animals. I think it makes us better friends."

Sarah-Bee merely shrugged, while Lizzie smiled, asking, "Do you do this often?"

"No, I hate it. My older brother, Nathan, usually does it, but he had to help Pa plow today."

Lizzie confessed, "I like the animals."

Sarah-Bee made a face, "I don't. I'd rather sew."

Changing the subject, Lizzie explained, "I have two older brothers. They're both plowing today."

"What do they plant?"

"Corn."

"My pa grows tobacco."

Lizzie was puzzled, "I didn't know you grew tobacco here."

"My pa does. He sells all he can grow. It smells odd. At first I didn't like it, but it grows on you. It's a good thing because at the end of harvest he dries it and puts it up in the barn. We'll have a whole crate of it."

Free of the burden of cow-pulling, Sarah-Bee became very talkative, and by the time they reached the meadow, Lizzie had heard all about her family with their eight children as well as town gossip and details on the other girls—and boys their age. Sarah-Bee looked over the meadow where the town sheep, having spent the night, were busy grazing while the local cows, having been milked, were coming to feed for the day. "Most of the animal work is done by the boys," she explained, "except when they are too busy—like today. The only other girl who does it regularly is Abigail Stebbins—she's our age. We call her Abby."

"I think my father knows Mr. Stebbins."

"There are two. They are brothers," Sarah-Bee instructed, "Mr. Benoni has a house inside the stockade and Mr. John Stebbins' family lives outside the stockade like our families."

"I think my father knows Mr. Benoni."

"I like him, he's funny—the other men are more serious. Abby's father is John. You'll see her out here most mornings." Sarah looked at the sky, "I better go. Ma doesn't like me to tarry, and I think it's going to rain. Thank you for the lesson in cow control."

Lizzie laughed, "You're welcome. I think I'll walk back by the river."

Making her way down to the bank, she removed her shoes and hiked up her dress. She walked a short way in the

17

sand before the lightning struck and thunder rolled. *Guess I'd better get home.* The downpour started before she was out of the meadow, but that didn't bother Lizzie. She had made a friend.

That evening when it was still light after dinner, Robert and the boys sat and smoked, discussing the progress in the fields, while Mary and Sarah set to spinning and sewing, which gave Lizzie the opportunity to go to the loft. Feeling about the straw-filled mattress, she found the hard mass and reached through a small opening. As she had hoped, it was a book!

Even more than the outdoors and animals, Lizzie loved to read. Her educated mother had taught her young, and she excelled in the Northampton school until she was 10 years old, the end of schooling for girls. The people referred to—in a pejorative fashion—as *Puritans* by the Anglicans, referred to themselves as *Independents*. Many of them felt the Bible was the only book suitable for reading.

Fortunately, her mother had some books and would also tell young Lizzie stories she had read in her youth, but this was the first volume that would be Lizzie's alone. On careful inspection she saw it was not a printed book, rather a handwritten journal. She paged through, finding only strange words. *French?* Apart from the script there were numerous line drawings. Eventually she tore herself away and cached the journal. She knew it was time to return to the family before she was discovered by her straight-laced sister who agreed if anything were to be read, it should be the Bible.

Chapter Four

Once Saturday's work was done, Sara organized the family for the weekly bath. "Cleanliness is next to Godliness," she would exclaim whenever protests were made. "And tomorrow will be our first day at Meeting. I expect us to make a fine impression."

Sarah set her largest wooden tub in a corner of the main room, hung a blanket to provide some modicum of privacy and heated a large cauldron of water. The girls were first. Prudish Mary insisted she be alone with her mother. Not so shy, Lizzie undressed as soon as her sister was finished. While Sarah put Lizzie's clothes in a second cauldron to soak, her naked daughter climbed into the tub. Sarah then dipped a pitcher in the heated cauldron and poured it over Lizzie, observing, "Elizabeth, I believe you are fully a woman now." Lizzie nodded. She had started her *monthlies* six months earlier, and she was also impressed—and pleased, at the changes in her figure.

Sarah handed her a bar of lye soap. "Scrub up. Then squat in the tub to do your privates."

Lizzie complied while smiling inwardly at her mother who still felt it necessary to explain the same routine they had followed weekly for almost 14 years. When she stood, her mother poured a second pitcher for rinse. Once Lizzie was dry, she took her clean *good* clothes from the chair and redressed. Each family member had two sets of clothes. Both the same, gray homespun dresses with a white apron and bonnet for the girls and rough trousers and a shirt for the boys, the only difference was age and wear. The better set was *good* for Meeting, weddings and other special occasions.

Before she left the bathing chamber, her mother put her hands on her shoulders. "Stand up straight and let me take a look at you, child." Lizzie obeyed as Sarah continued. "You always were a very handsome girl, Lizzie Price, and now you are becoming a beautiful woman." Sarah ran her hand through her daughter's wavy blonde hair with just a hint of her father's red. It always looked good even though it was generally covered with her traditional bonnet. Her skin was smooth, her teeth were straighter than most, and her eyes—a piercing green so that people, seeing her for the first time, could not stop looking at her.

Sarah continued, "I was a nice looking girl once. Often that is not easy, and sometimes it is almost a curse. You must be more careful around men than the others. Even in a Christian community as ours, you must always be on the guard around men." Lizzie nodded in her typical *yes mother* style and abandoned the bathing chamber to her brothers.

Once the girls were clean, Sarah proceeded to the boys who protested her presence and to which she always replied, "You were naked when I bore you. Nothing has changed."

The girls had retreated to the loft where Lizzie noticed she could actually watch from her perch in the rafters. She had often peeked in the more crowded conditions of Northampton and enjoyed both the view as well as excitement of the prohibited act. She also realized the boys likely had pulled the same shenanigans. This thought also gave her a forbidden thrill.

* * *

Sunday morning Sarah assembled her brood and marched them south on the town road. She even prevailed on her wayward husband to make an appearance for the sake of the children. Whereas most early Massachusetts residents or their ancestors had come with families from England to avoid what they saw as the excesses of the Anglican and Catholic churches, a few, like Robert Price, came as a single Englishman looking to find his fortune. He had also come to avoid certain unhappy financial circumstances in the old world.

By far the largest building in the village, the town hall sat in the center of the stockade. It served as meeting house on Sunday as well as the place of town meetings and the older boys' school. The boys were pleased to see a familiar face waiting on the town hall steps. "Well, lads, how nice to see you so bright and early for Meeting."

Ben, who escorted his mother, extended his hand and said, "Mr. Stebbins, this is my mother, my brother, Sammy, and sisters, Mary and Lizzie. I believe you know Pa and Johnny."

Benoni Stebbins was a head shorter than the two Field boys and a bit huskier. At forty-one he still had all of his dark curly hair and most of his teeth, which he constantly displayed with a devilish grin and a glint in his eye. Although he was a selectman of the town council and on the congregation board, he was hardly the most religious member of the congregation. In fact, he had been cited periodically in his youth for various mischievous acts. But here at the ends of civilization, a man of honor and trust was highly prized even if he did have a sense of humor.

Shaking Robert's hand, Benoni said, "I told your boys of our days together with Turner and the battle of the falls. I think we should get Nims and Wells and have a pint some night at the tavern. Whadda ya say?" Robert agreed as Benoni motioned them into the building. "Come, I'll introduce you to Mr. Williams."

Rev. John Williams was chatting with an older couple. Wearing the simple black robe of a cleric, he was taller than Benoni and, in spite of the robe, it was clear he favored his food. Once he had dismissed the couple, he said a few gratuitous words to Robert and Sarah, shook the boys' hands, nodded to the girls, and proceeded into the gathering congregation.

Ten years earlier, Williams had graduated from Harvard College. His wife, Eunice, came from a line of notable clergymen including Increase and Cotton Mather. As a result, Williams could have had his pick of comfortable congregations around Boston but elected to take his work to the far reaches of the wilderness—Deerfield. He was 22 at the time.

His service was vintage Independent—very long. As Robert had once said in a lighter moment, "These sermons show you the real meaning of *eternity*." Williams would read endless passages from the Bible and lecture on morality, never missing the chance to call out the satanic

Papists and the devil worshipers of the Church of England. The attendants would walk down the aisle armed with a long stick with a feather on the end to tickle the nose of any so irreverent that they would fall asleep. Lizzie busied herself by counting the number of rows and average number seated in each row eventually calculating the capacity of the facility.

Mr. Stebbins had told them the population of the village, and as she suspected, the building would not accommodate everyone if they chose to come. This, she theorized, lay waste the theory that attendance was mandatory. Mr. Williams realized this and that in the real world, an emergency at home, a sick child, or, almost as bad, a sick animal would take precedence. Of course, there was always the occasional person who simply chose not to attend—her father being a classic example.

At noon the congregation was excused to return home for a midday meal following which they were to return for more reading and preaching. Lizzie also did not mind the passages chosen by Rev. Williams as they tended toward hellfire and damnation which she found more entertaining. Finally the congregation was dismissed and poured out into the sunlight where they could visit, giving the Price family more opportunity to meet the neighbors.

Chapter Five

Bianca had become accustomed to the new routine. Once situated in her familiar section of the north meadow, she began to graze and no longer attempted to follow Lizzie, who reassured her bovine friend, "I'll come get you at milking time."

Heading toward the river, Lizzie began her customary route home when she heard the roar. Turning, she saw the source. She had seen the bull from a distance, but this was her first close encounter. There was little question what the creature had in mind. As he stalked Bianca, Lizzie stepped instinctively toward her, stopped only by a tug on her shoulder.

"I don't believe it prudent to interfere with Charlemagne."

Lizzie had not noticed the young girl when she entered the meadow. As Lizzie regarded her with her mouth agape, the girl smiled, "You must be Lizzie."

"Uh—yes."

"Sarah-Bee told me to look for you. I'm Abby." Pointing to a nearby tree, she suggested, "Let's go over there. It's interesting to watch, but you mustn't get too close."

Raised on a farm, Lizzie was no stranger to mating animals, however she had never seen anything this impressive. When Abby judged them to be at a safe distance, Lizzie asked, "You call the bull Charlemagne?"

"Yes, he belongs to my Uncle Benoni, but I named him. Do you know about Charlemagne?"

Lizzie answered with confidence, "He was King of all Europe."

"Do you read?" the surprised Abby queried.

"Yes. My mother has books."

"I wish my mother did," Abby replied, "Mrs. Beaman, the school dame, gives me one on occasion. Most of the town only reads the Bible, but I like to read other things."

Lizzie explained, "So do I." As the bull gave out a loud groan and the cow squealed, she added with a frightened frown, "Oh, dear! Is he hurting her?"

"I don't think so, they always sound that way."

"You ladies learning anything?"

Both girls jumped. In the excitement they had not heard the cart approach. Turning, they saw a small wagon driven by a gentleman accompanied by a young boy. Once Abby had caught her breath, she said, "Oh, Uncle Benoni, you nearly scared us to death."

"Well, you were preoccupied—but I suppose it is better you learn from the cows rather than the boys. Abby, I see you have met Miss Price." Addressing Lizzie, he asked, "So, Miss Price, how do you find our 'City on the Hill,' as they used to say in Boston?"

"Like John Winthrop?"

25

Benoni's smile widened, surprised that this young country girl should know the origin of the phrase. "How did you know that?"

Lizzie looked demurely at her feet while secretly smiling that she had impressed the man. "I read sometimes. My mother's great-grandfather knew Mr. Winthrop. She told me they came to New England about the same time—though she said her great-grandfather did not care for him."

Benoni smiled again, "Some did not, I daresay."

Pointing to the young boy in his cart, he said, "This is my son, Bennie. Boy, why don't you go check those two cows I told you about? I think I'll visit a spell with the young ladies."

Benoni surveyed the clear spring sky and pointed to an old fallen tree. "Too fine a day for workin'. Let's go set a piece. Don't worry about gettin' back, just tell your Ma that old Benoni came by and made you stay for a visit." Once he had found his perch, he lit a pipe. Looking up to exhale, he continued, "I always take pleasure in youngsters like you two who ain't afraid to have some fun or don't mope around with their heads down 'cause some preacher told them that's what to do. Why, when I was young—younger than you two, some friends and I in Northampton paid an Indian to take us to Canada to join the fur traders. Course, we hardly got outta town before we was caught. Whipped us good, too." He turned to lift up his shirt to show the ancient lash scars on his back. "Still, it was a grand adventure."

"Anyhow, I moved here with my Pa when I wasn't much older than you. The town used to be called Pocumtuck, for the tribe that lived here in the old days. After the white man first come, the Pocumtuck were struck with the pox—most of 'em died, so when the government needed new land, the tribe had vacant land to sell. They're still around from time to time—real friendly."

Looking to Lizzie, he went on, "So we was livin' here when your Ma and her husband, Zeke Field, come. He was a hell of a fellah, Zeke. When they found him dead, they said it was Indians—but not Pocumtuck. The next year we formed a militia with Captain Turner. That's where I first met your pa, Robert Price." He removed the pipe long enough to spit before resuming, "We raided this group of tribes camped at the falls just north of here. Lot of folks died—on both sides..." He looked down sadly, "Just stupid."

Benoni stood to stretch and spit again, announcing, "Well, I guess I'll go find my boy and see what he's doin' with my cows. This story is too long and too good to tell all at once. I'll tell you more when we have another visit."

As he turned, Lizzie asked, "But, Mr. Stebbins, how do you know the good from the bad Indians?"

Turning back, he explained, "When you see 'em, you just know." Then he shrugged, "Trouble is, once you see 'em, it's too late." Looking up at the sun and wiping his brow with a kerchief, he added, "Gonna be a hot one. In the old days, I'd go jump in the creek."

As they watched the cart lumber back to the town road, Abby suggested, "He's right, let's go down to the river."

Frowning, Lizzie answered, "I shouldn't. My mother is expecting me home to work the garden."

"Don't worry. Just tell her we met my uncle. Everyone knows how he talks, and I'm certain she would not want you to be rude."

Reluctantly, Lizzie answered, "Well, maybe."

"Good!" said Abby, pulling her hand to lead her, "I have a *secret place*."

She led Lizzie to a great willow tree, then through dense underbrush emerging at the bank, where Abby confided, "This is *very* secret, *no one* comes here but me."

Lizzie carefully took off her shoes and hiked up her dress to wade in while Abby laughed, "I thought we were going *swimming.*" Lizzie looked with astonishment as Abby removed her white bonnet, shaking out her long, dark wavy locks and proceeding to undress. Once she was in the water, she called out. "This is wonderful! Come in!" Lizzie was immobile, causing Abby to laugh, "Must I turn around?"

Accepting the dare, Lizzie threw off her bonnet and quickly disrobed before entering the stream. The water was still chilly but was clearing of the snowmelt silt; she could almost see her feet on the wonderful sand bottom. Abby walked over, staring at Lizzie through her dark-brown eyes. "See that wasn't so difficult. If I looked as good as you, I would never be so shy." When Lizzie splashed water in her face, Abby returned the shot, launching a session of splashes and giggles. Eventually Abby announced, "I suppose we should go, even Uncle Benoni doesn't talk this long."

Dressing quickly, they returned to the meadow where halfway to the town road they heard, "My word, what are you girls doing so far from home?"

In the heat of their conversation, they had failed to see Reverend Williams wandering along, his head covered with a wide-brimmed hat, reading his Bible. "I came down to stroll and find the Lord's inspiration. But should *you* not be home helping your dear mothers with the household duties?"

Lizzie was speechless, but Abby came to the rescue. "Yes, Reverend, but unfortunately the men of the families were so busy with the planting, they had no time for the livestock. In addition, my uncle was out and wanted to visit with us. You know how he likes to talk—we felt we could not be so rude as to excuse ourselves."

Williams did not seem totally convinced, but Lizzie found her tongue, adding in a docile voice, "Reverend, my dear sister Mary's health does not abide with outdoor work. I have always thought it must be God's will that I do whatever men's work needs doing."

Williams grunted and excused himself. Once they were clear of him Abby giggled, "I think *God's will* convinced him."

Lizzie began to relax. "I was worried he had been watching us swim."

Abby laughed out loud. "I am certain he would have enjoyed it, but I doubt his girth would allow him to descend the bank."

As Williams watched the two girls giggle their way up to the road, he was reminded of his own youth and the wonders of a warm care-free day. Although determined to keep his flock on the straight and narrow, he realized this congregation consisted of many second and third generation New Englanders living in a time and place much changed from the Old World. Life was different, as were the issues germane to their existence—especially here, at the ends of the frontier. These people did not come to Deerfield for religion. They came because it was one of the few remaining places they could have a farm and make a life. John Williams didn't necessarily like this fact, but there it was, and he had pledged to do his best.

When she arrived home, Lizzie was singing. Not only had she found another friend, but she had discovered a soul mate. The next Sunday the Reverend did speak at some length on the importance and sanctity of *women's work* and the folly of idling away the hours.

Chapter Six

Sitting just north of the stockade along the eastern side of the town road, the log building could be just another house but for the roughly-painted sign swinging gently in the July breeze—*TAVERN.* The door opened into a simple room with tables, chairs and a counter, behind which were two smaller rooms, one a guest chamber for the occasional visitor to Deerfield requiring lodging and a second, the residence of the current innkeeper, a man known only as Potter and his maiden sister, Lenore.

Robert sat at his usual table and signaled Lenore who could have scarcely missed him as he was the first patron of the evening. "The usual, Mr. Price?" He simply nodded as she continued, "You're a bit early tonight."

"Yes, I'm meeting some other gentlemen." Normally Robert came on Saturday night or nights after official town

31

meetings when the establishment was busy enough that he could find someone who would pick up his tab as a courtesy to a new neighbor. However, tonight, he had been invited by the members of his old militia company, and he knew he could come early for a few drinks that would be added to the group bill which one of his former comrades in arms would graciously pay.

Returning with a tankard of ale, Lenore asked, "Who are you meeting?"

Robert smiled. He was still handsome and had a wonderful smile that women, especially desperate single women, loved. "Members of my old regiment, we fought at Turner's Falls."

"Oh, I've heard about that. Were you injured?"

"Yes," Robert lied, "and decorated."

Lenore gave him her most adoring smile, "How heroic."

As he watched her walk away, he thought back to his first day at the Northampton Inn when still in uniform, he met the young, beautiful, widowed stepdaughter of the owner. He had her in the palm of his hand the first night and would have settled for free drinks and a brief liaison, but when he found that Sarah Field was respectable and had some means, he played the long game.

The marriage had worked out well as long as her money could cover his lifestyle and his debts, so he did not need to move on as he had previously in Sussex, England, then in Boston and later in rural Connecticut. The Sarah financial arrangement had worked for 18 years, and only now had things become desperate enough to abandon Northampton for Deerfield where Robert believed he could last as long as the Field boys worked for him and the citizens would extend him credit.

"Lost in thought, soldier?"

Shaken from his daydream, Robert stood, "Hello, Godfrey."

Both shoemaker and farmer, Godfrey Nims was a few years younger than Robert. He ordered a tankard while Robert ordered his second. Soon Captain Jonathan Wells appeared and on his heels, Benoni Stebbins. Once they were all served, and Robert served again, they each gave Robert a brief personal history update. Even though all three were younger than Robert, they outranked him in Turner's militia and had established themselves now as leaders in the community.

Robert gave his résumé, making it as respectable as possible. Interestingly, although everyone was under 45, all but Robert had already been widowed once, and all four were now married to women who were themselves widows. Such was the precarious nature of life on the New England frontier. Once histories were traded, Stebbins said, "You know, Price, we have our own militia here in Deerfield to protect our families against another possible Indian uprising. We could use a man with your experience."

Robert looked down, then finished his current tankard before replying, "I appreciate the invitation, Benoni, but I'm afraid after my injury and all, I'd be of little use."

"Well, think on it. Jonathan Wells here is our captain, and we train regularly inside the stockade."

"I will, Benoni. I will." Seeing that the party was winding down, Robert excused himself so as not to risk being stuck with the bill.

As Robert walked out the door, Captain Wells said, "Well, Benoni, no surprises here. I wondered why you even invited him. If Major Turner had not been killed at the falls, he probably would have shot Price for cowardice."

"I know the man is no prize, Jonathan, but Nims and I knew Mrs. Price's first husband, Zeke Field—as fine a man as we have ever met. His widow, Sarah, was and still is a gracious lady and her children are all people of worth, just like Zeke. I think they need our support."

Captain Wells stood to go. "Well, I'll help where I can, but I for one am pleased he did not take your offer."

Robert had strolled across the town road to a bench where he sat in the dark until his friends and the other customers had left the tavern. Then he returned to find Lenore cleaning up and lured her into the rental room for a brief but enthusiastic tryst. Although not particularly attractive, Lenore had other qualities. She was allegedly barren, desperate, enthusiastic and willing to overlook Robert's bar tabs whenever she could.

Chapter Seven

But Ma, Bianca hasn't been milked, and I can't leave her as long as it will take to go to Reverend Williams' lecture."

Sarah was at her wits' end. First, she could never get her husband to attend Meeting, and now her daughter had an excuse. "Lizzie, how will this look?"

"Ma, I saw Sarah-Bee and she said her father was not in from the field. So they will be going late, and she said she will stop for me. I can milk Bianca, dress and attend with the Beldens. Mr. Belden is a council member and they won't be critical of him."

Sarah sighed, still not convinced. "Very well, Elizabeth. But make *certain* you arrive with the Beldens."

Lizzie knew she was in trouble when her mother used her formal name. "Yes, ma'am, you can count on me."

Sarah gathered the rest of her children and headed to the town hall. She had no idea where her husband was. At the same time, Lizzie hustled to the barn to be greeted by Gwendolyn, the cat. Her litter had gone its own way and Gwendolyn had regained her pre-litter strength. A truly giant feline, she could bring in the largest rat without difficulty. Lizzie often wondered if she could bring down a raccoon. Purring, she rubbed against Lizzie's leg. Lizzie, in turn, scratched her head, "I don't have time, Gwen. If I don't get to the lecture on time, Ma will skin me alive."

Beginning to milk Bianca, she heard Hamlet barking in back. *I hope that fox isn't back, that's all I need.* Finishing as quickly as she could, she turned to put the bucket out of the way. When she turned back, she saw what had troubled Hamlet, and Benoni Stebbins' words flooded back to her, "You'll know when you see them—problem is, then it's too late."

His face was painted black, his body decorated in red, his hair shaved to leave only a sharp stripe down the crown of his head. "Those are Mohawk," Benoni had told her, "They are the worst."

She tried to scream but could not. She turned to run, but he grabbed her wrist with an iron grip. Suddenly his face went pale as he winced in pain. Releasing her arm, he tried to reach his back where Lizzie could see Gwendolyn clinging to his red-painted skin with her vicious front claws. Lizzie used those precious seconds of freedom to grab the spade and hit the savage on the forehead, knocking him to the ground. As he tried to get up, she prepared for another swing. Looking into his dark eyes, she realized he was probably no older than she. Suddenly he turned and fled the barn. Gwendolyn finally released him when well away from the barn and returned to Lizzie as the triumphant warrior.

While the cat sat cleaning the blood from her paws, Lizzie whispered, "Good work, Gwendolyn, but now what do I do? If I stay here, they may come back. They say if you run out, they catch you." She looked carefully out the barn door. Seeing no one, she thought, *I need to get to the meeting and warn the others.* Carefully she made it to her house. *If I go to the town hall, I'll be exposed for a long way.* Then she thought, *Of course! The Beldens. They are only a few houses away. Sarah-Bee's father will know what to do.*

Lizzie ran cautiously from house to house, avoiding the street while attempting to stay hidden in the high grass and bushes. Beldens' house was quiet. *Good. The Indians must not have been here.* She sprinted the last few yards to the house but tripped on something in the tall grass. Pulling herself up, she saw the blood—then the body. *Daniel!*

Daniel Belden was three years her senior. She knelt, examining his head where he had been hit, crushing his skull. Leaving her lifeless friend, she continued and found young John, only seven years old, with a similar fatal wound. Looking about she saw nothing else. *I must warn the town!*

Shaking with fear, she returned to her routine, running house to house, this time toward the stockade. Attempting to be as fast but also as invisible as possible, it seemed forever until she reached the open north gate of the stockade. Once inside and feeling safer, she sprinted to the town hall, bursting through the door.

Reverend Williams was droning on while his congregation, most of whom had worked all morning in the fields, tried valiantly to stay awake. Those conscious enough to hear, turned to see who had so rudely rushed through the door. At the same time, Reverend Williams began to admonish Lizzie when she screamed. "Indians! They've killed the Beldens!"

As the entire congregation jumped to its feet in panic, the militia took over. Captain Jonathan Wells stood on the pew shouting orders. Soon some semblance of order returned. As was their routine, militia members had brought their muskets which had been sequestered at the entry. Captain Wells, Benoni Stebbins and Godfrey Nims with a few others shouldered their arms and performed their studied drill of securing the stockade gates while inspecting for intruders. Finding none, they gathered at the north gate where Wells asked Lizzie, "Where did you see them?"

Emboldened by the men in arms, she stood tall and declared, "They are at the Belden house. I can show you!" Wells selected a few armed men to accompany them, and they retraced Lizzie's path to the Belden house, being ever alert for savages. Once there, Lizzie showed them Daniel and John's bodies before they began a careful search of the area. Lizzie followed Benoni, and eventually the group found the bodies of Samuel, age 9 and young Thankful, only one year old. Benoni took Lizzie to the barn where they heard some commotion in the loft.

Benoni had his musket poised when a small head appeared, "Please don't shoot me," whined six-year-old Abigail Belden. Lizzie rushed to her, "Abigail, did you see Sarah-Bee?"

Between sobs, she replied, "She brought me in here and hid me in the loft."

Lizzie heard some knocking from a large wooden chest. They opened it carefully to find her friend covered in tobacco. Sarah-Bee pulled herself upright, covered in the leaves of the dark, odiferous plant, and sobbed, "I didn't know where else to hide. Where are the others?"

Stebbins put his hand on her head, "We are looking for them, dear." He turned to Lizzie and produced his flint-lock pistol from his belt. "Do you remember when I showed you and Abby how to fire this?"

Lizzie nodded like a soldier, "Yes, sir."

"Well, then, you hold it and stay here with these two. I'll be back—but don't shoot me, only Indians."

Soon he was back carrying a body. "We thought this one was dead, but he's still alive. Lizzie, keep an eye on him while I help the others." He laid young Samuel in the straw and left again while Lizzie inspected the boy. He had a bad blow to the head where Benoni had wrapped a bandage. He was unconscious but breathing.

It seemed an eternity before Benoni returned with Godfrey Nims carrying a woman's body. Sarah-Bee shrieked as Nims laid her mother's lifeless body on the straw. Soon all three girls were wailing hysterically. Benoni took Lizzie firmly by the shoulders. "Stop it! Let her girls grieve—but *you* must remain calm. It's vital that you maintain a clear head. Do you understand?"

Lizzie nodded slowly, stifling a sob as he continued, "It would appear that the three children and their mother are the only dead. We suspect they have taken Mr. Belden, Nathan and the other girl your age—Hester, is it?"

Lizzie nodded, "Yes, sir." Then she stood straight and dried her eyes. "I'm all right, Mr. Stebbins. You can count on me now."

"Good, I knew you could do it. We are sending a group of the men north to see if they can find a trail. The rest will bring the bodies, and we will go with them to the stockade. "Can you still carry my pistol?"

"Yes, sir!"

With armed men in front and back of the sad parade, they made their way back to the north gate. While a group of women took the bodies to prepare for burial and Samuel was taken to Benoni's house to be nursed by Mrs. Stebbins, Godfrey Nims announced a meeting in the town hall for all adults. Lizzie asked, "May I please come to the meeting, Mr. Stebbins?"

He smiled for the first time that day, answering, "Yes, young lady, I think you have earned the right."

Once the townspeople were convened, Nims took the floor. "As of now we proclaim martial law as we did following the 1694 raid. The militia and town council shall make all decisions. This shall continue until we believe we are secure. All men working the fields shall bring their arms and we will have some militia watching the farms during the day.

"The stockade gates shall remain guarded and all persons shall be inside the walls by nightfall. Citizens who live outside the walls shall be billeted in the town hall or in homes lying within the stockade. The council will post a list of families and where they are to spend the night."

After questions, the town was excused to return to the waning daylight inside the security of the stockade. Once outdoors, Lizzie returned Benoni's pistol, asking, "Mr. Stebbins, what will become of those taken?"

Stebbins invited her to sit with him on the bench by the large sycamore tree standing guard over the town hall. "I was taken in a raid in '77. We were marched to Canada. Luckily, I escaped, but the others were placed with the French. Eventually English representatives secured their release and they returned home."

"How long did that take?"

"Within a year or so as I recall."

Not finding this reassuring, Lizzie stood, "I suppose I should find my family."

Benoni handed her the pistol. "Why don't you keep it for now? Give it to your Ma for protection."

Lizzie put on her best serious-adult face, "Yes, sir!"

Benoni excused himself and walked away, hoping she would not discover the one detail he had omitted—that Sergeant Plympton, who also been taken in 1677, had been burned at the stake. As Lizzie returned to the town hall to learn where she was to be billeted, she had a certain confidence in her gait—Lizzie Price was no longer a child.

Chapter Eight

As the townspeople were making billeting arrangements, an oblivious Robert Price wandered out the tavern door, squinting at the late afternoon sunlight. While his neighbors were at the lecture, Robert had taken advantage of the fact both his family and Potter were attending, leaving him and Lenore alone for an afternoon of drinking and debauchery—at Potter's expense.

Finding the streets vacant, he laughed, thinking, *I guess old Reverend Williams was particularly full of hot air today.* Seeing no other option, he began to stroll north to his vacant house. Once home he thought he would take advantage of the silence for a nap. As he entered the bedroom, however, he heard Hamlet barking in the barn. He peered out the small back window and gasped.

It seems the young Mohawk had thought better of his retreat from the crazed feline, realizing he should return to steal something so as not to return empty-handed and disgraced. Seeing nothing but worn farming tools in the barn, he decided to try the house. Turning, he saw his last sight on earth as Robert blew a large, close-range hole through his chest. Robert was as shocked as the young Indian as he suddenly felt sick, vomiting his liquid lunch onto the barn floor. In spite of his boasts in taverns, Robert had never fired his gun other than in target practice. Whenever Turner's militia came upon adversity, Robert was first to retreat. Once he regained his senses, he realized there could be more hostiles around. Circling to the front of the house, he came upon Captain Wells and a few local militiamen returning from their futile hunt for savages.

"Price! What are you doing? Why aren't you inside the stockade?"

Robert turned his dazed expression to Wells and simply answered, "I... I just shot an Indian."

The men rushed to the back to find the young brave. Wells turned to his men, "You two carry him, we'll take him back to the stockade—good work, Price." It had been many years since Robert had heard those words.

While they marched back to the stockade, they asked Robert for details which he provided. If Robert could do one thing, it was embellish a story. By evening, the unlikely Robert Price was town hero.

* * *

The first two weeks of martial law were chaotic. Each morning the militia would declare the town secure before the citizens could leave to tend their animals and crops. Although nerves were on edge, the presence of armed militiamen throughout the area was reassuring, although in truth, their training and skills were often marginal. Even Robert Price was persuaded to man the lines. Following dinner, the families would return to the stockade for the night. Conditions were extremely crowded to say the least, but various creative plans improved the circumstances. Young children and their parents were billeted in homes and the town hall. To make numbers manageable, the older children were camped in tents, boys on one end of the compound and girls on the other. They were all chaperoned, although some of the freer spirits occasionally crept away. In addition, some of the men wandered over to the nearby tavern in the evening.

Once Lizzie recovered from the shock of the attack, she found the compound with girls close to her age enjoyable as they began to forge new friendships. However, she remained concerned about her traumatized friend so she sought her new and first real adult friend.

"Mr. Stebbins, what's to become of Sarah-Bee?"

Benoni sat on a nearby bench to answer in his thoughtful and patient manner. "She'll be all right, Lizzie. She and her sister will live with one of the ladies who were close to her mother. The little girl is already improving and Sarah-Bee will eventually. She's good New England pioneer stock, like us—you'll see."

"What about Samuel?"

Benoni pulled out his pipe as though searching for inspiration. "Well, that's a bit more difficult. It seems the hatchet to the head damaged his brain. He'll stay with Mrs. Stebbins and me." Benoni stood and Lizzie bid him good day as she wandered back to the girls' compound, coming to the realization that being an adult could be more complicated than being a child.

Two nights later, three weeks from the day of the raid, the head selectman, Ensign John Sheldon, announced the end of martial law while assuring the citizens that armed militia would guard the town until the end of the harvest. The following week he announced his own exciting news that he was about to build the town's largest home.

Chapter Nine

<u>Late October, 1696: Deerfield</u>

Now that the harvest was all but over, the guards had been reduced to two at the stockade and three around the perimeter of the village, and life was as normal as it ever was on the frontier. Bianca and the sheep had been moved to their winter quarters in the plowing fields behind the barn, and Lizzie was relieved of her twice-daily trek to the north meadow. Sarah-Bee and her sister were living across the town road from the Price home with the school dame, Mrs. Beaman, who had no children of her own. Lizzie used her spare time to walk along the town road each day with her silent and withdrawn friend.

New England was at the pinnacle of autumn splendor with the forests awash in red, gold and orange punctuated by the occasional green conifer. The day was warm, the breeze gentle with the occasional small gust bringing down a swirling shower of color. Making the turn at the southern end of the road, the girls passed through the stockade gates and watched the construction of Ensign Sheldon's grand two-story home—the first in the village. They proceeded north toward their houses, kicking the piles of leaves as they went. As usual, Lizzie did the talking as she led her ever-silent friend while holding her hand. "My brother John has been to Northampton twice this week," she reported as she had the day before as well. "He's courting that Mary Bennett who was his girl when we lived there." Sarah-Bee did not respond, but Lizzie continued, "They're to be married next month at her father's house in Northampton."

They kicked leaves in silence while Lizzie waited hopefully as always for a response from her friend—a response that had not come since the raid. When none came, she went on, "The good news is they are moving back to Deerfield, and John is taking an empty house by us so he will share his fields with my father and they can work them together."

Reaching the northern extent of the street, Sarah-Bee pointed to a large fallen log and to Lizzie's surprise, spoke, "Let's sit here a while."

From the log they had a panoramic view down the plowing fields to the north meadow as it ran down to the river and woods. Suddenly, Sarah-Bee pointed, speaking almost in a whisper. "They came from there—from the woods at the river." Not knowing how to react, Lizzie remained silent until her friend added. "When I came down here to find out when Pa would be back for Meeting, I saw the Indians before Pa and Nathan did. I screamed, but they were too far away to hear." She pulled a kerchief from her sleeve and blew her nose. "Pa saw them and began to run. He was almost here when they grabbed him and Nathan and tied them with ropes. I had been so frightened, I had not moved, but realized I must go tell Mother. I ran back to the house, but I think they saw me. That's how they knew where to go." She started to sob.

Lizzie put her arm around her friend until she stopped crying to say, "Ma told me she, Daniel, and Hester would stay with Samuel, John and the baby. She told me to take Abigail and hide in the barn—that was the last time I saw them." She was quiet for a while before going on. "There wasn't enough hay in the loft to cover us both, so I covered Abigail and made her promise not to make a sound. Back on the ground, there was nowhere to hide—until I thought of the tobacco. I crawled in and waited—it seemed forever. Eventually I heard them, I prayed for Abigail to be quiet—I guess it worked. It was silent for a long time. When I tried to open the lid, it was stuck. I just lay there thinking all manner of horrid thoughts until you opened the lid."

When she began to sob softly, Lizzie embraced her. Suddenly Sarah-Bee stood, dried her eyes, blew her nose and declared. "I'm going to be all right, Lizzie. Let's go home."

Approaching the house, they could see Mrs. Beaman in the front, obviously wondering where they had gone. School had begun following the harvest. Mrs. Beaman taught the children under ten years old at her home, while Mr. Richards, the school master, taught the older boys at the town hall. Always pleasant and helpful, the school dame was loved by the entire village. A portly, apple-cheeked woman, she and her husband had no children so even with Sarah-Bee and Abigail there was room at her home for the school.

Waddling out to the road, she greeted the girls, "Ladies, I was becoming concerned."

Lizzie smiled. "We stopped for a chat."

The red-eyed Sarah-Bee added softly, "I'm going to be all right, Mrs. Beaman."

Putting her plump arms out, she embraced her charge, "Oh, Sarah-Bee, I am so pleased—I knew this would happen." Looking about, Mrs. Beaman said, "The children have already left and Abigail is in back doing her studies. Perhaps you could help her."

"Yes, I'd like that."

As Sarah-Bee went to the back room, Mrs. Beaman motioned to Lizzie to follow her into the yard where Lizzie gave her a summary of the day's events.

The school dame pondered a moment before replying, "She shall need something to occupy her. Perhaps she can help with the children." Thinking some more she added, "Lizzie, you are an intelligent girl. Perhaps you could come, when your mother can spare you, and help as well. It would be good for her to have a companion." She could tell from Lizzie's smile that she agreed.

Chapter Ten

<u>March 1, 1698: Two years later: Deerfield</u>

Sitting as quietly as she could while struggling with the embroidery she so detested, Lizzie sighed and shifted her position, drawing the disapproving stare of her mother. Lizzie tried to hide overwhelming boredom while their guest continued his story, "That is correct, Mr. Price, I plan to add more wheat to my field this season..." Samuel Smead and Robert were having a variation of the same conversation they had each evening since Smead first came courting Mary.

Lizzie was having the same fantasy she had had each time. The one where she stands and screams, "Don't you have anything of interest to say!" But she bit her tongue and stuck to her knitting—or embroidery in this instance.

Smeads were found in many corners of New England, and Samuel's family had been in Deerfield for some time. One of nine children, Samuel was the last of the family living at home and represented a good match by Robert's reckoning. He owned the family farm complete with a widowed mother as all of Samuel's siblings now lived on their own farms. He was enough in love that he was willing to accept the paltry dowry offered, and Robert had already decided he could get help both physical and financial from Smead once he and Mary began to have children.

As the waning sun approached the horizon, Smead rose. "I should be going. Thank you for your hospitality, sir." Mary accompanied him out the front door where Lizzie alone could just see them and the subtle un-Mary-like kiss she planted on his cheek.

Setting down her needlework, Sarah announced, "We should all be off, tomorrow will come early enough."

Sammy set away the leatherwork he had been learning from Mr. Nims and headed up to the boys' loft where he occupied the lone remaining bed while the girls left for their loft. Closing the curtain to their room, Sarah told Robert, "It will be so empty with only Sammy and Lizzie—and who knows when some boy will come calling on her?"

Sitting on the bed while removing his boots, Robert replied, "When he does, I hope I have some dowry money remaining."

"You should, dear. With Johnny just next door and his family already growing, and now Mr. Smead and our Mary just down the way, you should have plenty of help in the field." Maneuvering into her night shirt, she continued, "If only Ben had stayed." Her eldest son had left soon after Johnny's marriage to marry into the prominent Dudley family in the coastal town of Guilford, Connecticut. "However, I suspect he has a fine situation where he is."

While her sister crawled into her bed, Lizzie sat bolt upright cross-legged on hers. "Mary, how do you suppose you'll *do it* the first night?"

"Lizzie! What a thing to ask."

"You do know how to do it—don't you?"

"Well, Mother told me some."

"What if Samuel wants to do it some odd way?"

"I'll deal with it then." Mary covered her head, bringing an end to the conversation.

Lizzie wondered if she should share her French journal with her sister. She had only deciphered a few of the French words, but it was clearly a study of sexual acts and positions, and she had puzzled out most of them. But perhaps discussing them was not a prudent idea with her overly-prudent sibling.

* * *

At sunrise, Lizzie went directly to the barn to milk Bianca and feed the product of Bianca's episode with Charlemagne, a young heifer she had named *Kate*. At the same time, Sammy would feed the pigs and chickens and let the sheep out to graze. Following breakfast they would cross the road together to Mrs. Beaman's house where Sammy would be a student and his sister an assistant to the school dame.

A few months after Sarah-Bee and Lizzie had been enlisted by Mrs. Beaman, they were joined by Abby Stebbins. The three girls worked well together, strengthening their special friendship. A threesome was ideal as the class was divided into three age groups: 4 to 6 years, 7 to 8, and 9 to 10. Assigned to the middle group, Lizzie's charges included siblings of each of the three friends, Sammy Price, Abigail Belden and the most free spirit of the school, Thankful Stebbins.

The three girls had also formed a bond with Hannah Beaman. In her fifties, Mrs. Beaman had been in charge of the school for many years. Married twice and widowed once, she had been unable to conceive but claimed she had more children than any woman in New England. Hannah acquired a love of books and learning from her mother who was born and educated in England, and her small personal library was huge by New England standards. However, she was careful with whom she shared it as some of her neighbors still associated most books with the ever-present Satan.

Mrs. Beaman had conquered a few of the barriers to teaching in 17th century New England. Her husband, Simon, had cut smooth boards on which his wife had painted letters, numbers, words and simple arithmetic problems. He had also made small wooden squares stained black on which the children could write letters, words and numbers using a common local soft white stone then wipe the board clean with a simple piece of homespun cloth. She had even acquired a map of New England which she proudly displayed on her wall. Though it was rudimentary, it did show the towns, mountain ranges and rivers.

The school dame's most productive venture involved the only book outside the Bible totally endorsed by the congregation—*The Bay Psalm Book*, a collection of psalms edited to satisfy the standards of the *Independents*. Apart from the lectures and scripture readings by Reverend Williams, the occasional reading or singing of a psalm was the only other oration at meetings. Unfortunately, very few of these books made it to the frontier, limiting participation. Actually, singing was hardly accurate as no musical instruments were allowed. The tune was up to the privileged few *singers*. The leader was clearly the

Reverend's dear wife, Eunice, who, along with her strong position in the community had a very strong voice. Unfortunately strong only produced loud as the good Reverend's spouse could not carry a tune and was tone deaf.

So Mrs. Beaman wrote the words to three of the most common psalms on paper and along with her rare volume of the psalms book, she was able to help the older children read words that they had heard regularly at Meeting, allowing her to turn out a few more truly literate pupils. In addition, Hannah Beaman had some of the musical skill that Eunice Williams lacked. Having acquired a native recorder or Indian flute from one of the Pocumtuck squaws, she would play the tune for the children who greatly enjoyed truly *singing* the passages. They took this knowledge home to their parents, and over the first year, a much larger segment of the congregation knew the words and the tune causing an explosion of participation. Eunice Williams believed this was simply the congregation finally learning from her excellent example.

Chapter Eleven

Late April, 1698: Deerfield

Setting down her Indian flute, Mrs. Beaman clapped gently, "That was quite good, children, I believe you shall be ready by Sunday. Now if you will each take your boards, the girls are going to help you with your numbers." While she passed out the writing boards, there was a knock at her door. Not varying from her task, she ordered, "Sarah-Bee, will you see who is at the door, please."

"I can get it, Mrs. Beaman," Lizzie volunteered. "I'm closer."

"No!" Beaman said in an unusually stern voice. "Sarah-Bee will get it."

Opening the door she found Ensign John Sheldon, who asked, "Sarah-Bee, could you step outside for a moment?"

As she disappeared out the door, the house shook with her loud shriek that would be heard on both ends of the town road. Mrs. Beaman held up her hands, "Quiet, children, no need for alarm." Taking Abigail Belden by the hand, she, too, exited, producing a second cry. Soon Mrs. Beaman returned. "Very well, class. Now you may come see what the excitement is."

The cold cloudy April day with just a mist of drizzle in the air had not dampened the spirits of the people in the Beaman yard. The first thing Lizzie saw was Sarah-Bee hugging her father while sobbing hysterically. Then she saw Abigail with Nathan and Hester. They were all there! All home! All safe!

John Sheldon was accompanied by Benoni and Mrs. Stebbins who was holding the hand of young Samuel Belden. Since his injury, Samuel had not regained much use of one side and rarely spoke, but today even he was filled with joy. The drizzle turned to rain, causing Mrs. Beaman to invite the entourage into her home. Once calm was restored, Ensign Sheldon spoke, addressing his words to Sarah-Bee. "We heard of the return some days ago when we received word they were in Albany. We did not want to tell you until we were certain it was true. Mr. Stebbins and I left for Albany and were able to bring them home. Mrs. Stebbins and some other ladies have opened your old house, so you can all stay there tonight." Sarah-Bee just continued to sob tears of joy.

* * *

The following week marked the end of the school year as the planting season began, and with it, the expulsion of the grazing animals from the farm lots to the north meadow. The community had cared for the Belden animals following the raid, returning them when Mr. Belden came home. Lizzie and Abby had not seen Sarah-Bee since the day of her father's return, but today all three girls were in charge of leading the cows to the meadow. Sarah-Bee was filled with stories, and her friends were all ears.

"Pa told me when the Indians returned from the house, they tied their hands and put straps on their necks and led them away. They marched to Albany—that's near where the Mohawk live. He said they had other captives from other towns—he wasn't sure how many, but some man from Hadley started to argue with his Indian, and the Indian hit him with his hatchet and killed him. Pa said they just left him on the trail and moved on.

"They went away from Albany to the Mohawk River and the Mohawk camp where Pa, Nathan and Hester were put in a group that went north. Sometimes they walked and sometimes they went in canoes like the Pocumtuck have— but bigger. Nathan said the weather was good. He thought if it was winter, they would all have died for certain."

Arriving in the meadow, they left the cows to graze. Abby pointed to a log, "Let's sit there and you can tell us more."

"I guess they went up the Hudson River to the long lake. Remember when Mrs. Beaman showed us on her map? Well, they went all the way to the Saint-Lawrence River, where the Frenchmen live—to some kind of fort where they were separated into other groups—my family stayed together. They went to the Mohawk village across the river from the town of Montréal. Remember when Mrs. Beaman showed us where Montréal is? Anyway after a few days, they took Nathan and Pa to the town of Montréal and left Hester with the Indians in their town called Kahnawake."

"Oh my goodness!" cried Lizzie. "How awful. What did she tell you?"

"Nothing yet. She hardly talks. But she will, once she feels safer. You know how she likes to talk." Looking at the sky, she said, "We better get back. I have work to do. I'm the mother now, you know."

* * *

The next week Mary and her new husband came to dinner bringing Samuel's widowed mother. Considerably older than Sarah Price, Mrs. Smead moved slowly and rarely spoke. However, she did reputedly make the best pies in New England, so Lizzie, Sammy and Robert all looked forward to her visits. As with all gatherings of the week, the Belden family was the topic of conversation.

"Mr. Belden spoke at the council meeting this week," Samuel Smead reported, "He said once they arrived in Canada, he and Nathan were taken to Montréal. Hester stayed with the Mohawks."

"How terrible!" lamented Sarah, "What did they do to the child?"

"I hear they treated her as one of the tribe until a month before they were freed. Apparently she hasn't said much, but Belden says she appears to be intact."

In a rare moment, Mrs. Smead said, "I can only imagine what those heathens would do to such a child." Against his wife's better judgment, Robert had brought a bottle of local wine back from the tavern. He knew Mrs. Smead was not opposed to the occasional taste—or three, and he found it added some life to her visits.

Samuel continued, "Mr. Belden was taken to the home for the priests—Sulpicians I believe they are called. He did odd jobs around the place—he called it a seminary.

58

Anyway, he says he was well treated and thought they were not bad fellows."

"Odd group—all those men living together," Mrs. Smead declared as she drained her glass and placed it by Robert, subtly suggesting a refill.

Samuel continued, "Nathan was billeted in the convent with the nuns. Apparently he did odd jobs as well."

As Mrs. Smead emptied her second glass, she suggested, "I wonder what sort of *odd jobs* those desperate women have for a handsome young man."

Robert stifled his chuckle while he replenished the glass, and his wife said, "Poor Mr. Belden now with no wife himself."

Mrs. Smead said, "Don't worry, dear, some anxious young widow will snap him up." With another imprudent sip, she added, "Might give him a try myself," finishing with a belch.

Following dinner, crowned by Mrs. Smead's rutabaga pie, the Smead family took its leave while Robert excused himself for *a little walk.* Sammy had just retired to his loft when Sarah said, "Come into my room, Lizzie, I have something for you." Entering, she went to her chest. The ornate keepsake was as out of place in their frontier household as her husband was in Puritan New England. Lizzie knew it was a hand-me-down from Sarah's father who had received it from his grandfather who, in turn, had brought it to the New World from England.

The contents were clothes and some other household artifacts which Sarah removed, placing them on her bed. Then she pushed an obscure knob on the side and the bottom popped up revealing a second compartment hidden below. Lizzie looked down to the small cache of jewelry, scarves, and other treasures not used or appreciated at this time in Sarah's world. "Lizzie, these are things from my father's family. I knew your *prudent* sister would have little use for them, but that you would understand them better."

It was the first time Lizzie had heard her mother say something critical of her *can do no wrong* sister in comparison to her. "When I'm gone, these will be yours. I know you will appreciate them and, God-willing, perhaps you will live to a time and place where you can enjoy them publicly." Reaching under the scarves she retrieved a book. "This I want you to have in particular." Handing it to her daughter, she continued, "Read it, but don't share it with the locals. They won't have the appreciation you or I would have—or that the book deserves."

Lizzie stared at the cover, "*Romeo and Juliet* by William Shakespeare."

"Do you know about it?"

"Well, when I was little, you used to tell me some of his stories—and sometimes Mrs. Beaman mentions him."

"I doubt the town would approve of him, and certainly not this book. But read it. I know you will appreciate it. You know you are related to Mr. Shakespeare?"

"I remember you said something once, but…"

"I know I have only told you a little, but the story is this. My great grandfather, Sir Alexander Webb, came from England in 1629. Not to escape religious persecution, but to flee the change in government. He came with four sons and one grandson, my father." Sitting on the bed she motioned for Lizzie to sit beside her. "My great grandfather was very rich. He sold a large estate in England and brought the wealth with him. Over the years that wealth was distributed and inherited and sometimes wasted. Unfortunately, the contents of this box are all that remains for our family. I want you to have it because your father is—well, not a good steward of money. Anyway, back to the story."

Sarah picked up a pair of earrings from the box. Looking at them longingly, she turned them over again and again in her hands before returning them to their home while she continued, "My great grandfather was born and raised in Stratford-upon-Avon. His mother's name was Margaret Arden. Her sister was Mary Arden and Mary's son was William Shakespeare. He and my great grandfather attended the King Edward VI School in Stratford. They were friends as well as first cousins. My great grandfather had more than a few books of his plays, and they were distributed over the years to various family members. This one was my father's and is now yours."

Lizzie looked again at the book as her mother placed her hand on it one last time. "Read it, enjoy it, and guard it well. It is priceless on two levels." And with that she closed the secret compartment and the chest. "When you are done with the book, put it back. The chest and its contents are all to be yours."

Chapter Twelve

It was proving to be one of the warmest summers in memory, and Lizzie was happy to run her mother's errand after dinner. Now low in the sky approaching the tree line along the Deerfield River, the sun had lost much of its fury, while the steady breeze from the west brought blessed relief to those lucky enough to be out of doors. It seemed most of the village was fortunate, as each porch was lined with family members escaping the indoor inferno. Located south of the stockade, Mr. Gunn's store was as prominent as the tavern was obscure. A hodge-podge of articles not capable of being made at home cluttered his yard. Making her way through the maze of wagon wheels and other manufactured goods, Lizzie entered the emporium of smaller treasures.

"Ah, Miss Price, *vat* can I do for you?" Gunn spoke with an accent causing the occasional whisper that he may be *Jewish*. However, most citizens dismissed this as idle gossip and considered him a valued member of the congregation.

"Good day, Mr. Gunn. My mother said you had a new pair of scissors for her?"

"Ah yes." Reaching under his counter, he retrieved a small package along with a sheet of paper and a quill. "Please make your mark here." Money rarely changed hands in the frontier, and credit or trade for anything from other manufactured items to food or services were more common. Examining the bill, the shopkeeper commented, "Ah, how nice you *vrite* your name." Handing over the package, he added, "Zees is da best scissors—from Europe, no less. Be careful mit dem."

Lizzie merely smiled, thanking the old merchant and turned to come face to face with a friend. "Lizzie!" exclaimed Sarah-Bee, "What are you doing here?"

"Errand for my mother, what else?"

"I'm doing the same—but for my father. Wait, we can walk back together."

Lizzie left her friend to complete her business and strolled among the cornucopia in the yard. When Sarah-Bee appeared, package in hand, the girls headed north, passing the construction of the new school building soon to replace the classroom in Mrs. Beaman's home. Following a discussion of the oppressive heat, Sarah-Bee told her friend, "After Meeting Sunday, Hester started to tell me about her ordeal. I think she's getting better. I asked her to come with us tomorrow to the meadow. Maybe she'll have more to say." As they exited the stockade, they saw the giant wall of black arriving rapidly from the west. There was a wild gust of wind and the rain began in torrents. The girls spun around with their arms out, looking up with their mouths open.

"Relief at last," Lizzie giggled as they splashed like children through the puddles.

"Do you young ladies not have more productive activities?"

Turning in surprise, the girls had not seen Reverend Williams approaching from the north as they watched nature's storm approach from the west. Lizzie was the first to find her tongue. "Good evening, Reverend. We were just thanking the Lord for blessing our crops with his rain."

"Well, perhaps you should go home and dry off," he replied as he turned with his ever-present Bible tucked safely under his coat and his free hand pulling down on his wide-brimmed hat, attempting in vain to keep out the rain.

Sarah-Bee took her friend's arm and, with a soft chuckle, whispered, "Elizabeth, I wish I could think as quickly as you."

By the time they reached Sarah-Bee's house, they were drenched to the skin but still giggling.

* * *

Typical of New England after a drenching storm, morning was spectacular—the sky blue, horizon red, landscape green and filled with sparkle. Hester Belden was little more than one year younger than her current teenaged-companions, but she had always felt like the little sister. Her experiences of the past year and a half had certainly raised her to a greater level of maturity, but still she was excited to be invited today by the very same young ladies she had always admired.

Once they had turned their bovine charges loose on the Bay Colony vegetation, Lizzie asked, "Hester, what was it like? Can you tell us?"

Abby added, "Yes, we are *dying* to hear about it."

Suddenly Hester's ordeal became her badge of honor, and these older girls, whom she had always regarded in awe, wanted *her* to tell *them* something. It was all the encouragement she needed as she looked beyond the river, gathering her thoughts before beginning, "At first it was terrible—I don't remember everything. We were all getting ready for the lecture when Sarah-Bee came back and warned us. Mother sent her to the barn to hide with Abigail. Just then, the first one burst through the door. I was closest, and he put a strap on my neck pulling me outside. Several more Indians went through the door, but by then Daniel, I guess, had his gun and began to shoot. More Indians came and I was pulled out to the meadow where Pa was with Nathan. They, too, had straps on them.

"They pulled us north and crossed the river. We waited there a long time. I began to cry and my Indian slapped me—hard. Pa tried to help but they hit him with a stick and pulled out an axe. I thought they were going to kill him, but they did not. Eventually—I don't know how long, the other Indians came back from town but with no other prisoners. We marched until dusk, then stopped to camp."

She waited for a while, but her older friends were speechless, so she continued, "One of the Indians spoke some English. Actually my *master*—that was what they called the man who held your leash—knew a few words. Anyway, they took all our clothes and threw them in the woods. Then made us bathe in the river."

Abby was aghast, "Naked? In front of everyone?"

"Yes. I thought Pa might do something—I guess he learned from the first time he complained. Then they gave us Indian clothes."

"What were they like?" Lizzie asked?

65

"Made of animal skin. Nathan told me deer. Anyway, they were comfortable and easy to walk in." Looking at her current gray dress and apron, "Much easier than these. Mine had a skirt below my knees. This was good because when I had to do *my business,* I just had to squat."

Abby was in horror, "Had you no privacy?"

"None at all. The Indian who spoke English told us we must not complain and must follow right along. If we lagged behind or complained, they would kill us. That night my master tied my neck strap to a stake so I couldn't move."

The girls were speechless, Abby and Sarah-Bee were sobbing. Finally Lizzie said, "Oh, you poor thing."

Hester shrugged, "I suppose it could have been worse."

"What happened next?"

"In the morning we started to march straight away—to the west. I know because the morning sun was at our back for a few days. I don't remember how many. We met some other Indians with captives. We did not know them and were forbidden to speak. One of the men did complain and they cut his head with their hatchet—he died right away.

"Eventually we came to a river. Pa said it was the Hudson River and we were close to Albany, but we never saw the town. Here we found canoes and went north to another river heading west. They said that was the Mohawk River. From there, the canoes took us to a Mohawk village.

"Their village was something like ours. The houses are wood, but longer and hold many more people. The fire is in the center but without a chimney so the room is smoky. We only spent two nights. Then we were divided up again and headed north on the Hudson. My family was kept together, and I had the same master. We hiked some days but took the canoes a lot. The Indians had to work hard because the current is always to the south. We went through Lake Champlain which took several more days and even saw some traders in canoes. Sometimes they stopped to talk to the Indians. I couldn't understand—I think they were French. We stopped at a fort close to the Saint-Lawrence River. That night I asked my master what had happened to the rest of the family in Deerfield. He just shrugged and said, 'all dead'."

Hester stood and threw a stone into the stream. Seeing her older friends remain silent, she suggested, "We should go home. I feel better now. Maybe if I come tomorrow I can tell you about Canada."

The following morning, however, brought another torrential storm, and Nathan was chosen to bring the cattle to graze for the next few days. It was only the following week that Sarah-Bee and Hester could again come to the meadow. Abby suggested they go to her *secret place* on the river by the giant willow. Once there, they removed their shoes wading in the stream while Hester continued her saga.

"From the fort we went to the Mohawk village called Kahnawake. It was almost as large as the village near Albany and larger than Deerfield. It sits across the Saint-Lawrence from Montréal. Although the river is wide, you can see the island of Montréal. All the villagers came down to greet us. They were very curious and wanted to touch our skin and hair, but they were gentle. Then our group was taken, and the leader said we would *run the gauntlet*. I had no idea what that was—I was fortunate I did not."

Hester picked up a few stones, beginning to skip them before she resumed, "They took all the small children aside and made the rest of us strip. By now we were used to it. Then they smeared each of us all over with a red paint.

Soon a few men came and took me aside and examined me closer than I would have wanted, but then they put me with the younger children. Later I found it was because they determined I was not yet a woman. I had no idea how fortunate I was. The Indians formed two lines, each Indian armed with a stick or branch and each adult prisoner was made to run down the center while the Indians beat them."

When she stopped for a while to organize her thoughts, her friends stood silent with mouths open until Abby said softly, "My God, how terrible!"

"Yes," Hester went on, "Pa and Nathan came through easily but some of the older people fell and two were beaten to death. At that point an Indian woman came and took me to the river to wash off my paint. She spoke some English, explaining that she would be my *mother,* and I was to live with her until I was old enough to have a man." Suddenly she threw off her bonnet and skirt, "I'm going swimming!" She dove in like a diving bird and swam like a fish as her friends continued to stare in amazement.

Most New Englanders who lived near water could swim enough strokes to avoid drowning, but Hester swam like no one the girls had seen. Soon her friends joined her. When they finally came out, Lizzie said, "You're like the mermaid!" Realizing her friends had no idea what that was, she explained, "A story my mother told me—the legend of a creature, lady on the top and fish on the bottom—don't tell the Reverend about it. I don't think he'd approve."

The girls began to dress, but Hester simply sat naked on a log. "I lived in my new mother's house—actually it was her mother's house. The Mohawk are what they call matriarchal. That means the women are the family heads."

This information was more radical than anything the girls had heard. "I don't believe it!" Abby declared.

"It's true, when a man takes a woman, each continues to live in their own mother's house."

"But—what if they want to…"

"At night, the man goes to his wife's bed and returns to his mother's house when he's finished."

Lizzie pointed out, "But you said there was only one great room."

"It's dark."

"But…"

"You get used to it. At first it's interesting, then funny, then boring." She rose to get stones from the bank and began to skip them. "It's like clothes, after a while it's nice without them. If no one cares, what difference does it make? In the summer I would dress like this," she said referring to her nude torso. "Except once I began my monthlies, I wore a cloth on a string in front like the ladies."

She went to her clothes and began to dress. "A year or so later, my father came with a priest I have never been so happy. He said the Governor had released us and we were soon to go home."

With her dress in her hand, she stood silent for a while. "It actually occurred to me that if I would stay, I would be all right. One of the girls from Maine refused to go home." Hester dropped the dress and went to embrace her astounded sister, "But I could not leave my prudish sister and her silly friends." She sobbed for a while, until she stood straight and suggested, "Let's go home."

Hester rarely spoke about the affair again.

Chapter Thirteen

September, 1698: Deerfield

As the harvest neared its completion, the school year commenced with the opening of the new school house filling everyone with anticipation. The two individual classrooms allowed separate quarters for Mrs. Beaman's youngsters as well as Mr. Richard's older boys. The perennial school dame had passed the last half of summer carrying her classroom paraphernalia to the new building. Although the children eagerly awaited the new facility, no one was more excited than the dame.

Anxious to begin, Abby and Lizzie were on hand, while Sarah-Bee was taking the year off to serve as *mother* at home. At the close of opening day, the young children rushed off into one of the warmest and most glorious autumn days in memory, while Mrs. Beaman and her two assistants returned order to the classroom readying it for another day.

"Well, ladies, I believe we are done for the now, why don't you two go enjoy the gorgeous weather?"

Lizzie suggested to Abby, "Why don't you go ahead? I need a moment with Mrs. Beaman."

Once Abby had skipped off, Lizzie opened her bag which carried the items she needed for the day. Handing a book to the dame, she asked, "Can you help me with this?"

Mrs. Beaman looked at the tome with astonishment. "My God, where did you get this, child?"

As Mrs. Beaman held it to her ample bosom like a newborn, Lizzie told her, "It is from my mother. It comes from her family."

Beaman looked fondly at the book. "I first read this with *my* mother. She had a copy brought with her from England. It, more than anything, convinced me to do what I do today."

Pleased at her superior's reaction, Lizzie asked, "I have a few questions. I thought they would be better for you than for my mother."

Mrs. Beaman laid *Romeo and Juliet* on her desk with care. "I would be happy to try."

Lizzie touched the book and asked, "In the beginning, Juliet is being courted by Paris, who seems an excellent match. Why would she have interest in Romeo, an enemy of her family and someone she scarcely knows?"

"An excellent question, my dear, but we must ask *what does the author want to do?*"

Lizzie tilted her head in quandary. "What do you mean?"

"Well, dear, I think he wants to tell a story of love and passion beyond normal boundaries." Lizzie looked perplexed as her teacher handed her the book, saying, "Read on, my dear, and tell me what you find. For now, I believe Abby is waiting for you in the square. Why don't you go enjoy this spectacular day?"

Lizzie placed the book in her bag with care and walked into the sunlight. Before she closed the door, Beaman called out, "And do not forget—it *is* a tragedy."

Lizzie proceeded north into the stockade to find her friend seated on the bench beneath the giant sycamore. "What was that about?" Abby asked.

"I had some questions about a book." Abby suspected it was best not to pry further when Lizzie asked, "What happened to Thankful and Sammy?" referring to their siblings.

"They went home. It's a beautiful day. What should we do?" Lizzie shrugged as Abby suggested, "Let's go for a walk. We can go down to the river through my father's fields."

They walked past John Stebbins' house and barn to the plowing fields where most crops had been harvested, providing an easy path to the river. Discussing this term's pupils and their plans for the school year, they were soon at the bracken of trees shielding the river. Proceeding toward the path that led to the river bank, Abby stopped abruptly. "Listen, voices in the woods—it sounds like children."

Putting her finger over her lip, Abby motioned for her friend to follow her into the brush. Lizzie stopped and whispered, "Listen, that's Sammy—and your sister, Thankful."

Stifling their giggles, they moved forward, planning to spring a surprise, but when they moved into the clearing, the surprise was theirs, causing Abby to shout, "Thankful! What in the name of goodness?" Sitting around a pile of sticks were Sammy, Thankful Stebbins and Abigail Belden, all naked as jaybirds but for ropes around their waists suspending a few leaves.

The irrepressible Thankful rose and stated calmly, "We are playing Indian."

Lizzie's mouth still hung open while Abby demanded, "Playing what?"

The other two children stood behind their leader while Thankful continued as calmly as if predicting the weather, "Hester told us this is how Indians dress when it's warm, especially children. They believe clothes are only to keep you warm when it is cold."

Feeling some of her friend's confidence, Abigail Belden added with growing confidence, "Hester said she always went like this in the summer—and she has, you know—breasts."

Lizzie decided to step in before irate Abby could become violent. "Thankful, your mother will skin you alive if she learns of this. Now you three put on your clothes and we will go home together." Looking at Abby, she insisted, "And we shall *all* promise not to speak of this to anyone."

Once the children were clothed, they headed to the town road. When Lizzie and Sammy had delivered Abigail to Belden's, Lizzie scolded, "Sammy, I can't believe you would do this."

Her brother replied calmly, "I liked seeing the girls like that."

"But, *Samuel*, you can't..."

"I'm not the one with a book of naked drawings under my mattress."

Lizzie could not hide her shock. "But—how do..."

"Mother sent me to your loft to find something. I liked the pictures."

"But..."

"And you used to watch Ben and Johnny bathe—I saw you looking."

"But…"

"That's all right," her brother decreed, "I watched you, too. You were more fun to watch than Mary." He stopped and looked her in the eye. She realized he was approaching her in height. "But like *you* said, 'It will be *our* secret.'" With a sly grin he continued toward home.

Lizzie had always thought Sammy had favored Mary more than he favored her, but now she felt a bond forming between her and her young brother—a bond she and Mary never shared.

* * *

Three weeks later, Lizzie appeared early to school. When Mrs. Beaman saw her, she knew the reason and asked, "Have you been reading the book?"

"Yes, ma'am."

"And?"

"Why would they do this?"

"Do you mean why would they be so defiant?"

Lizzie thought for a moment. "Yes."

"Who and what are they defying?"

Answering immediately, Lizzie said, "Their families."

"Correct and what else?"

This time she pondered and slowly responded, "Society?"

"Of course. What else?"

This time she was puzzled so the dame suggested, "Think of the priest."

"Religion?" she answered triumphantly.

"Good," said the dame before asking, "And what is Shakespeare telling us with this?"

"I don't know."

"Of course, you do. Continue to read and think. Come back to me when you have an answer."

Two days later, Lizzie returned with confidence, "That love is more important than any of those other things," she reported.

The dame smiled and put her hand on Lizzie's. "Certainly that is how Romeo and Juliet felt in the book, but is it?"

Lizzie returned to feeling conflicted while her teacher smiled broadly, telling her, "I suppose everyone has their own opinion here, and at the end of the day there is no absolute answer."

Lizzie looked at her feet, "But…"

Mrs. Beaman gave her wonderful chuckle, "This, my dear, is the difference between a good book and a great book—maybe the same as between a good love and a great love. As you go through life, you will find your own answer."

* * *

October was as cold as September had been pleasant, causing all thoughts of swimming or any other clothes-shedding activities to be abandoned, while New England braced for one of the coldest winters in memory. The high point of the frigid winter of the final year of the century was the marriage of Daniel Belden, Sr. As Mrs. Smead had prophesized, he was *snapped up* by an anxious widow. Hepzibah Buell-Wells had lost her first husband to an

Indian raid bringing certain symmetry to the marriage, allowing Sarah-Bee to return to her preferred role as teenage daughter.

Chapter Fourteen

Autumn, 1701: Three years later: Deerfield

O n possibly the final warm day of the year, Lizzie realized it might be her last chance as she strolled past the large riverside willow into the cover of Abby's *secret place.* The girls rarely swam together any longer. At seventeen they were no longer children. Girls swimming together may be looked upon as a transgression comparable to swimming with boys. So the solitary Lizzie carefully folded her things on a branch before walking along the firm sand bottom. When she reached waist depth, she lay on her back floating peacefully, watching the autumn sun sparkle through the overreaching tree branches. Nowhere was she so able to examine her thoughts and her life as she was in this special place.

Lizzie had planned to help the dame this one last year at the growing school. Abby only came on occasion and a younger girl helped from time to time. Next year Lizzie realized she might be considered too old for such activities.

The aging Mrs. Beaman much appreciated the help and had suggested Lizzie consider becoming a dame herself. When she mentioned it at home, her mother was opposed. "That is only for old maids and barren women," she claimed, although Robert considered Lizzie bringing home income and not requiring a dowry as a viable option.

Sarah-Bee no longer helped as she was busy at home and considering suitors. Lizzie had been called upon by two young men but had rejected them out of hand. The local boys held no allure for her and the thought of spending her entire life with one of them held no appeal. Abby, on the other hand, liked all the boys.

Lizzie rolled face down and swam upstream, Having been instructed by Hester in *Indian swimming,* she had become proficient, and when she reached what she considered the end of her privacy, she turned face up to float back downstream. Reaching the starting point, she climbed back to the bank where she stood naked, drying in the sunlight. This favorite part of her private swim gave her a special thrill. She felt the defiant Juliet would have done this had she lived. And she wanted to be Juliet—but where was her Romeo?

Once her hair was dry enough to cover with her bonnet, she dressed and headed to the town road. She had promised Mrs. Beaman she would stop this afternoon and help her prepare for opening next week. As Lizzie expected, Mrs. Beaman was already hard at work organizing the classroom. "Oh good, my dear, you are just in time to help me move this large bench." Pointing to the floor, she asked, "Can you crawl under and get that book? My old knees are just no longer up to it."

Lizzie smiled and crawled under enough to grab the wayward tome. On her way up, she knocked off her bonnet.

Noticing the damp hair, Mrs. Beaman remarked, "Was it raining earlier?"

"Uh—no, ma'am."

The dame merely shrugged, before asking, "Did I ever tell you how I loved to swim when I was young?"

"No, ma'am."

"Well, I did." After a short pause, she added, "I wish we could do it more nowadays—but now it seems so—defiant." She smiled but made no further comment and went back to work. Lizzie loved the dame.

After they finished organizing furniture, Mrs. Beaman asked, "Have you given any more thought to becoming a school dame someday?"

"Some."

Sitting down to fan herself, Mrs. Beaman continued, "I was thinking—you could act as dame one or two days a week, and I could be the assistant. It would be good training and give you a better chance to consider it."

Not mentioning her mother's lack of enthusiasm, Lizzie replied, "Maybe."

"I could even pay you some. God knows the town doesn't pay me much, but I am blessed with Simon," referring to her husband, "who takes ample care of both of us."

Deciding she could convince her mother, Lizzie answered, "Yes, I'd like to try it."

"Good. Here's a decision you can help with. Your brother Samuel is on the cusp of grades. He could stay here for his last year or move up early to Mr. Richard's class. I think he's ready. What do you think?"

"I'll ask him. Let me consider it."

"Good. By the way, where is the boy? I have not seen him in a while."

"He went with our stepbrother, Johnny, to visit our other stepbrother, Ben, and his family in Guilford, Connecticut."

"I love the seacoast," Mrs. Beaman replied. "We lived by the sea when I was a little girl. When will they return?"

"Any time now—maybe today, they've been gone three weeks."

Mrs. Beaman stood, "Well then, you should be off. I believe we are done here. You don't want to miss the homecoming."

Lizzie passed her brother Johnny's house before coming to her father's. Peeking into the back, she was rewarded seeing the cart with the horse still in harness. Next to it was a similar but unexpected vehicle. "Well, look who's here." She turned to see Johnny and gave him a hug, asking, "How was your trip?"

"Excellent."

"How was Sammy?"

Her stepbrother chuckled, "I'll let him tell you."

Pointing to the other cart, she asked, "Whose is this?"

"Guess."

Suddenly, the house door opened, causing Lizzie to scream and jump into the arms of her other stepbrother. Having not seen Ben since he had left to marry and live on the coast, she smothered him with kisses, then stepped back, "I like the beard." Poking his mid-section, she laughed, "I'm not certain about this."

"It's just muscle," he replied. Then walking around his sister, he added, "Looks as if you have changed a bit. How does Pa keep the boys away?"

Giggling, she answered, "He manages."

The door opened again and a young lady came out holding the hand of a three-year-old boy. Ben said, "Lizzie, this is my wife, Mary, and son, David."

80

Robert had told the family they could not afford to travel to Guilford for the wedding, so this was the first occasion they had to meet Ben's family. Lizzie offered her hand to Mary, "I see we'll have some confusion with Marys."

Ben laughed, "Ma already has a solution—Mary-Ben, Mary-John, and Mary-Sam," referring to their sister, Mary.

Lizzie laughed, bending to greet David, "I'm Aunt Lizzie. May I hold you?"

He offered his arms, and she picked him up while he burrowed his face into her bosom. Ben laughed. "See, he noticed them, too."

"Ebenezer Field!" she scolded as young David began to fondle her.

Johnny said, "Ben and I need to take care of the horses. Then Ma is making supper for us all. Tomorrow we'll have a big meal out in back."

* * *

After morning chores, Sarah whipped the functioning members of her family into line for orders. The working women were spread thin as both Mary-Sam and Mary-John were in the last two weeks of pregnancy. But everyone knew when Sarah had a mission, no one was exempt. Even Robert, who commonly disappeared when work was at hand, knew enough to pitch in.

Tables, benches and chairs appeared from the Price, Field, and Smead homes, and a meal preparation worthy of a Grecian bacchanal was prepared in all three homes.

The confined Mary-John Field was aided by her sister-in-law, Mary-Ben Field, while Mary-Sam Smead was rescued by her aged widowed mother-in-law. Once the meal was served, everyone relaxed and the four generations, some of whom saw one another frequently and others who had never met before that day, strengthened the wonderful bonds of family. The fun ran into dusk when a second course was served. Eventually all four of the fourth generation children were asleep and soon everyone made their way back to their assigned beds, promising to return in the morning to finish cleaning up.

Once the Price household was quiet, Lizzie made a rare climb up to the boys' loft. Crawling in next to her brother she said, "Sammy, you didn't tell me about your trip."

Propping up on one elbow, her brother claimed, "It was wonderful. When I grow up, I'm moving to Guilford and becoming a fisherman."

Sammy had long sandy hair that was always falling into his face. His sister swept it back as she said, "Tell me more."

Sammy sat up, "It was great. Ben has friends who are fishermen and I went out with them."

"What did you catch?"

"Lots of things. First, we went for fish which we caught in a net..." After describing in detail the fish episode, he added, "Then we went and took the crab from the crab traps." He explained each part of the chore with care. Finally he said, "Then we went to the beach and found oysters."

Once he had explained the nuances of oysters, she asked, "What about shoemaking?"

Sammy sat up straighter, "I liked working with leather like Mr. Nims showed me, but fishing is way better."

As he continued to dissect the adventure for her, she realized that her older sister and two older brothers had all found what they had searched for, and now her much younger brother had hit on his passion, but she remained in total conflict. She put her arm around her little brother as he eventually ran out of energy and tales of the sea. She knew she should return to her loft, but she just closed her eyes.

Chapter Fifteen

April, 1702: Deerfield

While the last of her students departed, Lizzie began to straighten the classroom. Mrs. Beaman rose from the corner where she had been observing and came to help. "Lizzie, I believe you now do a better job with the students than I."

"Oh no, ma'am," she responded.

"Well, it's true, child, and after this term you should decide what to do. I believe you might seriously think of becoming the dame."

Lizzie stopped, looking at her feet as she replied, "I just don't know, Mrs. Beaman. I enjoy the work, but I believe there is something more in my destiny."

"Well, take your time, it is a big decision." Lizzie loved the way the dame had of giving advice without making demands. As she stored the last few items in their places, the door opened. Mrs. Beaman looked up, "Hello, Abby, how nice to see you."

Abby Stebbins had abandoned assisting to search for other prospects, such as marriageable men. Smiling, she reported, "I thought I would stop to see if Lizzie would walk home with me."

Adjusting her bonnet, Lizzie said, "I've just finished, let's go." Lizzie knew that Abby would not come just for company on the way home so she was anxious to see just what her friend was up to.

Once they were outside, Abby asked, "Did you hear what happened?"

Lizzie shrugged, "No, what?"

Her friend drew closer, lowering her voice. "Four strange men came into town last night—in a canoe! My Uncle Benoni said they are camped in a tent on the north meadow."

"So?"

"Well, my uncle says three of them are Frenchmen and the fourth is…," she lowered her voice to a whisper, "an *Indian!*"

Lizzie frowned, "Oh dear."

Abby took on an even more secretive voice, "The last time a Frenchman came to Deerfield, he was taken to Boston in chains, but my uncle says these men are interested in doing business with the town that could benefit everyone."

"And what would that be?"

"I don't know," Abby continued with enthusiasm, "but they are meeting with some of the selectmen on the steps of the town hall in a short while. Let's go see."

Lizzie frowned, "Won't they wonder what we are doing there?"

Clearly Abby had thought this through. "We'll stay out of the way by the sycamore."

Once they were inside the stockade, they took a position under the giant tree where they could watch the town hall inconspicuously. Soon a few of the town fathers appeared along with four strangers. All were wearing deerskin clothing, the shortest of the four wore a bright red hat and was the obvious leader. The other two Frenchmen were very large and equally dirty. Abby whispered, "They look as if they could break a man in two." For Lizzie, the most interesting soul was the solitary Indian. Wearing only deerskin trousers, there was little doubt he was the fittest *and* most attractive member of the group. He had a red-beaded band around his head, and his long shining black hair was arranged in a single braid reaching nearly to his waist. Although the girls had never seen one, he had the physique of an ancient Greek athlete. The shorter Frenchman would speak and the town fathers would respond. Before the leader would speak again, he turned to confer privately with the Indian. The two giants remained silent.

Once the parlay ended, the four strangers left for their tent in the north meadow, while the town fathers had a discussion after which they dispersed. The girls left quietly for home.

"So what was that all about?" Lizzie began.

"I am not certain," Abby answered. "But my Uncle Benoni was there. I'll go ask him tonight. Maybe he can explain to me what happened."

The next day, Abby again appeared at the end of classes. As she and Lizzie exited into a cold damp spring afternoon, she reported what little she had discovered, "My uncle said it has to do with the fur trade but was uncertain about the details."

Three days later the Smead family came to dinner at the Price household. Along with Mary, Samuel and their two small children was the Widow Smead, who came bearing pies and anticipating Robert's wine. After dinner, Samuel reported on the new residents of the north meadow.

"The leader of the group is this man De Noyon. He is a French fur trader with no small amount of experience." He waited for Robert to pour more wine for his mother before continuing. "It seems he has been travelling about New England for the past two years looking to open the area to the French fur trade."

Mrs. Smead put her glass down long enough to comment, "Frenchmen! I can't believe you men would put your faith in the likes of them—they're all Papists."

Samuel replied, "They say he has broken all contact with the French fur merchants and that he has even abjured the *Romish* faith. The other two men, called LeDuc and LeMieux, seem to be along to do his bidding but rarely speak."

Trying to remain nonchalant, Lizzie asked innocently, "What about the Indian?" Since the day at the town hall, she could not get this man out of her head.

Widow Smead interjected, "An Indian! Next you'll be inviting them to live with us."

"He seems the most mysterious of the lot," Smead reported. "He claims to be Abenaki but does not have the appearance of one. In addition, he speaks to no one but De Noyon and only away from other ears. This De Noyon has apparently set up a scheme to bring French furs to market in New England. Due to the market price, he would be paid more, and the English would benefit from a trade we have not as yet been able to secure. In addition, this may improve our relations with the Canadian Indians."

Later in the week, Lizzie discussed the strangers with her stepbrother. Johnny explained, "They seem to be forthright in bringing in outside trade, and there is little doubt that this would benefit the community."

Lizzie hesitated. Trying to sound matter-of-fact, she then asked, "What about this *Indian?*"

Her stepbrother shrugged, "What about him? He only talks with De Noyon. I suspect this is because he knows no tongues other than his own."

Nodding in agreement, Lizzie continued to daydream about this strange and lovely man. Although everyone seemed to agree he was an Indian, he did not look like any of the local natives and certainly not like the Mohawk of that terrible day six years earlier. At night she would search the journal hidden in her mattress for a figure of a man such as this Indian. She found none.

* * *

Two weeks later, Robert Price was sitting at his usual corner table at Potter's tavern. There were no activities in town that night, and Robert was the sole client. He had come thinking Potter would not be working due to the slow traffic and had hoped he could barter love for beer with Lenore. Alas, Potter greeted him at the door. It appeared he would be required to part with some of his cash tonight.

Soon the tavern door again opened, but very slowly as two men peered in. LeMieux whispered a rare sentence to De Noyon, "He eez zee man in zee corner."

The three Frenchmen then entered the establishment. De Noyon tipped his red stocking cap to Lenore as he headed for Robert's table. "Could I buy yew a drink, Monsieur?"

Robert never had to think twice about this question and simply motioned for the threesome to be seated. De Noyon was slightly shorter than Robert, and, in his mid-thirties, was in excellent shape. Women found his angular face attractive and his smile disarmingly charming. He offered his hand, "Jacques de Noyon."

Robert took it and introduced himself. De Noyon motioned to his two partners, "Zees are my colleagues, Monsieur LeDuc and Monsieur LeMieux." The pair did not speak but in turn offered the largest hands Robert had ever seen. They were as ugly as De Noyon was charming, and it was difficult to guess their ages. Both had great beards and long hair, none of which appeared to have seen a comb. Their skin was weathered and scarred, and both skin and clothes had not touched soap for some time. Both men were taller than Price and their shoulders were each at least an ax handle wide.

When Lenore came to the table, De Noyon flashed his most alluring smile, "Ah, zee lovely mademoiselle. Four beers *s'il vous plait.*" The smile had been enough, but his French almost put Lenore over the edge as she giggled, *"Oui, Monsieur,"* possibly the only French phrase she knew.

Once the drinks were delivered, De Noyon got down to business. "As yew know, meester Price, My friends and I are strangers een your town. More difficult still, we are foreigners." Robert nodded as the Frenchman continued, "Currently we are een a tent in zee meadow." We must move to more suitable quarters and need zee help of some one such as yourself."

Robert had seen most every scam and knew if they were looking for finance, they were barking up the wrong tree, but they were buying the brew, so he simply nodded as De

Noyon continued. "Zere ees an empty house and barn in zee very northeast corner of town. Eet ees on wooded land not suitable for farming. I believe zey call eet a *woodlot.*" Robert nodded again and motioned to Lenore for more drinks. He hoped to get as many as he could before they discovered he had no money.

LeDuc and LeMieux emptied their second glasses as quickly as the first, while De Noyon sipped his as if it were vintage wine. "Yew see, meester Price, zee local peoples are not likely to sell such a property to zee Frenchman, but eef yew were to purchase eet, we would rent eet from yew."

Robert would have liked to string him along further but decided to say, "I am sorry, Mr. de Noyon, but I cannot afford…"

De Noyon interrupted, "Zat ees no problem, monsieur. I will geeve yew zee money." He took a sack from his pocket. "I know zee man who owns eet and what he would sell eet for." Counting out actual English gold coins, he pushed the pile to Robert. "You go to heem and he will sell. Eet ees all arranged." He then counted out more coins, "And here ees zee rent for zee first seex months."

Robert was no stranger to scams, and this had all the hallmarks of a classic. However, he could not see a downside for himself, and he was now holding more hard currency than he had seen in his lifetime. So he pocketed the money, nodded and ordered more beer.

In the morning he rode Gilgamesh south to Hatfield where the owner of the woodlot lived. The deal was consummated quickly, and Robert returned home a property owner for the first time in his life. By his calculations, the rent alone would exceed his annual farming income by some. According to English law, the

Field boys owned their late father's house but Sarah had use of it until her death. Robert decided he would keep this deal to himself for the time being. By the end of the week, Deerfield had four new residents, while Jacques de Noyon had a new house with two *colleagues* and an Indian living in the large barn.

Chapter Sixteen

<u>May, 1702: Deerfield</u>

The water was gloriously cool as she floated on her back, only occasionally opening her eyes to watch the muted sunlight filtering through a canopy of leaves. The end of April had turned unseasonably warm, and this third week of May had been miserably hot. School was out, planting begun and with it came the return of farm animals to the meadow with Lizzie bringing the cows to graze. At eighteen, Lizzie was enjoying more freedom as her father had the field help he needed from Sammy, Johnny and Samuel Snead. Her father had also become suddenly less concerned about finances.

Rolling over, she swam back to her clothes and stood in the ankle-deep water allowing the warm air to dry her skin. Hearing a distant rustling, she looked along the bank expecting the mother deer that had been bringing her two fawns down to drink, but her eyes met an unexpected sight. It was him! De Noyon's Indian—who was equally naked.

He had apparently not noticed Lizzie as he dove out, swimming to midstream, then back to the bank where he bent to pick up stones to skip along the surface.

Lizzie stood studying, rendered immobile by this idyllic sight, when he looked up and waved casually to her. Shaken from her trance, she realized that she, too, was not dressed and grabbed her smock in panic to hold in front of her. As he approached, again giving a friendly wave, she shouted, "Sir! Avert your eyes!"

The Indian quickly turned his back to her. The muscular physique of his backside was every bit as pleasant as his well-chiseled front. She could not stop staring until he shouted, "May I turn around now?" To date, no one in town, including Lizzie, had ever heard the man speak. It was assumed he knew only his Indian dialect. But this was English—and good English with only the hint of an accent.

Suddenly she returned to her senses. Realizing she remained undressed, she shouted, "No! Not yet!"

Quickly throwing on her clothes, she scampered up the bank to the safety of the woods before answering, "All right!"

The Indian turned, and realizing she had disappeared, returned to picking up skipping stones. Lizzie moved to a position where she could watch without detection. She had never seen a man undressed other than the few glimpses of her bathing brothers. This was altogether different and gave her a new and strange sensation. As he walked closer to her perch, she turned and hastened to the meadow. As she left, confident he could not see her, he shouted, "Goodbye!"

* * *

93

Three days later Lizzie was the first person at the meadow. The temperature had moderated, and she had lost some of her enthusiasm for swimming. Scratching Bianca's ear, she gazed out, down to the woods where the Deerfield River turned to meet the Connecticut, dreaming of the wonders that must lie beyond.

"I had forgotten how odd the English are about clothes." She turned to see the speaker. It was *him* wearing his usual deerskin trousers and headband, his chest and feet were bare as usual. She was speechless, standing with her mouth open. "I am sorry if I frightened you," he continued, "I certainly meant no harm." Looking around the meadow he told her, "Soon the others will be here. You should not be seen with me. If you like, we could go sit in the woods and talk a bit." She was still without words as he added, "I will promise to keep my clothes on if you will."

He smiled for the first time, and her heart melted as she managed to squeak, "Yes."

Once they were in the cover of the forest, he sat casually on a log, "What is your name?"

Gathering her courage, she answered, "Lizzie— Elizabeth, Elizabeth Price."

"Ah," he replied, "Named for the Queen of England."

She smiled, "Actually it was for my mother's stepmother."

"You should say it was for the Queen, people would be more impressed—but *you people* don't care for impressing others, do you?"

Dumbstruck, she could only think to ask, "What is *your* name?"

He laughed. "I have many names."

"Many? Like what?"

Holding up his thumb he began, "First, I was Andrew Samuel Stevens, a name given me at birth."

"What else?"

"My Abenaki name is *Skagit*."

She pronounced it slowly, "Ska jeet. It's pretty—like musical. What does it mean?"

Laughing again he said, "*Skagit*—but in English one would say, 'Wild River'."

"I like that. What else?"

"My French name is *André Saint-Etienne*, which in English is Andrew Stevens." He reached up, gently touching a curl that had escaped her bonnet. "You have beautiful hair. Why do you wear this bonnet, Queen Elizabeth?"

"Because I am told to."

"Do you always do as you are told?"

She could scarcely believe she was having this conversation, answering, "Usually."

He touched the curl again. It made her tingle as he asked, "But not always?"

She impulsively removed the bonnet, asking, "Why do you have so many names?"

"That, pretty Elizabeth, is a very long story, and we must not tarry too long here. You would do well not to be seen with me. Do you come here often?"

"Almost every day during the planting and growing season."

"Will you be here tomorrow?"

Lizzie could think of many ways this could go badly, but she replied, "Yes."

"Come again very early so we are alone, and we can talk for a while. Now is anyone else in the meadow?"

She turned to peer out. Turning back, she said "Only..." but he had vanished.

In the morning Lizzie told her mother, "I awoke early. So I thought I would go early to the meadow." She rarely lied to her mother, but this seemed a harmless fib. The sun was just at the horizon when she reached the meadow with her cows. There was no one else, not even Andrew. *Maybe he forgot*, she thought.

"Good morning, Lizzie."

His voice made her jump. "Oh my goodness! I didn't see—where did you come from?"

Smiling, he replied, "From where I had been, of course. Don't you know Indians appear from nowhere?" He pointed to the forest, "Shall we go? I have discovered a very secure spot." He led a short way to a great thicket. Pulling back the branch of a large shrub he said, "Through here."

Amazed as she entered the clearing she had never seen nor would have found on her own, she exclaimed, "I have never seen this. It's like magic. How did you find it?"

Smiling a wonderful smile, he replied, "Indians are clever in the ways of the forest. No one will find us here." Lifting another branch, he revealed the river bank. "And we even have the river." Pointing to a fallen tree, he said, "Sit here—seating for two. So you want to hear my story?"

She loved his smile, "Yes."

"I was born in Pemaquid, in the province of Maine. Like most, my parents had come from England to escape the Anglicans. However, my father's family was originally from France—the sea town of La Rochelle. They were Huguenots—do you know what that is?"

"French Protestants?"

"Ah, an educated woman—how fine—and rare. They left France for England more than one hundred years ago to escape the persecution of the Catholics. Their name was Saint-Etienne, but they changed it to Stevens to avoid the French stigma. When I had about eight years, the Indians raided our town. They took captives. I was one, along with my older sister. We were marched north to an Abenaki village where we were given to a new mother. It was in the summer. It was there I became *Skagit*."

"What was your sister's name?"

"*Sakari*, it means *Sweet One*"

"What was her *real* name?"

"In Pemaquid it was Katharine."

"What happened to her?"

"She took a husband. I suspect she is still with the Abenaki."

"How awful, what of your parents?"

"I believe they were killed," he replied calmly.

Now in horror, "How terrible for you!"

He shrugged, "Actually, my Abenaki mother was better than my English mother."

"How could that be?" she demanded.

He looked away in thought, "I suppose she was not burdened by an oppressive society." He reached over and gently removed her bonnet, running his fingers gently through her curls. "Any society that requires something this beautiful to be covered is oppressive. The sun is rising higher, you should go. If you like, I will be here tomorrow." She bent to retrieve her bonnet. When she stood, he was gone.

Chapter Seventeen

The following morning: The north meadow

Wwhen I had about fourteen years, French traders came to our Abenaki village. We had seen them from time to time, but these were different." Looking up at Lizzie, he asked, "Can you take off your bonnet? Your hair is so beautiful." She removed it, shaking out her curly blonde locks as he smiled before he continued, "The leader of the traders came and spoke with me about who I was and from where I came. Even after six years, it was clear to him I was not of the tribe. That night he purchased me from my mother. He was Jacques de Noyon."

Aghast, Lizzie asked, "Your mother sold you! I thought you said she was a good mother?"

Rising from his seat on the tree, he looked out at the Deerfield River, "She was. She knew I was never going to *belong* to the tribe like my sister," he explained slowly,

"She knew there was another destiny awaiting me. So we left and made our way to Montréal."

"Have you *never* returned to the village?"

He replied without emotion, "No, never." Sitting next to her, he continued, "Montréal is a real town with many people and businesses—even some buildings of stone. De Noyon took me to the house of the priests and left me to live and work with them. He wanted me to learn the ways and language of the French. I went daily to the Sisters of the Congregation of Notre Dame who taught me well, not just school things, but how to live in French society. The leader of the sisters, Sister Bourgeoys, took a great interest in me, and I traveled with her as she taught the native children of the region. I always think of her as my third mother."

Putting her hands on her hips, she said with a frown, "But you were an Independent, and these people were *Papists*."

He laughed. "Actually at that time I was an Abenaki. Then the French baptized me André. You may not believe it, but these cultures are not so totally different."

Going to the river, he tossed a skipping stone before returning to his seat. "After two years, De Noyon and his men returned. I went with them. In Montréal I dressed like a French school boy, then I began to dress as they do—like a voyageur. We left for the west where I learned the way of the beaver trade along with ways of other tribes. De Noyon even engaged a man from the Mohawk tribe to come with us to teach me the Iroquois tongue. Two years ago we began to travel and trade among the English. That is what led me here—and to you."

Struggling to process all this information, Lizzie asked, "Why do you now dress like an Indian?"

He laughed once again. "I am his translator. He speaks to the English or the Indian and I quietly tell him in French exactly what they reply. Since I am now *the Indian,* the people we meet don't take me seriously. Nor do they realize De Noyon does not always understand their language. They take him for a brilliant man who speaks many tongues well." Standing, he asked her, "Why do they make you wear the bonnet?"

"If I did not, it would be looked upon as a sin," she replied sternly.

Running his hand tenderly through her locks, he smiled again, "I think it is a sin to cover something so beautiful. If God made your wonderful hair, how can it be a sin?"

Lizzie was having feelings she had yet to experience, but she hid them and only shrugged as he stood back. "Tonight we leave for the east on business. I don't know when we shall return, but I will look for you." He reached over to touch her hair one final time, turned and walked away. This time he did not disappear.

* * *

Early summer of 1702 had been unusually warm, and as July became August, no relief was in sight. Lizzie spent her free time visiting and gossiping with Abby and Sarah-Bee who were both greatly interested in suitors. Lizzie didn't show much personal interest, fearing it imprudent to discuss her own interest in Andrew with friends or anyone else in town. Since his departure in late May, there had been no word of the odd foursome. Each day she passed the deserted house at the end of the town road, always looking for some sign of life but to no avail. When she was alone in the meadow, she jumped at every stray sound, wondering if it could be him. She had even returned to swimming, hoping maybe this might bring him back.

One lonely evening at dusk she wandered down to the vacant house. Ascertaining no one was looking, she tried the door and found it unlocked. Silently entering, she looked about in the failing daylight, seeing only a few sticks of furniture, a solitary straw mattress, and a few papers with French writing. Finding nothing else of interest, she cautiously strolled to the barn. It, too, was open, and its contents less interesting than those of the house. Apart from three straw beds, there was nothing other than a few tarnished tools.

She was about to leave when she noticed the corner of a board sticking out from one of the mattresses. Carefully lifting the bed, she removed the board. More than a foot in length, it was well smoothed and someone had been deftly carving on it. There were five perfect letters, each carefully chiseled: E L I Z A. Clearly there was room for four more. She smiled as she held it, then carefully returned it to its cache before she went home and to bed. That night she had a dream that embarrassed even her.

Five days later she and her cows arrived earlier than usual in the meadow. At first she thought it was her imagination, but as the morning light improved, it was clearly him. Seated on a log at the entrance to the woods, he stared out quietly but made no move indicating he had seen her. Resisting the urge to run to him, Lizzie turned to the cows. When she turned back, he was gone. Soon she began to doubt she had even seen him. Eventually she walked to the log. There was no sign of life other than bare footprints in the soft soil. Determining there was no other sign of Andrew, she turned to go home, finding him standing two paces behind her.

"Good morning," he said with his wonderful smile. "Didn't you see me on the log?"

"No," she lied.

"Why did you go to it?"

She struggled to think of an answer causing him to laugh. "English women are such an *énigme.*"

"A what?"

"It is French. In English it is—like a question to which you have no answer."

"Like a puzzle?"

"Yes, a puzzle. I had lost the English word,"

"Can you stay and tell me of your trip?"

"No, sadly, I have work to do at the house. But if you come early tomorrow, I will try to be here." He reached out to touch her golden curl, whispering, "Until the morn." He turned and headed for the town road.

* * *

"So that's all it was, traveling about the colonies forming relationships at the various trading posts. De Noyon did the talking and I did the translating."

"What did your other two friends do?"

Andrew turned away, laughing, "Made certain no one killed us. Many Englishmen do not like French people, but not enough to want to fight those two." Turning back and staring into her green eyes, he asked, "And what did *you* do all this time?"

Lizzie thought before answering. "The usual—chores."

"And your two friends?"

102

"Looking for husbands. I think Sarah-Bee has found one."

"Who?"

"A man named Burt—Benjamin Burt. He is your age and comes from Northampton. He moved here at the beginning of winter."

"Yes, I believe he lives across the town road from De Noyon. He asked me to help him move some logs. A blacksmith, I believe, he is making some tools for De Noyon." He touched a curl escaping from her bonnet. "And have you found a husband, Queen Elizabeth?"

"No, I find most men boring."

"Like the first Queen Elizabeth?"

She laughed, "I suppose. I would rather sit and read."

"I wish I could read. The sisters taught me how to read some French, but not English."

"Maybe I could teach you. I know a good book."

* * *

"I guess that's enough for today," she said, as she stood from their log seat at the river.

Stowing the precious book safely back in its leather sack, she added. "You learn quickly."

"You're a good teacher, Queen Elizabeth."

"You are a good student."

"But the story isn't real."

She bit her lower lip in thought. "Well, it is fiction. It never really happened."

He smiled, "I know that. I mean it never *would* happen. Juliet has everything she needs, wealth, status, a good family. Yet she is willing to throw it all away for this man she doesn't know?"

"Let us say it is just a story," she suggested, changing the subject. "Let's talk about something else. What is it like to be an Indian?"

Andrew stood and stretched, looking across the river. "Easier than being a white man."

Looking perplexed, she asked, "What do you mean?"

"The white man wants more. The Indian wants enough."

"I don't understand."

Motioning to the town, he replied, "Look about you. These people want more land, more house, more animals, more money, more children. They work constantly trying to achieve it. Like your girl, Juliet. She has everything anyone could want, but she wants Romeo just because he is something she doesn't have. If the Indian has a place to live and enough for him and his family to eat, he is satisfied. He doesn't need to work more to achieve more than he needs."

She pondered a while. "But you said your Indian mother knew you were not meant for the tribe."

"That is correct," he answered, "It is because I want *more.*"

* * *

Two days later: The north meadow

"Today tell me what it is like to be a Frenchman. Is it easier to be French than English?"

He laughed at the question, "Maybe not easier, but certainly more fun."

"Fun?"

"Puritans would not know fun if it bit them."

Placing her hands on her hips, she protested, "We call ourselves, *Independents*—not *Puritans.*"

Mocking her with his hands on his hips, he replied, "Although you are anything but. You are tied to rules at every turn of your life. You must do this, you must wear that. Fun has been outlawed."

"So what is better in New France?"

"Church, for one."

"Church?" she asked, indignantly.

"Yes," he replied. "The churches are attractive and well decorated."

"With idols," she countered.

"With statues. They are art and make the place of worship more appealing than the blank walls of your meeting house. There is singing and the services are but an hour. Here they are endless and boring."

She had to smile, "I cannot deny that."

Continuing, he added, "In New France there are picnics after mass where the people gather in the square to eat, drink, visit, dance, play—even fight on occasion."

"Fight?"

"Usually in fun. In New France, men and women dress to be attractive, they talk, flirt—they even swim together." With his sly grin, he added, "Sometimes they even sneak away to secretly make love."

Blushing, she giggled, before changing the subject. "I am teaching you to read. Perhaps you could teach me to speak French."

"Perhaps, maybe I can also teach you Abenaki. You could run away and be a translator."

Chapter Eighteen

Over the ensuing weeks into midsummer, Lizzie and Andrew managed to meet regularly. Careful to avoid a predictable schedule, they had managed to elude the scrutiny of the townspeople. Generally they preferred their secret niche in the forest where Andrew had a clever knack of detecting people long before they were close, along with an uncanny talent for disappearing when necessary. Their conversations continued to center on each other and their life experiences although Lizzie felt hers were much less interesting than his.

"Tell me more about fun in Montréal."

Today they had dared to go wading in the river, the closest they had come to swimming since their original encounter. She skipped a stone across the water while he gathered his thoughts. Under his tutelage she had become very adept at this endeavor which Reverend Williams would consider poor use of one's precious time.

"The French love contests," he began.

"Contests?"

"Yes, to see who is best at something." With an impish grin he added, "I suppose around here, it would be who can suffer the most."

"What?" she asked incredulously.

"Just a joke," he smiled, and then added, "They have canoe races."

"Whatever for?"

"For Fun. To see who is fastest. They may paddle down a stream or across a river. There may be several canoes or perhaps only two. The French are expert canoeists, but not as good as the Indians. Sometimes the French race the Indians. However, the Indians almost always win. Sometimes they race in the rapids."

"Like by the mill at Hatfield?"

"Yes, but often bigger—like Lachine."

"A strange name."

"They say one of the early explorers named it as he thought it was the route to China."

"Is it really?"

He shrugged, "What it is, is the site of the worst of all Indian raids, but then by the English and Mohawks on the French—that's a story for another day. In winter they race with sleds pulled by dogs. There are games, too."

"Games?"

"Another concept foreign to *Puritans*," he said, stressing the pejorative term. "Games like *Lacrosse*. The word comes from the French for the stick with a net which is used to catch and throw a ball, trying to put it in a goal."

"Sounds frightfully complicated."

"It's not. Actually it's an Indian game and as always, they are the best."

Incredulous, she asked, "The French actually play with the Indians?"

"Frequently. The two peoples need each other. There is even a type of game played on frozen ponds in the winter."

"Seems as that would be terribly cold."

"They know how to dress for it, just like they dress for the heat, not for the way someone told them God commands them to dress."

* * *

She skipped the stone across the river, before turning to him to say, "The shadows are getting longer."

He smiled the wonderful smile. "Just as they always do in the autumn."

"Are you going away soon?"

"Yes. In a few days. We are heading west to trade for furs. We will return in the spring, probably to the market in Albany."

"When will you be back here?"

"After the market, in the spring I suppose."

Changing the subject, she asked, "Tell me more about Montréal."

"It is a large town on a larger island built on the bank of the great river of *Saint-Laurent*. From the bank the terrain climbs to a great hill. It is told when the explorer, Jacques Cartier, first saw it, he said it was a Royal Mountain. At first, the town was called Ville-Marie, but his term, which in French is Montréal, took hold."

"How large is it?"

"Not large like the great cities, but great by our standards. I believe almost 4,000 people."

"Goodness, that would be huge, like many Deerfields."

Laughing, "It is nothing like Deerfield."

"Are the buildings really stone?"

"Some, like government and church buildings—a few homes of rich merchants. Not long ago, the buildings were all wood, but there were many fires so they brought in and trained stone masons."

"Is there more than one road?"

"There are many and they are always busy. People are shopping or selling. There is always some market and each week there is a grand market. Many people are just out to walk."

Lizzie tried to imagine the sight. "How do people dress?"

"It depends. Clergy dress in black or gray robes, soldiers in colorful uniforms, Indians—like Indians."

"Are there Indians wandering the street?"

"Oh yes, many, they are a part of the city."

"What do the regular people wear?"

"Ordinary people wear ordinary clothes but not all the same like here, and the women have style."

"Style?"

"Something colorful, to make them look attractive, and different. Not like here."

"And the rich?"

"Ah, they wear elegant clothes, some drive in carriages instead of carts. The women wear jewelry and fine dresses."

"My mother has jewelry. She can't wear it here."

"She would wear it in Montréal."

"It sounds exciting."

"I suppose if you were from London or Paris, you would think it quite crude. But from here…"

Lizzie gazed over the river, suddenly deep in thought. Then she turned impulsively, gazing up with her green eyes, she said, "Take me swimming."

"Are you certain?"

"Yes, very."

Taking his hand, she led him to the bank where she began to undress. He did the same taking care not to look. "You can look at me," she said. "I want you to." He did as she watched him. When they were naked, she dove into the river, swimming to the center.

When she came up, he said, "You swim like an Indian."

"Sarah-Bee's sister, Hester, was taken by the Mohawk for a year. They taught her to swim and she taught me." He also dove in and swam off.

"You swim like a fish," she called out.

Laughing he said, "I was taken by the fishes and they taught me."

She splashed him and he splashed back. Following a series of playful splashes, she took his hands, "Hold me," she said. As they embraced, their wet skin engaging, she was filled with excitement, lust and terror at the same time. *How can this be wrong?* She thought, peering with her bright green eyes into his dark ones. "Kiss me." He did— for a long time. She had never had this experience. She could feel his excitement when he gently pulled her away at arm's length.

"We can go no further," he decreed. "I have seen what *your people* can do to a woman with child out of wedlock. You must *never* let it happen. Not with me—not with any man."

He led her by the hand back to the shore where they slowly dressed. "Will I see you before you go?" she asked.

"Perhaps it is best not to."

Trying to avoid desperation, she asked, "Will I ever see you?"

He grasped her shoulders with his hands. "Yes, I promise you."

"Then I'll be all right."

He kissed her gently on the forehead and walked away.

Chapter Nineteen

C ome on, girls, we haven't all day." Since Andrew's departure, the morning trip to the meadow had lost its excitement, just as Lizzie was beginning to lose patience with her cows. Entering the meadow later than had become her recent habit, she settled the cows in their usual spot before heading back to the town road where she saw another girl struggling with her animals. It reminded her of her first meeting with Sarah-Bee, and as she drew closer she saw it was one of the other *Sarahs*.

Suddenly Lizzie realized why the girl was here and that her own recent infatuation with Andrew had kept her from being a good friend. Feeling a little ashamed, she resolved to make amends. Walking to the girl, she waved, "Good morning, Sarah-Lynn. I haven't seen you down here before."

Sarah-Lynn Hurst stopped to catch her breath. Struggling with her words, she choked out, "I haven't before, well, now—you know."

Lizzie held her friend's hand and replied softly, "Yes, it must be terribly difficult for you now." Looking down the meadow, Lizzie added thoughtfully, "I bring the cows every day. Actually I like it better than housework. I was thinking, I have some extra time and it would be no trouble for me to come and get yours in the morning and bring them back with me in the afternoon."

"Oh, Lizzie, I couldn't…"

"I would be glad to do it. I love the cows. In fact, if you are too busy sometimes, I could even milk them as well."

Suddenly Sarah-Lynn burst into tears and hugged her. "Oh Lizzie, would you? It has been so awful…"

Lizzie took her kerchief to dry her friend's eyes. "Come, we'll get them down to the grass and sit a while."

The oldest of six children, Sarah-Lynn Hurst was two years Lizzie's junior. Her parents were younger than Lizzie's, but earlier that summer her father, Thomas, had taken ill, dying suddenly only three weeks ago. On the frontier, death was a common occurrence in all age groups, and although the town banded together for condolences, it was by necessity taken in stride. The Puritan religion considered death and burial a government rather than a church matter, just as they did with weddings and other practices common in other Christian faiths.

Once the cows were settled, the girls sat on a nearby log. Sarah-Lynn was just getting her grief under control. "Oh, Lizzie, it's been so hard. I'm oldest at 16 and the boys are only 10 and 8. Pa used to do so much and he was so strong. If Ma can't find another man, I don't know what we'll do."

Lizzie answered, "I know what Mr. Benoni Stebbins would say." Changing to a gruff voice she said, "You're good pioneer stock just like me. You can do anything."

Suddenly, Sarah-Lynn began to laugh through her tears and hugged her friend, "I can't believe you made me laugh."

The two chatted a while until Sarah-Lynn said, "I'd better get off home."

Lizzie stood and took her hand, "I'll go with you."

When they arrived, Mrs. Hurst, another Sarah, was hard at work in the garden with 14 year-old Elizabeth while her oldest son, 10 year-old Thomas, was valiantly trying to split wood. She stopped her labor to greet Lizzie, and Sarah-Lynn announced the plan.

"Oh, Lizzie, dear, we couldn't ask you to do that," Mrs. Hurst protested.

"You needn't ask, Ma'am, I volunteered. I have the time and I love cows."

Sarah Hurst wiped her hands and face with her ever-present apron and hugged her. "Thank you, my dear." Then looking into her green eyes, she added, "I only wish I had a son old enough to call on you."

Lizzie smiled graciously thinking, *that's all I need right now.*

* * *

Autumn of 1702 arrived in all of its splendor. The harvest came to a close, and school commenced, but for Lizzie and her close friends, the high point was the marriage of Sarah-Bee. Benjamin Burt, the young blacksmith who had recently come from Northampton, was instantly attracted to her and soon asked for her hand. In the weeks preceding the event, Abby and Lizzie met regularly with their friend and giggled and gossiped, sharing visions and fantasies of married life.

Puritan weddings were small civil affairs consisting of a short ceremony and dinner following. Only family and close friends attended, and when fellow blacksmith, Deacon French, who also served as magistrate, married the couple, Abby and Lizzie stood quietly in the back of the Belden family's main room trying to control their giggles.

* * *

The third week in December, winter arrived with a vengeance, and the frontier residents hunkered down for the season. Lizzie continued to walk past the house at the end of the town road, always on the alert for life which she knew she should not expect until spring. The high point of her winter was a stealthy visit to the barn where she found her entire name carved in the board which now sat beside one of the three straw mattresses. She lay on the bed, holding the board, and sobbed quietly.

Chapter Twenty

Vaudreuil entered the room in his usual hurried manner, declaring without any unnecessary niceties, "Gentlemen, you may be seated. We have a good deal to discuss." His officers and minsters obeyed, wondering how this new leader was going to affect them and their colony.

With the sudden death of the widely admired Louis-Hector de Callière, Philippe de Rigaud Vaudreuil had been called up from his position as Governor of Montréal to become the Governor of all New France. The two men presented a study in opposites. They had both been born and educated in aristocratic families in France, but the similarities ended there. The younger Callière was born in Normandy and Vaudreuil in the south of France. Callière was studied and well liked, while his successor was

116

impulsive and unpopular, but the greatest difference came in their philosophies on how to govern the colony.

Callière was a realist and knew that by sheer numbers alone, New France could do no better than to cooperate and coexist with New England. Vaudreuil, as they were soon to realize, felt much differently.

Drawing their attention to a map of the northeastern section of North America, he began to state the obvious. "New England is running out of room. Refugees fleeing the English Isle are arriving regularly and feel they must push farther westward—into *our* land! Land we need for trade and commerce. In addition, there is news of renegade French traders cooperating with the English to bring French furs to Albany. If history has taught us anything, it is we must constantly beat them back to maintain our position. I believe this is a crucial time to make a strong statement.

"First of all, New England has 15,000 soldiers where we have but 4000. Although many of ours are gentlemen, the numbers remain the same." A few of his military officers privately frowned, knowing that being a *gentleman* hardly guaranteed a good soldier.

"Now, even with these numbers, other circumstances help us. England is devoting more of its military attention to the current European conflict over the Spanish throne. Our recent treaty with New England's traditional allies, the Iroquois Five Nations, ensures they will remain neutral in any conflict. Do not forget how effective they were aiding the English against us at Lachine in 1689. We also have a number of native allies who will side *with* us for their own reasons." Here he resorted to reading from a list. "The Mohawk at Kahnawake, the Huron at Lorette, the Iroquois at La Montagne and Sault-au-Récollet and, of course, the Abenaki at Odanak as well as to the north and east."

Placing his list on a desk, he concluded, "In short, we are in an excellent position to produce a devastating raid."

"And where do we propose staging this devastating raid, Excellency?" asked a young advisor.

Pointing to the map, he replied, "In a small backwater of a village in western Massachusetts. We have had small skirmishes there before. *Guerrfille*, I believe it is called."

The young advisor looked at the map. "I believe that town is called *Deerfield*, Excellency."

"An even odder name," Vaudreuil decreed.

One of the officers asked, "Why there?"

Pleased with the question he wanted, the new governor answered, "As you know, in these raids the Indians take captives which they may keep for their own needs or more commonly sell to the French to be made productive citizens, ransomed for cash or traded for French hostages held by the English. Here is the critical part of my plan— Baptiste!"

Everyone understood. Pierre Maisonnat was a renowned privateer, a pirate who operated under the French flag to attack English ships. Called *Baptiste,* this man was the most valuable person in the French Marine. Unfortunately he was currently a prisoner of the English on Castle Island in Boston.

"They will never trade for him," challenged an advisor.

With a smug grin, Vaudreuil returned, "There is a clergyman in this town who is related by marriage to some of the most revered clerics in New England, and you know how these religious fanatics regard such people—in higher esteem than royalty. My sources say if we can capture this man, we can trade him for Baptiste and the whole venture is guaranteed to be a success."

Stepping back, he concluded, "I have chosen my officers under Jean-Baptiste Hertel de Rouville. We shall make our plans in earnest and prepare to attack by late summer. That is all." As abruptly as he had entered, Vaudreuil departed.

Chapter Twenty-one

February, 1703: Deerfield

Frowning as she looked out the schoolhouse window, Mrs. Beaman suggested, "Lizzie, the snow is so deep, I think you should walk the children home." Agreeing, Lizzie marshalled the *troops*, making certain each child was adequately dressed for the brutal frigid wind, organizing them in pairs, having each small child with an older partner, and placing the most reliable older girls at the end to deal with stragglers. Seeing all was in order, she marched them out to the town road. Thankfully, the driving snow of morning had abated, and the sun was peering out, but it provided little warmth as the north wind continued to drift the new blanket of white down the street.

Trying to keep her line in the rut packed down by the few wagons and pedestrians who had already braved the weather today, she would wait at each home for the children to be greeted at the door before marching on. The next to last house was that of Deacon Thomas French, and

Lizzie accompanied Abigail and Martha to the door. Mrs. French greeted them along with Freedom who had been the best student at school before graduating last year. Lizzie enjoyed the French family with the exception of their oldest daughter, Mary, who Lizzie found too serious for her tastes.

Finally they came to the Hurst home. Since Sarah-Lynn and her two oldest brothers were out back doing battle with the wood pile, Mrs. Hurst greeted Lizzie, inviting her in. Lizzie helped young Hannah off with her coat, while Mrs. Hurst walked the floor carrying her youngest, Benjamin, who had been born a few months before his father's death.

"He has an earache and fever," Mrs. Hurst reported. "I can't seem to quiet him." Lizzie offered to take the screaming infant, and the grateful Mrs. Hurst handed him over, thankful for the respite. When Benjamin pulled off her bonnet and played with her golden curls, she immediately thought of Andrew. He soon quieted, and she laid him on the main-room bed where Mrs. Hurst now spent nights alone.

Soon he was asleep and Lizzie rose, "Would you like me to fix some tea, Ma'am?"

"Oh, Lizzie, that would be wonderful." Normally a wife would never ask a guest to prepare anything, but Mrs. Sarah Hurst was obviously exhausted and at her wits' end. When it was ready, Lizzie set the tea on the table and sat with Mrs. Hurst, who whispered, "Thank you, dear."

Just then the door opened and a snow-covered form appeared. Carefully removing her outer garments at the door so as not to spread the snow through the house, fourteen-year-old Elizabeth Hurst declared with a sigh, "They are all fed, milked and watered—Oh! Hello, Lizzie, I didn't see you—everything is still all white."

"Lizzie was kind enough to see Hannah home and made me tea," explained her mother. "How are your sister and brothers doing with the wood?"

"Fine—now. Deacon French and Mr. Kellogg came over and helped them."

Looking at Lizzie, Mrs. Hurst said, "Everyone has been so kind, we are truly blessed. With Mr. Hurst's sudden illness and passing, we just had no time to prepare for winter. Our wood is a mess."

Three more snowmen appeared at the door. "Fortunately it is no longer a mess," groaned Sarah-Lynn, as she and her two brothers: Thomas, 10, and Ebenezer, 8, unloaded their outer garments at the doorway. She came over to hug her friend, saying, "Praise God, you made tea," and sat, pouring a cup.

* * *

Spring, 1703: Deerfield

Winter left as quickly as it had come, and on April seventh, spring had definitely arrived. Along with the warm weather, Robert Price came home with uncharacteristic enthusiasm. "Good news, Mrs. Price!" he said to his wife who was preparing dinner with Lizzie. "I have found the perfect husband for Lizzie!"

Trying not to frown, Lizzie knew it was not considered her place to criticize her father on this matter as her mother simply commented, "Oh?"

Robert sat, his enthusiasm unabated, "Yes, his name is Willard Otis, and he comes from a good family in Connecticut. He is currently visiting in Hatfield and

122

searching for a bride. A friend of mine told him about Lizzie, and he plans to call tomorrow evening. But the best part is he has some means and does not require a dowry for the *right* young lady."

"Well, that sounds promising," his wife replied. "Doesn't it, Lizzie?"

"Yes, Mother," she replied, failing miserably at her attempt to sound sincere.

That night Lizzie tossed into the wee hours considering her paucity of choices. It would be difficult to turn down a proposal without a dowry, and she knew her parents would not let her remain in the household much longer. Maybe Mr. Otis would be the man of her dreams. But she doubted it.

The following evening the stage was set. The family finished dinner early, Sammy was stationed doing leatherwork in the corner, while Lizzie and her mother did needlework by the fireplace. Robert sat in the best chair smoking his pipe while opposite him the next best chair awaited a victim. The knock on the door came at precisely the appointed hour. Robert rose slowly to answer so as not to seem too anxious.

"Ah, Mr. Otis, how nice to see you," he declared with a rare show of charm as he opened the door. "Please come in." As Otis entered, Robert began his introductions. "This is my wife, Sarah." Otis nodded as Robert continued introducing the family, "My son Samuel who is studying leather work, and *this* is Elizabeth."

"G-g-good evening," Otis replied, as Lizzie looked at her needle work. *My God, he stutters.*

Otis was seated, and Robert began the small talk. Eventually he was able to get the young man to choke out that his family owned a large plot in Connecticut which he and his two brothers worked along with their father. He indicated it was very prosperous. As Otis and her father droned on, she knew it was improper to stare, but she tried as much as she could to survey the lad. She found little to like. He was a head shorter than she and thin in the shoulders and legs, but portly in the middle. His clothing appeared dirty and in poor repair, and he seemed to be closer to her father's age than hers.

* * *

"Lizzie, wake up. I need your help!" Sitting up, it took her a few minutes to get her bearings. Since Mr. Otis's visit four days ago, her sleep had been fitful.

As her eyes adjusted to the moonlit loft, she asked her mother "What's the matter?"

"It's Johnny's Mary. She is in labor. I'm going to assist and think it is high time you helped with a birth."

Lizzie threw on her clothes and climbed down the ladder, seeing Johnny's oldest daughter, six-year-old Mary, at the table. "Mama's having another baby, and Papa sent me for Grandma," she reported.

The three generations left together. Bright moonlight allowed them to take the shortcut across the field to the house where Johnny greeted them at the door. Sarah went straight to work. Mary was in the main room bed, moaning while the fireplace provided a small amount of light. Sarah pulled back the covers and had Mary spread her legs. She pointed to the bloody mucous on the sheet. "That's her *show*," she explained to Lizzie, "it's the plug that is the first thing to appear. Have you lost your *water* yet, dear?"

"No!" Mary cried in pain.

Just then there was a flood of blood-tinged fluid into the bed. Lizzie felt faint. "Excellent," Sarah declared, "you're already well-dropped and with this being your fourth, the rest should go quickly." She reached over and took Lizzie by the arm. "Come here. You can do this one."

"But..." Lizzie whined.

"But, nothing. Put your hand here at the opening. Soon you will feel a hard ball. That's the head."

Lizzie complied with trepidation and gasped, "I feel it!"

"Good," her mother said with New England calm. "It will take a few pushes, but once the head is out, the rest takes care of itself."

Lizzie stood with her hand guarding her sister-in-law's *privates* while she felt sweat running down her head and back. Every few minutes Mary let out an ear-piercing scream, and Lizzie produced more perspiration. Suddenly it moved! Then it moved some more, until with one grand scream, the head was free. Before Lizzie knew what had happened, the shoulders were out and suddenly the entire baby was on the bed, nestled between her mother's thighs. It was now apparent the child was a *her*. "Fortunate she was in the bed and didn't fall to the floor," Sarah said, smiling. "Now take this, swaddle her and give her to her mother. Between the two of them, they'll know what to do." Lizzie wrapped the babe and put it in the mother's arms, thinking she could now relax until her mother added. "Now deliver the afterbirth."

This was news to Lizzie who looked questioningly at her mother. Sarah smiled, "Take the cord..." In the excitement, Lizzie had scarcely noticed the long rope-like structure still connecting mother to child. "...take the cord and *very* gently pull. The afterbirth will come free on its own and come out." It seemed an eternity, but eventually the cord came loose and a mass of tissue joined the other contents on the bed with more blood than Lizzie had seen in her life. This was the last thing she remembered. When she came to, she was in a chair, sunlight was just beginning to enter the room, and mother and child were sleeping, having completed their first meal. Sarah and young Mary had removed all the gore.

"Oh, dear! I must have…"

Her mother touched her shoulder. "Happened to me, too, my first time. You did wonderfully, Elizabeth. Come see your new niece."

Rising slowly, she recovered her bearings and walked to the bed. Mary smiled at her. "Thank you, Aunt Lizzie." She offered her the baby which Lizzie clutched to her bosom while Mary said, "This one will be Sarah, for her grandmother."

* * *

A few days later, the gnome-like Mr. Otis made his repeat appearance. This time Lizzie found him even less attractive. When she asked him if he knew Shakespeare, he replied, "Never met him. Does he live around here?" She asked if he liked to read, but he boasted he had no use for it, had never learned. A glare from her mother put a stop to further interrogation.

At the end of the evening, her father suggested she see their guest out, where she had a closer look and discovered, besides having no teeth, he smelled like something in a pig pen. Declaring he would be back within the week for her answer, he gave her a gummy kiss on the cheek. Once she was inside, Robert was smiling as he matter-of-factly concluded, "I guess that's all settled. I'm going over to Potter's to celebrate."

Once he was gone, Lizzie broke into tears. "Oh, Mama, I can't..."

Sarah took her daughter's hand, "Now child, he is not all that bad. He does have means and can take care of you. In addition, I think he is quite fond of you." In her stern tone, she added, "Let me tell you, many wives would gladly trade for that situation."

"But Mama..."

"Hush, go sleep on it. Frankly, I think you have no option. At least here is a man who will take you."

* * *

"He is simply awful. I don't know what I can do. I wish I could just go graze like you two and wait for a bull." All the way to the meadow she reviewed her plight with Bianca and Kate while the Hurst cows, who were not privy to such personal information, brought up the rear. Once they were in the meadow, the cows began to graze, and she continued to rant until she sensed another presence. Looking, her eyes widened. It was *him*!

Chapter Twenty-two

This time she did not play coy as she rushed to him. Pulling his hand, she ordered desperately, "Come with me." Once they were secure in their special clearing, she turned to him, looking up with those green eyes. "Kiss me."

He obeyed, it was long and tender. When they parted, he smiled, "Where did you get the new cows?"

"Oh, that's—that's another story," she blurted in frustration. "I have a terrible problem and don't know what to do."

She began to cry. He had never seen her this way, "Are you pregnant?"

"No!" Now she began to smile—he could always make her smile. "It's different. It's even worse."

"We better sit down." They sat on their special log as he put his arm on her shoulder, and in a concerned voice said, "Tell me."

Taking her kerchief, she blew her nose. "My father has found the *perfect man* for me—one who doesn't demand a dowry."

"Isn't that good? Is he like Juliet's suitor, Paris, in your book?"

Blowing her nose again, she whined, "No, nothing like that. He's the most disgusting man I have ever met."

Andrew held her tighter. Trying to make her smile again, he asked, "Have you met Monsieur LeMieux?"

Now she began to laugh, "I'd take LeMieux over him!" She put her arms around him, "I'm so happy you're back."

"Tell me all about him."

"Well, Father met him somewhere, and he was looking for a woman. He didn't require a dowry, so Father arranged for him to call." She continued into a litany of the shortcomings of Willard Otis, finishing with, "Both my parents say I *must* take him because he's the only man who will take me." Beginning again to sob, "The problem is, without a dowry, they are correct. Where would I find another man—especially on short notice?"

"Like Romeo?"

"Oh, Andrew, be serious."

He stood, pointing to his chest. "What about me?"

She blew her nose again, "Oh, Andrew, you're an Indian."

"No, I'm not."

"Everyone thinks you are and that's enough."

"Do you have scissors?"

"Scissors?"

"Yes, you know, to cut things."

"My mother does."

"Good, bring them early tomorrow morning."

129

She dropped her kerchief and bent to retrieve it. When she looked up, he was gone.

* * *

"What in the world is he going to do with scissors? How can they help him be a white man—cut out the Indian?" One thing Lizzie loved about the cows is they were wonderful listeners, and as she led her enlarged herd down the next morning, she was giving them an earful. "No one will let him marry a girl from the Congregation." Once they reached the meadow, she sat on a log, going on, "and if my mother finds I have taken her treasured scissors, she'll beat me until there is not left enough for even Mr. Otis." Standing again to face Bianca, she added, "And where is Andrew?" The old cow looked up with big sad eyes, chewing a mouthful of grass, but had no answer.

"Right behind you."

Lizzie jumped. He had not been there seconds before. "How do you do that?"

"Maybe I *am* an Indian."

He was carrying a package which he set on the ground before taking her in his arms. She rested her head on his chest. He was too tall to rest it on his shoulder. "Oh, Andrew," she whined, "No one will let me marry you."

Pulling away, he took her hand, "Follow me." Once they were in the safety of the forest, he asked, "Do you have them?"

She reached under her apron, producing the scissors which he carefully examined, before asking, "Have you ever cut a man's hair?"

"Of course—my brothers'. I still cut Johnny's."

Andrew removed his red headband and loosened his braid, shaking his long hair free. Hanging well below his shoulders, it was smooth, dark and shining. Sitting on the log, he said, "Cut mine like Johnny's."

Convinced this was folly, she began nervously, but once the coiffure began to take form, her confidence was restored. Finally she decreed, "That's it."

He stood and turned around. "Do I look like Johnny?"

"No."

"Do I look like an Indian?"

"Not really. But Andrew, this isn't going to…"

He put his finger to his lips to quiet her. "I'll look at my reflection in the water." He removed his deerskin trousers and walked down to the river. She could not take her eyes off him. Standing in the cold knee-deep water, he studied his image, then dove out and swam back, using his hands to comb his hair. Returning, he said, "It's perfect," and opened his package, containing typical New England clothes. Once dressed in sturdy pants, work shirt, shoes and socks, he donned a common hat. "How's this?"

"Good, but…"

He quieted her again. "Now tell me about Willard Otis."

"He's from Connecticut and is staying in Hatfield."

"When is he due to call on you again?"

"In four days—on Friday."

"Good, I'll see you here Friday morning." He planted a kiss on her cheek, picked up his headband and deerskin trousers and walked off to town.

* * *

Friday morning Lizzie waited anxiously in the meadow with her cows. Today, Andrew appeared at the end of the town road wandering into the meadow like any normal resident. "Good morning, Miss," he said, as he tipped his hat to her. "Fine morning, is it not?"

Standing with her mouth agape at the *new* Andrew, she sternly demanded, "Andrew, what did you do?"

He answered innocently, "Do? Why I did nothing. Why do you ask?"

Frowning, she sat as he stood before her. "Last evening, my father arrived home mad as a hornet. He had been to Potter's tavern, and by chance saw Mr. Otis who said he was to leave for Connecticut forthwith—on an emergency."

"How odd, anything else?"

"Just that he was doubtful he would be back. Then said he would be unable to call on me in the future. Papa was absolutely buzzing. He says he doubts he can ever find someone as suitable in the future."

"It would seem this will give you some more time."

"Andrew, did you go see this man?"

"I assure you I have never laid eyes on the gentleman."

"But..."

"Now that I think about it, I believe Messieurs LeMieux and LeDuc said they were in Hatfield yesterday and met a curious man."

With a suspicious stare, she stood with her hands on her hips, asking, "And what might *they* have done?"

He thought for a second. "I'm not certain, but what I have seen them do with people they meet is kill them, harm them greatly, or make an offer that, let us say, people might find—imprudent to turn down."

"Andrew!"

"Are you angry?"

"No." Putting her arms around him, she added, "I'm in love." Stepping back, she questioned, "But what are we to do? The town still considers you an Indian."

"I suppose I must convince them otherwise."

She embraced him again, "Will you take me swimming?"

"Not now, it was too cold three days ago." She pouted, but he became serious. "We must tell no one that we have met before. I will be around town and may greet you from time to time. If I wander down into the meadow, we may say hello. *If* we have the chance, we can go to the woods." He started toward the road, but turned saying, "You never told me where the new cows came from."

"Come back and sit, it's a bit of a story," Sitting with him, she embarked on the sad plight of the Hurst family.

When she was finished, he smiled. "This will be very helpful."

Confused, she asked, "What...?"

Putting his finger to his lips, he told her, "Later—I must go." Turning, he walked casually across the meadow and into town, like any good New England colonist.

* * *

As spring turned to summer, the new Andrew Stevens became a common sight in town, visiting with the town fathers and helping neighbors whenever he could. He had even met Lizzie and Abby by the town hall, introducing himself as though he and Lizzie had never met. When she called on the Hurst family, Mrs. Hurst was filled with enthusiasm. "Lizzie, do you know this Mr. Stevens?"

Trying to be nonchalant, she replied, "I have seen him. He said hello to me once."

"Well, he came to the door and said he heard I needed some assistance and asked if he could do anything. I didn't know how to react but mentioned a few chores—God knows we do need help. Anyway, he finished them all and has been by periodically to help."

Lizzie only nodded while Mrs. Hurst continued, "Mrs. Eunice Williams told me he had come with those Frenchmen and had dressed like an Indian." Lowering her voice, she added, "Mrs. Williams says she thinks he *is* one and is trying to pass himself off as a white man."

Feeling the need to make some comment, Lizzie merely said, "Oh?"

"She says the Reverend has met with him and his friends and remains skeptical."

Lizzie was hardly surprised that Reverend Williams' wife would maintain her prejudices and said, "When I met him, he seemed to speak perfect English."

"I thought he only said hello."

"Oh, uh, well—I heard him speaking—with some other men."

"Lizzie, I think white or red, he is a wonderful man and a true Christian."

On her way home, Lizzie began to consider this might work.

Andrew and De Noyon had even started attending Sunday Meetings. On occasion he strolled into the north meadow and tipped his new hat to whomever he encountered, including Miss Price with whom he now occasionally passed the time of day. Since Lizzie was nineteen, she was considered in danger of becoming an old maid, and the goodwives of Deerfield felt the occasional uncharoned contact with an eligible man was an act of desperation and not a total scandal.

Today was such a day when he mentioned in passing, "I'll be in the woods." He disappeared and she soon wandered casually into the forest where he was waiting on their favorite log.

Lizzie crept carefully, approaching him from behind. "Boo!" she called, causing Andrew to jump, turning to see his love bent over in laughter. "Maybe you *are* no longer an Indian," she giggled. They embraced as she said, "I've missed you. It appears you have been busy. You've even managed to go to Meeting. How did you win over Reverend Williams?"

"Telling the truth, of course."

"The truth?"

"Yes, that I was born in Pemaquid, Maine, and brutally kidnaped by Indians. Some years later, I was blessedly redeemed by Monsieur de Noyon who took me to the only place he could at that time, Montréal. Later, I worked for him *posing* as an Indian so I could act as his interpreter in all three cultures."

"And he believed you?"

"I think he is not quite convinced, but he'll come along—it is the truth."

"And why did he accept De Noyon as well?"

"We both went to him and abjured the *Romish* faith. The Reverend loves things like that. Moreover, De Noyon gave him a gift of money for the congregation."

"I can see where that may work," she said laughing. "Where did he get the money?"

"We had a very productive winter. We traded for as many pelts as we could manage and sold most of them in Albany at a premium. We also have a barn-load of furs left at the house. Furthermore, now that we are established, I no longer must be an Indian to translate."

"Why is De Noyon interested in the congregation?"

"He likes it here and plans to stay. De Noyon is not the sort to let religion interfere with business or his personal life."

Lizzie digested this information for a bit, then asked, "And what will you do now?"

Offering his hand, he said, "Take you swimming?"

* * *

The same day: Québec City, Canada

Vaudreuil stepped away from his map, "There you have it, gentlemen, in two weeks we will be ready to march. Hertel and his men have assembled 200 troops at Fort Chambly, and our native allies are in place—140 strong."

As the ministers and advisors prepared to leave, the door opened abruptly. "Excellency," the excited gentleman shouted. "I have just received this urgent message from Acadia. It is only a week old."

Irritated by the intrusion, Vaudreuil groaned, "What does it say?"

Knowing his superior did not like bad news, the man nervously announced, "There have been sightings of English ships approaching the *Saint-Laurent*."

Acadia sat at the entrance to the Saint-Lawrence River and the water route into New France. Vaudreuil knew its security was paramount to the safety of the colony, and a blockade or—worse yet, an attack would be a disaster of the first order. He left the room with his most trusted

136

advisors, only to return a short while later with an announcement. "Gentlemen, it seems we have no alternative but to send troops to protect Acadia. This means we must move many of Hertel's men east and postpone the raid. I should emphasize this is exactly why we need Baptiste freed. If his ship was patrolling the area, they would not even attempt such an act."

Chapter Twenty-three

<u>Late summer, 1703: The banks of the Deerfield River</u>

D o you remember the first day we saw each other?" she asked, as she ran her fingers through his short wet hair.

Smiling his wonderful smile, he answered, "I tried to look calm, but I wasn't. In the Abenaki village I had seen many naked women, but never one as perfect as you."

Returning his smile, "Do you remember what I said?"

"Sir!" he told her as he ran his hand down her wet back. "Avert your eyes!"

She giggled, "And you did."

As she ran her hand slowly down his back, he added, "It was difficult to do. I thought, *how foolish to turn away from such loveliness.*"

"I just stood and stared at you until you asked if you could turn around," she confessed. "I was still naked. When I did dress, I ran to the cover of the trees but watched you for a long while."

He chuckled, "I knew you were watching me."

"How could you have known?"

"Then I was an Indian, remember?"

She embraced him, holding her body to his for a long while. Lizzie would have gladly submitted to him, but he continued to caution her. "If we are to marry and live here, we must do it correctly. As tempting as it is, it would be a mistake."

Lizzie wondered if other men were this disciplined. "When will you ask my father to call on me?"

"Soon, I hope. Time should be right in about two weeks."

"I don't think I can wait much longer," she complained.

"Just a little while. We must be patient." Looking up, he added, "We should get dressed."

Putting on her best pouting expression, she asked, "Will you stay and talk?"

"For a short while."

When they were dressed, she sat on the log they now considered, *our log*. "What was it like to be *taken?*"

He looked up thoughtfully into the canopy of trees before answering, "It was a long time ago, and I was very young…"

"So you don't remember?"

"On the contrary, I remember like it was yesterday."

Standing, he looked out over the river as if to look into the past. "It was this time of year. I remember it was very hot—as hot as it ever gets in Maine. It was morning, but very early—still dark. We had left all the windows and the door open for the air. Our dog was first to know. A big black dog called *Blackie*—not a very creative name, I think I named him…" After a short silence, as if lost in memories, he continued, "My mother came to quiet him, but he would not stop, even when threatened with a stick— usually he was very obedient.

"My father got up. I think he was the first to realize what was happening. He was already dressed and took his musket from the hearth. He told my mother to bar the doors and windows and went out into the darkness—I never saw him again. We were all in our nightshirts as my mother barred the door and two windows. The noise outside continued to grow, war cries of Indians and screams of citizens, I guess."

He looked back at the river as if trying to collect his thoughts. "I hid under the bed while my mother and sister pushed furniture to the door. When the attackers reached our house, they had little difficulty overcoming the barrier. A single Indian entered and Blackie jumped on him, taking hold of his arm with his teeth. The Indian did not make a sound. He pulled Blackie off along with some of his own skin and shot him..." Pausing again, he added, "That was the only time that night I saw an Indian fire a gun. My mother began to scream and threaten him—he tried to subdue her. It was clear he wanted us all alive, but she had her large kitchen knife and cut him—badly. He continued to try to subdue her, but when she pulled away, she fell on the knife. I think she was dead right away. The Indian looked at her sadly and shook his head. I did not understand then, but now I realize he needed a wife."

Lizzie sat mesmerized as he spoke. When he seemed to stop, she prodded, "Then what?"

"He took Katharine and me and put straps around our necks." Smiling he added, "Like you do with your cows." For the first time she smiled as he went on. "He pulled us outside. There was no moon—the only light was from a few house fires. I had never heard the word, *chaos,* but

140

that's what it was. People—red and white, running and screaming. Some of the townsmen were shooting. Two bodies lay on the road—adults, children, Indians—I couldn't tell. We had to step over them, but it was too dark to know who they were. We were pulled to the edge of town where they had—maybe ten people from the village, and began to march us north, toward the blackness. We could see the fires in the village behind us until the sun rose."

Lizzie remained silent until he said, "We must go. It's been too long already." He turned and walked off while she waited the usual amount of time before she left in a different direction.

* * *

The same day: Québec City, Canada

As Vaudreuil entered the room, dropping into his chair, it was apparent the news was not good. "Gentlemen, Mr. Hertel reports that the long awaited attack of Acadia never occurred. He has, however, suggested he and his men remain until the weather changes, greatly lowering the risk of such mischief. This, of course, pushes our plans further into the future. As it stands we have fewer than 40 men at Chambly. On an even worse note, it seems some of our savage allies have broken ranks and gone on their own. I am told that the eastern Abenaki are now launching small raids on the frontier of the Province of Maine. So not only do we lack our own troops but those of our native allies seem to be scattering to the wind."

An advisor stood in the back, "Excellency, I am told that the Five Nations Iroquois have offered to help negotiate a peace between the French and the English."

As soon as the words were out of the advisor's lips, he could see he would regret it. Vaudreuil leapt from the chair pointing at the hapless subordinate. "How dare you suggest we negotiate with the help of the very savages who have raided us for a generation!" The advisor sat quickly as the Governor concluded, "Now gentlemen, if there is no *intelligent* discussion, we are adjourned." Turning abruptly, he left, slamming the door behind him.

* * *

Three days later: The Deerfield River

When a rabbit jumped out of the log, Lizzie jumped almost as high. Amused, Andrew simply laughed, "Maybe we'll have to fight for possession of our log." Becoming serious, he looked at the long-fallen tree, adding softly, "like the French and the English."

Lizzie giggled, "Well, it is ours for now." She sat on her customary side. Patting the spot next to her, "Sit, I claim possession for this morning. Now tell me what happened once you left your village."

"They put us in a line. Each of us had one Indian holding the strap placed around our necks. Marching north, we were instructed to obey all orders and keep pace with the group. Katharine and I were strong and healthy, but some were not. There were two small children whom the Indians carried as well as one old woman who was too weak. When she fell behind, her master took his ax and

142

calmly hit her on the head. She fell to the ground. We merely stepped over, leaving her for dead."

"My God, how awful!"

"A man behind her did protest, not physically, but he shouted at the Indian who turned with equal calm, killing him with the same ax."

"How vicious!"

"Actually, not vicious. In fact, he showed no more emotion than you would—just picking an ear of corn."

"But how barbaric—how could you *live* with these savages?"

Standing, he looked through the branches to the meadow. As their plan progressed, he was becoming more cautious of being discovered. Satisfied they were alone, he turned back to her. "That's what I thought—then. But after living in three cultures, I see it much differently."

"But how?"

"First of all, the Europeans have killed more Indians than Indians have killed Europeans."

She protested, "But how could that Indian have been so calm? Couldn't he wait for the old woman?"

"Like everyone, they had a job. In fact, they had a mission, and for soldiers—or anyone, the mission is most important. They realize they may be pursued, so they must keep up their pace."

Remaining doubtful, she asked, "Then what?"

"We continued north for many days. I don't know how many. It was summer. The weather was good. Eventually we reached their village by the *Saint-Laurent* River. Here Katharine and I were taken to the tent of our new mother. We were given Indian clothes, although in summer we wore little."

"Hester said the Indians lived in log buildings."

"Those were Iroquois. They are farmers. Abenaki are hunters so we would move the camp from time to time to follow the hunting. Our houses were—portable. A few weeks after we arrived, Katharine was given to her new husband."

With a look of horror, Lizzie questioned, "How did she take that?"

"Not well. However, she knew she had no choice."

"You seem to take it lightly," she replied with feminine indignation.

"Like most things in life, it worked out."

"How could that be?"

"He came to her bed the first night and they *coupled.*"

Again in horror, she asked, "In the same tent as you?"

"And our *mother.*"

"Hester told me about this but those Indians lived in a great longhouse—not a small tent."

"Yes, in the morning our *mother* spoke to her about family life. Katharine seemed to be all right by the end of the week."

"Hester said Indian husbands in her village each returned to his own mother's house when they were, uh—finished."

"That's because Iroquois are even more matriarchal than the Algonquin, like the Abenaki. After the first week, Katharine and her husband, *Yuma,* moved into their own tent."

"How did that work out?"

"All right, eventually. By the time I left with De Noyon, they had two sons. Katharine adored them, and I must say they had a better childhood than any child in New England ever had."

"And what is *matriarchal*?" she asked, "Hester used that word."

Smiling again, "Something you will never find in New England—the women are in charge."

Her mouth hung open until she replied with a grin, "Oh, yes, I recall now. Maybe the Indians *are* the more civilized." Pulling him by the hand, she said, "Enough history, this may be our last day to swim."

Chapter Twenty-four

<u>September, 1703: Deerfield</u>

Trying their best to keep the giggles to themselves, the three young ladies, arm in arm, headed south, along the town road. The source of their amusement was Sarah-Bee's description of the intimate wonders of married life along with tips for her yet-to-fall comrades. "I would definitely recommend a tradesman over a farmer," she counseled, as they neared the stockade. "Benjamin is so busy at the forge, he has been able to hire-out all our farm work." Adding with an impish grin, "That leaves me with free time—like today."

"The men in my family would certainly like that," Lizzie stated. "Pa, Johnny, Sammy and Samuel Smead are all working today at moving rocks. They have the horse and both cows in harness."

"Our men are starting next week," explained Abby. "Uncle Benoni says he believes the stones breed and give birth to new rocks."

While Abby and Lizzie laughed at the joke, Sarah-Bee announced suddenly, "*I'm* going to give birth"

The parade came to a screeching halt as her two friends turned and embraced her. "Oh, Sarah-Bee, that is *so exciting*! How long have you known?"

Pleased her secret was out, she replied, "I've just become certain. I've missed my last three *monthlies.*"

"When do you—expect?" asked Lizzie.

"Well, Mrs. Belden says first babies are always late, so I guess in March or maybe April." In deference to her late mother and the horrible circumstances of her death, Sarah-Bee had chosen to call her stepmother *Mrs. Belden* in place of *Mother*.

The topic of babies occupied the gossip for the rest of the walk. When they approached the north gate of the stockade, Lizzie said, "Look at all the people in the square. What could be happening?"

"Let's go see," Abby suggested. As they entered, the town square was buzzing with small pockets of conversation. Abby concluded, "I know how to find out." Working their way through the crowd, she found her source. "Uncle Benoni, what is going on?"

The sage of Deerfield looked up. "Oh, hello young ladies—rumors. I've heard a few versions. I'm not sure if there are multiple occurrences or if it's the same story being retold, but in a nutshell what they say is there have been some Indian raids on the Maine frontier."

"Indians?" exclaimed Abby. "Will they come here?"

"Too soon to say. I don't even know if the whole thing ain't just a bunch of smoke, or if there's fire in it."

"What are we going to do?" asked Sarah-Bee.

Benoni decided this discussion required some thinking, so he produced his pipe and lit it. Following that ceremony, he answered, "Deacon French is going to check the story and Reverend Williams is writing to Governor Dudley asking for troops. Captain Wells is going to put guards on the gates and sentries at each end of the town road. All in all, we gotta see what happens." After a long pull on the pipe followed by an impressive arcing spit, he added, "I already started—two weeks ago. Me and Bennie's workin' on the house. We're going to fortify it—make it gol-darn Indian proof."

"Can you really do that?" Lizzie inquired.

"Well, I can sure as hell try." Realizing his slip of the tongue, he looked around quickly for the Reverend. Not seeing him, he concluded, "Well, I gotta git. We got a council meeting. I'll let you girls know if I hear anything more."

The girls wandered about listening to the various stories and theories before they left for home. Lizzie remained uncharacteristically silent as they headed north, wondering about Andrew. She had not seen him in the square and wondered how this might affect him—or, more importantly, affect *them*.

* * *

Dinner at the Price home included Johnny and his family. During dinner, the men limited their conversation to the evils of the infamous New England rocks. Afterwards, the women retired to the hearth where Lizzie, her mother and Mary-John sat and sewed. Young Mary, 6, sat on the floor with her younger sibling, John, 3, while she held her baby sister, Sarah, already five months old. At the same time, the male conversation moved to a discussion of the rumors in the square. After reviewing the issues, they decided it was only a wait-and-see situation.

Eventually Robert excused himself and headed south on the town road. He knew this would be a busy night at the tavern, so he had purposely left early. In fact, he was first to arrive. Heading for his usual table, he waited for the crowd, especially someone who would graciously offer to pay his tab. The next three clients were men he had hardly expected to see that night. They headed directly for his table.

Offering his hand, the smallest of the three said, "Good evening, Mr. Price. I am Andrew Stevens. I believe we met briefly with Mr. de Noyon a few weeks ago."

Robert stood and took his hand, "Yes, I recall."

Andrew continued, "And I believe you have met Messieurs LeDuc and LeMieux." Robert nodded, and the two French behemoths merely grunted while Andrew added the magic words, "Could we join you and buy you a drink?"

Robert accepted, so Andrew motioned to Lenore. "Four tankards if you please, Miss." Andrew had been in the tavern twice. The first time Potter viewed him with suspicion, but after making inquiries, Potter decided there was no definite evidence that he was an Indian, and that he could allow him in as he saw fit.

Once they were served, Andrew continued, "Mr. Price, I have just purchased the vacant house two farms north of you. I noticed today you and your boys were moving rocks."

Wondering where this could be going other than more free beer, Robert simply answered, "Yes."

"Well, we have little to do on my place until spring, and I know how difficult the rocks can be. My father used to call them 'the curse of New England'."

Ignoring the joke, Robert answered, "Well, I'm afraid I couldn't pay…"

Almost apologetic, Andrew explained, "Oh, Mr. Price, this would simply be a neighbor helping a neighbor."

Robert's life experience had given him a healthy suspicion of friendly gestures becoming scams, but his house deal with De Noyon had been exactly as advertised. "Well, in that case…"

"Excellent! We shall be there at your service tomorrow morning," Andrew concluded, as he signaled Lenore for another round of beer.

As the evening progressed, the crowd grew to standing room only. Even Deacon Thomas French made a rare appearance. Usually conversation in the tavern consisted of pockets of small groups discussing various events of the day, but tonight it became a virtual forum, led by none other than Benoni Stebbins. The first round consisted of various stories of who heard what followed by a string of opinions. When the heated discussion began to cool, Andrew took his chance and stood.

Surprised by the move, the room went silent before he spoke. "Gentlemen, my name is Andrew Stevens. I have met a few of you. When I arrived last year, my unusual appearance was a concern to some, but I assure you it was for business reasons that will only benefit the town. That being said, I would like to explain my background. I was born in Pemaquid, Maine, to a God-fearing family of New England *Independents*. I was taken from my home and family at the age of eight in just such a raid as we are discussing tonight. I lived for some years in an Abenaki village until I was redeemed by Jacques de Noyon, who, I believe, many of you know. Recently I have purchased a farm on the north end of the village and hope to work it and become a productive member of your community. My two associates seated with me—along with Mr. de Noyon, stand ready to help Deerfield in any way we can. In closing, I should say that I would be happy to share with you any insight I have from my years with the Indians. Thank you."

As he sat, there was a hubbub of discussion before Benoni asked, "Sir, what do you make of these stories?"

Andrew could not remember ever being addressed as, *Sir*. Standing, he replied, "I'm afraid they sound legitimate. From the description and the location, I would guess they are Abenaki."

A second citizen asked, "How does that affect us?"

He thought for a moment, choosing his words, "If I had to be raided and taken, I would prefer Abenaki to Mohawk."

"Why so?"

As he thought, he realized he had never really understood why he had this feeling. Eventually he said, "With deference to my former Abenaki *family*, I believe the Mohawk are more clever—and more ruthless."

"What should we do?"

Andrew believed there was little they could do if a serious raid occurred, but he chose not to share this concern. "I think Captain Wells has laid out a good plan. Make the stockade strong and well-guarded." Eventually the conversation dwindled and participants went home to rest for another day.

In the morning, Robert announced they would have help in the fields. "It is going to be hot today. Lizzie, will you bring water down to us at midmorning?"

At the appointed time, she filled two large buckets at the well, attaching them to a yoke, which allowed her to carry them both on her shoulders, and began trudging down to the men. When she saw who was with them, she almost dropped the yoke, regaining her balance just in time. Going straight to her father, she put the buckets down. When the men came to drink, Robert told her, "This is Mr. Stevens." Pointing to the north, he added, "He is buying the old farm over there." She kept her head down both to keep her modesty but also to hide her expression as she merely curtsied. On the way back, there was a spring in her step which was not only due to the lighter load.

That evening, Sammy was more talkative than usual. "Ma, you should see Mr. Stevens' men work." Lizzie stared at her plate to appear disinterested as her brother continued. "One's called LeDuc, like a duck, and the other is LeMieux, like the noise Gwendolyn makes. We had one rock that Gilgamesh was having trouble pulling, and LeDuc—he just came, pick it up and carried it to the rock fence." After a few more bites of porridge, he suggested. "If we have one of those Indian raids, I want those men at our house."

Robert gave his son a rare smile as he said, "It's true they must be the strongest men in New England, although they are Frenchmen. This man Stevens is also a good worker and an altogether pleasant chap." Lizzie tried to hide her glee.

In the morning Robert said, "Lizzie, bring us water again today." When he was ready to leave for the field, he pulled her aside. "When you come today, I'll introduce you to Mr. Stevens again. Say hello and smile—you have such a beautiful smile. Maybe we can get him to call on you."

Lizzie could hardly remember the last time her father had complimented her. She answered simply, "Yes, Pa."

On her way to the meadow, she regaled the cows on what a genius her love was.

That evening Robert returned with enthusiasm. "Good news, *Elizabeth*, it seems you made an impression on Mr. Stevens. He has asked to call on you."

She looked at her feet, trying to cover her grin, "Oh?"

"Yes, we are finishing the rocks tomorrow, so I suggested tomorrow night."

Chapter Twenty-five

Mr. *Stevens* arrived at the Price home on schedule, finding the family in the same battle stations used for the abortive Mr. Otis episode. The similarities ended there. After being greeted by Robert, he complimented Sarah on her home. Looking at a solitary trinket on the mantle, Stevens questioned, "This is an interesting piece. Is it French?"

Sarah broke with protocol and rose from her chair to join him. "Yes. It was my father's. He brought it from England. He said it was made in France."

Looking closer, he asked, "Is it from Limoges?"

Shocked at the question, she said, "Why yes."

Smiling his wonderful smile, he said, "I suppose you wonder how I knew that—just a coincidence, really." Addressing Robert, he explained, "As you know, I traveled with Mr. de Noyon in the fur trade. The last time we were in Montréal, I met a French gentleman from Limoges, who had a similar piece." Looking at Sammy, he continued, "He had come with the military but said it did not suit him, so now he works as a cobbler, like you." Sammy smiled, pleased that Andrew had noticed what he was doing when Stevens added, "I think leather work is less heavy than rock moving. Don't you?" The smile widened.

Andrew sat in the appointed chair and conversed with Robert as expected, but he continued to engage the others in the conversation. Lizzie and her mother eventually set the knitting on their laps and listened, even making a comment when appropriate.

Eventually Andrew rose, turning to Robert, "I should be off, sir. Thank you for your gracious hospitality. You are to be congratulated. You have a wonderful home and family. I hope I was not too forward. As you know, I was taken from New England when I was young and sometimes do not have the proper manners." Turning toward Lizzie, he asked, "May I call on Miss Elizabeth again? Perhaps in a week?"

With a rare smile, Robert answered, "Yes, sir, a week from tonight will be fine."

Breaking protocol again, Sarah stood, "Why don't you come to dinner, sir? I will invite Elizabeth's sister and her family."

"Thank you. That would be excellent." He shook Robert's hand and was off.

Once he had parted, Robert went off to Potter's Tavern to celebrate, while Lizzie and Sammy ascended to their lofts. Once Lizzie was in bed, her mother appeared. Sitting on Mary's old mattress, she said, "My goodness, I'm out of breath. That ladder gets longer each year."

Lizzie smiled, but she noticed her mother had begun to look old. In her fifties, she was five years Robert's senior. When she had caught her breath, she took Lizzie's hands. "Elizabeth, what a wonderful man!"

Lizzie smiled, looking down as her mother continued, "Such manners, and intelligent—also pleasant to look at." Squeezing her daughter's hands, she said, "So much nicer than that awful Mr. Otis. I'm so glad we waited."

Lizzie decided it was imprudent to mention her mother's original comments on Willard Otis, merely whispering, "Yes, Mother."

"He reminds me of Mr. Field." Sarah stood, realizing she should not dwell on the differences between her first husband and Lizzie's father. "If this one asks for your hand, say yes."

Lizzie smiled, "Yes, Mother."

After her mother had struggled back down the ladder, Lizzie pulled her *French Journal* from under the mattress to read and dream.

* * *

October 8, 1703, One week later: Deerfield, the north meadow

Having delivered her cows for grazing, Lizzie was the last person leaving the meadow to head for home. Skipping and singing to herself, she could only think about Andrew and his planned visit that night. As she approached the town road, she saw two young men bringing their cows. Zebediah Williams and John Nims were the stepson and son of Godfrey Nims, her father's friend from Turner's Falls. When they passed, she waved and called out, "Better hurry up, boys, or the grass will be gone," and continued on her way. The lads were only a few years older than Lizzie, and she would not normally have been so forward. However today, she was on top of the world.

At home she began to help her mother prepare for tonight's dinner. Around midday, Sarah asked, "Would you look down on the field and see if Sammy and your father are coming up to eat?"

Walking around to the back of the house, she could see them making their way up from the cornfield. As she returned to the house, she heard the ringing. "Mother, is that the town bell?"

Sarah came to the door and listened. "Yes. It's signaling an emergency." She removed her kitchen apron and said, "We should go."

Entering the town road, they joined a few neighbors also responding. The *town bell* was not a genuine bell, as the community was still saving for that treasure, but Sarah-Bee's blacksmith husband had fashioned a temporary device more like a gong, ringing when struck with a hammer. Continuous ringing signaled an emergency, usually a fire. "I don't see any smoke," Lizzie noted as they approached the stockade. When they entered, an armed man stood at the north gate along with a group in the square being addressed by Benoni Stebbins who stood on a bench in order to be heard.

By the time Sarah and Lizzie could hear him, he was well into his report, "...so curfew and billeting will be much as it was in '96. We will have a list of billeting assignments this evening. You are encouraged to be here before nightfall when the gates will be closed."

Lizzie realized her wonderful day had turned dark. When Benoni stepped down, she asked him for details. "Indians," he said. "They took two of Godfrey Nims' boys from the meadow this morning."

"Oh!" she exclaimed, "I saw them entering with their animals as I left this morning."

"Well, my girl, you are very fortunate you left when you did. The only reason we know is the young Kellogg boy was playing at the end of the road and saw them. He says a bunch swooped down, tied 'em up and high-tailed it north. Captain Wells and Nims have taken a few men to try to find their trail, but I'm afraid them Indians got too big a start."

She thanked him while starting to look for Andrew. She was certain he would have been among the first to respond to the bell. After a while she began to worry. *What if they took Andrew and the Kellogg boy didn't see it?* Finally she decided to risk asking. Benoni was easy to find in the thick of things. "Excuse me, Mr. Stebbins," she asked, keeping her voice low. "Have you seen *that* Mr. Stevens today?"

"You mean the Indian?"

"Well, actually he's not really…"

Benoni chuckled, "I know, dear. Just teasing. My niece told me she thought you were sweet on him." She could feel her face turning red as he continued, "He went off with Nims and Wells and the others to search." Her fears were only partially alleviated.

In the morning Stebbins addressed those who had remained in the stockade. "Captain Wells and his men returned last night. They found no trail of the captives or evidence of any other Indians. The council has decided to continue the guards, but the citizens may stay in their homes as they wish." She and her family returned home, and she took the cows to the meadow which was guarded by two armed men, but she saw no sign of Andrew. *I should have asked if he returned, but I couldn't be so obvious.*

158

Returning home, she commenced helping her mother. Around noon, Sarah said, "Oh, Lizzie, while you were out, I took the liberty to call on Mr. Stevens at his new house. It is quite nice. I asked if he could come to dinner in two days. You don't mind, do you?"

Putting down the broom, she embraced her mother. "Oh, Mama, I love you."

Standing back, Sarah put her hands on her daughter's shoulders, "Lizzie, you have not called me *Mama* since I don't know when. You are taken with this man, aren't you?"

Lizzie nodded before her mother continued. "We'll give you a bath with a special soap I have in my chest. We shall make *certain* he asks for your hand."

Chapter Twenty-six

Sarah had instructed Lizzie to come straight home after delivering the cows to pasture. "We shall send the men out to the fields so you and I can prepare for the dinner. Sammy will retrieve the cows this afternoon."

A dinner at this stage of a courtship was uncommon and might be looked on by some as out of line, but Sarah had her mind set, and her plans left little to chance. She had arranged their table so it would accommodate eight. "We will put your father and me on the ends. Samuel and Mr. Stevens can sit facing each other on your father's end, You and Mary next to me and Sammy and Mother Smead in the center.

"I had Sammy lay up a large fire so we will have light, and I have been saving two candles for just such an occasion. You and I will prepare dinner today. Mrs. Smead is bringing her apple pies." Smiling, she added, "That alone should convince Mr. Stevens."

Surveying her room, she had a faraway look in her eyes. "When I was a young girl, we lived on the coast of

Connecticut—close to where Ben lives now. I remember going to dinner at my Grandfather Webb's home." Lizzie had heard this a long time ago, but did not interrupt. "My grandfather still had all his money. He lived in the grandest house in town. Made of bricks, it had a great porch with columns. Inside was a large room with a long table, used only for dining. There were rugs on the floor, paintings on the wall, and candles everywhere. He had a room for himself that was filled with books." Looking into her daughter's green eyes, she said, "Oh, Elizabeth, I wish you could have seen it."

Once things were ready, Sarah said, "Now it's time for your bath." Pulling out the large wooden tub, they went through the ritual, but Sarah had added herbs to the water and produced her long-guarded bar of perfumed soap. Once they were finished, she surveyed her daughter. "You are lovely, Elizabeth. It is a shame we cannot leave your bonnet off. Your hair is wonderful," adding with a grin, "But then Mr. Stevens will never want to go home."

She brought out her precious chest and produced a dress. "This was mine," she said, filled with nostalgia, "let us see how it looks." The garment was conservative but much less rigid than the girl's smock habitually worn. Then she produced something Lizzie had never seen, a gold chain with a green pendant. "This was my grandmother's—it will match your eyes." Then with a laugh, "Don't ever let Mrs. Williams see it." Placing it on her daughter with a tear in her eye, she claimed, "I never realized how much you look like my mother—she, too, was a beauty."

As the appointed time approached, the family gathered. Mrs. Smead had brought the pies and Robert had brought some wine which he promptly served to the thirsty old lady. At last the knock sounded on the door, and Andrew was ushered into the arena. Robert shook his hand, saying, "You know Samuel Smead, this is our daughter, Mary, and *this* is Mother Smead."

Mrs. Smead set down her empty wine glass, giving Andrew a conspicuous once-over. "Don't look like much of an Indian," she reported.

Mary's face went pale, while Lizzie responded with a smile, "He's not really an Indian, Mother Smead, that was a, uh—disguise."

"So why was he runnin' around all year half-naked like an Indian?"

"As I said, Mother…"

"What's your name, boy?"

"Andrew, Ma'am."

"Scottish name—mine's Elizabeth, like Lizzie, here— named for the Queen. Bend down here, lad, let me see your face."

Andrew complied while he stifled a chuckle and Robert refilled Mrs. Smead's wine glass. It was a significant bend as Andrew towered almost two feet above the diminutive old lady. Reaching up she grabbed his chin and then his cheek. "Seems to have a beard," she declared, "Indians don't have beards. 'Course, could be a half-breed."

Mary was looking for somewhere to hide, while Lizzie could see Andrew was actually enjoying this and struggling not to laugh. "Where ya born, boy?" Mother Smead asked.

"Maine, Ma'am—Pemaquid, Maine."

"Well, there's Indians in Maine. Me, I was born in Plymouth." Before he could respond, she added, "My man, William, he was born in England. Came over on the boat— should a stayed there. They ain't so weird in England."

Giving another once-over, she said, "Turn around." As he did, she squeezed his buttock. "Good firm butt. That's good. I think Indians don't have firm behinds. My man, William, he had a great one. Hard as a rock, it was. You can always tell a good man because of his butt." Mary wished *she* was in England, while Lizzie was in fear of wetting herself because of laughter. Andrew seemed to be enjoying the show.

Mrs. Smead handed her empty glass to Robert and ordered, "Let's eat."

Dinner was excellent by frontier standards. The men discussed the ongoing Indian worries as well as the usual town issues. Eventually Andrew stood and excused himself. "Mrs. Price, the dinner was wonderful, and Mrs. Smead, it was a pleasure meeting you." He shook hands with the men and tastefully took the hands of Mary and Lizzie as he said his goodbyes. Lizzie decided to be forward and see him out into a grand autumn evening with a gentle breeze and only a sliver of moon vaguely illuminating the growing heaps of fall color.

"Andrew, you were perfect," she declared taking his hand. "I'm sorry about Mrs. Smead."

"Don't be. She was the highpoint of the evening."

"She never used to be like this."

"Sometimes when folks grow older, they begin to say what they have been thinking all along, and she's been living in a world where women cannot speak their mind. She would make a wonderful Frenchwoman."

"Don't tell *her* that," she cautioned. Then with anticipation, "When will you speak to my father?"

"As soon as possible, maybe tomorrow at Meeting."

"He sometimes misses."

With confidence, he replied, "I'll find him."

Squeezing his hand tighter, she looked up, asking, "When shall *we* meet?"

"Come to the meadow early Tuesday," he suggested before kissing her on the forehead.

Continuing to look up with a grin, she challenged, "You can do *better* than that."

He looked around at the darkness before he took her in her arms. When he released her, he repeated, "Tuesday morning," and turned toward his new farm.

When Lizzie returned to the house, Mrs. Smead said, "You were gone a long while." Lizzie looked down, blushing as the old lady continued. "Don't blame you. I'd have stayed out longer. Elizabeth, Indian or no, he is a beautiful man, the kind that makes a woman moist between her legs."

"Mother Smead!" Mary scolded at her wits' end. "Please!"

Looking at her overly-prudent daughter-in-law, she replied, "Well, he is. He did for me—first time since Samuel's father passed, and I'll wager a pound he did for Miss Elizabeth, too." Looking at the blushing Lizzie, she questioned, "Isn't that right, dear?"

Lizzie continued to study her shoes, while her sister replied, "Samuel, we must be going." Kissing Sarah's cheek, she concluded, "Thank you for a grand evening, Mother." And she marched Samuel and Mother Smead out the door.

Robert sat in his best chair, roaring with laughter, more than his family had seen in a long while. "Mrs. Price, you can invite her any time you like." Turning to Lizzie, he said, "I hope you won't go moping about this one, girl."

She knelt at his knee and took his hand, "No, Father. I think he is perfect."

Putting his hand on her head, he asked, "Will wonders never cease? There is a man who suits you."

Sarah rose from her chair. "Elizabeth, come help me clean up. I agree he is wonderful." Looking at her husband, "And I think Mrs. Smead is correct."

Chapter Twenty-seven

Three days later: Deerfield, the north meadow

Leaving her cows to graze as the sun broke the horizon, Lizzie entered the thicket—their thicket. Anticipating she was early, she was surprised to find him on the log—their log. She rushed to him as he stood, taking her into his arms. "Oh, Andrew, Father told me."

Sharing her excitement, he replied, "Yes, I saw him Monday at Mr. Potter's. I asked for your hand straightaway, and he agreed." Then with a coy smile, "He told me he was certain you, too, would agree."

Nestling her head on his chest, she asked, "Can we get married right away? I don't think I can wait any longer."

Holding her out at arm's length, he looked into her green eyes and told her, "Now that the news of our betrothal is out, I think it would be prudent to wait a few weeks."

Frowning, she whined, "A few weeks! Why?"

He sat on the log, patting it to invite her to sit. She remained defiantly standing while he explained, "There are still people who believe I am an Indian. *We* need to give them time to realize otherwise."

"But..."

"I discussed this with Deacon French, he has been very helpful. He believes it would be a good idea." Pouting, she finally sat on their log as he went on. "In addition, the rumors of raids in Maine continue. The town council has decided to reinforce the stockade, and I have agreed to help. Furthermore, I must travel to Northampton to buy livestock and supplies for my farm—our farm."

This made her smile, but she persevered, "But, Andrew, how does this all affect us?"

Taking her back in his arms, he replied, "It does. And it is important that we do these things properly. It is only a few weeks and we are talking about *the rest of our lives.*"

Stepping back, she took her kerchief and blew her nose. "All right, but I don't think I'll make it."

"I'm certain you will. From now on we can meet in town as long as we don't get too close."

"How will I kiss you?" she pleaded, pushing her body against his.

"Maybe we can meet here occasionally."

"Kiss me *now*," she ordered.

* * *

November, 1703: Deerfield town road

Taking advantage of the unusually pleasant weather, Lizzie and Abby had decided to visit the square to survey the progress on the new stockade. "Andrew has been working here nearly every day," Lizzie reported.

"My pa said he's a good worker," Abby added. "They particularly like that he brings those two men, LeDuc and LeMieux."

Lizzie chuckled, "Andrew says they each can lift one of the new pilings by themselves."

Approaching the nearly completed structure, Abby said, "Look how high it is! No one will *ever* be able to climb over that."

As they passed through the new north gate, Captain Wells was ringing the gong to signal the noonday break. In addition to head of the militia, Wells was a carpenter and in charge of the construction. Some men left the square for home, while others sat on the green to eat.

"There's Andrew," Lizzie said. "He's with that Frenchman, De Noyon." Although Andrew had mentioned De Noyon from time to time, she still had not decided how to regard him.

When they approached, the men stood and removed their hats. "Good day, ladies," Andrew said in a very formal fashion. Motioning to his companion, he added, "This is Mr. de Noyon." Then addressing the Frenchman, "This is my fiancée, Miss Price, and her friend, Miss Stebbins."

De Noyon bowed deeply, oozing his reply as only a Frenchman can, "*Enchanté.*"

Lizzie giggled to Abby, "That means *pleased to meet you.*"

De Noyon replied, "I have already met Mees Stebbins—and now I have zcc privilege of zee acquaintance of zee two most beauteeful women een all New England."

Beauteeful women entered the air with the consistency of honey.

Standing at a respectable distance, they chatted for an appropriately short time before the ladies excused themselves. As they proceeded to the south gate, Lizzie declared, "Mr. de Noyon is quite the elegant gentleman. When did you meet him?"

"He called on me once," Abby answered casually.

"He did?" Lizzie replied in disbelief. "I can't believe your father would—I mean, he's a *Frenchman*! I would think that worse than an Indian—which Andrew is not. It's like, like—Reverend Williams' Negro, Frank."

"Well," Abby began, "He is now a respected member of the congregation, has abjured Catholicism, and is *very* rich."

"Rich?"

With her nose in the air, Abby answered, "Apparently he's one of the richest men in Canada."

"But he lives here…"

"He can get his money anytime. He has even been teaching me French. I knew what *enchanté* meant."

"I thought he called on you *once*."

Abby lowered to a whisper, "I have been meeting him *secretly* for months."

Lizzie's eyes grew wide, "Does your family know?"

"Of course not, only you. By the way, how did you know what *enchanté* meant?"

"Well…"

Keeping to a whisper, Abby said, "I know you've been meeting Mr. Stevens in the woods for a long time."

"You…do?"

With a sly smile, Abby confessed, "I even watched you swim. It was *so* romantic!"

Losing her cheerful calm, Lizzie blurted, "Have you...?"

"Told anyone? Of course not, silly. In fact, Jacques and I have done it, too. So it can be our little secret—forever." She extended her hand and Lizzie shook it before they turned back north, walking arm in arm.

* * *

Working his way farther into the thicket, he could not believe he was lost, but every turn was a dead end. Finally, he saw the back of a female figure behind the next bush. "Lizzie," he whispered.

She turned slowly. It was not Lizzie. "Skagit," she said softly, "how you have grown."

"Adsila," he called to her. She had not aged a day since he had last seen her.

"I approve of your woman," she said looking down, which had always been her habit when thinking. "However—remember, nothing is certain but today."

After she disappeared into the thicket as only Indians can do, the silence of the dark forest was broken by a loud pounding.

He looked around but saw no source. Suddenly he sat bolt-upright. In spite of the cold night, he was covered in sweat. It took a moment for him to realize he was in his own bed, and the noise was a knock at his door.

Opening it cautiously, he saw her. As he stared in amazement, Lizzie pushed her way in, shivering. She wore only her thin nightshirt. "Hold me, I'm freezing."

He held her, rubbing her to restore warmth. The night shirt was thin. Bringing her to the fireplace, he stoked the dying embers and placed another log. "Why are you here?"

170

Lizzie embraced him again, sharing his warmth as she said, "I had a strange dream. I was looking for you in the thicket, but I was lost. Then I saw this young Indian woman. She said—this was very odd—she said, 'Remember, nothing is certain but today.' Andrew, I was so frightened, I did not know what to do, so I came here."

"But, what if you were seen? What will your parents say?"

"No one saw me. There is no moon. My father was at Potter's earlier, nothing will wake him, and my mother is getting too old to climb to the loft."

"You must leave before you are discovered."

She gave him her saddest look, "Let me stay a little while. Lie with me in your bed."

"We mustn't…" he began.

Pleading, "Just for a while, until I am warm. We can talk, nothing more."

Against his better judgment, he agreed. She lay on the bed as he held her in his arms feeling the beat of her heart through the thin frock. Looking into his eyes by the faint light of the fire, she said, "Father told me there was more talk of Indian raids today. Andrew, why can't these people get along? English, French, Indian—why must they always fight?"

As he sat up in bed to think, she laid her head in his lap, looking up while he began, "Deacon French explained it to me. He said in the Old World, England and France frequently go to war over various issues, and that spills into the New World."

Now interested, she sat up. "But why must Old World battles affect us?"

"He says it does. He told me that now they are fighting over who will be King of Spain."

171

"That makes absolutely no sense," she complained.

"That's what I said, but he contended it does. He told me that in the New World, each side has differences on additional issues."

"Like what?"

"He explained it like this, France has interest in trade—furs, fish, lumber. For this trade, they need a great deal of wild land. England, on the other hand, has interest in colonial settlements—like Deerfield. They send many people to make this their permanent home—people like you and me. However, the English do not have enough land for these people to farm. In the next generation, there will be far more people, but no more land. France controls the land to our west, and we need it."

She nodded, "I see, but what about the Indians?"

"That is easy to understand. The Indians see it all as their land—which it is, or was. The French have been, by comparison, friendly to the Indians as they need them for their trade, and they are willing to share the land with the Indians. The English have little or no use for the Indian."

"But don't some Indians side with the English?"

"The Mohawk and the other Five Nations of Iroquois sometimes, but *they* truly resent all the Europeans."

Yawning, she lay back in the bed. "This is too complicated. It has made me sleepy."

Andrew leapt to his feet and pulled her onto hers. Looking sternly into her deep green eyes, he ordered, "No, you must go home—*now*."

When he pulled her to the door, she whispered, "Kiss me again." He did, running his fingers through her blonde, bonnet-less curls while she asked softly, "Who could the Indian woman in my dream have been?"

Still stroking her hair, he answered, "*Adsila,* she was my Abenaki mother."

"How can you be certain?"

"I had the same dream."

"What could it mean?"

"I have no idea."

She thought for a moment before whispering, "When we are married, you can teach me things every night." Running her hand to the bottom of his back, she said, "Mother Smead was right—it is firm." He opened the door and she left.

Hurrying home across the cold ground, she entered quickly and climbed silently to her loft.

* * *

In the morning she came to breakfast as if nothing had happened. Sarah asked, "Did you sleep well, Daughter?"

"Yes, Mother, but I had strange dreams."

After breakfast, she and Sammy went to tend the livestock. Once away from the house, Sammy said, "So you slept well?"

"Yes, why do you ask?"

"Mother awoke last night and called up to see if we were all right. You didn't answer. So she sent me to check on you."

Lizzie blushed and was uncharacteristically silent as her brother finished with an impish grin, "I told her you were sound asleep—but I knew where you really were."

"Oh, Sammy, thank you."

"Maybe you can do a favor for me someday, Lizzie."

* * *

Four days later: Deerfield

Weather had changed dramatically as the last few
pleasant days turned to early winter blizzards. When Lizzie
looked out from the barn where she and Sammy had been
tending the livestock, she saw the solitary figure trudging
down from the town road through the deep drifting snow.
She only recognized him a moment before he entered the
barn, shaking the snow off his hat and coat. She wanted to
embrace him and knew Sammy would not tell, but decided
to be prudent, greeting him, "Good morning, Sir."

"Good morning, Miss. Good morning, Sammy." Sammy
only waved while Andrew continued, "Is your father
home?"

"He is."

"Good. I will go speak with him, but I saw you and
thought I would tell you first." She waited impatiently
while he paused, not knowing what would be the nature of
the news to bring him over on such a day. "I have seen
Deacon French who said..." he searched his coat pocket for
a scrap of paper, "...that he will marry us in two weeks—
December the sixth."

Lizzie quickly changed her mind and threw prudence to
the wind as she rushed to embrace him.

Chapter Twenty-eight

December 06, 1703: The Price home, Deerfield

Closing his book, Deacon Thomas French signaled the end of the short civil ceremony typical of marriages in *Independent* congregations. Shaking Andrew's hand in congratulations, he turned to Lizzie. "Elizabeth—I mean, *Mrs. Stevens*," he added with a rare grin. "I was pleased that you married before my term as magistrate was finished. Your influence on my three youngest girls, Freedom, Martha, and Abigail, was very much appreciated. None of the three had the interest in education that Mary, our oldest, had. They credit your influence making reading enjoyable."

Lizzie thanked him with appropriate modesty as her mother inquired, "Deacon, will you join us for a small dinner?"

"Thank you, Mrs. Price, but Mrs. French insisted I hurry home to help her. I would, however, like to address the gentlemen."

Since marriages were small intimate affairs and New England farm houses small, marriage gatherings were necessarily limited. The male attendees included only Robert, Andrew, Johnny, Samuel Smead, and Sarah-Bee's husband, Benjamin Burt. Once they were gathered, French told them, "Men, I was advised only today that Governor Dudley is recalling most of the soldiers from Connecticut and Massachusetts who have been guarding the stockade. This means we will be calling on you to take more guard duty."

The men nodded in agreement as Lizzie's prudent and shy sister, Mary, asked a rare question. "Deacon French, is withdrawing the soldiers a wise decision?"

French scratched his chin before answering, "I suppose we would like to see them stay, but the town and homes are crowded with the billeted men, and that will get more cumbersome as winter descends. History tells us that raids of note are unheard of at this time of year. In addition, we do have the improved stockade." With his same grin, he added, "Also I don't think the government assigns much weight to what *we* think." Starting for the door, he stopped suddenly. "Oh, I almost forgot." Turning to the new couple, "You must sign the town register."

He produced a small ink bottle and quill and they signed in turn. As French went to close it, Andrew said, "I signed it so people will remember who I was."

French read the entry and smiled, "Actually I don't know if anyone will ever read this book. Even Reverend Williams rarely looks at it." Chuckling, he added, "Although sometimes I think he is beginning to take strange pride at having a Frenchman and an *Indian* in his congregation." When he returned the book to the town hall, he read it once more with a smile, *Andrew Stevens - the Indian.*

When the evening came to an end, the newlyweds walked to their new home through the light covering of snow. Taking his bride easily in his arms, Andrew swept her across the threshold. "What were you talking to Mother Smead about?" he asked as he stoked the dying flames in the fireplace.

"She was giving me advice."

"About what?"

She came behind him, massaging his shoulders, "About what to do with you tonight. The old woman never ceases to amaze me."

* * *

December's weather was merely average, the days short, nights long, and temperature cold. Snow fell regularly keeping the ground covered although not deep enough to impair travel. The new couple was invited for dinner at the Field, Smead or Price residences, and Lizzie even gathered her courage to reciprocate on occasion. During the evenings that Andrew was assigned town sentry duty, she would dine and stay with her parents.

Andrew was as organized and hard working as her father was not. Their larder was stocked with food, the barn with feed and the woodpile had fuel enough for the winter. As a result, they had an abundance of glorious free time.

One afternoon she produced her mother's *Romeo and Juliet.* "Let's see if you can read this to me *without* my help," she challenged, as she laid the book in his lap. Later, when the light faded, she suggested, "Now you can teach me more French. We don't need light for that."

"Why are you so interested in French?" he wondered.

With her nose in the air, striking a haughty pose, she answered, "I have always regarded people who speak two languages as very intelligent, and I want to be very intelligent." When she tired of French, she would take his hand with her most mischievous face, "Come, I know something else we can do without light." Lizzie felt she was in paradise. As December came to an end, she announced, "I predict 1704 will be the best year ever!"

* * *

"Dear God," she sighed, as she rolled off him. "It is January and I am soaked with perspiration." Feeling his chest, "So are you." Rolling back, she put her head on his chest. "Do you suppose making love is this good for everyone?"

"I don't know," he said, "I've only made love to you."

Propping up on her elbows, she looked at him through the flickering light of the fireplace. "Really?"

"Of course. What did you think?"

Now sitting up, stroking his chest, she replied, "Well, you lived with the Indians, and the *French.*"

"I'm sorry to disappoint you, but you were the first."

She put her head back on his chest, "Don't be sorry, I just thought..." Rolling onto her back, she put her arm around his neck. "As a girl, I remember hearing the ladies gossiping when they thought I wasn't listening—about what a chore love-making was."

"And what do you think now?"

Sitting up, cross-legged, she said, "I think it is... what would Shakespeare say? *Ecstasy?* I like that word. People in New England don't seem to use it—what do they say in French?"

Now he sat up and thought, *"ravissement."*

She repeated, *"ravissement*—I like that even better." She lay back with her head on his chest while he stroked her golden locks. "Andrew, tell me about that China place."

"The place on the other side of the world?"

"No, the one by Montréal—where they had the terrible raid."

He sat up, "You mean *Lachine.* It's a village southwest of the city."

"Yes."

"It's a terrible story."

"Tell me anyway."

They both sat up in bed and he put his arm around his wife as he began. "As I told you before, there are two groups of Indians, the Algonquin are hunters and trappers—like the French. The Iroquois are farmers—like the English. The two tribes have always been at odds as the Algonquin want free access to land, and the Iroquois want control of their land. When the Europeans came, the two tribes formed allegiances—the Algonquin with the French and the Iroquois with the English. In the mid 1600's, the French sent an army to fight the Iroquois, and in doing so killed a great number of people.

"The Five Nations Iroquois set out to fight the French and around 1690, they attacked the village of Lachine. There were many more Indians than Frenchmen. The result was a true massacre. Many French were killed—burned, shot, or killed with the ax. Many more were taken captive and few ever returned. The numbers are unknown, but I have heard numbers from a hundred to a thousand. Eventually peace talks were held, but the tension between Iroquois and French remains. Since that time, the French and their Indian allies have made raids of varying size on New England."

Lizzie sat up and straddled her husband, looking at him intently. "What do *we* do if there is a raid?"

He held her by the shoulders, peering into her green eyes. "This is very important. If you are ever taken, you must do exactly as you are told—no matter how awful it is. If not, they will kill you. *You must stay alive at all costs!"*

"What if *you* are not taken?"

"You stay alive. I will find you. I will rescue you."

She bit her lip as tears began to cloud her eyes. "But, what if you...don't survive?"

"I will. If not, you must *promise* me you will live— making the best life you can." She looked down and remained quiet until he again took her shoulders, looking into her wet eyes as if he could see into her mind. "Promise me!"

She fell into his arms, sobbing softly and without conviction, whispered, "I promise."

* * *

Late January, 1704: Deerfield Town Hall

Not uncommon for New England, January had turned bitterly cold, and along with it came a greater than normal snowfall. However, as if God had deemed it, this Sunday was bright and sunny. When the congregation exited the town hall, heading home to the midday meal, they were temporarily blinded by the intense sunlight reflecting off the snow.

Once their eyes had adjusted, Lizzie and Andrew headed out the north gate where Godfrey Nims stood guard. "Good day, Mr. Nims," Lizzie said as they approached the gate. "Is there any word of your boys?"

Nims set his rifle against a pole as if he couldn't speak while holding it. "No, Mrs. Stevens, thank you for asking. Ensign Sheldon has been making inquiries, but little can be done until the weather breaks."

"We shall keep them in our prayers," Lizzie promised as they exited the stockade. Turning to Andrew, she noted, "It seems so odd being able to address the adults—and being called *Mrs. Stevens.*" Taking Andrew by the arm, she added, "I like that." The parade of citizens formed a line in the center of the road where foot and cart traffic had packed down a path.

"Lizzie!" A voice called from behind, causing her to turn.

"Look, Andrew, it's Sarah-Bee and Benjamin. Let's wait for them."

Once their friends caught up, the men took the lead to discuss the farms and town matters while Lizzie and Sarah-Bee followed behind discussing *ladies' issues.* Lizzie put her hand on her friend's enlarging abdomen which was becoming prominent even under her heavy coat. "It appears you are coming along nicely."

Sarah-Bee put her own hand on her front and responded, "Mrs. Belden says it should be in about two months. Fortunately, she says I'm doing well."

Lizzie put her face to her friend's ear and whispered, "I missed my last *monthly.*"

Her friend squeezed her arm, "Oh, Lizzie, that would be wonderful. Our children could be best friends." Looking more serious, "But Mrs. Belden says missing is common in the first months of marriage, even when there is no baby."

Lizzie held her arm more tightly, "I guess we shall wait and see."

Changing the subject with enthusiasm, Sarah-Bee asked, "Did you hear about Abby?"

Lizzie's ears perked up, "No, I have scarcely been out of the house with all this snow."

Pleased she was the first to know, Sarah-Bee said, "Well—*that* Mr. de Noyon has asked for her hand, and her father has *agreed.*"

Lizzie took her friend's arm in both hands, stammering with a quizzical look, "Is...well, can they..."

Anticipating the question, Sarah-Bee answered, "Apparently they went to see Reverend Williams and he agreed—he has even agreed to do the marriage in place of the magistrate!"

"Oh, my goodness."

Sarah-Bee added in a whisper, "They say De Noyon *is* one of the richest men in Canada."

"Yes, I've heard. When will it be?"

"In early February. Oh, Lizzie, wouldn't it be fun if we all had children and they could be friends as we were?" When they reached the Burt home, Lizzie and Andrew bid their friends goodbye before hurrying across the road to theirs.

While they ate, Lizzie related the gossip to her husband, particularly concerning Abby and De Noyon.

"I doubt he is the richest man in Canada," Andrew told her, "but he did make a lot of money from furs and still has a barn full of them which he plans to take to Albany this spring."

As she cleared the table, she looked out their solitary glass pane, "The sun has disappeared and clouds are gathering. I think it is going to snow again." Coming up behind Andrew, she massaged his shoulders, "Do you think anyone would notice if we stayed home from Meeting this afternoon?"

He reached over, taking her hand, "Maybe not. However, we *must* return. I want us to be the most dependable couple in the village."

* * *

February arrived in a tempest. Snowfall surpassed anyone's memory as storm after storm pushed the drifts as high as some roofs. The day of the marriage of Abby and Jacques de Noyon did not escape nature's fury. In spite of this, many neighbors including her two best friends and their husbands trudged to the Town Hall to bear witness to the event which was indeed conducted by the Reverend Williams himself.

In spite of the weather, the newlywed Stevens couple forged ahead with their new and wonderful life. They would bundle against the elements and march out hand in hand to care for their livestock each day and managed to have dinner with family each week. In spite of this, they had time to enjoy each other as they planned for each and every aspect of the future in joyous anticipation.

Lizzie's French improved as she also learned some Abenaki terms, and Andrew successfully read *Romeo and Juliet*. "I should return this to my mother," she announced after his completion. "I haven't seen her for a few days. The snow has stopped, and it might be a good time for me to run over there." She bundled up and putting the beloved volume inside her coat, headed out. In spite of the clear day, the snow banks remained formidable, but she made it down two doors without too much difficulty.

"Come with me and we shall put it away," her mother said, leading her daughter into the bedroom. Pulling out her precious chest, she opened the secret door. Setting the book carefully among the other treasures, she instructed, "There it is—where it belongs, and you know that when I am gone, you are to take the chest."

"Yes, Mother," she answered, as her mother pushed the chest away.

"Come have a cup of tea," Sarah suggested, as they returned to the main room. "Your brother is helping Johnny while your father went to Potter's to hear the latest news." As she poured the tea, she continued, "He says there is still talk and concern about raids. He says everyone is uneasy."

Lizzie stirred her cup as she replied, "Andrew says raids don't happen in the winter, especially with snow like this."

"That's what I thought, too," Sarah agreed as she poured more tea. "I think people just worry too much."

When Lizzie returned home, she asked Andrew, "At what time of year was the raid on Lachine?"

"Summer—August, I believe."

"Oh, Good," Lizzie replied in relief. "We will be safe this winter."

Chapter Twenty-nine

<u>Monday February 29, 1704, 4:00 AM: Deerfield—Day 1</u>

A ndrew, wake up," she said, shaking her sleeping husband's shoulder.

"Huh, what?" he responded, not half-awake.

"You are snoring, roll over." He obeyed and immediately fell back to sleep.

"Andrew!"

Now awake, he sat up. "What now?"

"It's something else, listen."

Returning to his pillow, he answered, "It's only the wind."

"Go look," she ordered.

Knowing he had met his match, he staggered to the glass window and opened the inside shutter. Turning back he yawned, "It's only the…" He was interrupted by the sound of the town gong. "Listen, is that the *bell?"*

Now Lizzie sat up. "I think so, but it only sounded once."

Taking his coat, he said, "I'll step out and look." He returned right away. "I think I see a fire in the stockade, I'd better go lend a hand."

As he quickly dressed, putting on his heavy coat and boots, Lizzie came to the door. "Be careful and take your musket."

Donning his heavy hat, he kissed his wife. "Yes, ma'am. Bar the door as soon as I leave."

She secured the door and looked through the window into the blackness. As she returned to the remaining warmth of their bed, she heard a loud knock. "Who is it?" she asked coyly.

"It's me." His voice filled her with fear.

She carefully opened the door and he entered abruptly, returning the bar to the door. His command was frightening, "Hurry, get dressed, put on your warmest clothes, coat and heavy boots."

Going from coy to terrified, she asked, "What's wrong?"

"I think I see two fires, and there are tracks in the snow."

"There were people walking out there before dinner," she explained, trying to remain calm.

"Some are on the side of the road and they are *racquet tracks.*"

"What is that?" she asked, becoming more nervous.

"Shoes to walk on the snow."

"Maybe somebody has them?"

Becoming very serious, "English don't use them."

Even more concerned, she asked, "Who does?"

Staring sternly into her green eyes he said softly, "Indians."

Panic spread across her face. "What will...?"

He took her firmly by the shoulders. "Do as I say. You are going to your father's house."

"But why?"

"Just do it!"

She had never heard Andrew angry before and pulled on her clothes. As they left the house, he ordered, "Leave the door open!"

"But..."

"Do it!"

As they stepped into the snow, she shouted, "Wait a second!" She turned and reentered the house as he stood impatiently at the door. Going to the fireplace she removed its single ornament from the mantel—the carved board—*Elizabeth*. She stuffed it under the mattress and returned to Andrew.

Tears were forming in her eyes as they struggled through the three-foot snow blanket to her father's house two doors away. They had to knock persistently before they heard motion inside. The door opened a crack. She could see her father's face. "What?"

"Mr. Price," he said abruptly, "it is Andrew and Lizzie, let us in."

Her confused father opened the door, "What the...?"

"Sir, it appears there is an attack on the town!"

"What?"

Andrew closed and barred the door. "There are fires in the stockade and Indian *snow slipper* tracks in the road, many of them—all going south. You are all to put on your heaviest boots and coats."

Robert looked out again. "If it's Indians, why didn't they stop here on the way in?"

Andrew became stern, "Sir. There are a great number of tracks. This is not a few renegades picking off two boys in the meadow. This is a big attack and they want to hit the stockade first. But they will likely be back this way. Now everybody get dressed. Sammy, you and your father bring your guns and everyone follow me."

Once they were dressed, he led them out the front. "Leave the front door open. Everyone make your own set of tracks to the road, angle toward the village." They complied until they reached the ruts in the road, and Andrew ordered, "Now follow me *exactly* in my tracks." He turned, leading them north, then on a circuitous route arriving at the back door of the Price barn. Once they entered, he explained. "Now there are no fresh tracks leading from the house directly to the barn, and it looks as if you left the house in a hurry, running to town. Sammy, you take Lizzie and your mother to the loft where you are all to hide until someone you know, hopefully us, comes back."

Sammy objected, "Can't I come with you?"

"No! You have a more important job. Hopefully they will pass the house by. They may burn it. If they do, they do. If you are faced with a lone Indian, Sammy, you shoot him. If there is more than one, put your gun down and surrender."

Sammy's face was beginning to reflect his horror. "But…"

"Sammy, if there is more than one and any of you do *anything* other than *exactly* what they order, you will all die. Now we must go. We will stop for Johnny and Samuel Smead and do the same with their families." Looking up the ladder to the loft, he whispered softly to himself, "God help us." The two men marched off toward the stockade.

The threesome gathered in the corner of the barn loft, shaking from fear and cold. It seemed like an eternity before Sarah whispered, "Mary won't have to go to the barn. Mr. Smead has that cellar that is perfect—no one would find it."

As the minutes dragged by, the sounds became audible—then they became loud. Screams, war cries, shooting. Lizzie thought of what Andrew had called *chaos*.

It seemed forever before they heard motion below. "Maybe it's the men," Sarah whispered. Lizzie merely shook her head. She could still hear the fighting in the village, and she soon heard people speaking below the loft. They did not speak in French, and she did not think it was Abenaki. As they heard the steps on the ladder, Sammy pointed his musket. Lizzie quickly pulled on the barrel, whispering, "Sammy, they were talking. There is *more* than one."

He reluctantly obeyed with a frown and set the weapon aside. As the first head came through the opening, Lizzie's fear increased—he was Mohawk. He motioned for them to follow him down. She had expected to be dragged, but remembering Andrew's advice, said to the others, "Just follow me and *do as they say*."

When they were down, the Indians put straps around their necks and Lizzie was struck with the bizarre thought that she was suddenly relieved her father had decided to butcher the aging Bianca who did not live to witness this.

Led out to the road, they headed toward the fires raging above the stockade. Indians were roaming over the road, checking houses to find those who had not moved to the fortification. Flames were rising from Mrs. Beaman's house, but De Noyon's place at the end of the road still stood. As they headed south, they passed Johnny's house where Indians were pulling his family out of their sanctuary. Young John and Mary walked bravely in front of their mother who carried baby Sarah. She stumbled in the snow almost dropping the infant when her captor pulled the baby from her arms, hit the child with his ax and discarded her casually in the snow. When the child's mother, Mary, tried to protest, the Indian threatened the other children with the ax, causing her to stop.

"Mother! Say nothing," Lizzie ordered, as she saw her own mother ready to act. Thinking to herself, *God, help me be brave,* she shed a tear for the child she had helped bring into the world.

Samuel Smead's house was in flames. *Dear Jesus, I hope they did not go to the cellar.* Sarah-Bee's father's house was smoldering but no one was around.

Finally they came to the stockade. The snow bank had drifted up to the top of the north wall, and with the glow of the firelight, she could see the *Indian slipper* tracks going right over it. Both gates were wide open. The interior was littered with bodies, debris, and ash from burning houses. Reverend Williams's house had burned almost to the ground while more than half the other homes in the compound were aflame including that of Benoni Stebbins. They were led into the town hall. Packed with citizens, many on Indian leashes, the building reeked of blood and human waste as well as fear. As they were herded into the hall, they were pushed into the French family.

"Lizzie, how is your family?" the Deacon asked softly. She told him what she knew, and he reported, "I saw Andrew and your father as we were brought here. They were still up and shooting."

She took that as the best she could hope for before asking about his family. Pointing around he explained, "We all got out." She looked, seeing his children along with their wailing mother. Deacon French added, "except for the

190

baby, John. He was just one month…" Suddenly he broke into tears, sobbing, "They pulled him away, killing him like an animal." Lizzie embraced him as he wept on her shoulder. She never thought she would see this grown man of authority cry.

When he quieted, she asked, "Are there any more people captive?"

Grateful for another topic, he replied weakly, "Yes, I hear there is a group at the Sheldon house."

Lizzie tried to look about, attempting to see who was present and who was not. In her terror she could not remember everyone's name. She did see Sarah-Lynn Hurst, her mother and siblings including two-year-old Benjamin.

"Lizzie!" Turning, she saw Abby along with De Noyon and the two giants. Abby reported her father's family seemed to be intact but had no further news of Robert or Andrew. "I did see Sarah-Bee and Benjamin over in the corner." She mentioned a few more names but Lizzie was losing her concentration to fear and confusion.

Suddenly the mass of humanity started to move as they were led into the square, then north on the town road. There were a few bodies to step over, some she recognized, and some she did not. The house fires were almost burned-out. Her house and her father's remained standing, but Johnny's was now in flames. As they passed her father's house, the first rays of sunshine arrived, allowing her to see a Mohawk coming out the door carrying her mother's beloved chest. She wanted to scream, but she had promised Andrew who had sworn to rescue her.

Some of the English prisoners had been given *Indian slippers*, but they clearly did not have enough. As a result, she and her family had to trudge on without. Fortunately, Andrew had made them dress warmly and take heavy boots. Many of her neighbors were hiking in simple indoor clothes and shoes. Lizzie was beginning to suffer the cold and realized how much worse it must be on them.

Once they left the town road, entering the north meadow she knew so well, they were no longer aided by the ruts in the road. Only able to follow the much more difficult path cut by the Indians, Lizzie followed Sammy who followed their mother. She could already see her mother failing and soon she stumbled and fell. Sammy rushed to her aid, but his Indian held tight to his tether. Sarah's Indian merely pulled out his ax and struck her on the head. Blood poured forth as the woman who had given them birth, fell silent. Her Indian tried to kick her body off the path but the snow was too deep. They were forced to step over. Sammy began to react. Fortunately Lizzie could reach him, saying with a calm that surprised even her, "Sammy, do nothing—remember what Andrew told us." In spite of her calm words, violent thoughts were filling her head.

As they neared the bank of her beloved Deerfield River, they heard a ruckus from behind. It appeared a group of citizens, aided by a force from a nearby community, were coming to save them. As her hopes rose, a small army appeared from the woods in front of them. She had forgotten about the French. She had only seen the Indians sent to raid, kill and pillage while the French soldiers sat on the outskirts ready to repel just such a pursuing force. Within a few minutes, the English posse retreated south, and the dejected prisoners crossed the frozen river, heading north. Two miles and two hours later they reached a clearing known as the Petty Plain where the attackers had camped before the raid. Now protected by the French-Canadian troops, the Indians began to make camp.

Route of the Captives

F

Day 45 Montreal

Day 26 - Chambly

Day 22

E

Day 17

D Day 14 Day 12

B

G

C

Day 9

Day 6

A

Day 4

Day 1 Deerfield

B

A - Deerfield River
B - Connecticut River
C - White River
D - French River
E - Lake Champlain
F - Odanak
G - Green Mountains

Chapter Thirty

March 3, 1704: The Connecticut River Valley—Day 4

As Lizzie awoke, she felt the empty space beside her. *Andrew must already be up.* Then reality struck like a thunder clap. Andrew was not here. Nor was anyone else in the small tent. Her new *master,* who had lain naked with her last night, must be up. She opened the flap slightly. Peeking out, she saw only snow illuminated by very weak light. It must be daybreak. Pulling the deerskin blanket over her head, her mind began to clear, as she realized she had slept—soundly. Surprisingly, she felt rested though her memories of the past three days remained hidden in fog.

Suddenly the flap pulled back as her master entered with a basin. Setting it down, he motioned for her to kneel as he did. This was as close to standing as one could get in the small enclosure. She wondered how he could do it with his crooked leg. Handing her a cloth and what seemed to be a type of soap, he made bathing motions. Once it was clear she understood, he left her alone.

The water was surprisingly warm, and the *soap* had a strong scent of sage. It was glorious. Finishing her torso, she washed between her legs where she had been forced to soil herself during first day of the march. As she finished, she looked for her clothes, but they were gone so she returned to the deerskin. Soon he returned with an armload of skins—her new garments. He had her lie down so he could help her dress in the close quarters. She found this embarrassing but realized modesty had become a thing of the past.

There were deerskin trousers much like Andrew's except the crotch was open. She realized why, recalling her conversation with Hester Belden a few years before. She had thought it odd at the time but now considered it a good idea. There was a deerskin dress to cover her and a pair of deerskin boots, the softest, most comfortable shoes she had ever experienced. He indicated she should go out.

Dotted with small tents, the camp stretched as far as she could see. She tried to identify who was there, but in the dull morning light, she could not. There were a few small fires where water was heated and food prepared. She only remembered the piece of leathery meat, but this morning her master handed her a small bowl of porridge. To her surprise, it was good.

She spooned it down quickly and was soon sorry as she felt a wave of nausea and vomited. Generally Lizzie had a strong stomach, although even in the few days before the raid she had experienced the wave of nausea in the morning. Her master remained calm, took her bowl, rapidly folded the tent, and replaced her leash. In a matter of minutes, they headed north.

Once her nausea had passed, she began to feel stronger as they continued over the rolling forested terrain, always going up or down—never level. Though the woods were thick, they moved quickly. As Andrew had once told her, Indians had an instinctual knack for finding a trail where none was apparent. The sky was clear and the air warmer than before. Unfortunately this changed the hard snow to slush—even more difficult to negotiate.

In spite of this hardship, her memory began to return. She vaguely remembered the first night when they had killed Reverend Williams' Negro man, Frank—for no apparent reason. That night one of the young men ran off. She seemed to remember it was Joseph Alexander, only a few years her senior. She recalled the Reverend announcing the Indians had made it clear if there was any more such mischief, they would burn the lot of them alive, dampening any thoughts of escape.

There were more murders that day, including three or four small children. She still could not remember who died with one exception. Reverend Williams' wife, Eunice, had been just ahead of Sammy who was ahead of Lizzie. Having just given birth a few weeks before, she remained weak. She was also quite heavy and when crossing a stream, she broke through the ice and was submerged in the frigid water. Her master pulled her out but she continued to struggle in the thin jagged ice. Reaching the bank, she fell again and her master struck her with his ax. As Lizzie passed her, Eunice's eyes were wide open as blood flowed over them. She seemed to be staring at Lizzie across death and Lizzie feared she would never lose this horrid spectacle.

Lizzie saw no murders today, but she could hardly see the whole procession for the trees. Her new clothes were warm and comfortable and her deerskin boots were amazing. She felt better and better as the day passed, beginning to believe that she would survive. She must. Andrew could appear at any time to rescue her.

That night they halted to camp on the bank of a small easterly-running river flowing to meet the larger Connecticut. Apparently the raiders had camped here on their march to Deerfield as they had provisions stored and guarded by a few Indians as well as two Frenchmen. Along with food and more clothing, they had a few sleds and dog teams to pull them. Lizzie flashed back to Andrew's description of dog sled races. In addition, their captors had more *Indian slippers* including a pair for her. Her master attached the *racquets* to her boots and showed her how to walk in them. She instantly understood their importance. He efficiently constructed their tent while she tried to survey the surrounding area, trying to make a mental note of who she recognized. She was relieved when she saw Sammy who was no longer in line with her. There were a few small fires and her master visited one, returning with two pieces of what appeared to be fowl. She resisted devouring it, eating slowly, making certain she left no morsel. When finished, she broke the bone and sucked the marrow.

Sitting on pine branches as they dined, they carefully studied one another. Older than her master of the first two days, she judged him to be in his forties. Tall and thin, he had a jagged face and sharp jaw. Like most Indians, he showed little, if any, emotion. He would have been tall but for the crooked leg which made him six inches shorter when he stood on it. She had guessed he was Abenaki or at least some sort of Algonquin. The difference from her early Mohawk master was striking. The first man was brusque and cruel as he pulled her leash constantly, occasionally causing her to fall. He would criticize her loudly, kicking her to get up and even threatening her with his ax. She had great hopes not to encounter him or his tribe again.

As the sun set, her new master led her into their tent and again had her undress so they could once more share their heat. Tonight she was surprisingly calm, appreciating the human closeness.

* * *

March 5, 1704: The west bank of the Connecticut River—Day 6

Her master was gone when she awoke. It amazed her he could leave such cramped and intimate quarters without disturbing her. Struggling into her clothes in the small tent, she crawled out to greet the early dawn, and walking behind a small bush, she squatted to *do her business* with as much privacy as the circumstances afforded. Returning, her master presented her with a morsel of meat which she put in the pouch in the front of her dress. She had decided it was best to wait for her stomach to settle in the morning before eating. Surveying the camp she saw Reverend Williams walking with two Indians.

After they stopped, he called out over the camp, "Today I have convinced our captors to allow us a day of rest to observe the Sabbath. Once you have eaten, we shall gather in the clearing to praise the Lord." Andrew had told Lizzie that the French and many of the Indians were Catholic and also observed Sunday as a day of rest. However, she would allow the Reverend to take credit—and certainly had no objection to rest.

As they gathered in the clearing, Lizzie found herself on high ground with her first real view of the entire crowd. Trying to compute its size as she often did when bored at Meeting, she was suddenly struck by the enormity of the group and the implications for Deerfield. Watching Reverend Williams struggle to the center, she could see how badly he was walking and wondered if his late wife's fate also awaited him. As Williams surveyed his flock, Lizzie suddenly began to sob.

The sermon was vintage Williams as he chose *The Lamentations of Jeremiah,* one of the most depressing passages in the Bible. Lizzie began to wonder if he was trying to blame the congregation for their current plight. After about an hour, one of the English-speaking Indians came to him and asked him to sing a song. He announced his selection and led the congregation in their typical lack-luster rendition. Following this, the Indians sang their own hymn. It was quite lively and well performed. At the end it was clear from their smug demeanor, they felt their song was superior.

Lizzie smiled to herself as she recalled Andrew's description of French and Indian love of contests and became further amused when they decided this was a good time to end the service. Obviously they thought an hour was long enough, although the Reverend believed he was just getting warmed up. Her master pointed toward the river and took her hand leading her to an area where they could sit on the bank. A tear came to her eye as she recalled the many times she had done this with Andrew.

Mammoth compared to the Deerfield River, the Connecticut was almost a quarter mile wide at some points.

The banks varied in height. Here they were low and the river valley was wide. From her vantage point looking across the river to the east, Lizzie estimated it was almost two miles before the valley floor began to ascend into the hills. When she could see through the trees to the west, the valley was narrower but its eventual ascent higher as it reached for the foothills of the Green Mountains.

In the summer the river would flow calmly, but today it was covered with ice. Unlike the covering of smaller streams, this could not be easily crossed as the ice was broken and piled frequently with free ice floes in some small treacherous areas of open moving water.

"Well, hello, Elizabeth." Lizzie startled at the voice and turned quickly to see Mrs. Beaman with her master who had sat next to Lizzie's. From their appearance and dress, she judged the two men were from the same tribe, and they began to visit, giving her a precious opportunity to talk to her old school dame.

"How nice to have this day to rest," Mrs. Beaman said casually as she sat, adding, "A nice service, don't you think?" Lizzie nodded and noticed the dame's subtly sly smile as she told her, "My departed father said, 'few souls are saved after one hour of preaching.'" Lizzie actually smiled as the dame continued, "How are you getting on, dear?"

Lizzie answered and once they were confident they were free to converse, they turned to more serious matters. Although Mrs. Beaman and her husband were older and stouter than the Reverend Williams and his wife, they were apparently stronger as they were keeping up with the group. "However, I must confess that yesterday they let me ride a while on a dog sled with some of the children—it was quite a thrill."

Finally they came to the terrible but inescapable list of those they each knew to be dead. Lizzie told Mrs. Beaman about her mother and baby Sarah Field along with a few others while the dame shared her sad list. "Sarah-Bee's stepmother, almost all the Hawks family, and four of the Nims children. Of course, only today Mrs. Nims was killed." Lizzie's brief smile had disappeared and her eyes filled with tears. Then the dame asked the sensitive question, "What of your young man, dear?"

"I don't know. No one seems to," she explained, choking back the tears. "He went off with Mr. Smead, my father, and my brother, Johnny, to fight. I have not seen any of them here."

Mrs. Beaman almost smiled. "Oh, I heard…from Mr. Brooks that he saw a group of men with guns escaping through the south gate just in the nick of time to save themselves." She thought for a moment, "Let's see…there was Mr. Smead, your father, your brother, Johnny, Captain Wells, Ensign Sheldon and several others he had not the time to recognize."

"Maybe if I asked him," Lizzie suggested with new vigor.

The dame nodded, "I haven't seen him since we spoke in the town hall, but I shall keep an eye out for him."

The two Indians rose, signaling it was time to go, and Lizzie followed her master back to camp with renewed hope.

Chapter Thirty-one

March 8, 1704: Connecticut River Valley—Day 9

T hough it was early afternoon, it appeared they had stopped to make camp for the night. The past three days had been long, the terrain difficult, and Lizzie knew all would welcome some additional rest. Before them was a river entering the Connecticut from the west. By Lizzie's memory, it was the fourth such stream they had encountered. Wider than the others, it would likely be more difficult to cross. Most of the other streams had been frozen enough to allow walking on the ice, two had required a brief search for a place to ford.

As the Indians set their tents, there seemed to be more conversation than usual, a few French officers had even made a rare appearance.

"Oh, look! There she is!" Lizzie immediately recognized Abby's voice and was shocked to see her descending a small rise along with Jacques de Noyon and his two large sidekicks. Abby sprinted ahead of the others almost knocking Lizzie over as she rushed to embrace her. "I'm so glad we've found you. I knew you'd be somewhere. They couldn't kill *you*."

Lizzie stood silent with her mouth open as De Noyon had a brief conversation with her master, following which he walked over, removed Lizzie's leash and tossed it to her master. He then suggested to her, "Come and seet over here. We can veeseet." Lizzie looked to her master, who nodded while De Noyon assured her, "Eet will be all right."

Sitting on a rock by the confluence of the rivers, he told her, "I know dees man's tribe. Dey are Abenaki from around Odanak northeast of Montréal. I have had beesness weet dem een dee past. You are fortunate to have heem for your master."

Lizzie felt relieved as Abby said, "We are with the French. They recognized Jacques and took us. We even managed to get them to take Sarah-Bee and Benjamin as well. I tried to get them to take you, but they told us, 'no more'. So we are pleased you are at least traveling with Abenaki."

Ecstatic to see her friends, Lizzie began with the key question, "Have you heard anything about Andrew?"

Abby answered, "We did hear he was with a group who escaped to the south. That's all."

Lizzie smiled and asked, "Why did we stop early today?"

De Noyon said with authority, "Ah, I believe eet ees here we will spleet up. Dee old people and dee children will go down deese branch called dee White Reever because in dee spring eet has dee rapids dat make dee water white. Dee rest will go up dee beeg river. Eet ees faster but more deefficult because we must climb dee Green Mountains. Now you will tink eet ees white mountains, but in dee summer dey are green. Eet ees why dey call dis place *Vermont*. Eet ees *vert*—French for green, and *mont* for mountain. Some of dee udder tribes will go alone. Dee food is scarce and dey needs to hunt een small parties."

"Will *we* stay in the same group?" Lizzie asked.

He shrugged in French fashion with his outreaching hands palm up, "We must wait and see."

"Won't they tell you?"

He laughed, "Dey tells me nothing. We travel wit dem so dey can keep dee eye on me. I tink dey want when we get to Canada to have me shot."

"Oh, my!"

"Not to worry," he said with a grin. "Dey needs me too much."

* * *

In the morning, the English captives were indeed separated into smaller groups. The older people and small children followed White River with the dog sleds while a few smaller groups headed north. Sammy had been taken with the young group along with Abby's sister, Thankful. De Noyon reassured Lizzie they would be safe. Lizzie stayed with the largest cadre and their masters who were joined by a group of French soldiers who led the way as they continued the march north on the western bank of the great Connecticut River.

* * *

<u>March 11, 1704—Day 12</u>

The weather had returned brutally cold with a strong north wind delivering pelting snow into their faces as they struggled along to the north. Grateful for the hood on her coat which kept much of the blizzard out of her face, Lizzie worked to keep up. Today was made more difficult as her stomach problems had increased. She had developed cramps at midday, but unlike her nausea, they would not subside. To add to her misery she had learned Mr. Brooks was with another group and with him had gone any hope of learning more about Andrew.

They encountered a new river branch entering the Connecticut from the northwest. Crossing it, they left the great river and followed this smaller tributary to the north and east. Becoming more irregular, the terrain began to climb. Rocky outcroppings became more common and the bare deciduous trees gave way to more conifers. Two hours after leaving the Connecticut River, they stopped to camp. Happily, her master chose a site to the south of a small rock cliff giving respite from the blowing snow.

As he assembled their meager lodging, she went to relieve herself. As she squatted, she knew something was not right. It felt like the beginning of a particularly painful *monthly,* but she had not had one for almost three months. When she stood, she saw the blood. *Maybe it is a monthly,* she thought, until she looked closer. It was not just blood. She screamed and began to sob, bringing her master to investigate.

He, too, knew what it was. He put his arm on her shoulder in a tender gesture, motioning to her to wait as he disappeared into the tent. Returning with a leather cloth, he knelt in the snow gently scooping the tiny lifeless fetus onto the leather which he carefully folded, then tied. He led her under a spruce tree whose branches had kept the snow from collecting around its base. Kneeling beneath the tree, he took his knife and ax, carving a small grave in the frozen earth. Laying the leather sack inside, he chanted a few words, obviously a prayer, before he covered the sack. He produced a stick and leather strap. Carefully fashioning the stick into a cross, he secured it with the leather and placed it at the head of the tiny grave. Making the sign of the cross, he rose and gently held the sobbing Lizzie in his arms. Consumed by her own grief, she failed to realize he was also shedding tears, not only for her loss but for his and a history he had kept hidden.

Eventually he brought her back to the tent and fed her a piece of dry meat. She had no desire to eat but knew she must. When she had choked it down, he poured a yellow liquid from a leather sac into a small wooden cup, offering it for her to drink. It was herbal in taste and burned on the way down. She tried to hand it back, but he insisted she finish it. Once she had, he laid her down and covered her with a second deerskin, while he sat as cross-legged as he could with his bad leg and watched over her. She sobbed softly, she had lost the child she did not know she had—Andrew's child. Maybe she had lost Andrew as well. She said a prayer as her master's hand stayed gently on her shoulder, protecting her from whatever else the world had to offer.

When she awoke, he had not moved. *How could anyone sit like that all night long?* He had her spread her legs and wiped her with a cloth. Fortunately there was not much blood. He fashioned a pad which he tied between her legs to collect any further blood. She wanted her mother more than ever in her life, but she was amazed there was a man in the world who could—and would do this.

He helped her dress and gave her another piece of meat. She ate it and did not feel nauseated. She realized now why she had been sick in the mornings. He took her out to help her walk. She was weak but could do it, and knew she would have to do it, as *he* knew she must. The group began to move, the snow had stopped, and the sun was out although the bitter cold remained. At first she just trudged on. She didn't care.

Soon she realized, *If Andrew is alive and trying to find me, I owe it to him to remain alive!* And she quickened her pace.

Chapter Thirty-two

March 13, 1704: The Green Mountains—Day 14

As they followed the new river to the northwest, the uphill grade became steep as the foothills worked their way up to the true mountains. The river was as rough as the terrain. The water was generally open as the much faster current caused frequent violent rapids. Here there was no river valley and the path was steep, narrow, and littered with obstacles such as large rocks, small cliffs and ever-present fallen trees. The temperature was warmer and the few short snow flurries wet as Lizzie followed her master ever upward. Today he had dispensed with the leash. It was clear she was not about to run off.

By mid-morning they were in the upper reaches of the mountains, the view ahead continued constantly up through the dense conifer forest. The river had disappeared. They had either turned away from it or passed its source. By midafternoon, the terrain became a bit more level and it seemed the summit was at hand. By late afternoon the view began to look slightly downward. Lizzie thought it was odd that anything concerning this ordeal could seem hopeful, but the thought of the climb ending pleased her.

They soon stopped to make camp, a chore becoming almost automatic as they were set up within minutes. The temperature had continued to ameliorate and the snow had stopped. Lizzie reflected on what both Andrew and Nathan Belden had said about their treks, "*Had it been winter, we would have surely died.*" She was beginning to believe she was about to survive, but realized had she been left in her Deerfield garments, she would certainly have perished by now.

Her master presented another piece of the same dried meat which had deteriorated daily. As she took it, he pointed at her and said something that sounded like, "*ariweeiswee?*" Thinking back to her brief Abenaki lessons, she thought it might mean, *name.*

She pointed to herself and replied, "Lizzie." He repeated it with as much of a chuckle as she had heard from an Indian. Apparently he found it an amusing name. She pointed at him attempting, "*ariweeiswee?*"

Laughing at her pronunciation, he answered, "*Makya.*" She repeated it. She thought it seemed a noble name. He said a few more words, none of which she grasped when she was struck with an idea. She still had no idea if this man would protect her or would eventually slaughter her—perhaps if they could communicate she could convince him to do the former.

"*Parlez-vous Français?*" she questioned, as his face lit up. It had never occurred to him this English girl would know French.

With enthusiasm he replied, *"Oui!"* Holding up his thumb and forefinger as to indicate a small distance, he said with less enthusiasm, *"Un peu."*

"Moi aussi, un peu," She uttered, indicating that she, too, only spoke a little. Pointing to him again, she queried, *"Qu'est-ce ça veut dire, Makya?"*

Pointing up, he responded, *"Chasseur d'aigle."*

"The Eagle Hunter," she whispered, "how grand."

Pointing to her he asked, *"Qu'est-ce ça veut dire, Lizzie?"*

She pondered a moment before responding, "Elizabeth."

He stood silent for a while, as if he realized they could now communicate but could think of nothing to say. Finally, he said, *"Demain, la chasse. Nous restons ici."* Some of the Indians would hunt tomorrow, but she and Makya would stay put. She tried to smile.

He had her undress as had been the routine and she crawled into the tent. He removed the pad between her legs as he had the last two nights. There was no blood. He showed her and lay it aside, then lay next to her under the blanket wearing only his medallion. He patted her shoulder but did nothing more and was soon snoring. Lizzie was still afraid of the future, but for tonight, for the first time, she was not afraid. She said a prayer for Andrew and Sammy—somewhere between *Dear Lord* and *Amen,* she joined Makya in slumber.

* * *

At daybreak, a few select Indians carrying muskets and bows departed in three separate groups in three separate directions. Lizzie had stopped bleeding, and for the first time since before the raid, she felt close to normal. Alone in the tent, she examined herself, her muscles were harder but she had lost considerable weight and her skin almost sagged. Her mother would have said, "Child, you are nothing but skin and bones." The thought brought tears to her eyes, but she exited the tent to conquer whatever faced her today. Makya handed her another morsel of the dreadful meat, saying with assurance, *"Ce soir—mieux."* Not certain tonight's fare would indeed be better, she dutifully swallowed it.

Makya took her hand and motioned to the clearing. When they entered it, she realized they had allowed the prisoners some latitude as some stood visiting. She also noted they had been rejoined by one of the smaller parties and she saw Mrs. Beaman again—behind her was Mr. Nathaniel Brooks!

Rushing to him, she cried out, "Mr. Brooks!" Looking up, his face became lifeless, as she asked, "Tell me about Andrew—my husband."

Brooks took her hand with a solemn expression. "Well, I saw him and the others going out the south gate..."

"So he's safe?" she asked, with hope overflowing in her voice.

Brooks looked down, "Mr. Hoyt was with them, but he was later taken. I saw him the night we split up. He said an Indian aimed his rifle right at your brother, Johnny, but Stevens pushed him out of the way so the bullet hit him."

Her world was collapsing, "Was he...hurt?"

"My dear, he is dead. But he saved your brother's life. He died a hero." Lizzie was unimpressed as she began to wail. Brooks continued as she clung to him, "I know. They killed my Mary the day before the Sabbath."

Looking up through her tears, "Mrs. Brooks is...?"

"Dead? Yes. I know this is doubly hard for you after your sister and all."

Looking back in horror, "My sister? What about her?"

Brooks wished he was on another planet. "Oh God, you don't know?"

"Know what?"

He took her in his arms again, "Mr. Smead put his family in the cellar and locked the Indians out." Her horror grew as he finished, "The Indians burned it. Your sister, the children and Mother Smead. All gone."

She pushed him away. "I hate you!" Looking about, "I hate you all!" and she ran to her tent, falling into a quivering, wailing ball. Soon Makya opened the flap and she threw a small pack at him, "Get out of here, you filthy, murdering heathen. Go rot in Hell!"

Eventually her wailing turned to sobbing, finally subsiding into a fitful sleep. Around midday she was awakened by a hand on her shoulder. "Andrew?" She sobbed as she looked up at the dame.

"There, there, child," she said, taking Lizzie in her arms and holding her against her ample breasts. "Let it go. Cry it all out. You deserve the chance."

As she sobbed, Mrs. Beaman rocked. When she was four, Lizzie had broken her arm and her mother held her like this to comfort her. The pleasant thought of her mother was very fleeting as her death came crashing back. "Mrs. Beaman, what can I do?"

"What would Andrew want?"

"*I* want to die." Lizzie declared with conviction.

"Would Romeo have *wanted* Juliet to stab herself with that dagger? What would your mother want? What would your sister want? What would your suffering friends want?

I for one want you alive, Elizabeth. I cannot abide another dead loved one."

Lizzie continued to sob while the dame continued to rock. At dinner time the dame coaxed her out to eat something. The hunters had triumphed and she was served an entire turkey leg. She sobbed as she ate it, but knew she must if she was to remain true to Andrew, and she still had Sammy to worry about.

That night she crawled into the tent waiting for Makya. When he did not appear, she peeked out the flap. He was lying directly in front of the tent, protecting it from intruders while wrapped in a skin reclining in the snow. She returned to her skin and to tormented dreams.

* * *

March 16, 1704: The Green Mountains—Day 17

It was that special sort of day when winter finally begins to loosen its grip, and one can feel the early spring seeping in from all sides. The sky was clear, the southwest breeze pleasant as the captives were finally able to loosen their coats. Lizzie had even removed her hood allowing the breeze to blow through her golden curls. This would have been forbidden in New England, but today Lizzie didn't care as she marched on in fits of depression interspersed with bursts of courage to keep the promise she had made to her dead husband. Her fellow captives were all in their personal purgatories, marching expressionless, fearing where the next year, month, day, or passage would lead them.

Today, the trail took them ever downward as they followed a new river they had encountered two days before. A big river, although not as wide as the grand Connecticut, it flowed to the west. Its ice was breaking into floes that grew smaller as they descended down the mountain slope, meandered along with the current. Makya had told her it was called the French River as it was a common path for the French traders traveling west to the large lake and the fur trade. Coming into a clearing, Makya told her it was here they would make camp and stay an extra day to hunt.

The flat meadow ended abruptly on the western side with a sheer rocky cliff descending about 100 feet to a valley below. From their vantage point, there was a spectacular vista of the largest body of water New Englanders who had not been to the sea had ever seen. The dame told her this was Lake Champlain, named for the French explorer who had founded Québec a century before.

While Makya assembled the tent, Lizzie sat quietly on a flat rock staring at a panorama more inspirational than anything she had seen. She could hear her husband's words, *"You must promise me that you will stay alive and find the best life you can."* As the tears formed in her eyes, she whispered, "I promise."

Going to the center of the camp, Makya returned with a piece of rabbit. As they sat carefully cleaning the bones, she pondered a question she had formed during today's march. It was a question no one else would dare to ask or that she would have asked a few days ago for fear of the possible consequences. But now her life was hers alone and she alone would suffer them, so in her halting French she gritted her teeth and asked, "How could you have been so kind to bury my unborn child yet evil enough to kill innocent women and children?"

Obviously taken aback at the query, he thought for a long while, staring into nature's pallet before replying in his French which she now realized was superior to hers. "When I was young man, I had wife. I had also child. He had two years. One day, English soldiers came to our village and killed many, my son and wife among them. They took me captive, but I escaped going to new village." He thought more before continuing, "I have killed no one." He shrugged, "Who is to say who is innocent?"

He rose and walked into the woods as darkness surrounded the camp. Lizzie crawled under the deerskin and lay awake thinking. Suddenly, she recalled Andrew's story of his mother fighting an Indian in their home. *"It was clear he wanted us all alive, but she had her large kitchen knife and cut him—badly. He continued to try to subdue her, but when she pulled away, she fell on her knife. I think she was dead right away. The Indian looked at her sadly and shook his head. I did not understand then, but now I realize—he needed a wife."*

Andrew had explained that Indians took captives for varying reasons: to sell for money, to use as slaves, to trade for Indian captives, or to replace a lost loved one. How could she have been so oblivious? Makya was civil to her from the beginning because he wanted her to be his wife. He did not violate her because, like Andrew, he wanted this to be according to the mores of his society. She did not see him until morning when he was sitting awkwardly cross-legged on the flat rock.

* * *

215

The weather had continued to improve since they reached the bank of Lake Champlain three days before. The final hike down the rolling forested foothills of the Green Mountains had marked the end of strenuous travel as the wide banks of the lake were flat. In fact, they were the flattest terrain Lizzie had ever seen. Nights and mornings were cold, but the days were almost pleasant.

When they reached the mouth of the French River as it emptied into the big lake, they found canoes that had been stored along the tribe's way to Deerfield. Some of the less agile captives were now transported in them along with the small tents and skins as well as the plunder from Deerfield.

Although she still faced the frightening uncertainty of her future, she had become secure in the present. She had resolved herself to the death of her mother and sister, but Andrew still visited each night in dreams, assuring her that he would reappear as her savior. Each morning, however, greeted her with reality. Her worries were now centered on Sammy. During the climb in the mountains when daily survival was her own greatest fear, she had little time to agonize over him. De Noyon had assured her he would be safe with the children, and at 13, he would be one of the oldest and strongest. However, she now realized this guaranteed nothing.

The lake was calm today, but two days before, the north wind blew and the waves were impressive. Lizzie thought *this must be like the ocean.* Some ice still remained, clinging desperately to the shore, occasionally breaking loose as a small floe to travel north to the Saint-Lawrence River eventually to disappear into the sea.

At midday they came to long islands in the lake, bisecting it longitudinally. At one point they were less than a mile from the shore, and Lizzie saw what appeared to be an Indian family with a tent on the island. Going about their daily life, they seemed to be fishing. As she watched them toil, uninterested in the captives and masters on the mainland, Lizzie realized they were the first civilization she had seen since Deerfield three weeks ago. Soon they stopped and Makya assembled the tent before going to the fire returning with two pieces of boar. When they finished, Lizzie asked softly in her ever improving French, "What happened to your leg?"

She was a little concerned this may be a sensitive question, but he did not appear upset as he looked away in thought before beginning in French, "When I had about eleven years, I followed my father on hunting trip for deerskins. At that time, our village was at end of great river French call *Saint Laurent*. We went farther, beyond mouth of river into bay with large island known for fine deer herd. We collected many skins and were deep in forest by great tree fallen into another in storm. I tripped by tree—enough to make it fall all way to ground. Sadly, my leg was under it.

"I was in terrible pain. My father tried as much as he could to move tree, but he could not. He began to panic. He realized if he could not free me, I would die. Suddenly white man appeared from nowhere. Apparently lost, was French. He and my father struggled and moved tree just enough for me to pull myself out. My leg was very crooked, but they were able to bind it with branches and vines enough that I could be moved."

He looked off into the distance as Lizzie sat captivated, asking, "Then what?"

Makya's attention returned to her. "My father wore wampum of wood and beads that his father had given him for luck. He never removed it until that day when he gave it to the man in gratitude, who looked puzzled but then removed medallion from his neck, giving it to my father. He told us his father had given it to him for luck. Soon we parted. Later, we discovered the man had come on great boat from France on other side of world. We even saw boat next morning. It was larger than boats that come to Montréal."

Reaching around his neck, he removed the medallion she had always seen on him. "When my father died, he gave it to me," he said as he put it in her hand.

She jumped, "It bit me!"

He smiled. She had never seen him really smile before. "Sometimes it does that."

The medallion was silver with the figure of a man dressed in a robe with one outstretched hand which seemed to be pointing. Makya took it back and returned it to his neck. "My father said it was magic."

Lizzie knew the Reverend would say it was possessed by the devil, but knew it would be best not to discuss it with him.

Chapter Thirty-three

This morning they hiked to an apparent narrows between the east and west shores of the lake. Canoes transported them as they began to ferry the group to the western side. More stable and maneuverable than she would have thought possible, the native craft amazed Lizzie. The Indian crew's considerable skill and strength hearkened back to Andrew's description of canoe races.

From the landing point, they hiked westward, soon arriving at a narrow body of water. They were not on the opposite bank of the lake, but on a peninsula which they now crossed and began to set camp. Still early afternoon, the camp took on a casual air as mingling was permitted. Soon Abby and De Noyon came to visit. Jacques explained their current circumstances. "We are now very close to Montréal. We have, perhaps *tree* days hike up *zees* reever," he explained, pointing to the stream running north from the lake. "Een *tree* days we shall be at dee fort, called Chambly. Der we will gather and go on our separate ways."

"What of the other groups of captives?" Lizzie asked with nervous anticipation.

De Noyon gave the French shrug. "Eet ees hard to say. Many will come der. Udders will go directly to der villages."

"But what about my brother, Sammy?"

Again the French shrug, "Hopefully he will come. We must wait and see."

Lizzie was becoming quite agitated as Abby took her hand and said, "It should be all right. My sister, Thankful, is with the same group. Right, Jacques?"

Shrugging again, he changed the subject. "Zees stream we will follow ees called dee Richelieu Reever, for a famous Cardinal and Meenister of France more den feefty years ago. He was famous, yes, but also evil." Pointing to Lizzie, he continued slowly and thoughtfully, "He ordered dee killing of many French Protestants. Some Protestant peoples escaped from France to come to New England." Lizzie suddenly flashed back to Andrew's story of his Huguenot ancestors.

* * *

March 25, 1704: Fort Chambly, Canada—Day 26

Long treks had filled the past three days. Although the terrain along the Richelieu River was flat and steady, the distances, along with occasional dense forest on the banks, made for exhausting days. Anticipation of an end to the long ordeal was offset by uncertainty of what was to follow.

Midday on the 25th, they had come to something they had not seen since that awful day they last saw Deerfield— a road! Only a small dirt path wide enough for a small wagon, still there was no doubt this led to civilization. Lizzie was struck by an almost giddy sensation as they began to tread on the flat surface nearly devoid of obstructions. For a few moments she almost forgot her overbearing concern about Sammy.

Within an hour they came to a narrows where they crossed to the western shore of the river. Soon they came to a clearing from which they could see Fort Chambly. Larger and more substantial than the Deerfield stockade, not only was this more fort than she had anticipated, but it was surrounded by a town. Not with a single road as in Deerfield but many crossing roads and more houses, some more substantial than even the grand structure of Ensign Sheldon. As they entered the town, Indian leaders were replaced by French soldiers who marched them to the gate.

Along the way, Lizzie saw the river rushing as wild rapids into a small bay, while the prominent fort sat strategically on the point formed by both. In the distance two large mountains watched over the bay and the fort. Most of the snow and ice was now gone from the valley, but the mountains retained their winter blanket.

The French troops marched them through the gates without fanfare. Larger than Lizzie expected, it was not a simple stockade. Inside grounds were lined with small buildings constructed as lean-tos against the inside walls. Their leader was a young man who disappeared into what was likely headquarters. Lizzie would soon learn he was Jean-Baptiste Hertel de Rouville, commonly referred to simply as *Hertel*. Soon he reappeared and found Jacques de Noyon who led him to Deacon French. The three men disappeared back into the office.

Lizzie had been studying her group along the way. She had calculated there had been more than one-hundred captives at the beginning and more than eighty had survived. But there were now only about fifty in the compound. It appeared their group was the first to arrive and the smaller bands were hopefully on their way. She prayed Sammy would be in one. Soldiers began to organize them into sections, assigning each to a building. Eventually De Noyon and Deacon French came out and began to circulate among the captives. Finally De Noyon reached Lizzie.

"So zees ees how eet works," he began carefully to explain what was going to happen. "Each captive ees zee property of hees master who may sell or keep heem as he weeshes. Eef dey wants to keep, dey may leave now. Doze not yet here may not come at all."

Lizzie could see this was complicated, but important. With a furrowed brow, she asked, "Who do they sell to?"

"Dee French. Den dey will keep as French ceetizen or perhaps some of der family from New England will *redeem* dem."

Frowning, she inquired, "You mean buy them back?"

"Yes. But you see, dee Iroquois do not like so much to sell, especially da childrens. Dee Abenaki, dey are more likely to sell except da young childrens or if dey needs da slave or da wife."

Pondering, Lizzie thought she must cut to the chase. "What will happen to me?"

De Noyon winced while giving the French shrug. "I am tinking he is wanting a wife." She frowned as he added,

"He will stay here for some times. He ees from da nort at Odanak. He will not go until all hees peoples do."

"What about Sammy?" she asked in a frightened voice.

Again the shrug. "He ees wit da Abenaki, too, but not wit your man's tribe, hees master ees way from far nort. He will sell eef he ees not wanting slave."

Desperate for help, she asked, "Will you be able to help talk to these people?"

He laughed. "I weesh. Dey is taking me today to Montréal to stand trial." With an impish grin, he added, "Happily dey does not want to shoot me."

"Thank goodness."

"No, dey wants to hang me."

"Oh, no."

He laughed again. "Not to worry. Dey needs me too much."

Lizzie was beginning to understand, realizing at this point there was nothing for her to do but wait and see.

* * *

April 8, 1704: Fort Chambly—day 40

After two weeks, life at the fort was becoming routine. She slept inside rooms for the women—with bunks, actual beds. Initially, those in the bunkhouse included Lizzie, Abby, Sarah-Bee, Dame Beaman, Mrs. Sarah Hurst, Sarah-Lynn, and Elizabeth Hurst among others. They still belonged to their masters and saw them on occasion although they no longer shared quarters. Last week a priest from Montréal came and took a few women including Mrs. Beaman and all three Hurst women. Periodically some of

223

the smaller bands arrived and with them came a few children, but it was apparent that many of the children, especially those with the Iroquois, had gone straight to various Indian camps. Her fear for Sammy was growing daily.

"I think spring is really coming."

Interrupted from her thoughts, Lizzie turned to see Abby. "Yes," she answered without enthusiasm.

"Let's go sit a spell," Abby suggested, "Like my Uncle Benoni would say."

Taking a sun-exposed seat on the benches along the walls, she placed her hand on Lizzie's. "Worried about Sammy?"

Lizzie's eyes began to tear, "Yes, he should be here by now."

"Jacques said it would be a while, not to worry."

"I know," Lizzie said in frustration. "I wish Jacques were here."

"Not as much as I," her friend returned with a smile.

"Oh, Abby, will Jacques be all right?"

"He says he will. You know none of my younger siblings have come, nor Freedom, Abigail and Martha French, or your brother, Johnny's family."

"I know, Abby," she said in resignation. "It's the wait. I think it is harder than the march."

Abby smiled, "I think you have a short memory. Oh, look, there's a cart, maybe they have someone."

Two carts entered the yard as the girls moved to investigate. Coming close, Lizzie whispered, "Mohawks! They frighten me," and held back.

"I have an idea," Abby declared, as she ran into a nearby building, soon exiting with a friend. "Monsieur LeMieux will come help us look." The giant Frenchman accompanied them to the carts which to their disappointment contained no captives, only booty from the raid.

Studying the contents from a safe distance, Lizzie gasped, "My mother's chest!" Turning to LeMieux, she asked in her ever improving French, "Monsieur, can you ask them about that chest?"

Surprised by her French, he nodded. Approaching the wagon, he had an animated conversation with the driver in a mélange of French and Iroquois. Finally he returned. "You can't reason with the Iroquois," he reported, "This one doesn't want to talk."

They moved away as a few soldiers came out of the office to view the loot. Lizzie was still not ready to quit as she left the fort for the small Abenaki camp the masters had set up against an outside wall. Finding Makya, she explained her dilemma. He escorted her back to the fort, instructing her to sit on a bench as he approached the Mohawks. Following a very spirited exchange, he came back to sit on her bench.

"He is going to sell it, but you could not begin to buy it."

"How will he sell it?"

"To some rich lady in market."

In desperation she asked, "Did you tell him…"

He shrugged, "You cannot talk to Mohawk." Patting her hand, "I'm sure it is empty in any case."

"But it has a secret compartment."

He *almost* chuckled, "That may fool Englishmen, but not Iroquois."

Standing, he patted her shoulder and headed back to the gate. As she watched him lurch away, she realized she missed his company, and although she could never admit it, she missed the nightly intimacy and warm security lying with him gave her on those awful nights. Maybe being an Indian wife would not be so terrible—maybe.

Chapter Thirty-four

Last night's heavy rain had stopped, allowing the sun to reappear, warming the spring air. Lizzie and Abby sat together on a bench enjoying the warm rays of sun and the lack of activity in the yard.

"Monsieur LeDuc says Jacques' trial is almost complete, and there is no question but that he will be acquitted."

"What will happen then?"

"He will return to rescue me." Abby declared, with an impish grin. "We will move to his grand home in Montréal where I shall be lady of the manor."

"Can I come visit?"

"Yes, in fact you can come and work for me. I shall need an English serving girl." Laughing, Abby embraced her friend, "Of course! Come anytime."

Lizzie frowned, "That is if I can ever come."

Suddenly the door of the headquarters opened, and a man came out heading toward them. It was hard not to

227

recognize Jean-Baptiste Hertel de Rouville. Young for an officer of rank, he looked even younger, always dashing in his dress uniform. Approaching the girls, he bowed elegantly saying in surprisingly good English, "Ladies, I wonder if you can be of service to me. It seems one of your group is great with child and appears to be ready to give birth…"

"Oh, Sarah-Bee!" Abby exclaimed in glee.

"Yes," he responded, "but it seems we have no women in the camp but you two. Our surgeon is on maneuvers with the men and all of your other women have left. We have not even Indian squaws."

Abby grew pale, but Lizzie told him, "I have some experience, sir."

"Well, Mademoiselle, that makes you our local expert. Please follow me."

They followed him to a door with a cross and the word *Clinique.* Entering they saw Sarah-Bee groaning on a stretcher with two helpless, terrified young soldiers at her side. "These ladies will take over, men." Hertel explained in French, causing the two warriors to bolt for the door. Lizzie turned to him and in her improving French, asked, "Where is her husband?"

"Uh, next door I believe."

"Good. Keep him there. Can you get me some hot water and towels or sheets?"

The commander of the troops looked bewildered, "Yes, Mademoiselle. Right away." And he scampered off on the errand.

Lizzie put her hand on her friend's forehead, "Sarah-Bee, it's Lizzie and Abby. We are going to deliver your baby."

Trying to sit up, she asked weakly and without confidence, "You are?"

"Yes, I've done it before," she claimed before fibbing, "Many times. It's easy."

Sarah-Bee moaned, "Doesn't feel easy."

"Did you lose any water or mucous?"

"Some water."

"How much?"

"A whole lake!" She began to groan louder.

"Good, that means you are ready."

A soldier arrived with the water and the towels. Apparently Hertel had resigned as assistant. When he left as quickly as he had entered, Lizzie looked about the room. The solitary window let in precious light, and let out the strong smell of rubbing alcohol pervasive in the room. There was a cupboard of red and blue glass bottles with French labels that Lizzie would not have understood had they been in English. Above the stretcher hung a frightening crucifix. *I hope you can help,* she thought as she stared at it. Lizzie pulled down the sheet and had Sarah-Bee spread her legs before applying the warm damp towels to her *privates.* "Ma says this loosens you up for the baby to get out."

"Good, use a lot."

Abby remained speechless while Sarah-Bee moaned loudly with every contraction. "Ma says the closer together the groans come, the closer the baby is to out." Lizzie declared with false confidence. They sat nervously with their friend for what seemed like hours without the groans becoming closer together. Then she changed from groan to scream as the pains arrived more quickly.

"This is good, Sarah-Bee, you are almost there." The encouragement was a little premature as they progressed

229

through the next hour. The new assistant put his head in from time to time. When they told him they were all right, he needed no further encouragement to leave.

Finally Sarah-Bee gave a loud, "Oh my God!"

And Lizzie asked, "Do you feel like you have to push?"

"Yes!"

"Good. Do it!"

Suddenly, Lizzie saw the head beginning to crown and Sarah-Bee's *privates* beginning to tear and bleed, but she was resolved not to pass out this time. Finally the head began to move and with four more screaming contractions, it was out. With Mary, the rest was very fast, but today the shoulders took a few more pushes. Once they were out, it was over. Lizzie was thrilled.

Taking a towel, she wrapped the baby and began to hand it to its mother. "Give it a breast."

"Is it a boy or a girl?" Sarah-Bee moaned with a tinge of relief.

Lizzie quickly unwrapped the towel. "A boy!" she claimed, as she handed him back to his mother. Then she remembered the cord. As her mother had instructed, she held it firmly until it came loose. Once it was out, she realized she had missed the next step when she fainted at Mary's. Turning to Abby, she whispered, "Run outside to the Abenaki camp and get Makya!" As Abby left, Lizzie hoped her master was more skilled in this than the soldiers.

He was, as he took the placenta in one hand and tied a knot close to the infant. He then produced his ever-ready knife and cut the cord. Putting away the blade, he put his hand gently on Sarah-Bee's forehead, whispering in French, "I had son—once." As he left the room, Lizzie began to sob, but it only lasted a minute until she dried her eyes, and went to the proud father. Walking back into the

spring day, she knew life would be worth living and that
Andrew again was right.

* * *

April 11, 1704—Day 43:

After visiting their patient and determining all was in
order, Abby and Lizzie sat in the courtyard to enjoy another
spring day. Today they had a special treat as there was to
be a game of lacrosse. Lizzie was particularly enthused as
Andrew had given her a brief description of the game, and
she could flaunt her knowledge to Abby.

"The two boxes of net at either end are called *the goals*.
Each player has a stick with a net to hold, throw, or catch
the ball. If one team gets the ball in the other team's goal,
they get a point."

One team was from the local tribe and the second from
Makya's Abenaki camp. The soldiers, captives, Indians and
local citizens turned out for the match. The girls were
shocked by the skill of the players as they seemed to float
from one end of the field to the other, while using their nets
to control and move the ball. Even Makya with his crooked
leg could play skillfully. They were further entertained by
the fact the Indians were naked but for loincloths. Abby
whispered mischievously to Lizzie, "I hope Jacques gets
back soon."

The Abenaki tribe beat the home team in a close match,
but the competitors all seemed to leave the field friends and
in a good mood. *Fun*, Lizzie thought, *like Andrew said.
This is fun.* When the game was over, the victors took on a

231

team of soldiers. To the dismay of the girls, the soldiers remained dressed.

The game was more lopsided. As Andrew would have predicted, the Indians were more skilled in their native game. The soldiers were good sports, however, and everyone parted friends and *happy*. Sitting in the wonderful spring afternoon, Lizzie realized all three of the civilizations represented were having a good time in a friendly atmosphere. Even the captives, who had been forced from their homes to endure unspeakable hardship, were smiling. *"These civilizations are not so different,"* Andrew had told her. She began to shed tears for her loss of this wonderful man.

After the field was cleared, the fort returned to normal until two carts entered, this time followed by a parade of ragged children. The remaining captives flocked to see who was here, but also who was not. While Lizzie searched frantically through the group, she saw Thankful Stebbins, her three siblings, along with Freedom and Martha French, but no Sammy Price.

Panicked, she went to Thankful. "Sammy was in this group, Thankful. Where is he?"

Thankful drew herself back from the excitement of reunion with her family and thought. "His master took him. He said they were going north."

Not giving up, she raced to find Makya in the Abenaki camp. She explained the situation and he came to investigate. When he was finished, he told her. "His master is northern Abenaki. He lives far from here. He may yet sell the boy, but there is no way to know."

Lizzie sputtered, "But…how will I find him? How will I know?"

Makya put his hand gently on her shoulder to deliver the awful truth, "You may never find him." She collapsed, wailing in his arms. He held her until she was quiet, before delivering her to her bunk. Again she had gone from joy to misery in a few hours.

Chapter Thirty-five

<u>April 12, 1704: Fort Chambly—Day 44:</u>

The sun rose on a day as gloomy as Lizzie's state of mind. Cold and foggy with an annoying drizzle, it matched her perfectly. She began with a visit to Sarah-Bee who was now up walking the baby with her proud husband. Having heard about Sammy, Sarah-Bee did not flaunt her happiness, she only gave condolences and thanked her friend again.

As she left the *Clinique,* she was greeted by Abby with her own news, "Jacques was acquitted! He should be here in a few days."

Lizzie expressed her happiness and shared a bench with her friend who tried to reassure her, "There are still many people missing, Lizzie. Abigail French, Eben and Hannah Hurst, little Eunice Williams, and a lot more. You'll get Sammy back. Jacques will help when he returns."

Looking up with sad eyes, she said, "Who knows where I will be, Abby. My mother, Andrew, my sister, little Sarah

Field—all dead, and no one has seen any of Johnny's family."

Abby was silent for a while. She wanted to console her friend but knew she had nothing more to offer. Eventually Lizzie rose and headed to the gate.

Makya was sitting in front of the camp in his awkward cross-legged position. She sat to join him. This odd man had come with men who killed her family and friends and dragged her away, but there seemed to be good in him. He may represent her best chance of survival. They remained silent until she asked, "Will you walk with me?"

He rose to his feet quickly, which always amazed her. Extending his hand, he pulled her up. "Let's walk along the basin," she suggested. He complied while remaining silent. The drizzle had stopped, but the day remained cold and gloomy. There was little if any view through the fog, but she didn't care. "Tell me about your wife," she proposed. He continued to walk in silence, thinking before he began to speak.

His wife was younger than he, from the same tribe but a different village. Makya knew her brother as a boy. They were married and lived contently. They worked well together. They had a son they both adored. Then the raid and they were dead. He had condensed their five years into ten minutes when he asked her, "Tell me of your husband."

She also thought for a while. "When we first met, we were both naked..." She told him about their early relationship and what an enigma he had been. Meeting secretly, swimming, talking and being in love. They stopped to sit on a stone where she told him of Andrew's career with De Noyon and his two odd friends, and how he played Indian so people would not know he was the one who spoke three languages. A few days before, she would not have dreamed of sharing this intimate information, but somehow she felt she needed to get it out.

She explained his wisdom and how he had explained it to her, drawing from his life in all three cultures. "I taught him to read English, and he taught me to speak French." She related the Mr. Otis debacle and how Andrew saved her, how he morphed back into an Englishman and won the town over so they could marry. She told of their passionate three months and ended with his heroic death saving her brother. Her description took over two hours.

When they arrived back at the camp, he stood a while, studying her before he said, "We shall leave first thing in morning," and disappeared into the camp.

* * *

April 13, 1704—Day 45:

He was waiting outside her door at first light, or what would have been first light were it not for the weather. Still cold, but bearable, the air was filled with a fine drizzle, and the combination of thick clouds, haze and fog limited visibility to a few yards. She had abandoned the smock she had been given at the fort and wore her Indian clothes. She had said goodbye to her close friends last night, knowing it might well be for the last time.

He simply indicated she should follow and led the way. He had a small sack while she was empty-handed. She had anticipated going directly up the Richelieu River, but he led her into the woods. Due to the lack of sun, she had no idea of the direction but assumed it was north and east. The thick forest soon became passable and in the first hour, they came to another small road. From then on, travel was easy.

Remaining silent, he left her to her thoughts. Last night she had not slept as she agonized over her plight and future, finally concluding that things were not so bad. Makya was a good man and he cared about her. She doubted she would go cold or hungry. She might even see Sammy again. Andrew had once told her, *sometimes you have to do with what you have*. Certainly she was better off than Mrs. Eunice Williams—or was she?

At midmorning they stopped and he gave her a piece of dried meat. It was slightly better than the fare on the march. Soon they were again on their way and in early afternoon came to a body of water. It seemed to be a river traveling to their right as they faced it. She had no idea of its size due to the persistent fog. Makya pulled aside a bush to expose a canoe, indicating she should climb in. She did and he pushed off. Again she was amazed at the speed and dexterity of the craft, especially when paddled by Makya. There was a definite current, and some waves indicated this was a large body of water. About an hour later, they came to the other bank which, due to the continuous fog, Lizzie only noticed when the canoe struck it. They stepped onto firm ground, and Makya pulled the canoe up on the bank. Straining her eyes, she barely made out a wooden palisade.

"Makya, where are we?"

He looked ahead, motioning she should follow as he answered, "Montréal."

She had to hurry to keep up as he entered a small gate in the palisade and crossed a road. The building appeared to be gray. Never having seen such building, she touched it—stone! He led her to a wooden door and pulled a chain, ringing a bell. The door opened as an older woman in black greeted them.

She smiled saying, "Pierre-Henri, what a surprise."

He stepped inside and began to speak to her in French. It was very fast. Lizzie only caught a few words. She did notice a sign next to the door. *La Congrégation de Notre Dame*. The lady stepped away from the door. "You may say your goodbyes here."

He turned to Lizzie and held her shoulders in his hands as Andrew had when he had to make a point. She said, "Makya, what…?"

"Listen, Elizabeth," he ordered. "You belong here. Not with me. You are intelligent and educated, you read, you want to learn. You need—*more!*" The word rocked her soul as her eyes shed tears. "And you will need good fortune." With this he removed his ever-present medallion and placed it around her neck.

She felt the tingle as it touched her skin. "Will you go home, Makya?"

"No."

"Where will you go?"

His dark eyes pierced her green as he said, "To find your brother." Turning, he disappeared into the fog.

Tears filled her eyes, as she whispered, "Good luck and be well, Eagle-hunter."

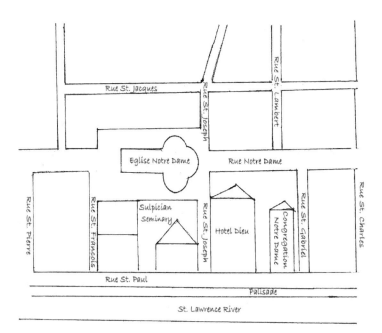

Montreal City

PART TWO—MONTREAL

Chapter One

April 13, 1704: Montréal, Canada

Although Makya had soon disappeared into the heavy fog, Lizzie watched quietly long after he was gone. Finally the lady in black spoke, using good English, "Come in, my dear."

Lizzie entered the hall of the convent. The poor visibility had hidden its size, but from the inside, she judged it was large. The spacious entry hall was decorated with paintings, Indian art, two statues, and a large carved crucifix, certainly more art than she had seen in her lifetime. Three hallways led to the unknown and a staircase to the upper levels.

The older lady took her hand, announcing, "Welcome to the Convent of the Congregation of Notre Dame. I am Sister Marie-Angélique and shall be in charge of you during your stay. I know you have many questions, but there will be ample time for them during the next few days. I also suspect you are exhausted and nervous, but rest assured you are welcome and safe in this house."

Putting her hand out, she indicated that Lizzie proceed down the first hall. Soon they encountered a girl about Lizzie's age. "Ah!" said Sister Marie-Angélique, "This is Marie-Joseph. She will be your companion for now." The young lady took Lizzie's hand as the older woman continued down the hall.

Marie-Joseph was slightly shorter and a bit stouter than the emaciated Lizzie. She wore a simple black dress with her head uncovered, exposing her long dark hair for all to see. She was pretty, not beautiful, and her English was good. "Come, we shall get you settled and washed. Then you can get to bed. I suspect you are exhausted. You'll want to sleep for a week. I know I did when I first came." They headed up the longest staircase Lizzie had ever seen as Marie-Joseph led her to a door behind which they found a small room with fireplace blazing. A solitary large tub of water sat in the corner.

Marie-Joseph instructed, "Get undressed, climb in the tub and sit down. I'll turn while you undress. Tell me when you are in."

Reflecting on the past weeks, Lizzie thought, *why bother turning around?* However, she complied. The water was warm! "I'm in."

Marie-Joseph opened a cupboard and brought soap and a bottle. Handing Lizzie the soap, she poured oil from the bottle into the water. Lizzie wondered if this was how heaven smelled. "What is that?" she asked.

"Perfumed oil. Sister Marie-Angélique's family sends it to us." Marie-Joseph explained. "She was born in Paris, the

241

most beautiful city in the world, and her parents are *very* wealthy."

With a pained, quizzical face, Lizzie questioned, "Why is she *here?*"

"She had a calling."

"Calling?"

"Yes, you'll learn about it later. You will have a million questions. I did, and I was only seven." Bending to pick up the deerskin clothes, she explained, "I shall store these and bring you more comfortable things."

Once alone, Lizzie surveyed the room. There were a few wooden chairs against the wall, a small desk, a single window, a few cauldrons, a painting of a lady in black with a strange black shawl on her head, and a carved crucifix over the fireplace. The singularly most impressive object was the mirror. Two feet in length with an ornate frame, it was placed so she could not see her reflection from the tub.

Mary-Joseph returned, setting a bundle on one chair while pulling another up to the desk. "I need to get some information. Are you up to it?" Lizzie nodded and Marie-Joseph began questioning about herself, her family, what she knew of their status, etc. When she finished, she brought the chair to the head of the tub. "Rest your head here and I'll check you for ticks, lice and things."

As Marie-Joseph inspected her hair, Lizzie asked, "How do you get so much hot water up here?"

"Everyone asks that," Marie-Joseph answered with a grin. "We have a rope and pulley behind the fireplace which lifts and lowers buckets to and from the well below. We keep a cauldron heating at all times. We only have one such room here, and it is used by all, so it is in use almost constantly. Unfortunately, we can each use it only once a week at the most and not for long. Your first bath is always special, so it is longer. You don't get the oil each time, either."

"Were you a captive?" Lizzie inquired.

Marie-Joseph chuckled, "Did my English betray me?"

"Yes."

"Lay your head back into the water, I shall tell you my tale as I wash your hair. You won't get this service again either." Lying back, Lizzie wondered if this was how one was admitted to paradise. "I was a captive. My mother, sister and I were taken from York, Maine, in 1692. I was seven and my sister, Mary, eleven. We lived in the Abenaki village for a month or so, until one day a priest and two nuns came in a canoe and brought the three of us here. Our mother was redeemed and returned home two years later, but my sister and I decided to stay."

Lizzie suddenly sat up with her head full of suds, "Why?"

Marie-Joseph shrugged, "There was little for us to return to at that time. Just before the raid, our mother had taken a new husband—her fourth. He did not care for us. Frankly, we liked Montréal better." She stood, putting her hand on Lizzie's head and pushing down playfully, she ordered, "Rinse your hair and you can dry with a towel. When you stand, check the hair between your legs for lice. I'll turn away."

Standing, Lizzie complained, "I can't really see this."

Marie-Joseph turned back, "I can help." Once she had searched, she declared, "No creatures anywhere—must be the winter. We came in summer and had many of them." As Lizzie continued to dry, she walked into the viewing field of the mirror, almost non-existent on the New England frontier. Reverend Williams had added them to his long list of *instruments of Satan.* Her mother had a small cracked looking glass in her now-pilfered chest, but Lizzie had only seen a reflection of her body in the rippled waters of the Deerfield River. She was even more frightfully thin than she had imagined as her skin and breasts drooped from her skeleton.

Realizing modesty had been abandoned, Marie-Joseph walked behind her. "Isn't it interesting? This was another gift from the family of Sister Marie-Angélique. She put it in here because, she said, 'The girls and women should have the opportunity to see themselves as God made them'," adding in a whisper, "She is less strict than the other sisters." Looking into the mirror, Marie-Joseph noticed the medallion. Touching it, she jumped. "What is this? It stung me—like a bee."

"My Indian master gave it to me."

Marie-Joseph continued to study it. "Looks religious," she decided. Pointing to the bundle on the chair, she ordered, "Get dressed and I'll take you to a bed chamber to rest. Tonight you can be alone. Tomorrow I will get you in the morning, and we will start your orientation."

They ascended to the third floor where Lizzie was deposited in a tiny room with a small dormer window and single mattress. In the dark of her solitary quarters, she began to wonder about Makya and Sammy, but she was soon asleep.

* * *

"Elizabeth, it's time."

Totally disoriented, she looked around. The small room was dark but for a single candle lighting the face in front of her. *Where am I? Heaven? Maybe Hell!* Suddenly her mind cleared. She had never slept so soundly—or so clean.

"It's Marie-Joseph, Elizabeth. Time to rise. I'll leave the candle and you can get dressed. I'll wait outside your door."

"I need to use the privy," Lizzie said with some urgency.

Marie-Joseph instructed quietly, "You can use the chamber pot, over in the corner. Just put the cloth over it when you are finished."

Mystified, she asked, "What do I do with it then?"

"Leave it, someone will collect it." She giggled, "Don't get used to it. Soon you shall be helping with that task."

Descending the stairs, Marie-Joseph told her, "First we go to the chapel for Mass, then to the dining room for breakfast." Handing her a gray scarf to match her new grey smock, she explained, "Cover your head with this in the chapel." Lizzie thought of Andrew, *these religions are not so different.*

The chapel was large enough for one hundred but was only half-filled. Although still in darkness, some light was provided by a fireplace as well as more candles than Lizzie had seen in her lifetime. Candles were a rare and valued commodity in Deerfield, apparently not so rare here. Soon a man in a colorful robe came down the aisle accompanied by a boy in white. They walked slowly to the altar.

"That is Father Mericl," Marie-Joseph whispered, "You will get to meet him—he's very nice."

When he started to pray, Lizzie understood nothing. Then she remembered Andrew explaining no matter what the local language, the Mass was always in Latin. Soon he faced the congregation and spoke in French. She was pleased that she understood most of it. He welcomed the new people, had a few announcements and gave a short lecture on God's plan for man on earth. It was over in fifteen minutes. Lizzie smiled, wondering how much Reverend Williams could condense into that amount of time. The rest was incomprehensible Latin, although there was some chanting and a group of women in black sang in Latin while one played an Indian recorder similar to that of Dame Beaman.

Within an hour the service was over, and they headed to the dining room. There was now enough light to see the interior of the highly ornate chapel. Decorative painting surrounded it along with paintings of people in robes. At the altar there was a large crucifix with a statue of Jesus attached. On its right was a statue of a woman holding a child and on its left, a man with his arms reaching out.

The dining room contained rows of tables and benches, only half of which were occupied. The ladies in black with the headpieces like Sister Marie-Angélique sat in front, while Sister Marie-Angélique and two others sat at a head table with Father Meriel. The group filed along in line and each person was provided a spoon and bowl which was then filled with porridge. As they went to the tables, Lizzie saw the Hursts and Mrs. Beaman on the other side of the room. Marie-Joseph suggested, "Let's sit alone so we can chat. You'll have time later to meet the others."

Once everyone was seated, Father Meriel stood, made the sign of the cross and said grace, ending again with the sign of the cross. "Am I supposed to do that?" Lizzie asked.

"Not yet, don't worry, things will become clear. When we first came, I was totally confused." The congregation began to eat and Marie-Joseph explained, "The women in front are the Holy Sisters. In French they are *religieuse,* in English, nuns. Behind them with simpler gray habits are *novices*, studying to be nuns. The rest of the people are captives like you, residents like me, or externs who go to the country and work with the sisters. After breakfast, you will go with Sister Marie-Angélique and she will explain more."

"How were you taken?" Lizzie asked.

Marie-Joseph was very casual as she explained, "The Indians came at night and took many of us from our beds. My mother, sister and I marched with them to the Abenaki village at Odanak—north of here. It was summer, I don't remember much anymore. We lived with the Indians about two months until a priest came with a nun and a few Indians. They brought us to the convent, much as you came yesterday. My mother left and my sister decided she had the calling to join the Holy Sisters. She now works with the Indians at a mission north of here. We don't see her much."

"Tell me about this *calling*," Lizzie asked.

"Sometimes a girl decides she wants to devote her life to Christ." Marie-Joseph explained calmly. "They work and study as a *novice* for some time. Eventually they take their vows and become a Holy Sister."

"Vows?"

"Poverty, chastity and obedience," Marie-Joseph recited. "They swear to live a life without a man, without money and within all the rules of the church—it's not for everyone."

Lizzie could see this may not be the career path for her. "What is to become of you?" she asked. Marie-Joseph shrugged, "I can remain a helper of the Sisters, marry, or go home to Maine. I haven't decided, but I can stay here and work as long as I like."

Lizzie processed this before asking, "Why does Sister Marie-Angélique speak such good English?" Marie-Joseph

247

shrugged, "They say she grew up with private tutors. She also speaks German, Italian and Latin."

Father Meriel stood and gave a final blessing after which the women returned their bowls and went off to do their daily work. Sister Marie-Angélique came for Lizzie. Following a brief tour of the convent, Sister Marie-Angélique took Lizzie to her small office. "The mission of the Congregation," she began, "is to work among the population, spreading education and the word of God." Pointing to a painting of a lady in black, she continued, "Marguerite Bourgeoys came from France almost half a century ago. She was not a nun but an extern, one who aids the Holy Sisters. In those days, nuns were cloistered—they stayed in the convent isolated from the outside world. They spread their word through externs, like Sister Bourgeoys." Standing to look out the window, she continued, "She helped found our congregation and suggested our nuns should not be cloistered. Now we go out to work among the people, particularly the natives. We leave our habits," motioning to the garb she was wearing, "inside and dress in ordinary clothes. In addition, we offer help to people like you, trapped in the cultural battles of our day." A tear came to Lizzie's eye as she remembered Andrew's story of Sister Bourgeoys.

Sitting again at the desk, the nun explained, "While you are here, you will have classes in French culture and language as well as the Catholic faith. What you do with this is up to you. Some choose to stay, becoming French and Catholic. Others do not and may return home if it is possible. This will become clear as time goes on. You may go out if you have finished your duties, but at first you are to go with one or more of the experienced women. Do you have questions?"

Lizzie had many questions but one was burning. "Sister, my brother Sammy, is…?"

The nun interrupted, "Pierre-Henri explained it to me and he is going to try to find him. He is very competent. I will let you know as soon as I hear anything."

"Why do you call him Pierre-Henri?"

Smiling, she replied, "He accepted the Catholic faith like many of the natives. That is his Christian name. He sometimes uses his Indian name among his people. You were very fortunate to fall under his care." Standing to end the visit, she concluded, "Marie-Joseph will be your mentor and answer other questions. If she cannot, my door is open." Extending her hand, she added, "Again you are safe and welcome with us."

Marie-Joseph was waiting for her outside the office door. Filled with enthusiasm, she suggested, "We have today free, so we can do as we please! Let's start on the roof." She led the way back to the stairs. On the third floor they found a different stairway. The door at the end led to the roof. The day was as clear as yesterday had been foggy. Marie-Joseph said, "Wait, we are not there yet." A narrow tower with a ladder on its side stood in the center. Marie-Joseph began to climb. "Follow me."

The top was a platform with conical roof supported by pillars. In the center, hung a great bell. Suddenly Lizzie and her new friend were standing in the sunlight with a gentle breeze in their hair and a 360 degree view of the entire world! In front was the great river flowing to the sea and behind a small mountain rising gradually to hide the northwestern branch of the river behind it. Below was the city! Buildings large and small with streets running east-west and north-south, streets filled with people, horses, carts and commerce.

"This is the river *Saint-Laurent*," Marie-Joseph began, "I should probably start using French names."

"I do know some French."

"Good, that will help." Pointing, "We are looking east. The convent is on the northern end of town, and the two villages across the river are Longueuil and Boucherville. In back is Mont Royal from which the town takes its name. Beyond that is the other branch of the river. Montréal is an island—a big one. The large building to the south is the hospital, called *Hotel Dieu.* The next large stone building is the Seminary of the Sulpicians, priests and monks. In Québec they have Jesuits, you'll learn about that in class. The male captives tend to be housed in the seminary. Then the great building behind it is the main church where we shall attend Mass on Sunday. You have never been in a more beautiful building. A few of the other larger buildings belong to the government and the rest are homes and shops. In the next few days, we should get to go out. As you will see, this is not a small village like Deerfield."

Leaning over the edge of the railing, Marie-Joseph pointed out the fine points of Montréal, what the smaller buildings were and what the hubbub of humanity was doing way below. They were shaken from the lure of civilization as the great bell began to chime. "My goodness!" Marie-Joseph reported, "The Angelus already."

"The what?"

"It's a prayer to the Virgin said three times a day. It is signaled by the bell. You were too asleep to hear it this morning." Taking Lizzie's hand and leading her back to the ladder with a smile. "It also means it's time to eat!"

Lizzie followed her new friend as they snaked their way down the ladder, stairs and hallways to the dining hall. The ladies distributing the food were dressed much like Marie-

Joseph apart from a plump woman in the sister's habit. Marie-Joseph whispered, "That's Sister Marie-Clare, head of the dining hall." Each woman had a bowl, and as they passed Marie-Clare, she loaded a ladle of porridge, along with a generous slice of bread being cut from giant loaves.

Marie-Clare reminded Lizzie of Mrs. Beaman, her enormous bosom was apparent even in the habit. Before Lizzie could move on with her bowl, Marie-Clare reached out and stopped her. Then looking her over, up and down, she grunted, *"Trop mince!"* and ladled a second helping of porridge and second slice of bread. Marie-Joseph led the way to a table trying to control her laughter. When she sat down, the young woman across from her asked in English, "What's so funny?"

Stifling her laugh, Marie-Joseph said, "It seems Sister Marie-Clare is making it a mission to fatten-up Lizzie."

Their tablemate grinned, "Be careful, she'll make you as big as she is." Extending her hand, she announced, "I'm Catherine Dunkin, taken from Billerica, Massachusetts, in 1695." The girls began to chat as Lizzie felt herself oddly transported from grieving young widow to school girl. Taking the first bite of the porridge, she was astounded. In Deerfield, porridge was porridge, but this had more tastes than she could identify. "Good, isn't it?" asked Catherine.

"Yes, what is it?"

"One of Sister Marie-Clare's many secrets. The woman is a master of herbs and spices—the bread is even better."

As Lizzie began to add back her pounds, Catherine reported. "I met some of your friends today, the Hursts."

"I know, I've seen them. When will we get to visit?"

Marie-Joseph answered, "You'll have plenty of time once you start your classes. You will all be together. Outside of classes the sisters would like you to get to know the others, like us. Once your French is better, we will introduce you to the French women."

Catherine told them, "I hear they are expecting a large number of people from Deerfield. Sister told me they will likely need to put the younger children with families."

Once Sister Marie-Angélique had said a brief prayer and dismissed the group, Marie-Joseph said, "Let's continue our tour. We can see a lot before dinner."

When Lizzie rose to follow her, she felt her stomach as full as it had been the last time she saw Mrs. Smead's pie. Marie-Joseph continued a tour of the nooks and crannies of the convent including the grounds and gardens still sleeping from winter. Lastly they made their way down dark and dank steps for two floors into the earth. "This is a crypt," Marie-Joseph explained. "The Congregation began about fifty years ago and since then some of the nuns have been buried down here. Sister Bourgeoys was buried in the cemetery, but…" she paused with a spooky expression and whispered, "her heart is buried down here." Then with more mystery, "Don't come down here alone unless you relish playing with ghosts."

She motioned for Lizzie to lead the way back up. As they started the climb, she pulled hard on Lizzie's smock. "Boo!" she shouted. Lizzie jumped and screamed while her new friend bent over in laughter before continuing their ascent.

Dinner was no disappointment, the porridge looked the same but it was again deliciously different. Along with the bread came a small piece of meat and a generous slice of cheese with a small dish of fruit preserve. Marie-Joseph led her to the dormitory where she was able to say hello to some of her Deerfield friends, but her bunk was away from them, close to Marie-Joseph. As she drifted off to sleep she thought, *maybe, I will be all right.*

But she was not. Her dreams were filled with pain, death, and ghosts of friends and family. She awoke screaming at least three times, each time to be rescued by Marie-Joseph. In the morning she assured Lizzie, "Don't worry, everyone goes through that."

Lizzie was not entirely relieved. "When does it end?"

Her usually upbeat new friend frowned, looking her in the eye. "It doesn't"

Chapter Two

As the sun worked its way above the horizon, the entire congregation was dressed and ready to go. Joining the crowd, Lizzie stepped onto the streets of Montréal for the first time since she was left by Makya. Turning south, they followed the Rue Saint-Paul with the palisade to their left and buildings to their right. Sister Marie-Angélique had told Lizzie and Marie-Joseph they could walk together, talking quietly so Marie-Joseph could point out areas of interest. The first large stone structure was the back of the hospital called the *Hotel Dieu,* and past this was the large fence-enclosed seminary where the priest and monks lived. The *Hotel Dieu* was one floor higher than the convent and the seminary reached a dizzying five stories. She had already learned in class the Sulpician order had come from a Parisian parish named Saint-Sulpice. Clearly the quarters and grounds of the men surpassed that

254

of the women. "The male captives are brought here," Marie-Joseph reported.

Turning right at the next opportunity, they found narrow Rue Saint-François, which soon opened onto the largest square Lizzie had seen. Although the centerpiece church of Notre-Dame seemed enormous viewed from the roof of the convent, it appeared even larger from the ground. The square was filling with church-goers, some entering and others standing to visit in the square. Sister Marie-Angélique led her flock directly into the building. The stone edifice was even grander from the inside. Walking down the long aisle, Lizzie could not stop staring at the high colored windows illuminated by the morning sun. She and the other lay members sat on the side before a second aisle crossed the center forming a cross. The altar was much higher and more decorated than the chapel of the Congregation. The statues and paintings were much larger and better done. The crucifix looked frighteningly real.

A group of gray-clad monks sat in the center while the sisters went to seats on the side of the cross aisle from where they would sing. As the rest of the parish filed in, Marie-Joseph whispered that the rich families would sit in front and the less fortunate behind. Once the crowd had gathered, the steeple bell rang, and as the priest and servers began their march to the altar, there was a loud sound like the horn of a giant. Marie-Joseph whispered above it, "That's a thing with seven large pipes. It's called an *organ* and I heard it was one of just two in Canada. It only arrived two years ago. It plays wonderful music."

Mass was longer and more complicated than the daily celebration at the Congregation, but Lizzie found it more enjoyable, although she knew Reverend Williams would hardly approve. When the priest left the altar, Marie-Joseph

255

motioned for Lizzie to follow her, whispering, "Sister said we did not have to come back with the group as long as we are back before the noonday Angelus." She quietly led her down a side aisle and subtly ducked out a small side door. Emerging into the sunlight, she told Lizzie, "This way we can go watch the people come out." They hurried to arrive at the main doors just as they opened, allowing the parishioners to pour into the square. Those seated in back exited first. Lizzie was surprised at the number of Indians. Marie-Joseph told her, "Most Christian Indians attend Mass at one of the mission churches, but those who are in town are welcome here."

Next came the working class—the largest segment of the parish. Some men wore deerskin, but most a simple cloth coat. The women had covered their heads with shawls much as Lizzie and Marie-Joseph had done. When they came out, some put them on their shoulders like a scarf. Soon there was a flow of elegantly dressed people followed by the priest.

"Oh look," whispered Marie-Joseph. "That is Monsieur and Madame Le Moyne. His family is very rich. They have a large estate in Iberville and a mansion in town by the convent. They sometimes house captive children." Lizzie watched in amazement, the difference in Deerfield between the richest and poorest was not much. "And that's Monsieur Le Ber, a widower who also has an estate across the river and a mansion on Rue Saint-Paul." Looking on as if she was identifying songbirds, she again whispered, "That is the new Governor of Montréal, Ramezay—oh my God! He's with Vaudreuil. He was the Governor of Montréal but is now Governor of *all* New France." Vaudreil came close and tipped his hat with a flirtatious wink. As they moved on, Marie-Joseph exclaimed with a smug air, "Did you see that? The most powerful man in New France!" Lizzie did not realize, nor would she ever, that she had been flirted with by the very man responsible for the death of her family members.

While they were star-gazing, a female voice came from in back. "Why look. It's Esther."

Turning quickly, they saw another prosperous couple. Marie-Joseph curtsied and changed to French, "*Bonjour*, Madame Roi."

The elegant lady on the arm of an equally prosperous man said, again in French, "But it is no longer Esther, is it?"

"No, Madame, it is Marie-Joseph."

"And who is your friend?"

"This is Elizabeth, Madame—a new English girl, living at the convent."

The grand lady switched to halting English, "Hello, my dear."

Marie-Joseph explained, "Elizabeth speaks some French, Madame."

Going back to French, Madame Roi exclaimed, "How nice. You must be very intelligent." Then taking Marie-Joseph's hand, "My dear, I will be at the Montréal house most of the season. When you and your friend have time, please stop by. I would love a visit."

As they moved on, Marie-Joseph told Lizzie, "Le Bers, Le Moynes and Rois are all very good to the Congregation. They have helped many captives. I stayed with Madame Roi for two years after I was taken." Looking off in thought, she added, "We are taught the French are bad and they are taught we are bad, but in truth we are all people."

"My husband used to say that." It was the first time Lizzie had referred openly to Andrew.

They looked at some shuttered shops along the way while Marie-Joseph suggested, "When we have the opportunity, we shall come by when they are open."

Lizzie nodded and looking ahead saw something which made her mouth drop. "Monsieur LeMieux!"

As he stopped, equally surprised, she greeted him in French. Delighted that they could communicate, he answered, "*Bonjour*, Miss Elizabeth."

"What are you doing now?" she inquired.

Pointing at the departing Roi couple, he told her, "Monsieur Roi's young son, Jacques, is a master stone mason building a new house for new Governor Ramezay. I am helping along with LeDuc."

This was more than Lizzie had ever heard him say. She asked, "Do you know how to cut stone?"

He laughed, something else she had not heard before, "No, but I know how to lift it."

"What about Monsieur de Noyon?" Lizzie inquired.

Scratching his giant chin, he reported, "He has joined Alphonse de Tonty in his *troupes de la marine*."

Alarmed at this, she asked, "What about Abby?"

He shrugged, "I think she may be coming to the convent with you." After a pause, he added, "LeDuc and I are staying in a shed by the new construction of the mansion. If you need us, Miss Lizzie, just come get us."

Suddenly Montréal seemed safer.

As they approached the convent, Marie-Joseph said, "A strange man—and a big one."

"Yes, I'll tell you more later. What was that about *Esther?*"

"It's my name, or it was in York, Esther Sayward. When you are baptized Catholic, you sometimes take another name. You'll learn about it in your lessons."

Turning onto Rue Saint-Paul, they heard a bell. "Oh, dear, the Angelus, we need to run!"

* * *

May, 1704: Montréal

"This will be a perfect day to see the finer side of Montréal!" Marie-Joseph was even more enthusiastic than usual as she and Lizzie started down Rue Saint-Paul. Madame Roi had repeatedly asked Sister Marie-Angélique to allow the girls a visit, and the nun finally acknowledged Lizzie was ready for the adventure. Excelling in her French language and culture lessons, she was even coming to grips with the labyrinth of Catholicism. Of course, Andrew's tutelage had been more than helpful.

During class she had reunited with the Hurst women, Mary French, Dame Beaman, and Sarah-Bee who had arrived recently with young Christopher, while Benjamin was housed and worked at the Sulpician monastery. Several of the other children were living with prominent French families, while several more remained mired with the Indians. Sammy and Mary Field along with her children, John and Mary, remained among those unaccounted, although Sister tried to assure Lizzie they were likely safe.

Spring did not announce itself as dramatically in the urban area of Montréal as it did in the meadows and forests of Deerfield, but the sun was warm, and pockets of *printemps,* as the French called the season, displayed itself in the small gardens and orchards surrounding the great, ornate three-story town residences along the Rue Saint-Paul. As the girls worked their way up this grand street,

259

Marie-Joseph pointed out the homes of Le Ber, Le Moyne and other prominent families, while she explained to Lizzie that these were used when the family was in town. For the women, this was much of the time, but the men spent more time in the country estates in towns across the river like Boucherville, Longueuil and La Prairie where they oversaw the management of farm land and the other businesses, primarily the fur trade. Not trapping or trading with natives, but selling the valuable cargo in the rich markets of Europe.

Finally they came to the Roi residence, every bit as magnificent as the neighboring mansions, it boasted spacious grounds running all the way to Rue Notre Dame, providing space for the stables and large gardens. A black female *servant*—the French avoided the term, *slave,* greeted them at the door. Already *au courant* with who they were, she bid them enter.

Lizzie found the entry nothing short of breath-taking. Floors of varnished boards were adorned by luxurious rugs while paintings on the walls could be illuminated at night by the chandelier overhead. A grand staircase led to unknown wonders on the floors above.

"Ah, ladies! Welcome." Lizzie brought her gaze back down to earth where she saw Madame Roi. In a colorful lace gown, her hair styled, wearing tastefully ornate jewelry, she was everything Lizzie expected in an elegant French lady. Putting out her arms to greet them, she took Lizzie's hand. Surprised at the roughness of the grand lady's palms, Lizzie merely smiled. Madame continued, keeping her French slow and simple. "Come in—please." Turning to the servant, "Babette, would you please serve tea in the drawing room? And ask our *new girls* to come down."

260

As she was escorted, Lizzie could scarcely keep her head on as she tried subtly to see as much of the grand home as possible. Her mind flashed back to her mother's description of her grandfather's home, *"Oh, Elizabeth, I wish you could have seen it."*

Soon they were seated on upholstered furniture while Babette brought the tea service on a silver tray. Sister Marie-Angélique had given her a crash course in etiquette and Lizzie obeyed, not doing anything until her host did it first. Although her mother had alluded to it, she had never seen tea in a cup *and* saucer. Madame Roi picked hers up, as did Marie-Joseph, Lizzie followed, struggling to mimic their actions. "Elizabeth, my dear, how are you getting on in these new surroundings?"

Lizzie's moods changed constantly from panic to relaxed, excitement to depression and acceptance to rebellion, but she simply smiled, reporting, "Very well, thank you, Madame." Babette reappeared with two young girls. Looking up, Lizzie could scarcely recognize Martha French and Elizabeth Corse. Between eight and nine years old, the girls were dressed in crisp gray smocks with lace embroidery. Their heads were bare, their hair curled and both looked freshly scrubbed. Once they realized who was visiting, they lost their polite demeanor, rushing to embrace her.

"My goodness, you must have been a popular young lady," Madame Roi guessed.

Martha French turned, recovering her polite pose without letting go of Lizzie's hand, and explained in English, "Lizzie was our school dame. She taught us to read and write."

Madame Roi smiled at Lizzie remarking, "My, what an accomplishment for such a young age."

Lizzie could not hide her grin as she explained her actual role with Dame Beaman. Madame Roi became even more enthusiastic and lapsed back into French. "Oh, my dears, how exciting!" Sitting back down, she retrieved her cup and saucer before continuing. "My oldest daughter, Marguerite, is with the Holy Sisters. She works with the Congregation teaching the natives in the reservations to the north. Some of the ladies and I join them from time to time. I will go tomorrow and speak with Sister Marie-Angélique. You must accompany us, it is a grand experience, and you would be wonderful—I am certain." Setting her cup down she pondered a second, "I know. I shall bring Madame Le Moyne with me. Sister would never say no to her."

The visit continued as Madame Roi explored Lizzie's background briefly while explaining some features of Montréal. Following an appropriate period of time, she rose, thanked them, and asked Babette to show them out. Once back on Rue Saint-Paul, Marie-Joseph looked up at the sky and determined, "We still have time, let's see some of the city."

Turning inland on Rue Saint-Charles they followed the fence surrounding the Roi gardens all the way to the wide Rue Notre-Dame turning back toward the city center. Soon they encountered the bustling construction of the Ramezay mansion. In the forefront of the action was the hulking LeMieux who was loading enormous stones into a rope net while his partner, LeDuc, was on the next story, pulling them up with the help of a rope and pulley. Once the stone was up, he placed it at the direction of a young man next to him.

"Your friends are very strong," observed Marie-Joseph, stating the obvious.

Lizzie nodded, "Who is the boy?"

"That is Madame Roi's young son, Jacques."

"He looks so young."

Marie-Joseph agreed, "Yes, younger than me. He was at school when I lived at the mansion. His father wanted him to continue his studies in Paris, but he chose a trade in stone."

"His father must have been upset."

"At first, but soon stone buildings became very popular. In fact, the government is trying to ban new wood structures."

With a quizzical look, Lizzie asked, "Why?"

"We have many fires every year. Stone doesn't burn. Anyway, young Jacques now seems to be the most gifted stonemason in Montréal."

As she looked up, LeDuc saw her and waved. She impulsively blew him a kiss. She felt safer with them around. As they turned away, she asked Marie-Joseph, "Does Madame Roi have many children?"

Marie-Joseph laughed, "More than I can count. I don't know all of them. They were usually away at school in Québec City—except Pierre." She began to giggle. "He's a little different."

"What does he do?"

Marie-Joseph pondered, "He's an—adventurer. Now he's off in a wilderness outpost called Détroit. I think he has an Indian wife."

Heading toward the church, Lizzie countered, "I had an Indian husband."

"His wife is a *real* Indian, and he is… well, you will have to see for yourself, he comes home from time to time."

263

The next few blocks were lined with small two-story houses. "This is the Artisan district," Marie-Joseph explained.

"They are tradesmen and shop keepers. The upper story is the house and the lower level the shop and store." As they passed, they could see the various wares displayed outside and often the tradesman toiling inside. Marveling at the sight, Lizzie thought back to Deerfield where the cabinetmakers, shoemakers, and others had small side businesses in the barn along with a small farm. Here each home was an enterprise, and it seemed anything one could desire could be found among these rows of manufacturing.

Stopping in front of a cobbler's store, Lizzie watched the man inside toiling at his trade. About her age, he looked up and smiled, he was very handsome. She returned the smile. Suddenly she felt guilty and began to sob.

"What's the matter?" her friend asked, putting her hand on her shoulder.

Lizzie looked at the ground, "Sammy wanted to be a shoemaker."

Marie-Joseph tightened her embrace, "And he shall, Sister said Pierre-Henri will redeem him." Then she warned, "But he may be far away and it may take time. I have seen people redeemed two years after capture." Lizzie stifled her sob and nodded but was far from convinced.

Reaching the church square market, Lizzie was shocked. There were stands of every size selling everything imaginable, farm tools, candles, silk dresses along with all manner of spring produce, meat, fish, dried and preserved food. As they wandered through the bazaar, she recalled the small shop of Moses Gunn as Sammy faded to the back of her mind.

Chapter Three

<u>Two weeks later: Montréal</u>

S he *could hear but could not see them. No matter how much she pushed her way through the thicket, she could not find the clearing. Looking down, she saw blood on her arms and legs from the thorns. Stopping, she listened carefully—laughing. She knew it was Sammy and Thankful out playing Indian again. "Sammy, where are you?" she shouted. "Thankful! Your ma is going to give you what for—you two come out right now!"*

Finally she found the clearing. Pushing through the thorn-covered thicket, she saw them—nuked as she had expected, but they were standing. As her eyes adjusted, she realized they were not standing, but hanging from the bushes—blood dripped down their bare chests from the long gashes on their throats. She screamed to no avail. Then the Indian appeared. "Remember, nothing is certain but today."

"Lizzie! Lizzie! Wake up!"

265

Opening her eyes, she again began to scream, but someone quieted her. It was Sarah-Lynn's mother. The room was dark but for faint moon-glow though the dormitory window. Sitting up, she began to orient. Her bedclothes were soaked. Mrs. Hurst sat on her cot, holding her as her mother had when she was small, while Marie-Joseph and Catherine Dunkin stood by. "You had another nightmare, dear," Mrs. Hurst whispered, as she rocked her on the cot.

Marie-Joseph took her hand, "Come with me, Lizzie, I know what to do" Handing her a robe, she led her out the door and down two floors to a small office. Inside, two candles burned, illuminating a nun sitting behind a desk, reading.

"Why aren't you two in bed?" she asked in her classic stern-nun voice.

"Sister Marie-Marguerite," Marie-Joseph explained, "Elizabeth had another nightmare."

The nun rose, "Very well, have a seat." She disappeared and returned with a teapot. Pouring three cups she said, "Tell us about it, my child."

She explained the dream and Sister Marie-Marguerite suggested, "These are normal at first, dear. It is a pity, as no one deserves to go through what you have."

"But Sister," Lizzie added, "Last night I dreamed of Andrew—my husband. We made love and he told me everything would be all right. Just when I think I can survive, I have another *terrible* dream."

Patting Lizzie's wrist, Sister Marie-Marguerite concluded with the classic nun answer, "The Lord works in mysterious ways, my child." Then standing, she added, "I have just the thing for you." Disappearing to return a few minutes later, she opened a bottle and checking that

Lizzie's cup was empty, poured the yellow liquid. "Try a taste of this, my dear." She poured a portion for both her and Marie-Joseph. Lizzie took a sip. Her green eyes opened wide as it burned down to her toenails. She also felt her hair was taking on a new curl. Setting the cup down, she was speechless.

Sister Marie-Marguerite asked, "How was that?"

Lizzie tried to respond but the words could not work their way out, and Sister Marie-Marguerite poured a second cup. "This is made from apple cider. In France it is called calvados after an area in Normandy. It is said to *cure what ails you*." When Lizzie appeared to have recovered, Sister Marie-Marguerite asked, "How are you now, dear?"

Lizzie finally choked out without conviction, "Better?"

"Ah good, now take the second dose and all will be well." Holding her own glass up to Marie-Joseph, she added, "Drink up as well, dear—*santé*."

An hour later the threesome was finishing a wonderful session of soul searching and confession when Sister Marie-Marguerite rose and took their arms, "We should be off to bed. Do not forget, we are going to the mission in the morning."

* * *

She was lying next to Andrew when the bell chimed. Suddenly sitting upright, she looked—he was gone. Her head hurt. Then she remembered the episode with Sister Marie-Marguerite. Her dreams had been pleasant since then, maybe the nun would give her a bottle of calvados to keep under her cot. She rose to dress, straighten her cot and follow her dorm mates down to chapel.

Following breakfast, she proceeded with Marie-Joseph to the entry of the convent. To its north stood a large archway that led to a courtyard and a second archway that led to the convent grounds with the kitchen garden, barn and stables. Here they found Sister Marie-Angélique and Sister Marie-Marguerite who had abandoned their habits for working clothes, directing two Indian men loading supplies into a cart while a third man was attaching two large white draft horses. Lizzie thought instantly of Gilgamesh, wondering what might have happened to her old friend.

"Do you like horses, Elizabeth?"

She turned to see Sister Marie-Angélique, "Oh, yes, Sister, I love all animals. These are enormous."

"Yes," the nun replied, "These are *Perchon* named for a region in Normandy. They were a gift from one of our Normand patrons." Addressing her and Marie-Joseph, she told them, "You two ladies are to travel with Madame Roi. You should wait for her by the front entrance."

Soon a cart stopped at the entry. It was not the elegant carriage Lizzie had envisioned but a simple working cart much like her father's, and it was not driven by a uniformed chauffeur, rather it was Madame Roi herself in the clothes of a farming woman. Now the rough hands made sense.

"Climb in, ladies," she ordered, looking about, "I believe we have one more—oh, there she is." As the nun climbed on board, Madame Roi said, "Elizabeth, have you met my daughter, Sister Marie-Marguerite?"

"Uh, yes I have. Last night."

As the nun climbed up, she looked at the two young women, asking, "Did you ladies sleep well last night?"

They both stifled laughs to answer while Madame Roi suggested, "Elizabeth, why don't you sit up with me and we can visit."

As they headed south on Rue Saint-Paul, Madame told her, "Today we are going to La Montagne. It is an old mission and not too far. Its people are mainly Iroquois, mostly of the Mohawk tribe." Lizzie's fear of Mohawks was only slightly tempered when told, "It's an older mission and the people are quite civilized. It was one of the first places visited by the Sulpicians."

As they left the city gate through the unfinished palisade, Madame related, "Sister Marie-Angélique told me you are married."

"*Was*, Madame, he was killed."

Stumbling on her faux pas, Madame said, "Oh, I am so sorry. Was he a good Puritan man?"

Lizzie smiled slightly at the question and answered by summarizing Andrew's past. When she finished, Madame asked, "What was his name?" When Lizzie told her, Madame looked shocked. "I knew him! He was a wonderful man. Oh, my dear, I am doubly sorry. Do you have anyone left?"

Lizzie hesitated, "Only my father and… I don't know."

Madame Roi was silent for a while before saying with encouragement, "Montréal and all of Canada are the land of opportunity, especially for women."

Lizzie looked at her as though she were mad, "For women?"

"Oh my, yes."

"How can that be?"

The older woman paused for a moment, "When France first came to Canada, it sent only men, assuming they would marry the natives. In short, it did not work out. Forty years ago the crown began to send young women promoted by their local priest to marry. They were called *Filles du Roi,* the King's daughters. For ten years, more than 700 young women came from France to Canada. In spite of that, there is still a great shortage of marriageable women," adding with a smile, "especially intelligent beauties."

Madame Roi extolled the wonders of the farm land as they passed many large tracts. Eventually she continued, "Canada is indeed a land of opportunity. What do you suppose my husband's circumstances were?"

Lizzie took a chance, "He was rich?"

Madame laughed, "He came from a coastal town of France, La Rochelle. He came as an indentured man and owed Monsieur Le Ber, now our friend and neighbor, three years' service. At the end, he stayed on and joined in some enterprises until today he is quite successful."

Lizzie pondered, "Were *you* rich?"

Again Madame laughed, "No, dear, I was one of those girls, a *fille du Roi.*" She reached over and touched Lizzie's golden locks, "Elizabeth, *you* would be well sought after."

The road had been flat but now began to climb. Lizzie had been surprised by the number of productive farms in the area. In New England, she had been taught Canada was nothing but empty wasteland. Reaching a high point, they could see a large mountain range to the north with peaks still covered in white. "Those are the Laurentian Mountains," Madame explained. "We will soon be at the mission. You will see it is not very large, many of the natives are moving to a new mission, at *Sault-au-Récollet* to the north."

"Why is that?"

"It's closer to the northern branch of the *Saint-Laurent,* and there is more land." After some thought, she decided to

270

be candid, "Actually the government wants this land for colonial settlers, something like New England." Coming around a bend, Lizzie could see the town when Madame announced, "This is it."

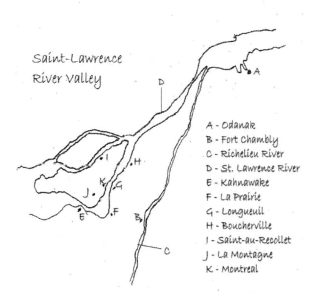

Saint-Lawrence River Valley

A - Odanak
B - Fort Chambly
C - Richelieu River
D - St. Lawrence River
E - Kahnawake
F - La Prairie
G - Longueuil
H - Boucherville
I - Saint-au-Recollet
J - La Montagne
K - Montreal

Chapter Four

June 1704: La Montagne

ike Deerfield, La Montagne was a collection of buildings surrounded by farming fields. Perched on a rise with a spectacular view of the countryside, the buildings were log longhouses without windows or chimneys. A larger, more traditional structure stood on a small hill at the end of the houses. The crucifix clearly identified it as the church. Barns and pens of animals sat on one end without any connection to any of the residences.

While the wagons pulled into a central location, the residents left their various activities to welcome the visitors. When the four women climbed down from the wagon, they were surrounded by children, most of whom were naked on this warm summer day. It was apparent both Sister Marie-Marguerite and Madame Roi knew almost all of them. Women came behind the youngsters, most bare-breasted. The men, dressed like Andrew when he first came to Deerfield, stood farther away.

Moving away from the wagon, they were greeted by an older lady. Wearing a brightly beaded vest providing more ornamentation than modesty, her skin was deeply tanned and weathered, her straight white hair tied in a long single braid. "This is Marie-Geneviève, but she prefers her native name, *Ojistah*," Madame Roi explained. "She is a tribal leader who will give us a brief tour of her village." They shook hands with Ojistah who greeted them in passable English and a grin exposing three ragged teeth, while Sister Marie-Marguerite excused herself to attend to her work.

Leading them into a nearby longhouse, Ojistah began, "It is here we sleep in good weather and stay, cook and eat in bad." Always the calculator, Lizzie estimated it was several times the size of a Deerfield home. Lined with cots on the perimeter, the center was clear for sitting and cooking. Wooden walls were packed with mud, surprisingly there was almost no light coming through cracks. Various food products along with many other unrecognizable items hung from the ceiling. A large fire pit sat below a circular opening in the ceiling above. "We have no chimneys as you do," Ojistah told them. "Some smoke goes out here," pointing a crooked finger toward the hole, "and the light comes in. In winter there is much smoke, but we are accustomed to it—very warm."

Exiting to a large open square surrounded by houses, she continued, "Here we can meet, play, celebrate or simply relax." Pointing across the square, she added, "There are ovens where all food is prepared in summer, and baking is done all year." A few women were occupied rolling loaves and loading them onto the fire while several children stood by, perhaps hoping to get a fallen corn cake.

"Beyond here," she went on, "are the barns and pens of the animals." As they passed, they saw three women caring for the stock. "And here," she claimed with a sweeping motion of her gnarled hand along the horizon, "are our fields." Lizzie could already tell they had corn, wheat, melons and some of the vegetable crops she knew from Massachusetts. The two obvious differences were that the fields seemed to be all commonly run, and only a few women and two men were tending them. Viewing the scene, she considered that in Deerfield, every soul over four years would be engaged in caring for the fields, animals, or cooking. Here only a few were so occupied. Andrew's words came hauntingly back. *The English want more, the Indian only enough.*

Struggling to keep up with the agile Ojistah leading them up the incline, they entered the church. A more traditional European structure, it had windows and an altar complete with crucifix and a small statue of the lady with a babe in arms. However, there were no pews. By the altar, Sister Marie-Marguerite and another French woman were seated on small stools, surrounded by native women sitting on the floor—cross-legged as Makya had done.

Ojistah told them, "These ladies are having a religion class. Later today, the children will assemble for lessons." Staring at the altar, she added, "Some time ago we had Mass almost every day, but now that more people have left for Sault-au-Récollet, the priest comes only once a week."

On the far side of the church ran a small river feeding a sizeable pond where they found more activity than in the rest of the village. Women washed clothes, men fished and children swam along with some adults. All bathers were naked regardless of age or sex. "You ladies may join them if you wish to cool off," Ojistah informed them. Lizzie was tempted but thought Madame Roi and Sister might not approve.

As they were about to turn back, they heard, "Lizzie!"

Turning, she saw eight-year-old Hannah Hurst sprinting to her, dripping wet and naked as the day she was born. "Oh, Lizzie! It *is* you!"

As they embraced, Lizzie asked, "Hannah, how are you? We have been so worried."

"I'm all right," the child reported, "But I miss my family. Do you know where they are?"

"Yes, Hannah, they are all with me in Montréal. Your mother will be pleased to hear I found you." She did not know if Hannah realized her baby brother had been killed but thought it best left unsaid.

"Tell her I miss her, Lizzie. Maybe she can visit, like you. But tell her not to worry. I'm having fun." Stepping away and looking down at herself, she stated the obvious with a grin, "We don't even have to wear clothes here." Turning, she ran to the pond and vaulted in, hitting the water as a great ball. While they returned to the village, Lizzie pondered how she would edit this story for Hannah's mother.

"From here we shall return to the church," Madame Roi instructed, "where you ladies can observe the lessons for the children. We will spend a few days, giving you the opportunity to see a good deal. The sisters, externs, priests and monks do the work as you will see. We lay folks are here to show our support to the natives and gain an appreciation of them."

That evening they joined the tribe in the square for dinner which was a cross between picnic and feast. Hannah brought a few of her equally naked friends to meet Lizzie who realized she had seen more fun today than she saw most years in Deerfield. Following the meal, Madame Roi suggested that although the French generally camped in tents, the two young ladies could spend the night in a longhouse for the experience.

Ojistah and another woman took them to assign cots. June on the island of Montréal provided daylight well into the evening, and as their eyes adjusted, they could see well enough. Eventually the men entered and made their conjugal visits. Lizzie and Marie-Joseph fought valiantly to control their giggles. When the visits were over, the men left as expected. That night Lizzie had a wonderful dream about Andrew, the best since that fateful day in February.

* * *

During their third day, Sister Marie-Angélique came for Lizzie. "One of the Indian ladies is about to give birth. I heard you have some experience bringing children and thought you should come." The nun led the way to a longhouse with a small gathering outside. Entering they found the mother and three other women. The mother sat on a reclining wooden chair with her legs bent and spread apart. The wet floor indicated her water had already broken, and her breasts suggested this was not her first child. Two women stood beside her for support while Ojistah was attending to the delivery.

As she saw Lizzie, she motioned for her to come close. Holding out three fingers, she explained, "Third baby." The head soon appeared and Ojistah put two fingers into the birth canal, expertly bringing the head. Manipulating the shoulders, she delivered them and the rest was automatic. Lizzie noted there was no tearing of tissue as she had seen with Sarah-Bee. The infant released a scream to make any

Indian proud, and Ojistah handed him to Lizzie while she attended to the cord and afterbirth.

The child tried valiantly to suck, so Lizzie put a finger in his mouth which satisfied him momentarily. She showed him to the mother and two attendants who all hummed an approval. As she held this new bundle of life, she reflected on the three births she had attended, one in each of the three cultures. All three groups celebrated the birth and life of the child. Then she considered her own sad loss on the march as well as the numerous children who had been destroyed along the way here and elsewhere.

As the tears filled her eyes, she whispered, "What is wrong with this world?"

Once things were stable, Lizzie followed Ojistah out of the longhouse. As they stood, getting adjusted to the bright sunlight, the old lady took Lizzie's hand in her withered paw. Looking into her green eyes, she said, "You have now helped with a birth of the tribe. You should have Indian name." Thinking for a moment, she put her hand on Lizzie's forehead, "I shall call you, *Kahente.*"

Lizzie pronounced it slowly and asked, "What does it mean?"

The old lady pondered the translation, then replied, "Before her time."

Smiling, she thanked Ojistah, and walked with her toward the square where dinner was being prepared. Perhaps she was before her time. At any rate, it seemed she had just been baptized into a second culture.

* * *

Five days after their arrival, the Montréal residents boarded their carts for the ride home while Sister Marie-

Marguerite and the other workers remained to continue their work at the mission. Madame Roi had accomplished her goal of introducing the young English ladies to the native culture and workings of the mission. At the beginning, Lizzie had been fearful of the *evil* Mohawks, but she now realized they were people too, again as Andrew had told her, "*People and their cultures are not really so different.*" She also realized they were not necessarily lazy, but had different goals in life. Again, they just wanted *enough*.

Chapter Five

<u>One week later: Montréal</u>

A ided by Andrew's tutelage in French language and culture, Lizzie progressed rapidly in her lessons, including those in religion. Having mastered a few basic prayers, she had become comfortable with crossing herself, genuflecting and other activities important to Catholics. She had never taken her New England religion as seriously as her peers and maintained the same nonchalant attitude toward this new cult. However, she realized regardless of where the future would lead, being comfortable in the religion of the time and place could only work to her advantage.

Today she was assigned the unenviable task of emptying chamber pots. Fortunately the same ingenuity that allowed water to be delivered to the bathtub was used to send the sewage outside where the rain would carry it to the nearby river. While she emptied her final load, one of the young novices came looking for her. "You have a visitor waiting for you in Sister Marie-Angélique's office."

Returning the last chamber pot to its position before heading downstairs, she pondered, *I wonder who it could be?* She had prayed daily for her brother's return but knew if this had happened, the message would have been delivered by one of the nuns. Approaching Sister's door, she recognized the voices causing her to quicken her pace to enter the room. "Abby!" she shouted, rushing to hug her old friend.

When Lizzie finally let go her embrace, the nun commented, "I didn't even hear your knock, dear."

Blushing she stuttered, "Oh, I'm sorry, Sister, I was…"

Brushing it off with a wave of her hand, the nun replied, "Very well, Elizabeth, I know how you have wondered about your friend, but here she is—safe and sound."

Realizing she had trampled on etiquette, Lizzie looked quietly at her feet while the nun continued, "I suspect you and Madame de Noyon have much to discuss. It is a lovely day. Why don't you take a day from your lessons for a visit? Go show her the city, but be prudent and back by the evening Angelus—and Elizabeth, remember to knock."

Arm in arm, Lizzie led her friend down Rue Saint-Paul to see the fine homes. "Well, *Madame de Noyon*," Lizzie asked with a giggle, "how is it to be a rich lady in the countryside?"

Abby stopped and responded with a frown, "I wouldn't know. You see, after Jacques' trial, they took almost everything he owned. I don't even know what it all was. Anyway, he went off straight away with this man, Tonty, to an outpost called, *Détroit*. There is a small property of his that pays a little rent, but that is all."

"Where do you live?" Lizzie asked with concern.

"At first I lived with Jacques' widowed mother in Boucherville—a small town across the river. It was awful. I was the serving girl. Then I moved in with Jacques' sister. She is married to a prominent fur trader, Michel Charbonneau. Her home is better than Jacques' mother's, but Boucherville is not much better than Deerfield, so she suggested I come to Montréal. She gave me the name of a friend I may stay with. Apparently her son in Détroit knows Jacques. In the meantime, Sister Marie-Angélique said I could stay at the convent." They walked on, admiring the mansions before Abby added with a sly grin, "Oh, yes, I'm pregnant."

Lizzie felt a pain from the memory of the small grave under a spruce tree, but recovered to congratulate her friend, "Oh, Abby, how exciting—when?"

"The end of the year, I think. It would be more exciting if I had a man around."

"Well," Lizzie countered, "Sarah-Bee has her little Christopher at the convent and Benjamin lives at the seminary."

"Marguerite, that's Jacques' sister," Abby explained, "says in this culture, if a woman is married and her man is gone most of the time, people don't object if she has a— *friendship* with another man."

Aghast, Lizzie countered, "Do you mean…?"

"Well, that is what she said. She told me she does it on occasion."

This astounding statement changed the conversation, and Lizzie retreated to tell her friend about her experience with the convent, life in Montréal, and her visit with the Indians as they made the rounds of the city returning to the convent just before the Angelus.

Lizzie appeared at the bathing chamber at her appointed time. Entering, she took a seat to wait her turn for an eagerly anticipated weekly bath. Next to her was Abby, who, as usual, had news. "I have met with Marguerite's friend, and she believes she may be able to take me in." Lizzie nodded and Abby continued. "I hope so, I've met a man and it would be much more convenient if I lived on the outside."

Aghast, Lizzie asked, "But Abby, what if something happens?"

Her friend laughed, "What's to happen? I am already pregnant."

As Abby rose to take her turn in the tub, Lizzie asked, "Who is this lady?"

"A Madame Roi, she lives nearby and her son works with Jacques."

Lizzie sat with her mouth open, while Abby took her turn in the tub. Soon, she was joined by Mrs. Hurst. Lizzie asked, "Have you heard any more about Hannah?"

The older lady replied, "Yes, Sister is trying to arrange a visit. She told me the Mohawk are reluctant to let the children out of the village. She says Hannah is happy. Looking back at our life since the death of Mr. Hurst, I'm not certain what is best for her—or any of us."

Soon Lizzie had her turn in the tub. The water was now lukewarm as it was only changed occasionally, but it was still a treat as she lay back for her precious few minutes. When she left, she walked by the mirror where she was pleased to see her weight and figure had returned. Leaving the room, she encountered Sister Marie-Angélique.

"Lizzie, what is that around your neck?"

She had generally kept the medallion beneath her clothes but in her haste to dress, it was exposed. "It was given to me by Makya—I mean, Pierre-Henri, Sister." She proceeded to tell the story.

The nun asked, "Does it tingle?"

Surprised at the question, she replied, "Sometimes."

The nun took it and turned it in her hand. "When I was a girl in Paris, my father had a very wealthy friend with a similar medallion. He claimed it was handed down through his family for generations and had been given to his ancestor during a crusade by King Louis IX, now Saint-Louis. There were three such medallions for three knights charged with bringing the true crown of thorns from the Holy Land."

Lizzie was mystified, but the nun concluded, "Probably just a legend. We can talk about it some other time."

Late July, 1704: Montréal:

Madame Roi did invite Abby to live with her which certainly gave the young lady more freedom. However, she didn't have the life of a rich wife she once thought awaited her. Nor was she simply a guest. Madame charged Abby with some of the care of the young Deerfield girls as well as the six youngest Roi children, ages 7 to 13 when they were at home and not away at school. Afforded some free time, Abby remained a frequent visitor to the convent.

It was on one such day in the throes of summer heat that she appeared to visit Lizzie, clutching a letter. "This just came to Madame yesterday!" she exclaimed, out of breath. "It's from Madame's son, Pierre, in Détroit." Before Lizzie could even ask, Abby answered, "He's coming to Montréal with Monsieur Tonty and Jacques!"

With enthusiasm slightly tainted by jealousy, Lizzie responded, "How nice."

"The letter was sent just before they were to leave, so they should be here in a few days!"

"Can Jacques stay?"

Abby frowned, "Only for a while. He and Tonty have business with the Governor. But here is the important news—Madame Roi is going to give a *soirée*."

Lizzie's French hadn't included this term and she looked puzzled, so Abby explained, "It's an evening party." Lizzie had only an inkling as to what *a party* was. They certainly didn't have such things in Deerfield. Abby tried to explain, "Men and women come all dressed up. They have food, music, dancing…"

Suddenly Lizzie understood. "Like the beginning of *Romeo and Juliet*!"

Abby continued, "And Madame wants to invite you, Marie-Joseph and Catherine Dunkin!"

Lizzie started to panic as her mind raced, "Oh, Abby, we couldn't—I mean what would we do—or wear?"

Abby's enthusiasm began to build. "That is the best part! She is going to have you over all this week to get ready."

"But what would the Sisters say?"

"Madame says it's not a problem. Some of the nuns and the priest come to her *soirées*."

Lizzie began to reflect amid this flurry of information, *maybe the cultures are **not** so similar.*

Chapter Six

<u>August 1, 1704: Montréal</u>

When Lizzie arrived with Catherine Dunkin and Marie-Joseph, they found Abby sitting in Sister Marie-Angélique's office. "Please have a seat, ladies," the nun instructed, as she rose from her desk. Sister Marie-Angélique always stood when she was about to make an important point. "It seems Madame Roi's guests from Détroit have arrived, and she has asked we have you ladies prepared for her *soirée* by the end of the week. To that end once you have completed your chores and lessons today, you are to proceed to her home. Do you have any questions?"

Though hesitant to ask, Lizzie realized this was her best opportunity. "Excuse me, Sister, but why is she inviting *us*?"

"Why wouldn't she?"

"Well, Sister, we are just—common girls."

The nun smiled while she answered the question she hoped for. "Do not forget, Elizabeth, Madame Roi herself was once *just a common girl.* New France needs strong, healthy, intelligent young women if it is to prosper, and although you may not realize it, you ladies are just that. When young women and girls are brought to us we believe they have three options: return to their homes, stay and join the Sisters, or enter into Canadian society. Many of the girls who have come to us in the past have done the latter and some have entered at each level of society. Catherine and Marie-Joseph have expressed no interest in returning to New England, and Elizabeth, you have expressed no opinion as yet. In addition, I have not noted a strong indication of any of you being called to the Sisterhood."

The girls tried to hide their giggles as the nun continued. "I realize this event is something you ladies have not experienced, and Madame Roi is going to show you what to expect. I have every confidence that you will behave perfectly. Now if there is nothing further, get on with your duties and meet back here after the midday meal."

Lizzie's chore for the day was tending the kitchen garden behind the barn. Trimming, weeding and gathering vegetables even on a hot August day allowed her to be alone with her thoughts. Although excited about the prospect of this special event, she had little interest in finding a man. Convinced she would never find one to replace her beloved Andrew, she also realized she could not stay in the convent forever—and there was little reason for her to return to Deerfield. After the midday meal, Lizzie rushed to wash and don a clean smock before meeting her three friends in Sister's office.

"Where have you been?" asked Abby.

"Cleaning the manure from my shoes." Lizzie answered with a hint of sarcasm.

Once outside, Lizzie asked, "What did *you* do this morning, Madame de Noyon?"

"Made love to my husband," she responded proudly.

The two other girls giggled but Lizzie was silent. Realizing her *faux pas*, Abby said, "Oh, Lizzie, I'm sorry…"

"Don't be. I understand." In an attempt to change the subject, Lizzie asked, "I still don't know why we are invited or even why Madame Roi is having this—*soirée.*"

Happy to move on to a new subject, Abby told them, "Jacques said it's all about politics."

"What is politics?" questioned Catherine.

Abby was only too anxious to show off, "Well, Jacques said because Monsieur Tonty is here—and Jacques, of course, Madame Roi can invite all the important people including the ministers and the Governor himself. This helps Monsieur Roi gain influence for his various businesses." With her sly grin, she added, "He also said having lovely young ladies will influence these men."

Madame Roi greeted them at the door. Catherine and Marie-Joseph had lived with her during their early days in Montréal and were well acquainted. Ushering them into her grand ballroom they were met by four young men, all no older than Lizzie. "Ladies, this is my son, Jacques Roi, and three of his old school friends: Messieurs Tremblay, Renaud and Charbonneau."

The afternoon began with the etiquette of meeting someone, conversation, and general social behavior. The second half was dancing. Lizzie had always associated dance with one of Reverend Williams' quickest routes to the Inferno, but she had always secretly wanted to learn. A young lady appeared with a recorder and began to play as the ladies were instructed in the fundamentals. Lizzie found it easier than she had expected and more fun than she had imagined. Once Madame Roi was satisfied with their progress, she excused the young men.

"Ladies, let me explain a little about *decorum*. The standard of behavior expected is not the same for all of you. Because Abigail is married, she can do as she pleases—well, almost anything. Catherine and Marie-Joseph are unmarried and should stay close to me so that I can nod an approval to any invitation—if you are asked to dance and the like. Elizabeth, you are different. As you are a widow, you are held to much the same standard as a married woman, but I think at the beginning of the evening, you should stay by me with the other two ladies. Now tomorrow we shall work on your *toilette*. I will expect you at the same time as today." Lizzie had learned the French word had little to do with the English *toilet,* and understood it referred to dress, makeup, hairstyle, and jewelry. Returning to the convent the girls were filled with giggles as they looked forward with a strange combination of excitement and dread.

* * *

The *toilette* phase was even more fascinating than the social lessons. Prior to the raid, Lizzie had never seen women wearing anything but a smock, apron and bonnet. Madame Roi was assisted by two other society ladies and three serving girls. They worked on their hair, jewelry and makeup—an entirely new concept. Finally they came to the dresses. Madame Roi told them she considered the dress,

289

the most important. Lizzie was particularly amazed by the *bustier,* an undergarment that fit snuggly around her torso while pushing her breasts up to an unnatural and prominent position. When she donned the dress she looked in the mirror exclaiming, "I look naked from the waist up!"

Madame Roi assured her, "Most of the ladies will be dressed like this—they just won't be as lovely." Lizzie thought the Reverend, however, could probably send her to Hell with a mere glance. Eventually they were deemed prepared and returned to the convent.

* * *

Two days later the three serving girls arrived at the convent to help the Sisters dress their charges. The nuns seemed to be enjoying the event more than anyone. When Lizzie viewed the finished project in the convent mirror, she was shocked and delighted. Certainly this must be the way Juliet looked on the night of the Capulet party. Once they were prepared, they went to the street for the short walk to Madame Roi's led by Sister Marie-Angélique who marched in front like the leader of a charge, prepared to slay any riff-raff that might trouble her lovely lasses.

As planned, they arrived before any guests other than Jacques and Abby. Jacques, whom Lizzie had not seen since Chambly, greeted her just as she had been told to expect. This time he oozed French, "How lovely you look, Madame," kissing the back of her hand softly. The house was decorated and more elegant than usual. Even as the sun set, it was still light due to the legions of candles and chandeliers. Lizzie remembered the two precious candles her mother had used on the night of the dinner with

Andrew and Smeads. Captivated by the sight, she thought there were probably more candles here than in all of western Massachusetts.

As the parade of guests began, Lizzie's hand was kissed by the well-known and well-to-do of Montréal including Governor Ramezay, Monsieur Tonty and Father Meriel. Once the line diminished, Madame Roi suggested they go into the ballroom where beverages and hors d'oeuvres were served. Although Sister Marie-Angélique had cautioned the girls about drinking too much, Lizzie thought she had already learned that lesson from Sister Marie-Marguerite and the calvados.

When a bell rang signaling dinner, Madame Roi came to show the convent ladies to their seats. Lizzie was seated between Jacques de Noyon and Joseph Parent. About Jacques' age, Parent explained he worked in Détroit with Madame Roi's son, Pierre. He was married and had a family in Montréal whom he only saw on occasion. His wife had not accompanied him. "Pierre and I were in Détroit before Cadillac came," he boasted. As dinner progressed, he told her of his life in the wilderness and finally quietly confessed, "The only reason I'm here is Pierre. Actually I'm not very comfortable around *these people*." Lizzie felt herself bonding with him.

Dinner was spectacular, although she had little idea what it was. Parent continued to fill her glass, helping her to relax. Upon completion of dinner, a small orchestra began to play and the guests retired to the ballroom. Parent told her, "I don't know about this kind of dancing."

Embolden by the alcohol, she replied, "I just learned. It isn't hard, I can show you." Parent shrugged as Lizzie began her first dance as the instructor. Soon other men, generally much older, asked her to take the floor with them and aided by the drinks, she did. During a break, Abby appeared with a man in his thirties, "Lizzie, this is Monsieur Joseph-François Hertel. Thankful is living at his estate up the river. He is going to bring her for a visit."

"Oh, that would be wonderful," Lizzie replied with a pang of worry about Sammy. She recognized the name, Hertel but would only later conclude he was the brother of Jean-Baptiste Hertel who had led the raid on Deerfield.

As Hertel wandered away, she heard, "Aye, there's some good-looking women." She turned to see who would make such an out-of-place statement. He was large, muscular, and very rugged. His clothes fit his body poorly and apparently fit his nature worse. He smiled, revealing a few gaps from missing teeth. "I'm Pierre."

"I'm Elizabeth." At first she was startled by his appearance, but his disarming smile made her reconsider, "You may call me Lizzie."

Pierre then noticed Abby and asked, "Aye, is this the one you told me about?"

Abby could not help laughing, "Yes. Lizzie, this is Pierre Roi. He works with Jacques."

Pierre took her hand in his meaty paw and kissed it. His beard was rough. "*Enchanté.* Ma always tells me to say that to people when I'm in her house." The music began and he suggested, "Aye, let's dance."

Taking her hand, he led her to the floor. To her surprise, he danced very well. "Ma made me learn to dance like this. It's all right, but not much fun." He looked down at her dress as if he could see to her navel or below, "Nice dress."

"Thank you."

"Looks good on you." He held her closely and his hand wandered down to her buttock. She knew she should protest but decided not to. "I saw you talking to Joe Parent," he told her. "We work together."

"Oh?"

"Yeah, we went west a few years ago—to the big lakes—Michilimackinac first. Then we went south, where Détroit is now. We was there when Cadillac arrived. I found my wife down there—Miami tribe."

"My husband was an Indian."

He stopped dancing, as he realized, "You were married to Andrew Stevens, right?"

"Yes."

"I loved that guy," he said impulsively.

"So did I," she replied with a sad face.

"I'm sorry, I shouldn't have said anything."

She held him a little tighter. "That's all right. It's nice to meet someone who knew him."

The music stopped and he said, "Thanks for the dance."

"Thank you."

"But, you know what?"

Puzzled, she asked, "What?"

He smiled, "When a guy puts his hand on your butt like that, kick him in the balls."

She laughed out loud, "Thank you, I will."

When he brought her back to Abby and Jacques, Pierre said, "Aye, you want to go to a really fun *soirée*?" They were silent as he continued, "Yeah, there's one at the guildhall on Saturday. They have *real* dancing there."

Lizzie frowned, "I don't know—Sister might not approve."

"Hell, leave Sister Marie-Angélique to me. We go way back, she used to whip my butt regularly in school."

* * *

The following morning, Lizzie was summoned to Sister Marie-Angélique's office where she found Jacques. "Monsieur de Noyon asked to speak with you," the nun explained, "I will be in the classroom."

They spoke in French so it was now she who had the accent. "I didn't want to tell you this until after last night," he began. "A couple months ago we had a party traveling to Massachusetts. I asked them to stop in Deerfield and see if my furs were still there. They told me your father had sold the house and the furs and left for parts unknown." Before she could respond, he said, "I don't hold anyone responsible for this, but I thought you should know."

Thoughts of Sammy and all the family flooded in, but she took her handkerchief and dried her eyes. "Thank you."

As he stood, he said, "I spoke to Sister Marie-Angélique about the *soirée* at the guildhall. She said if you girls wanted to go, you had permission."

"Yes, I'll go."

"Good. Abby, Pierre and I shall pick up you and your two friends. Sister said as long as you are with Pierre, you are safe."

While she watched him walk out the door, she realized there was no longer anything for her to return to in Deerfield.

294

Chapter Seven

Saturday: The Guildhall

A large half-timbered building in the *artisan* center of town, the guildhall was one large room built before the advent of stone construction. Jacques had explained that in France, *guilds* were groups of tradesmen who bonded together to protect their industry. There were guilds for carpenters, furniture-makers, shoemakers, rifle-makers, candle-makers, stonemasons and most other skilled professions. However, in New France guilds were outlawed as were attorneys, and just as attorneys were replaced by *avocates*, guilds were replaced by *confraternities* which served much the same purpose. In spite of this, *guildhall* was a term understood by all.

"Each confraternity has its own meetings, rules and ceremonies," Jacques explained, "but due to the small size of the groups and the community, they share one large hall and occasionally have a *soirée* for everyone. Frenchmen believe the larger the party, the better."

Pierre opened the door with a flourish and the group entered. Although neither Pierre nor Jacques was a member of a local confraternity, they were welcome, especially because they had brought young women. The hall was brightly decorated with banners while illuminated by candles and curious cups of flaming liquid. Pierre pointed to one of the *torches*, explaining. "It is this device that will make my brother a rich stonemason." Looking at the bright flame, Lizzie understood this could certainly be a source of fires in wooden buildings.

A sizable crowd had already gathered, and the sight, sound and smell of the building were in sharp contrast to the quiet elegance of the Roi mansion. Pierre went to the table where drinks were being served by none other than Messieurs LeMieux and LeDuc. He soon returned to a table with mugs and very small glasses. Handing each a mug of beer, he poured yellow liquid into each glass. "This is how we drink on this side of town," he announced as he swallowed the yellow liquid in one fearless gulp, washing it down directly with the beer, then slamming his mug on the table. Pointing to Lizzie, he declared, "Shot and a beer— your turn."

She carefully took the ominous-looking yellow liquid and began sipping it. It burned to her toenails as he ordered, "No! One swallow." When she gathered her courage and did it, she felt as if she had swallowed the torch. "Now wash it down—quickly!" he shouted, as he handed her the mug of beer. She obeyed and as she set it back on the table, she could scarcely see for the tears forming in her eyes. He clapped, shouting loudly, "Bravo! Now the rest of you ladies!"

Each took her glass in turn and accomplished the act. Marie-Joseph was last and once she had recovered, Pierre shouted, "Now you are real Frenchwomen!"

Soon a group of musicians with strange homemade instruments set up in the corner and began to play. This was certainly not the waltzes of Madame's parlor, but loud, fast, pulsating and wonderful. Pierre grabbed Lizzie and pulled her onto the dance floor as she protested, "I don't know how to do this."

Answering loudly over the din, he said, "No one does, just follow the music with your feet." While they began to gyrate around the floor, everyone joined in, and soon Lizzie was dancing with men she had never seen before. One particularly gruff fellow took her out and placed both hands firmly on her rear. Emboldened by the drinks and the atmosphere, she brought her knee quickly into his groin. The large fellow bent over in agony, as Pierre arrived to raise Lizzie's hand in celebration and danced off with her.

"These are my kind of people," Pierre claimed when the music stopped.

She smiled and replied, "I think they are my kind, too— just a little more—enthusiastic than I am used to." Pierre went for more drinks, and soon she knew she had had too much, but the feeling was pleasant—like the ambience of this party, and she really didn't care.

"Would you dance with me?"

The man was thin, not as tall as Andrew, but very attractive. His dark hair was cut short, he was clean shaven and wore small round spectacles. Nicely dressed, his quiet demeanor made him seem a little out of place. Her dance with the groper had made her a little hesitant, but this man looked trustworthy. "Yes. Thank you."

He took her hand and led her to the floor. This was an unusually slow tune and they danced much as she had at Madame Roi's. Her partner was an excellent dancer. He had a pleasant odor—*leather*, she thought. When the music stopped, he asked, "May I get you a drink?"

"Oh, I've had…"

"What I have in mind is not strong." He went to the bar returning with two glasses of pale yellow liquid. Looking at it, she remembered the calvados, but he smiled. "This is a local wine. It reminds me of my home in France." He touched her glass with his, and they took a sip.

"This dancing is fun," she commented, "I've never seen it."

"It's what we called in France, folk dancing," he answered. "The dance of the common man." Taking another sip, he looked about the room. "Sometimes the French-Canadians get a little out of hand as the evening progresses."

She only smiled as she took another sip of wine. "It's good," she said.

"Yes," he answered. "What is your name?"

"Elizabeth—Elizabeth Stevens. My friends call me Lizzie."

"Are you married?"

"I was—he died."

"Oh, I am so sorry. Where do you live?"

"At the convent."

His expression changed. "Were you a captive?"

"Yes."

He looked down sadly. "Oh, I am so sorry."

She shrugged before asking, "What is your name?"

"Jean, Jean Fourneau. My friends call me *Brindamour*."

She had learned of the odd French-Canadian custom of using a name other than one's family name, occasionally relating to a place, activity or some other feature. She was becoming very relaxed, "What does that mean?"

He smiled—a beautiful smile like Andrew. "*That* is a long story."

"What do you do, Monsieur Brindamour?"

"I'm a simple cobbler."

Suddenly she thought of Sammy. Then she remembered. "Oh you were the man…"

"In my shop this May—yes. I remember seeing you through my window. I have been hoping we should meet sometime."

They finished the wine, and he said with a frown, "I fear it is late. I promised the Father I would help him early tomorrow before Mass. I must go. I hope to see you again." He had soft green eyes, as soft as hers were bright.

As he turned, she said impulsively, "Oh…" He turned back and she finished. "Are *you* married?"

He smiled again, "No." She watched him leave just as a very large man challenged Monsieur LeDuc to a sort of wrestling match. While the crowd moved in for the spectacle, she felt a hand on her shoulder, and Abby said, "Jacques thinks we should go. Things might get a little rough, and remember we have to be up for mass in the morning."

* * *

Sunday Morning: Montréal

When the morning Angelus rang, she felt the bell was inside her head and opened her eyes with repentance for the excessive consumption of beverages. Catherine, who was no better off, sat up groaning in bed, and they began to dress for Mass. As they assembled downstairs, Sister Marie-Angélique looked at the three girls. "How was the guildhall, ladies?" They all gave weak smiles indicating it was fine. The Sister, who missed nothing, returned a broad "I-warned-you" grin and turned to lead the troops.

Mass seemed as it would never end as Lizzie tried to decide whether her head or stomach was most unhappy. Finally they were dismissed and spilled out into the fresh air of the square where she saw the large man and Monsieur LeDuc leaving together like best friends. Neither looked any worse for wear other than a few facial cuts and bruises. Suddenly she was greeted by Father Meriel himself. "Good morning, Elizabeth, what a fine morning!" Wondering if she looked as green as she felt, she merely nodded hoping not to vomit on the clergyman. "Sister Marie-Angélique tells me you are doing well in your catechism."

She squeaked out a yes, while he continued. "We must speak soon about the possibility of your conversion." She nodded and was saved by one of the society ladies seeking the priest's attention.

Two days later she was working in the kitchen when she was summoned to Sister's office where she was greeted by Meriel himself.

"Elizabeth, I have been discussing your studies with Sister who tells me your work is exceptional."

Pleased to be in better condition today, she smiled and thanked him before he continued. "I think it is time for you to consider conversion. On one hand, I do not mean to rush you, but I am certain you know by now that to remain in Canada and become a citizen, you must convert. I don't *entirely* agree with the rule, but there it is. You are a strong, intelligent lady, and if I may say so, a very lovely one. There is much you have to offer us and we to offer you."

Lizzie had given no small amount of thought to this situation but had not reached a conclusion. "Father," she answered, "I am giving it much thought and prayer…" She realized the priest liked to hear about the prayer, "I hope to have a decision soon."

"Well, if there is anything I can do, I am at your service." He dismissed her and she returned to her studies. *Maybe I need a sign from God. Reverend Williams and Father Meriel both seem to put stock in that.*

* * *

Three days later: Montréal

Lizzie was up to her elbows in dirt when the novice summoned her to Sister's office. *I hope it isn't Father Meriel again,* she thought as she wiped off her hands and headed in. She knocked on the office door and when it opened, she smiled, taking his hands, "Makya! How wonderful." She had only seen him twice since coming to the convent. When she let go, she added, "Should I say, Pierre-Henri?"

"They are both my name." he replied with a smile, showing he was equally pleased. "You are looking fine, Miss Lizzie. I have news."

She became rigid, not knowing what to expect, as he continued, "I have met with your brother. He is good and wishes to join you."

Overwhelmed with joy, she hugged him. "When?"

"This man who is his master is stubborn, but I believe I will prevail. I came to Montréal for the one thing I need to convince him. I hope to have your brother here soon."

She took his hand again, "And how are you, Makya?"

"Good. I have new wife."

"Oh?"

"Yes, good Indian wife. Young, from tribe of your brother's master. She now carries my child."

"I should like to meet her sometime."

"Yes. Well, I must go." And he was gone, quietly disappearing as only Indians can.

As she left, humming her way back to work, she realized—she had her sign.

Chapter Eight

<u>September, 1704, several weeks later: Montréal</u>

L ost in her thoughts, Lizzie crawled along the garden row, digging the late-season beets. Pulling along two buckets, one for the beets and one for the occasional pesky stone, she smiled each time she removed a stone, recalling the enormous, infamous and ever-present boulders of western Massachusetts. She scarcely noticed the moccasin-clad feet in her way. Wondering which friendly native had stopped by, she looked up, smiling.

He was a full head taller than when she last saw him, his bare chest deeply tanned and his sandy hair almost to his shoulders. She sprang to her feet, praying this was not another dream—overturning both buckets in the process. It was not a dream. As she embraced him tightly, she realized how tall he was and how hard his body had become. He even had an early beard.

"Oh Sammy, it *is* you," she said softly as she began to sob, "Thank God, thank God."

Finally she released him and, brushing the dirt from her hands, pointed, "Let's sit on that bench. Tell me everything."

He began with the three-week trek to the north and his master's tribe. "His name is *Dyami*," Sammy explained. "His people live in a large village. He is not a Christian Indian which made him harder to deal with. Some people who wanted to bring me here came to his village from the Catholic missions, but he did not want to deal with them." Describing the village, he told how people lived in tents, a nomadic tribe, moving about with the seasons.

"Dyami is a hunter and fisherman," he explained, as he told how he helped his master with his work. "It was hard, but some of it was fun. I really liked the fishing. I'm pretty good at it."

Hugging him again, she asked, "Oh, Sammy. Was he mean to you?"

"Not really. He is stern—kind of like Pa. Actually he is a lot like Pa—I don't think he is even well-liked by the tribe. It wasn't until Makya came that he considered ransoming me. Makya married his sister, *Sakari*, which means *sweet* in Abenaki. But it wasn't until Makya returned the last time with his *secret weapon* that Dyami agreed to terms."

Hanging on every word, she asked, "What was the secret weapon?"

He grinned, which gladdened her heart, as he replied with a chuckle, "He brought Monsieur LeMieux." She began to laugh out loud as she embraced her brother again.

"I see he has found you."

Looking up, she saw Sister Marie-Angélique followed by Makya and a young Indian woman.

Jumping up to attention, she said, "Yes, Sister." Turning to her old friend, "Makya, how can I ever thank you?"

He shrugged, "It was my pleasure. It is Monsieur LeMieux you should thank." Pointing to his companion who was no more than 18 and obviously with child, "Besides, I have found my new wife," After introducing her, they made polite small talk until Makya abruptly announced, "We must leave."

As he turned, Lizzie asked, "Makya, what does *Dyami* mean?"

He turned back with his sly smile. "The Eagle."

Lizzie laughed again. "I guess that has certain symmetry." Walking over and kissing him, she whispered gently, "Thank you again, *Eagle-Hunter.*"

As her friend walked to the door, Sister Marie-Angélique told her, "I explained to Samuel he may stay to dinner tonight, but then we shall take him to the seminary with the other men."

Lizzie frowned, "Can't he…"

Sister smiled, "My dear, I could not even control the older nuns with a handsome man like this around."

That night Lizzie was afraid to sleep for fear of awakening to find the day had been a dream. Eventually she did pass into slumber and awakened to a bright autumn day. All seemed right with the world—at least that day, it seemed that way.

* * *

Mid-October, 1704: Montréal

Autumn color had reached its peak as Lizzie and her brother strolled down Rue Notre Dame arm in arm. As they approached the church, Lizzie began to explain, "They say the original church was wood, but a few years ago…"

"Lizzie," her brother interrupted. "You already told me that."

His sister had reveled in Sammy's return and took him walking at every opportunity to show him their new city. He had settled in nicely at the seminary where several Deerfield boys were living including Thomas Hurst and Thomas French, Jr., both his age and good friends from home. In addition, Deacon French was there and served as an anchor for the lads. When they reached the square, the church bells rang, signaling the Angelus.

"We'd both better go home," Sammy said, as he pecked his sister on the cheek. "It's time to eat."

Arriving at the convent, Lizzie hurried in to avoid being tardy.

"Oh, good, I was looking for you, Elizabeth."

Surprised to see Sister Marie-Angélique waiting for her, Lizzie merely said, *"Bonsoir,* Sister."

Taking her hand, the nun said quietly, "We have a problem. Perhaps you can help me." She led Lizzie to her office where a young boy sat quietly in the corner, clutching a small rag doll. She had not seen young John Field since the raid but recognized him immediately.

Rushing to him, she swept him into her arms, "Oh, John!"

He looked at her calmly, "Hello, Aunt Lizzie," as though they had never been apart.

Looking to the Sister, she stressed, "He won't be a problem."

"No," agreed the nun as a knock came at the door. Opening it, she said "Please come in, Madame Hurst," as the elder Sarah Hurst entered. Walking to Lizzie, Sister addressed the boy. "John, Mrs. Hurst will take you to dinner while I visit with your aunt."

As they left for the dining room, Sister motioned for Lizzie to sit. "Some of the missionaries ransomed him and his mother from one of the northern tribes and brought them here."

Lizzie became excited, "Where is Mary?"

"Upstairs—actually she is the problem." As she rose, she added, "Please follow me."

Entering one of the private bedrooms on the third floor, Lizzie found her sister-in-law standing in a corner. As quickly as she had recognized John, she might not have known Mary Field had she met her on the street. Her previous shining sandy hair was nearly all gray, contributing to her appearing years older. She was pale and gaunt, a feature made more obvious as she was stark naked. Her clothes lay strewn on the floor.

Mary, on the other hand, recognized her visitor. "Oh, Lizzie, it's about time you got here. Where is Johnny?" referring to her husband, "and where are Mary and little Sarah?" She began to pick up her clothes complaining, "They always want you to go naked here."

Sister Marie-Angélique picked up the remaining garments, handing them to Mary as she said, "Mrs. Field, as I told you, you are no longer with the Indians. We prefer you remain clothed. As for the children, young John is here, and we are trying to find the other two."

Suddenly Mary changed as she flung her things back onto the floor, screaming at the nun, "You lie, you papist whore! You have my girls! Give them back! Lizzie, you tell her."

Lizzie took a shawl and draped it over Mary's shoulders, "Calm down, Mary. You are safe here. These people are our friends. We need to help them find Mary."

Suddenly she slapped Lizzie across her face. "You lie! You're in league with them, you and that papist savage husband of yours!"

Sister Marie-Angélique took Lizzie by the hand, "We must go." Turning to Mary, "Try to get some rest, dear."

She shut and locked the door, leading the way back to the office. "Oh Sister, what's to be done?" Lizzie questioned once they were in the office.

The nun was not as concerned, "We see this from time to time, and I have definitely seen worse. She will improve. The Sisters are quite adept at dealing with it."

"What about little John?" she asked nervously.

"I would not worry about him. Children do well. He is already getting accustomed to us, and the Sisters will spoil him awfully. He is almost seven, that's the age we generally send them to the seminary, but we can make an exception." Sitting down, she added, "You did say the baby was killed?"

"Yes, we saw it happen as we were led away."

"We will address that when the time is right. For now, we do not know where the other daughter is. What is her name and age?"

Lizzie thought, time had passed, "Mary—she would be eight now."

"If she is alive, she will be with one of the Mohawk tribes. We know everyone who is with the Algonquin."

Lizzie stood to pace, "Can we find her?"

"Perhaps. There are several children at Kahnawake."

Still agitated, Lizzie inquired, "Is that good?"

The nun shrugged. "The children do well there. In fact, they usually stay. Frequently they refuse to go home."

This did not calm Lizzie, "How can we find out?"

"Normally we would send someone with one of the missionaries, but the Mohawk of Kahnawake are quite independent and don't respond well..." She pondered for a while before suggesting, "I know, why don't we send you with Pierre Roi? He did not return to Détroit with Monsieur Tonty."

"Why him?"

"I think they hold him in high regard. He has traded furs with them for some years."

"Excellent! When could we leave?"

"I shall make inquiries right away." Sister stood, "I believe we are missing dinner."

Chapter Nine

Late October, 1704: The Saint-Lawrence River

Massive by any standard, the river named in 1535 by Jacques Cartier flows north and east from the lake called Ontario where it receives the enormous flow of the Great Lakes basin. Gathering more water from countless mountain ranges, it builds in size and power for one-thousand miles until it spills into the ocean. It was this wide waterway that allowed the French to settle much further inland than their English counterparts and had allowed them to keep that much larger adversary at bay for 170 years.

Although ubiquitous in Montréal, canoes continued to amaze Lizzie along with the skill and strength of men like Pierre Roi, who could single-handedly move the craft against such an impressive current at a reasonable rate of speed. Pierre had provided Lizzie with a paddle and a brief tutorial in its use, but, try as she might, she realized she was contributing little if anything to the effort.

He had also spent the previous two days explaining the nature of the people they were going to visit. "No matter how you cut it, they are Mohawk—Mohawk from the New York area. Don't tell our other native friends—or my Algonquin wife, but I believe they are the most clever and successful of all the tribes—also the group you least want to cross."

He told her how various Iroquois had migrated from their traditional land to escape abuses by the English. "They have settled along the river and allowed the French to put missions in their villages, but they are not as— compliant as the Algonquin." Lizzie was always surprised when Pierre spoke like an educated man. "They accept the church and the missionaries, but it *never* holds sway over the Mohawk ways."

He had also explained that the Kahnawake were the most independent and successful of the lot. "I know you went to see the Iroquois of the Mountain with my sister, Sister Marie-Marguerite, but you will find these people more independent. I should also warn you that they rarely ransom a captive, especially a young child. The tribe had the pox here a few years ago and lost many children," he said, "so they are anxious to replenish the tribe." Lizzie protested, saying that was not fair to the child, but Pierre was convinced that the children generally preferred to remain with the Kahnawake.

At the docks of Montréal, the river ran north and south, but further inland, it made a right angle around the island to go east and west, becoming much wider. "It looks more like a lake." Lizzie observed.

"Enjoy it while you can," said Pierre with no further explanation.

Pierre never missed a stroke and never stopped to rest. She had heard how voyageurs could paddle all day without rest, and now she believed it. Finally the river started to narrow, but as it did, the current increased its resistance. Eventually she saw the whitewater.

"That's the rapids at Lachine," he shouted above their roar. She recalled how Andrew had told her that Cartier thought this was the route to China, hence the name. She also recalled it was the site of a terrible massacre of French by the Iroquois. She began to see the French town of Lachine on the island, but Pierre had told her Kahnawake was across the river on the mainland side.

As they came close to the mainland coast, the ride became wild. Although they avoided the worst section of the rapids, she could imagine how terrifying it would be in the center. Lizzie saw a low point on the bank with a few beached canoes. While Pierre pulled the craft onto the shore, she asked, "Aren't you afraid someone might take it?"

He laughed, "Here, someone may steal your money or your woman—or slit your throat, but no one is low enough to steal a canoe." Pointing to a path through the forest, he directed, "This way."

Walking along the well-worn path where the trees shed their final autumn cloak, they encountered a clearing. Lizzie's jaw dropped. This was not a village—it was a city, stretching further than she could see. The longhouses looked more modern and substantial than those in La Montagne, some had chimneys and a few were made with some stone. A large square held a sizeable church and some other public buildings. The crop fields were very large, and there were people everywhere.

Proceeding to the square, they were greeted by an older man who had a conversation in Iroquois with Pierre while ignoring Lizzie. Eventually he shook Pierre's hand and wandered off. Pierre said quietly, "That was *Waneek*, a tribal elder."

"What did he tell you?" she asked anxiously.

"Nothing useful," he muttered as they proceeded along.

"Ah, Pierre Roi!"

Pierre turned and greeted a younger native man in French, "*Bonjour, Jean-Claude.*" They spoke for a while, and although Lizzie struggled to hear, she could not. When Pierre returned, he told her, "This man can help us. We'll meet him back by the canoe."

Jean-Claude was waiting when they arrived. He and Pierre had a long conversation. Lizzie tried to listen, but they continued to ignore her. When he left, Pierre reported, "He said there are a number of Deerfield children, and he can take us to see them tomorrow."

"What did you tell him about me?" she inquired.

"I said you were my new woman, and we were headed to Détroit."

Lizzie was dumbfounded, "What?"

"Believe me, it will work better than the truth. If they think you are here for the girl, it will all be over." Taking her hand, he said, "Come, we are invited to dinner."

The full moon lit the cool late autumn evening. Dinner in the square involved only a small segment of the community where various men came to speak with Pierre and a few women came to examine Lizzie's blonde hair. One man who came to see Pierre moved around behind Lizzie and firmly grasped her breasts. She did her best to remain calm until he let go, putting his thumb up to Pierre in obvious approval.

She was aghast as Pierre laughed, whispering softly to her, "Don't take it personally. They are curious."

"Where do we sleep tonight?" she whispered.

"In a longhouse. We'll have a bed of distinction."

"We?" she whispered.

"Just play along. If we don't, they will be suspicious."

They were led into a large longhouse and taken to a bed in the center of the room. "Get undressed and get into bed," he explained. She removed her smock and began to lie down when he took her arm, whispering, "I mean *undressed*."

She complied and as she went to lie down, a strong hand took her by the arm. Turning she saw Waneek looking her over. He spoke to Pierre, who answered. After a short conversation, he released her arm and moved away. Pierre whispered, "He wanted to exchange women. I told him, no. Get into bed quickly before he returns." She did and the bare Pierre lay down, covering them with a blanket. Turning to face her, he ordered quietly, "Make noises like you're having fun."

"I'm not having fun."

He laughed, "Me neither, but convince them—it's important."

* * *

The following morning: Kahnawake

Just before daybreak, the slumbering natives came to life. To Lizzie's horror, Pierre threw off their cover. Standing to stretch, he reached down for her. "I'll dress down here," she said quietly.

He took her hand and yanked her to her feet. "Act calm. Some of the women may come to see you." Three women did come and inspected her while chatting in Iroquois before they left. "They approve of you," he declared, "especially the blonde hair—all of it."

"Can I get dressed, now?" she pleaded.

"Yes, but slow and casual. Pretend you're at home, alone in a room."

"I can't be that deceitful," she whined.

"Try."

She complied, and he led her out to breakfast where a few men came to visit him. When the meal ended, he told her, "You impressed them last night. That's good." Standing, he continued, "Let's go meet Jean-Claude."

Returning to the trail they entered on, they took it in the opposite direction arriving at the side of the church building where Jean-Claude was waiting. He led them to a small side door. Inside they found a group of young children sitting in a circle around two nuns. In spite of tans, longer hair and different clothes, Lizzie identified some of the Deerfield children among the natives—Eunice Williams, Abigail French, Mercy Carter, and a few others. When she saw Mary Field, she almost cried out, but Pierre had cautioned her to remain silent. When the nuns saw them, they said something to the children causing them to rise, and the native children to leave.

Once the Deerfield children recognized Lizzie, they rushed to embrace her. She had known each of them from Mrs. Beaman's classes, and now they were all eager to tell her how they were doing. None of them mentioned going home or even asked about family and friends. As the nuns excused everyone but Mary, Lizzie remembered when Andrew, Catherine and Marie-Joseph told her how they had decided against returning. Mary, now eight, also seemed happy and healthy.

"Mary, your mother and John are with me at the convent. She wants you to come, too, and wants to take you home."

Mary looked at her feet, shuffling them before replying, "Aunt Lizzie, I like it here. We all do."

"But Mary, don't you want to see your mother?"

She paused a moment before answering, "Yes, tell her to come visit, but tell her I'm happy here. *Kahn-Tineta,* she is my Indian mother, wants me to stay."

"But Mary…"

"Aunt Lizzie, we have fun here. No one is mean. We help, but we can play more. They don't keep telling us everything is a sin. Even Eunice," referring to Reverend Williams' daughter, "wants to stay here. We're—happy. We like it here."

The nun came and asked Mary to leave, but before she did, she turned to say, "Aunt Lizzie, tell Momma and John I love them. Tell my daddy, too, if you see him." And she was gone.

"You see what we are up against, Madame Stevens," the nun explained. "We don't like it either, but in truth, most of these children do not want to go home. All we can do is try to make them good Christians."

As she returned to the village with Pierre, he told her, "My pa told me the first priests to come here were the Jesuits, who are still in Québec. They only wanted to make the natives Christian. The Sulpicians, like Father Meriel, want to make them Frenchmen as well. This plays well to some of the Algonquin like the Abenaki, but not to the Iroquois—and especially not to the Mohawk."

Chapter Ten

<u>Two days later: The Saint-Lawrence River</u>

Having spent one more night in Kahnawake, they returned to Montréal while Lizzie pondered how to tell this story to her sister-in-law. The trip back was quiet and tranquil as the current carried them downstream faster than Pierre had moved them up. While he sat in back, only using his paddle to adjust their heading, they had ample opportunity to discuss the issues.

"I agree with Sister Marie-Angélique," Pierre asserted. "Your sister-in-law will never recover from this, but she will come to accept it. Tell her the girl is doing well and in no danger, but be supportive." Lizzie looked skeptical as he added, "Were the parents of any of those other children taken?"

She thought for a moment, the first month had been so chaotic and now seemed a long time ago. "Mrs. Carter died, Mr. Kellogg was taken, but I'm not certain where he is. Eunice's father, of course, Reverend Williams, but we haven't seen him since he was taken away with a small group early in the march."

Pierre stopped paddling, "He's the one this was about!"

"I beg your pardon?" she asked in surprise.

Pierre thought for a moment, "Well, see—this might sound strange, but there is this man, Pierre Maisonnat. They call him Baptiste—I don't know why. But he is what's called a privateer, kind of a pirate who raids English ships for the French—both sides have them." He made a few course-correcting strokes before continuing. "The English captured him a while ago and the French want him back—badly. For some reason, they decided that this Reverend of yours is someone for whom the English might trade prisoners."

Lizzie frowned, "That makes no sense."

Pierre made another correction before laughing, "Does any of this?"

She almost smiled, "I don't—oh, there is also Deacon French. He is at the seminary. His daughter, Mary, is with the convent; his son, Thomas, is with him; Martha is with your mother and Freedom is with the LeBer family—and Abigail is in Kahnawake."

"I met him at my mother's," Pierre told her, "when he was visiting his daughter. He seemed a reasonable sort. I'll go see him at the seminary. He probably doesn't even know where his Abigail is. Maybe he can help with your sister-in-law."

By the time they arrived at the canoe livery, darkness had fallen along with the last leaves of autumn as winds of winter approached. "I think you missed dinner," he observed, looking up at the stars.

"I'll survive."

"Sister doesn't know when you're coming home. Why don't we stop at Fortin's Tavern? They'll feed us."

"Do they serve ladies?"

"They serve women—I guess they serve ladies."

By now, Lizzie had not only become accustomed to Pierre's humor, she loved it. Taking his arm, she ordered, "Lead the way. I guess if I slept naked with you I can have dinner with you."

Tucked away north of the church square sat an inauspicious log building. Lizzie had only seen the interior of Potter's Tavern in Deerfield once—when she was sent searching for her wayward father. As soon as Pierre had swung open the door into Fortin's, it was clear it had a far different ambience. Lit by a roaring fire and a few candles, the room was filled with tables, most of which were occupied, and the air was filled with conversation, laughter and fun. A young man sat by the bar playing folk music on an Indian recorder, while his companion drummed an overturned bucket with sticks. A few people danced in the small space in front of him. The room smelled of smoke, beer and roasting meat, and yes, there were women present.

As usual, Pierre seemed to know everyone as he introduced Lizzie to a few folks, explaining they had been on a mission for Sister Marie-Angélique. When a man introduced to Lizzie as Gervais Fortin came to the table, Pierre simply ordered, *the usual*. Soon Gervais returned with two small glasses of yellow liquid and two mugs of beer. Pierre lifted his glass, pronouncing, "*à ta santé!*" He quickly disposed of the calvados and washed it down with the beer. Lizzie duplicated the feat, this time she did not blink, and as she set down her mug, she smiled. "I'll have another, please." Pierre slammed the table as his laughter shook the room. When Gervais returned with two plates of hot steaming meat, Pierre ordered another round.

Lizzie regarded the plate with suspicion but cut a small piece and put it in her mouth. Once she swallowed, she asked, "How do they make everything taste so wonderful?"

Pierre shrugged, "They are French."

Once they had settled down and their third round of shots and beer arrived, Pierre said, "You know I'm sorry I had to put you through the ordeal in the longhouse, but..."

"I understand, Pierre," she interrupted, "It's all right. What's wrong with standing naked in front of an entire tribe?" Her eyes sparkled with her humor.

She told him about sleeping with Makya during the retreat. "People's lives have been saved by that skin-to-skin technique," he explained, while signaling Gervais for another round.

When it arrived, she asked, "Tell me about your wife."

He thought for a moment before saying, "She's about your age. She's not certain—Indians don't keep track of things like that. I met her when we were trading in the Ohio country—that's where many of the Miami live. I brought her to Détroit. We were married there. It was very impulsive—like everything I do."

"What's her name?"

"Ouabankekoué."

She smiled, "That's a mouthful, but when you say it, it's like poetry. What is she like?"

"Like poetry—like you. She's young and beautiful, and she keeps her own counsel. Her Christian name is Marguerite, like my sister. We had a little girl in April, also Marguerite."

She frowned, "Isn't it hard being away from your family so much?"

Pierre shrugged, "It's my life." He looked away for a moment before continuing, "Let me give your some advice. *Never love a voyageur.*"

She finished her drink and put her hand on his, "Let's dance." In her life she had never been this bold.

The first tune was lively, but the second was slow. He held her close and she said, "This is very pretty."

"It's an old French ballad."

She put her head on his shoulder and asked, "What's it about?"

"What all French ballads are about—love."

Returning to their table, he asked, "Can you handle one last round?"

She looked at him with confidence, "Certainly!"

Even Pierre was feeling the effects of drink as he leaned closer and told her quietly, "You know, the children wanting to stay—there is more than meets the eye."

"I don't understand."

"The nuns—and the priests—they are good people, but they can be very persuasive, particularly with children. They very much want to convert people whether they stay with the Indians or go to the French community, and they find the children to be the easiest candidates." She looked unconvinced as he added, "Between Father Meriel and Reverend Williams, who do you like the most?"

She hedged, "Well, they are both men of God."

"All right, which do you *fear* the most?"

She laughed, "That's easy, Reverend Williams."

Pierre finished his beer, "Both these men tell you bad things that will happen if you're bad, and good things if you are good." She nodded as he went on. "Your reverend dwells on what bad things happen if you sin. The priest tells you more about good things that will happen if you are good." She nodded without conviction when he asked, "How many Indians went to your church in Deerfield?"

"Well, we don't call it church and only Andrew—of course he wasn't an Indian—I guess none."

Pierre rose, "How many have you seen in churches around here?" Putting some coins on the table, he said, "Think about it. I believe we should go before the sun rises."

When she stood, she regretted her decision about the last round. "I don't think I can walk."

"Then stagger," he suggested, putting his arm around her waist more for balance than familiarity. "That's what I do." Stepping onto the unlit Rue Saint-Lambert, the cold air awakened her—a little.

* * *

The following morning: The Congregation of Notre-Dame

Slowly opening her eyes to the morning Angelus, she took a moment to orient. She knew where she was and where she had been but could not recall getting here. Everything hurt as she sat up. "Oh Lizzie, I have a message." She only nodded to the young novice who told her, "Sister Marie-Angélique said you came in very late from your journey, and I should tell you to stay in bed until you are rested."

Lizzie nodded again as she fell onto her pillow. "*God bless you, Sister*," she whispered. Suddenly the bell rang a second time. *That's odd.* Then looking around the empty dormitory, she realized to her dismay, this was the noonday bell. Sitting on the edge of her cot, she knew she would not get another reprieve, so she stood to dress. Her smock reeked of smoke and beer, but she hadn't another. So she threw it on and left for the Sister's office.

"You were late arriving home last night. Was it difficult canoeing in the dark?"

Lizzie considered potential excuses, but settled on the truth, "We landed at dark—missing the evening meal. I went with Pierre—I mean Monsieur Roi, to a tavern where we ate." She finished quickly with, "And we danced and drank—a great deal."

"Ah," sighed the nun, "confession—it is good for the soul. Well, I suppose you were entitled. What have you to report?"

Lizzie sat. She was afraid she could not stand much longer. She gave a rather complete synopsis of the trip and even decided to tell about the sleeping arrangements.

"Oh, to be young," Sister swooned with a gleam in her eye. "What you report is what I expected." She stood and continued, "Madame Field is making some progress. She is in the garden. I wouldn't say anything about your trip unless you are asked."

When they entered the garden, Lizzie was surprised to see Mary sitting on a stool, watching Sammy and young John toss a ball. Apart from her gray hair and gaunt face, she looked almost normal and leapt to her feet as soon as she saw Lizzie. She rushed to embrace her, sobbing, "Oh Lizzie, I'm sorry I was so bad. I was—confused." Before Lizzie could respond, Mary continued, "Did you go to look for her?"

Uncertain how to answer, Lizzie looked silently to Sister Marie-Angélique who nodded and mouthed the word, "*truth.*"

Lizzie stepped back and looked into Mary's eyes, "Yes."

"Did you find her?"

"Yes."

Mary remained calm. "Where?"

"A place called Kahnawake."

Mary frowned, "They don't give back children, do they?"

Lost for words, Lizzie looked to the nun who nodded. She replied, "Not usually."

Mary went to John and ran her fingers tenderly through his long sandy hair. "We'll just have to see." She sat down and remained silent.

* * *

Following the evening meal, Mary came to Lizzie, asking, "Can we go back to the garden?"

Lizzie found their coats and when properly bundled for the cold, they returned to the bench. The night was frigid and quiet, one might expect snow, but the sky was clear and the half-moon lit the way. Mary looked up, "That's the same moon they're seeing in Deerfield." Lizzie nodded and Mary continued slowly, stopping frequently to compose her words as well as her fragile emotions, "When we split away at the White River, we went with Reverend Williams. In a few days he went away. It was very confusing. I didn't see John or Mary again. I tried to find them but couldn't—I knew I could do nothing." The sobs returned, forcing her to wait. "I became worse each day. I barely remember Chambly. I think we were only there one day before they took us to the Indian camp."

She began to sob again. Lizzie started to speak, but Mary interrupted, "I'm all right—let me talk." She took a slow deep breath. "At the camp I was given to a man who would be my new husband. He *took* me. I should have protested but I didn't—I submitted." She was silent for a while before continuing, "Thank God, I'm not pregnant." She stood and looked away. "Some time later—I don't know how long, these priests came and told us we were to go with them to Montréal. I didn't care. I wanted to die." She walked over to a small apple tree and touched its bark. "I just followed as we walked along the river." Turning back to Lizzie, she explained, "It was young John who found me—can you believe it?" She sat again. "I didn't even recognize him, I was so lost. Thank goodness, they believed him and kept us together until we got here. It wasn't until I saw you—I'm so sorry how I acted. But when you left, I started to come to. When Sammy came, he spoke about our trip to Connecticut to see Ben—the light began to come back."

Before Lizzie could speak, Mary stood again, "How was my daughter?"

Lizzie told her. She was totally honest. "Well, I guess if she is happy," Mary replied, "Sister told me I could sleep with the others tonight. She put a cot by you."

Lizzie embraced her, "Good."

Mary almost smiled, "I promise to behave."

* * *

<u>Early November 1704: Montréal</u>

Following the midday meal, Lizzie presented to Sister Marie-Angélique's office as requested. "Come in, Elizabeth, Monsieur French is going to join us in a while, but I thought we could visit beforehand."

"Thank you, Sister," she said as she sat.

"Your sister-in-law is doing better each day."

"Yes, Sister, thank you."

"She is still not at peace with her daughter—I doubt she will ever be. I suspect you are not either, so I thought I might share an experience with you." Lizzie nodded and the nun went on. "I was born in Paris. My father was extremely wealthy and sent me to the finest schools for girls. When I reached 12 years, he sent me to a cousin in England where I attended another fine school for young ladies.

"You may not believe it, but my family was not particularly religious. In France we were Catholic, but in England I went to my cousin's Anglican Church. He said it was like the Catholics without the guilt." She swallowed a chuckle before continuing. "I had the opportunity to also attend the services of a small independent congregation, something like yours. We called it *Puritan*. At thirteen I found it terribly boring—I always left the service feeling worse than I had come."

Finally she stood, "Now I know this was the view of a foolish young girl, but I remember lamenting there was nothing to look at when bored except one's feet. I think many of the English children we see here have the opposite reaction to the Catholic Church where there is a great deal of beauty and décor. Again, I know this is not what religion is about, but we are talking about impressionable young children."

She was interrupted by the knock at the door which she opened to greet Thomas French, Sr. "Ah, Monsieur French, please come in." Lizzie had not seen Deacon French for months. His color and weight had returned, and he again looked like the man she knew in Deerfield.

"Thank you, Sister." Turning, he greeted Lizzie, "You are looking well, Elizabeth. I was very pleased to hear of the return of your sister-in-law and her son." He went on to explain that Pierre had come to see him and told him of their visit to Kahnawake. "He said he was returning to Détroit immediately so he introduced me to this Indian fellow, Jean-Claude, who was able to take me to see my Abigail. Unfortunately, I heard much the same story as you, and sadly, she also seems to have no interest in returning."

French went on to say, "Yesterday I received word that Ensign John Sheldon is arranging to come to Canada this winter to negotiate releases with the French and the Indians. I am only hoping that he can shed some light on this issue with the children. I have just come from visiting Mrs. Field and have told her we shall do everything in our power to get the children back."

Eventually French returned to the seminary while Lizzie went to prepare for dinner. *I can't believe Pierre left for Détroit without telling me.* Then she remembered his words at the tavern, *"never love a voyageur."*

Entering the dining hall, she sat with Catherine and Marie-Joseph. "It looks like we are getting some snow," said Catherine.

"That doesn't bother me," claimed Lizzie, "You should see the snow we get in Deerfield."

Chapter Eleven

December 22, 1704: Montréal

When the noonday Angelus signaled a reprieve from stacking firewood, Lizzie began to trudge through the drifts to the convent door. She had begun to regret her earlier statement about Massachusetts snow since the local cover was almost as deep as she had ever seen at home, and today's storm threatened to raise it to a new level. *No wonder the locals are so skilled with snowshoes,* she thought shaking and brushing off before entering.

Shedding her outerwear, she made her way to the dining hall where, as usual, she found Catherine and Marie-Joseph. "Are you getting excited, Lizzie?" Catherine asked, joining them with her tray. The girls had been telling her about the celebration of Christmas in Canada for days. In New England, the date was considered *ahistorical* by the clergy and the celebration of Christmas had once been outlawed as *pagan*. Although it was no longer considered a crime, the day was ignored in Deerfield.

"My sister and I were skeptical about it at first," Marie-Joseph related, "but now I love it. I think it is my favorite day of the year."

Catherine added, "Sister Marie-Angélique said we could be in charge of the tree this year—you can help, too, Lizzie."

Nodding in agreement, Lizzie was still not clear on these new and strange concepts. "The tree?" she asked.

"Yes. They say in Europe it is a tradition, especially in the land to the east of France. You'll see—a man from the parish is bringing it right after the meal." Sister stood for the blessing, putting a halt to all conversation.

Following the meal, they went to the convent entry hall. Catherine opened the door to peek out while admitting a cloud of powder. "I see him coming down the street," she reported. Opening the door again, she allowed a snow-caked figure to enter, pulling an equally encrusted conifer.

"Excuse me," he said, as he looked at the tree. "I must get rid of some snow." Exiting, he shook the tree vigorously before returning. The girls laughed. There was more snow than before. Looking up he lamented, "I guess this is as good as it will get outside. Tell Sister I'll clean the floor." And he shook the tree until the green was again visible. Leaving his hat and coat on the snow mound, he asked, "Where should we put it?"

Marie-Joseph led the way to the dining hall and the place of honor reserved for the tree. The man attached it to boards that held it erect. Standing back, he adjusted it before declaring, "Perfect." As Lizzie puzzled at this tree standing indoors, she was still not clear on the appeal.

"Will you help us decorate it?" Catherine asked the tree bearer. He nodded and Marie-Joseph produced a large box from which they produced colorful bows of ribbon which they placed on the tree. When Catherine put the largest bow on top, she declared, "Wonderful, better than last year."

Lizzie escorted the man back to the door where his coat lay in a pile of water.

"I'll take care of this," she told him, but he insisted on helping.

He began mopping the flood, saying, "You don't remember me, but..."

Suddenly she looked past the soaked hair and shirt. "I do! From the guildhall—Monsieur Brigand."

He smiled the wonderful smile. "Close—Brindamour."

"Oh yes." They stood in the wet foyer with the uneasy nervousness of two people who want to speak but are afraid to do so.

Finally he broke the silence, "I was wondering if you would allow me to escort you home from Christmas Mass? If it is acceptable to you, I will ask the Sister's permission."

Rarely was Lizzie lost for words, but she stammered, "Oh, yes, well, I mean, you don't—I'm a widow," she blurted, "I don't need permission."

The wonderful smile again, inquiring, "Yes, you don't need permission? Or yes, I may?"

She boldly took his hand, "Yes, you may."

Looking around, he concluded, "Wonderful. I shall see you Christmas morning." And he exited into the blizzard. Lizzie watched until he disappeared into the snow squall and returned humming. Already she loved Christmas.

Christmas Morning, 1704: Church of Notre Dame, Montréal

Marching down the center aisle to the customary seating, Lizzie searched for Monsieur Brindamour without success. Decorated with colorful ribbons and holly, the interior was more beautiful than ever, and many women wore sprigs of holly with ribbons attached to their coats. Although brief by New England standards, the service was longer than usual. Father Meriel read the Biblical story of Christmas in French while his sermon was filled with joy. She could not help reflect on Reverend Williams' frightening sermons of damnation called *jeremiad*.

Exiting into bright sunlight, Lizzie stood on the steps, staring out at the crowd for Monsieur Brindamour. As she peered over the mass of celebratory humanity who showed no intention of leaving the square, she had almost lost hope when she looked down and saw him smiling a few steps below her. She waved enthusiastically and began to descend, suddenly worrying she had been too enthusiastic. He produced a holly with ribbon, explaining, "This is for you—a lady in the square sells them." She beamed as he placed it skillfully into the upper buttonhole of her coat. Suddenly the bells began to ring in ear-splitting jubilation. Pointing to the side, he took her arm. Once they turned the corner, she could hear again.

"Today the bells will ring all morning," he shouted. "We can go this way to the convent."

"I don't have to go back right away," she told him, again hoping she was not too forward.

He knew this, but he, too, had not wanted to appear overly bold. "Very well, let's head north. The packed snow can be slippery. Perhaps you should hold my arm." She took his arm with both hands as he continued, "There is a café on Rue Saint-Charles that is open on holy days. We could stop for a cup of tea."

"I would like that."

The painted sign read simply, *Jean-Paul's,* and most of the tables in the small shop were taken by church-goers with the same idea. "We can sit here," he told her. "I come here when I don't want to cook for myself." Jean-Paul brought tea and asked if they wanted to eat. Lizzie did not object, so Brindamour said, "Do you like *pain perdu?*"

She couldn't imagine what *lost bread* could be. "I've never had it."

Nodding to Jean-Paul, who soon returned with two plates of odd-looking hot bread and a small pitcher, Brindamour explained, "They take stale bread and dip it in eggs and milk with spice and fry it." She regarded it with suspicion, as he took the pitcher, announcing, "Then the *pièce de résistance,*" as he poured the brown syrup.

Cautiously she took a bite. "It's delicious—is this maple syrup?"

"Yes."

"We have—had it in Massachusetts, but it was bitter. How do they..?"

He gave the Gallic shrug, "They are French." Remembering Pierre, she grinned.

Heading back to the convent, he told her, "We are having another party at the guildhall next week. Would you like to go?"

"Yes," she answered without hesitation. Then she asked, "You still haven't told me what Brindamour means."

"It is still too long a story. Let us say, my family name is Fourneau, and I would very much like you to call me Jean."

"Only if you call me Lizzie."

Ultimately, they returned to the convent. "My feet are freezing," she said as they came into the entry.

"Let me see your boot," he suggested.

Looking around, she hesitated, "I don't…"

"Just your boot, no one is watching." She stepped out of it and he knelt to look at it and her foot. "It's worn," he declared, "perhaps heavier stockings."

Stepping back into the boot, she said, "Thank you for the meal, and this," pointing to the holly.

"It's called a *boutonniere*," he explained, "because you put it in your buttonhole—I've noticed the ladies wear them at Christmastime, and thought you might like one."

Taking his hand, she replied, "I do like it—very much. Thank you." Looking into his pale green eyes, she had a sudden impulse to kiss his cheek but realized it would be beyond the pale at this time and in this place.

He, too, looked into her eyes, feeling at loose ends, not wanting the day to end. Finally he said, "Thank you for a wonderful day—Lizzie. I will call for you at six in the evening one week from today."

"Thank you," she said softly, "—Jean."

She went straight away to the dormitory. Sitting on her cot, she removed the boutonniere. Although she wanted to wear it, she didn't know if it would be appropriate. She could store it in her small locker at the foot of her bed, but decided to lay it on her pillow where her friends would inquire about it that night. She would tell them—she was dying to tell them.

December 27, 1704: Montréal

"You sent for me, Sister?" The nun looked up from her desk, peering over the spectacles she never wore in public.

"Yes, Elizabeth, we have two new residents arriving next week, Freedom French from the LeBer home and Thankful Stebbins from Hertel's." Putting down her paper, she commented, "Strange names these Puritans give their children. I am going to make Christine Otis their companion. She has never done this before but is now fifteen, slightly older than the other two and has been here forever." Removing the glasses, she continued, "However she is young and as you probably know, prone to mischief, so I want you to help keep an eye on all three."

Christine tended to stay with the younger girls, and Lizzie rarely spoke to her. Lizzie also feared she may be related to her former suitor, Willard Otis. Christine had come to the convent as a captive at the unusual age of 3 months. Her mother had subsequently married a Frenchman and now lived in town with their three living children.

Before Lizzie could comment, Sister added, "We have another piece of news. Yesterday your friend, Madame de Noyon, had her child."

Showing her excitement, Lizzie asked, "Oh, what was..?"

The nun interrupted by standing, "We must go visit and get all the details."

"Now?"

"Of course, follow me."

Lizzie followed the nun as they hastened to get their coats and departed for the Roi residence. Sister Marie-Angélique trudged through the knee-high snow like a well-seasoned draft horse as Lizzie worked as hard as she could to keep up. Babette greeted them at the door with Madame Roi just behind her. "Sister, Elizabeth, what a pleasant surprise. You have no doubt heard our joyous news."

"How is Abby, Madame?" Lizzie asked anxiously.

"Why don't you follow me and see. Babette, take their coats, please."

Following Madame up the grand staircase, they entered the first room on the second floor where Abby lay sleeping with the small bundle cradled in her arms. She startled awake as they entered. Lizzie thought she looked as bad as she had at the end of the march. Abby whispered, "How nice of you to come."

Looking at the bundle, Lizzie asked, "A boy or girl?"

Abby grinned, "A boy, Jacques-René, Father Meriel told me those are both saint names."

"Does Jacques know?" Lizzie asked.

Before Abby could respond, Madame Roi answered, "Oh, no. We sent word today, but in winter he will not get it for some time."

Abby spoke, half whisper, half exhausted groan, "Hold him, Lizzie."

Lizzie took the small parcel. As she looked down, he opened his eyes and seemed to look up as her mind bounced about, from the children she has known at Dame Beaman's, to the infants she delivered and finally to that small sad cross likely lost forever in the snowy mountains of Vermont. They passed Jacques-René around and made the standard comments and cute sounds women make at such gatherings until Sister Marie-Angélique deemed it time to leave.

They trudged a while until Sister broke the silence, "You looked quite natural with the infant, Elizabeth."

Lost for words, Lizzie replied, "Sister, do you ever...?"

Before she could finish, the nun answered, "Every day, my dear—every day."

Chapter Twelve

In preparation for the special evening, Lizzie had managed to trade bath times with Catherine. Finishing her bath, she donned her robe and took advantage of the mirror to arrange her hair, a task rarely necessary in Deerfield.

"Something special tonight?" Turning she saw Sarah-Bee. Always busy with the baby or going to meet her husband, Sarah-Bee seldom visited with her old friends.

"Yes," Lizzie replied, "I'm going to the guildhall."

Sarah-Bee took the comb, "Let me do that." She began to fashion Lizzie's hair saying, "I wish we could get out more, but it's difficult with our living arrangements. Sister is looking for a place for us to live together, and we have spoken to Deacon French. He is hoping to be ransomed and thinks he can include us. Have you talked with him?"

"A little. Actually I think I may stay."

"Stay?" Sarah-Bee sounded aghast.

"Yes, the only person I have left is Sammy, and he is here and…"

"Is there a man?"

"Not really. I am going out tonight but it's nothing special."

Her old friend smiled at her in the mirror, "So there *is* a man."

"Well, maybe…"

Sarah-Bee hugged her old friend, "Good luck, and be careful—I hear these Frenchmen are outrageously forward—and very sexy."

When she was happy with the hair, Lizzie retreated to the dormitory to dress. She had noticed ladies still wearing their Christmas boutonnieres and took hers from the locker, fastening it to her coat.

"Lizzie, this came for you."

She turned to see one of the younger novices with a package. "What is it?" she asked in amazement.

"Don't know, why don't you open it?" Lizzie pulled off the wrapping and the young novice gasped, "They're beautiful! Like the rich ladies wear." Lizzie inspected the boots which were definitely superior to anything she had ever seen. "Put them on!" her young friend suggested. Sitting down she slipped them on effortlessly. Lined with fur, they fit perfectly and were comfortable beyond belief. As she stood, the novice bent down to carefully touch them. "How do they feel?" she asked.

Lizzie thought for a minute, "This must be what it feels like to step into heaven."

Her young friend swooned, "Who are they from?"

"I'm not sure. I know a man who is a cobbler."

"He must want to marry you!"

"Oh, I don't think so." As the Angelus rang, she said, "Oh, dear, I'm going to be late."

When she arrived at the entry, Jean was waiting on a bench. "Sorry I'm late," she gasped, out of breath. He stood, "It's no problem. You look wonderful. You even wore your boutonniere."

She stood silently and finally asked, "Do you like my boots?"

"Are they new?"

She rolled her eyes, "Oh, Jean, you shouldn't have. They are far too good for me."

He smiled, "Nothing is too good for you. Your old boots were worn, did not keep you warm, and were putting a sore on your toe."

"But..."

"It was nothing," he continued, "just extra materials I had in the shop."

"I love them! I think I'll wear them to bed," adding with a worried look, "Do I dare wear them in the snow?"

He laughed, "They're boots— made for the snow."

They stepped out into a clear, frigid evening. The moon lit the way and the streets were crowded with celebrators. The concept of New Year's Day was even more foreign to Lizzie than Christmas as a holiday. England remained one of the few European countries to celebrate it in March, and of course, the Puritans celebrated nothing. "What a nice coincidence you brought the tree," she said.

He smiled, "It was no coincidence. I went out of my way to volunteer in hopes that I would see you again."

Entering the street, Lizzie took his arm, "I don't want to slip."

"You won't slip in those," he said with assurance.

She took his arm with both hands, replying coyly, "I just don't want to take a chance."

The guildhall was more crowded than it had been with Pierre. "I had them hold a small table for us so we can talk," he explained, escorting her to a corner.

"How do you do that?" she asked.

"I paid the manager." Lizzie continued to marvel at the things she never knew.

"Did you enjoy the wine last time?" he asked. Lizzie scarcely remembered it after the shots and beers, but she nodded. "I'll get some." He told her, going to the bar, returning with two glasses and a pitcher.

They touched their glasses in French style and after a sip, she declared, "Now you can tell me about *Brindamour*."

He took another sip before beginning, "A few years back, in France, I decided I wanted to come to the New World. There were three ways to do this: One could be rich—this was unfortunately not me. One could come as an indentured man for three years which was not appealing, or one could join the military. So I did and sailed to Canada with the Company Beaucourt. In the army there is this strange custom of assigning *dit* names. I believe you would call it *nickname* in English. Often it is the name of one's town in France, or sometimes something totally unrelated."

He poured more wine before continuing. "You know what *amour* is?"

She smiled, "I think so."

"Do you know *brin?*" She shook her head. "Well, it is a thin stem—like the stem of your *boutonniere*." She looked perplexed. He continued, "A *brin de paille* is a stalk of straw, and a *brin de fille* is beautiful young girl."

339

Grinning, she asked, "So you were the lover of a beautiful young girl?"

He smiled back, "Not until now."

Her heart skipped a beat, and she felt her face turn red. "At any rate," he concluded, "I am called Fourneau—like the stove, or Brindamour. Like it or not, forever I answer to both."

"What should I use?" she asked.

"I told you before, Jean."

She sipped more wine and inquired, "Did you like the military?" He gave a Gallic shrug, so she asked, "What did you do?"

"Fortunately the army has many boots to be repaired and many feet in need of boots. My father and grandfather were *cordonniers,* who you call cobblers or shoemakers. They had trained me, so I was able to spend most of my time at my trade. At the end of my tour, I left and set up my small shop."

Reaching across, she boldly took his hand, "If my feet are any judge, you are the finest *cordonnier* on earth." Squeezing her hand, he replied, "And you, Madame, are the finest *brin de fille.*" Following a long pause, he suggested, "They have food at the bar, should we go see?" Since most the food she had consumed in France was served by Sister Marie-Clare, she was pleased to have Jean make suggestions. While they ate, she continued to marvel at the food, while Jean explained what they were devouring. They danced, drank wine, talked, held hands and visited with the occasional person who stopped to visit with Jean. It did not escape Lizzie that almost all of them seemed to know who she was.

Leaving the hall, they were greeted by a lightly falling snow, while the moon still made a faint impression in the sky. Looking up, she sighed, "How lovely. Montréal must be the most beautiful city on earth."

He chuckled, "I think there are a few in Europe—but tonight you may be correct." She held his arm even closer. By the time they reached the convent, it had turned to a blizzard as the wind rose and the snow obscured vision at a few feet. Nonetheless, they stood in the tempest staring into each other's eyes. "Thank you for a wonderful time," she whispered.

"Thank you," he replied. And following a moment of indecision, he gave her a brief peck on the cheek. She, in turn, put her arms around his neck and kissed him with a passion. His lips were easier to reach than Andrew's. When she stepped away, they stared again into each other's eyes and she said, "I'll look for you at Mass." And she disappeared into the convent.

In spite of the late hour, she was surprised to see Sister Marie-Angélique sitting on a bench. "Did you have a good time, Elizabeth?" Her smile was still glowing, "Yes, Sister."

"That was quite a kiss." Lizzie's jaw dropped. "I don't miss much," the nun continued. "Who is your *young man?*" Lizzie told her and her expression changed to positive. "I hear he is a fine young man, and the *best* cordonnier in the city."

Holding up her foot, Lizzie supported the nun, "He made my boots."

The nun knelt to examine them. Lizzie had never seen the sister on her knees except to pray. Looking up, she reported, "These must have cost a fortune! How did you pay?"

"They were a gift."

The nun stood, becoming stern, "Oh my, this *is* serious." Leading Lizzie into her office, she said, "If you are contemplating marriage, you must first be baptized. These things take some time. If you like, I shall talk to Father Meriel."

Lizzie was still pondering this but replied, "Yes, Sister."

As she turned to leave, the Sister said, "And Elizabeth."

She turned back, "Yes?"

"Be—careful. I know you have been married, but children out of wedlock are still frowned upon here, just not as much as in New England. Nonetheless, *soyez prudente.*"

Lizzie gave her best *oh, Sister* face and left for bed thinking, *that is one smart woman.*

Chapter Thirteen

Late February, 1705: Montréal, Jean-Paul's Café

The brutal cold having finally ameliorated, snow falling outside the café was actually wet. French toast and tea had become a common after-Mass event for Lizzie and Jean, and although she could not avoid flashes of that terrible time just one year ago, she was doing her best to follow Andrew's order and find the best life she could.

"How are your classes coming?" Jean asked, as he poured the maple syrup. Lizzie had told him in January about her decision to convert. Although he understood the implications for himself, he never mentioned them.

"Very well, Father Meriel says I'm his star pupil."

"I would have expected no less."

"I must say," she added, "Catholicism is much more complicated than Puritanism." She had decided to use the pejorative term as it was better understood in Canada.

"Oh?"

"Yes," she replied, "The only rule Puritans have is, *don't have any fun.*" He grinned, having become accustomed to her sharp wit. When Jean-Paul came with more tea, she changed the subject. "Did you like the army?"

The grin disappeared, "Not at all."

Surprised at the answer, she merely replied, "Oh?"

"Actually, I hated it. I thought armies were to protect people." After a sip of tea, he added, "That is, of course, naïve. If that was all they did, there would be no war. Actually, armies do more harm than good." Reflecting a bit more, he said, "Of course, if they did not, I would have never met you—life is strange."

On their way back to the convent, he said thoughtfully, "I hope I didn't upset you with the talk of armies." Holding his arm tightly, while realizing had it not been for armies and war, she would have never met Andrew, she lied, "Not at all,"

Arriving at the convent, they were greeted with pandemonium as the three young girls were taking advantage of the soft snow, having a snowball fight with boys from the seminary. Lizzie was particularly alarmed when she realized it was Christine Otis and five children from Deerfield. Bursting into the fray, Lizzie shouted, "Stop this at once!" The battle waned as Christine, Thankful and Freedom stood on one side, and Sammy, Thomas French and Thomas Hurst on the other. "What are you children doing? What will Sister say?" At that moment, a snowball struck her directly on the back of the head. Furious, she turned, "What in the world…"

She was silenced by the sight of Sister Marie-Angélique bending to make another snowball. She approached Lizzie, whispering, "Why don't you take Monsieur Fourneau inside, dear? You can *smooch* in private there. I don't want the children corrupted by snowballs and public displays of affection at the same time."

As they entered the vacant foyer, Jean broke into laughter. It was the first time she saw him more than chuckle. "You should have seen your face when you saw Sister."

"Well, I..."

"I guess this is not something they do in Deerfield."

She returned his smile, "Let's *smooch*."

Following a passionate kiss, she said, "I guess I will see you next Sunday. I have work to do."

He buttoned his coat, "I think I'll go out and throw some snowballs."

She laughed, "I guess I'll go with you. If I'm going to be Catholic, I guess I should learn how to have some fun."

* * *

March, 1705: Congregation of Notre Dame, Montréal

Assigned to housekeeping, Lizzie was cleaning the third floor rooms. They were all vacant so she was surprised by a noise coming from one. *Not another raccoon,* she thought. She knocked at the door as Sister had taught her. Hearing no response, she opened to find a surprised Thomas Hurst, buttoning his shirt. "Thomas, whatever are you doing up here?"

"Uh, well... I was helping some of the girls with their lessons and my shirt needed— straightening." Having dealt with Sammy enough to recognize the cat that had swallowed the canary, she scolded, "Thomas, you know you are not allowed up here. Get down to the study room immediately."

Thomas did not need further encouragement as he was out and down the stairs in a flash. Lizzie went immediately to the small anteroom where she found none other than Thankful Stebbins. "Thankful, what are you doing up here?"

"I, uh, came to find Thomas. He had to—straighten his shirt."

Lizzie sighed, "Thankful, you know you are neither supposed to be up here nor fraternizing with the boys."

"Lizzie, we're old enough for boys. This isn't a prison."

"No, it's not, but get back to your studies—and Thankful..?"

Ready to escape, Thankful turned, "Yes?"

"Your smock is on inside-out."

Looking at her dress with chagrin, she thought a minute before entering her defense. "Lizzie, I'm not a child. Abby told me you swam with Andrew before you were married— naked, and she said she did the same with Jacques."

As Lizzie made her own way downstairs, she smiled. Father Meriel had told her that after her baptism, her soul would be clean and she only needed to confess sins committed after that time. Going to the kitchen she found Christine Otis. Having determined that neither Christine nor her mother knew a Willard Otis, Lizzie was more comfortable interacting with them.

"Christine, you are supposed to be in charge of these two new girls. I just found Thankful in the closet with Thomas Hurst."

Christine replied casually, "Lizzie, *these children...*" Lizzie smiled at her attitude to the two young ladies one year her junior, "have never been allowed any freedom. It's

346

natural." Before Lizzie could sputter a response, Christine added, "Besides, I heard you swam naked with your husband before you were married."

Lizzie sighed in desperation, wondering if there was anyone Abby had not shared this information with. "Well—just keep an eye on them."

She abruptly left the room, running into Deacon French. "Oh, Lizzie," he said, "I need a word with you." She waited in anticipation until he whispered, "Can we go into the courtyard?"

The weather had turned delightful. The snow was gone along with most of the ice on the river. Once they were seated on a secluded bench, he reported, "I have just received word from Ensign Sheldon. He and Captain Wells have arrived from Albany. They are currently in the north at Québec negotiating for our ransom. Try to spread the word to *our people* and I will let you know as soon as I know something more. Apparently Sheldon has already found his daughter, Hannah—soon we may be able to go back!"

Lizzie nodded and agreed before escorting him to the door. Once French had left the convent, she returned to the entry thinking to herself, *go back to what?*

"Oh Elizabeth, may I have a word." As she looked up at Sister Marie-Angélique, she reflected on what a busy day this had been. The nun invited her into her office. "I have just spoken to Father Meriel who says you are doing very well in your studies and that he would like to plan your baptism for the end of April. Now there is the question of sponsors, and I suggest we have someone from influential families who can be helpful as life goes on. I have asked Monsieur Pierre LeBer, the painter, along with our novice, Damoiselle Elisabeth LeMoyen. Is this acceptable?"

347

She nodded and was excused, realizing it may no longer be politic for her to spread Deacon French's information. She went to visit Sarah-Bee who graciously agreed to be the messenger.

Chapter Fourteen

April 23, 1705: Congregation of Notre Dame, Montréal

It reminded Lizzie of the fuss and preparations her mother made the evening of the dinner with Andrew and the Smeads, but today she had multiple mothers as a group of nuns and novices gathered to assist dressing her in the Congregation's special white baptismal robe. Prior to the ceremony, Father Meriel had discussed her baptismal name. She knew some of the ladies adopted these names and others continued to be known by their given names.

Marie-Joseph told her, "My given name was Esther. I hated it so I was glad to change."

Father Meriel told her she should take two names and suggested Marie as the first. "The name of the Virgin is very popular and many, if not most, Canadians choose it first. Elisabeth will be fine for the second."

"Was Queen Elizabeth a saint?" she asked.

Meriel looked as he had sudden chest pain. "No, definitely not! *Saint-Elisabeth* was the mother of the Virgin."

The chapel was filled with most of the members and some locals in back including Sammy, Madame Roi and Abby holding young Jacques-René. Behind them sat Jean Fourneau with Makya by the door. As promised, Damoiselle LeMoyen and Monsieur LeBer stood at her side. Father Meriel gave a sermon on the importance of the sacrament that Lizzie feared might rival Reverend Williams in length. Finally he came to the climax, and as he began to pour water, saying, "In the name of the Father…" young Jacques-René de Noyon let out an opera-quality scream. Completing the blessing, Meriel whispered in her ear, "A screaming child is the sign of good luck." Lizzie struggled to suppress her laugh.

Following the ceremony, Meriel led her to a large book, announcing, "You can now enter your name as a church member." Taking the quill, she began with an E. "No!" He said. "You start with Marie." And he took her hand in his and wrote the name. Irritated, she retrieved the quill and began writing Elizabeth. Again he interrupted, "No, the Saint spells her name with an *s,* not a *z!*" Again he took over. When it was done, Lizzie thought it looked like a child's writing, but she was in no position to object.

Following the ceremony, there was a meal in the dining hall where Lizzie sat at the head table with Sister Marie-Angélique, Father Meriel and her two sponsors. Father Meriel gave another overly long blessing and speech on the importance of the event following which Sister Marie-Angélique invited Lizzie to join her in her office.

"Come in, my dear. A beautiful ceremony if I do say so myself—please sit down." As Lizzie sat, Sister stood.

"Now that you are a member of the church your position changes somewhat. We will, of course, aid you on your journey through the other sacraments, but you are now more independent. As long as you live in the convent, you are required to do your work, but you may come and go in your free time as you please—of course, I do like to know where my ladies are."

A knock came at the door, and she rose to answer. "Ah, come in Pierre-Henri." As he entered, Lizzie rose to embrace him, "Makya, how wonderful of you to come—oh, I mean Pierre-Henri."

Sister Marie-Angélique laughed, "You may call him Makya if you like—just don't let Father Meriel hear you."

"Where is Sakari?"

"Home with my *son,*" he announced proudly.

"I'm so pleased."

"I have this for you." He handed her a small package.

Unwrapping it, she said, "It's beautiful!" It was a thin leather strap connected to a very small intricately carved cross. She slipped it over her head. He came to show her, "Medallion under dress, cross on top."

She kissed him again, "I shall never take either off."

He waved off the compliment, "When you have jewel to wear, take it off. Now I go back to my son." And he was gone. She opened the door to watch him leave. Returning to the office, she had tears in her eyes.

"Why, my dear, whatever is the matter?" asked the nun.

Lizzie returned to her seat, "Sister, I have never told this to anyone, but on our march to Montréal, I became sick each morning…" And she continued to relate her story of the grave beneath the spruce tree.

The nun rose and put her hand on Lizzie's shoulder. "And you say Makya said a prayer?"

"Yes, Sister."

She squatted to look Lizzie in the eye. "Praise God. Don't you see? He baptized the child. If you continue on the right path, you shall go to heaven someday, and he or she shall greet you at the gates."

Lizzie dried her eyes and excused herself. As she returned to the dormitory to get her normal clothes, she did not entirely buy the concept but had to admit, she felt a great weight had been lifted.

* * *

May 12, 1705: Montréal

As spring entered full bloom and the hours of daylight expanded, Sammy would come regularly to take his sister on an evening stroll through town. Only a few days before, an agitated Deacon French had arrived at the convent to report that Ensign Sheldon had left for New England. "He managed to secure the release of two of his children, Hannah and Ebenezer, as well as Esther Williams, but that is all—and he will not return until at least next year. It appears there will be no more freedom until then—at the soonest."

But today Sammy seemed excited, "Did you hear there is more news?" He proceeded to tell his sister, "Four of the boys have escaped—Tom Baker, Joe Petty, Marty Kellogg and John Nims who got taken in '03 with Zeb Williams."

"How could that have happened?" Lizzie challenged. "They weren't even staying in the same place."

"Well, I heard," Sammy began, "they all got permission to go to town for that parade two days ago."

"You mean for the Feast of the Blessed Sacrament?"

"Yes, I get those days mixed up," reported Sammy, who was not as up to date on holy days as his recently *saved* sister. "I heard they stole a canoe somewhere."

"A canoe?" she asked incredulously.

"Yes, Brother Guillaume, who grew up with voyageurs, told me they haven't got a chance of surviving without a guide."

She put her arm through her brother's, recognizing he was now taller than Jean. She sighed, "Oh, Sammy what are we to do?"

"What can we do, Liz? I don't even know what we would go home to. Johnny's the only one left, and we aren't even sure he's alive."

"Sammy, what a thing to say!"

"Well, it's true, and he will have his own problems— and Mary, I wouldn't be surprised if she jumps in the river someday."

"Sammy!" She began to understand that her brother had been worrying about the very things she was trying, obviously in vain, to shield him from. He went on, "Hell, Liz…"

"Sammy!"

"It's all right, Sis, you just can't take the *Lord's* name in vain."

She didn't know whether to smile or frown that her brother was now correcting her on commandments. "There is just not any reason to talk like that, Samuel." *Dear God, I sound like our mother.*

"Lizzie, I think we need to make a go of it here. The only thing is I need a job, but my French is not nearly as good as yours."

Lizzie's wheels began to spin. "Very well, Samuel. Today, we've done nothing but speak in English. From now on it's only French. *D'accord?*"

He shrugged in agreement. *"D'accord."*

Chapter Fifteen

Although still cool, the trees were in leaf, the flowers in bloom, and the sky blue, as Montréal again transformed from frozen wilderness to paradise. "I can't wait to see what it's like," Lizzie told Jean while they strolled down the Rue Saint-Charles. Sister Marie-Angélique had finally found a place for the Burt family to live, and Sarah-Bee and her son, Christopher, were now reunited with Benjamin under one roof.

"Oh look," she exclaimed when the new abode came into sight. "He has a shop below, just like you."

Walking up creaking steps to the second floor above the shop where the family lived, they found Sarah-Bee opening the door before they could knock. "Please come in," she invited with enthusiasm.

As roughly built and basic as anything in the city, the residence was a single room. Sitting area and kitchen shared the hearth where a cauldron of food hung cooking, and a bed and small crib were tucked in the corner. Even so, Lizzie swooned, "Oh, Sarah-Bee, it is magnificent!" Benjamin and Jean shook hands while Christopher toddled over and pulled on Lizzie's skirt. She scooped him up for a kiss, setting him down before he could object.

"Come," Benjamin said to Jean, "I'll show you my shop."

All five descended the stairs to enter the main floor. Another single room, even more basic, held a fire pit and a few tools. "It belonged to a harness maker," he explained. "Last year his wife died in childbirth, and this winter he fell though the ice and drowned. A blacksmith down the road had also died last year, so I was able to buy his tools with an agreement to pay his widow as I go." Such was life on the frontier. "What is amazing," he added, "is that at two weeks, I already have work."

Following the brief tour, they returned to the second floor where Jean pulled a bottle out of his pack. "A housewarming gift," he told Benjamin.

"Whatever is it?" Sarah-Bee asked.

"Calvados." Lizzie told her. "It's French—made from apples."

Sarah-Bee took the bottle, "Should we drink it now?"

"Probably not," Lizzie answered with a subtle grin, "It's pretty strong."

After they visited a while, discussing the current poor prospects of ransom, Sarah-Bee served her stew—made in the English fashion—bland. They each finished sipping a small taste of calvados with the responses expected from the hosts. Eventually the two couples said goodbye.

356

On the way home, Lizzie asked, "How can Benjamin be busy? He is foreign and hardly speaks French."

Jean laughed, "Montréal is growing by leaps and bounds. We have added nearly 500 citizens this year alone."

Thinking for a moment, she replied, "That's more people than live—lived in Deerfield."

"Correct. My business is bursting at the seams. I don't know how I will continue without an assistant."

She considered this statement and paused for a moment before making her decision. "My brother, Sammy, has done some leather work."

Jean stopped and stared at her, "You've been keeping this from me? Send the lad over, I'll put him to work."

* * *

One week later: Montréal

It would be considered a bit risqué for Lizzie to visit Jean's house alone, but with Sammy in tow, it was acceptable. A two-story artisan's house like Sarah-Bee's, it was larger and more soundly constructed. Entering through the shop's public door, they found the room clean with the scent of leather. A stove sat in the center while counters ringed the room. Most held works in progress. A large window allowed ample light to enter.

"Greetings," welcomed Jean.

Lizzie tried to look calm. "Have you met Samuel?"

Jean smiled. "Yes, in the snowball fight." He proceeded to give them a tour. Lizzie was pleased Sammy showed great interest and asked several appropriate questions before Jean told him, "I can pay you according to your work. The confraternity of Saint-Crépin has a proposed scale depending on level of skill, but we can determine that after you begin." Following this, Jean asked, "Would you like to see the upstairs?"

"Yes," Sammy answered, taking the pressure off his sister.

Jean led them up the stairs which they found much sturdier than the Burt's. Fronted by a full-length front porch with chairs, it boasted a reasonable view of the neighborhood. The large main room had a table, benches and chairs. It shared the space and the hearth with a well-organized kitchen. Two large windows provided excellent light.

"May I go back down and look at the shop some more?" Sammy finally asked. Lizzie wondered how to reward him.

Jean continued to the bedroom which also opened to the hearth. "It must be warm in winter," she remarked.

"Not if you are all alone," he answered with a telling grin.

There was also a second small room and two diminutive lofts reminiscent of her home in Deerfield. She continued to wander about, attempting to inspect without prying. Seeing a ceramic piece on the small desk, she questioned, "My mother had something like this. Where did you get it?"

"From home, in France—it was a gift when I left for Canada."

"Where did you live in France?"

"A city in central France, called Limoges."

It struck her like lightning. "Did you ever meet an Andrew Stevens?"

He thought for a minute. "I knew an *André Saint-Etienne.* I believe he was an associate of your friend, Abby's, husband—seemed a nice fellow."

Trying to control her emotions, she said softly, "He was my late husband."

The pieces began to connect. Carefully choosing his words, he said softly, "Oh, I see why you miss him so."

She began to sob, collapsing into his arms.

* * *

July, 1705: Montréal

"Sister, in Canada, how does a man ask for a woman in marriage?"

Sister Marie-Angélique suspected Lizzie had stopped by her office with a purpose. "If she lives with her parents," she began, "the man will ask her father."

"What if she has no parents?" The nun had anticipated this question. "Well, if she is of age, he may simply ask her. Why? Do you have something in mind?"

"Oh, well, I don't…"

Sister stood, "I have seen Monsieur Fourneau around a certain amount."

"Oh?" Lizzie asked, trying to appear surprised.

Sister Marie-Angélique could no longer control her laughter. "I've seen this man look at you, dear, and believe me, he is interested. As you may know, young women are a premium in Canada, and you are—well, let us say, this man *will* ask for your hand."

"Then why hasn't he…"

"Oh, he won't ask for a while. You see, when a lady such as you takes the religion, to marry soon after looks as though she was trying to snare the man. I doubt he will ask before Christmas."

Lizzie's disappointment was palpable. "Oh, Sister…"

She took Lizzie's hand. "Be patient, dear, it's not so long—you have your whole life ahead of you."

"Sister, that is what I was told with my first—and he died three months after the marriage." She plopped in the chair, trying to control her sobs.

Sister Marie-Angélique stroked her head in a maternal fashion. "I am confident it will work out, Elisabeth." Looking out the window, she added, "I believe Father Meriel is in our chapel hearing confessions even as we speak. You should hurry along and not miss him."

* * *

At the same time, Jean Fourneau was examining Sammy's work. "This is better, Samuel, but for *this* shoe, the stitches need to be closer and perfectly spaced."

Sammy replied, "When I worked with Mr. Nims in Deerfield, he never made stitches any better than these."

"That may be true for a worker's shoe, but this is for Monsieur Pierre LeBer. He is the man who has done all those paintings in the seminary and convent—as I recall, he was your sister's sponsor at baptism. His family is very rich. He dresses elegantly." Thinking for a moment, he continued, "He is a little *unusual*, however—doesn't seem to have any interest in women. But at any rate, he demands excellent workmanship and is willing to pay dearly for it."

Sammy nodded and Jean added, "We should finish soon. Your sister will be here to walk you home."

Putting the shoe down, Sammy looked up at Jean. "I don't know why she thinks she needs to do that. I can find my own way home."

Jean sat down in a fatherly fashion. "She was very concerned all that time she did not know where you were, and now she is frightened you might disappear again."

"Yes, but she doesn't have to—Did you ever have an older sister?"

Jean laughed, "I had two in France."

"Did they ever treat you..?"

Interrupting with a sly grin, Jean asked him, "Why do you think I came to Canada?"

* * *

Kneeling in the convent's confessional, she began, "Bless me Father, for I have sinned. My last confession was last week." Lizzie found confession the most curious aspect of Catholicism. Instead of asking God for forgiveness, one had to go through an intermediary, and she never knew exactly what to confess. In addition, Sister required that they all confess each week, so she didn't know why she needed to say how long it had been. "I told a lie," she admitted.

"What sort of lie?" Father Meriel asked.

"I told Catherine I liked her hair, but I didn't."

Due to the thin curtain separating sinner from confessor, she did not see his smile as he counselled, "That is sometimes merely an act of kindness and not a lie." It seemed to fit the definition of a lie for her, but she remained silent while he asked, "What else?"

"That's my only sin this week, Father."

"Are you certain?"

"It's only been one week, Father."

"No impure thoughts?" he inquired.

"Oh, no, Father!" Now she had another lie to confess next week.

"Very well," he continued, "say the Lord's Prayer five times and one rosary."

Exiting the confessional, she knew she would have to rush through the rosary to be on time for Sammy.

* * *

By the time she reached Jean's shop, he and Sammy were sitting on the second-floor porch sipping a drink. "Why don't you come up?" Jean called to her. When she reached the porch, he said, "We are having wine, would you care for a glass?" She nodded, and he directed, "Have a seat," as he disappeared into the house. She had not realized on her first visit, but from this vantage, she could see past the houses and the palisade to the river.

When he returned, she complimented the view, and he suggested, "Come, I want to show you something." Sammy stayed seated until he was invited as well. They went up a ladder to one of the lofts where there was a trapdoor to the roof. Through it they found a small platform with a view of both the city and river rivaling that of the convent.

"Jean, this is spectacular."

He put his arm on her shoulder. "I'm glad you like it."

Sammy looked at them and said, "You can kiss—I won't tell."

So they did.

Turning around, she saw a large vacant lot in back. "Is that your land?" she inquired. He nodded and she declared, "Why, you could have a wonderful garden there."

"I know," he admitted, "but I have no time. It is more economical to work more on shoes and buy food at the market or eat at Jean-Paul's." Returning to the house, he suggested, "It is such a gorgeous evening, why don't you and I take a stroll. I suspect Samuel can find his way home." Suddenly he had made everyone happy.

Once they were alone on the walk, he told her, "Samuel's work is quite good for a beginner. I think he has a real talent—if he will pursue it."

"Oh, I think he will." She decided not to mention Sammy's love of fishing.

"Lizzie, I think you need to stop treating him like a small boy. He's actually quite mature and capable."

"Who made you father?"

He laughed, "Sometimes it's good to have a third party."

She took his arm, "I'd like to make you father." He did not reply, and she suddenly realized how that sounded. Fortunately she had another subject to which she could retreat. "I visited Abby yesterday and Madame Roi is having a *soirée*."

"A *soirée*?" He questioned as if it were *castration*.

"Yes, because her son and Jacques are coming home with Monsieur Tonty to see the Governor. She had one last year and invited some of the girls from the convent. She told me I could invite you this year."

"But why would a shoemaker like me go to a rich party?"

"Why would a poor widow like me go?" she countered.

"Poor women are acceptable if they are beautiful. Besides, what would I wear?"

"You *are* going to be rich, look at your shop, and you could wear your army dress uniform—some men did that last year."

"I'll never be rich enough to live in a mansion on Rue Saint-Paul," he replied, "And the uniform gives me nightmares."

She stopped and stepped in front, facing him. "I know— you said you had a formal suit to wear for the special meetings of the confraternity." Sorry he had shared that bit of information, he knew he would not win. "Very well."

Embracing him, she delivered a passionate kiss. "Thank you. I'll do anything you ask."

"Excellent, let's go to Jean-Paul's and have a glass of wine. I need it. In fact, I'll buy you dinner." As they proceeded to the café, she confessed, "The reason I come for Sammy is to see you each day."

Chapter Sixteen

<u>July, 1705: Montréal</u>

O
h, look." Lizzie pointed as they strolled, arm in arm, down the Rue Notre Dame. "A new shop—it seems new places are opening everywhere."

"It's true," Jean replied. "The city is growing in leaps and bounds. I hear there were more than ten new businesses last year alone." In hopes of keeping everyone happy, Jean had suggested that Lizzie call at his shop each day at closing. Once she had ascertained her brother was doing well, he could return to the seminary on his own, and she and Jean could take a nightly promenade.

Reaching the northern extent of the city, they turned as he told her, "I want to stop at my place on the way back, I have something for you." Entering his shop, he took a package from the counter and handed it to her. "These are for you."

"Oh, Jean!" she exclaimed, unwrapping the paper. "They're beautiful, but what would *I* do with such shoes?"

Setting the elegant evening slippers on the counter, he smiled, "Wear them to the *soirée*."

"But…"

"If any of the ladies admire them, tell them they were a gift from me." She shrugged in agreement while he opened the door. Clutching her gift with both hands, they headed towards the convent. She asked, "Did I tell you I convinced Madame Roi to invite Sarah-Lynn Hurst to the party?"

"No—why?"

"She and I were friends at home. Since we came to the convent, she rarely speaks. She's always sullen and withdrawn."

"That doesn't seem too odd—under the circumstances."

"Yes, but her entire family was taken, and they seem to be doing well. Sarah-Lynn says she wants to go back—yet there is nothing for her to return to. I thought if she could meet someone, it might help improve her attitude."

Jean nodded, knowing he should keep his opinion to himself, but finally said, "I always find it's safer to stay out of my friends' affairs." When they reached the convent, she offered, "Well, maybe that's all right—for men."

* * *

One week later: Montréal

"Sarah-Lynn, you look absolutely elegant!" Lizzie told her friend, while they stood admiring themselves in the convent mirror. "I don't know, Lizzie," Sarah-Lynn whined. "I don't think I belong there. What will I do? How will I act?" Looking back in the mirror, she added, "And I look naked!"

"Listen," Lizzie reassured her, "just do as Madame Roi told you and you will be fine. All the ladies dress like this. You'll be surprised. And I'll be there with Jean—just come to me if you have a problem."

Madame Roi and her friends had decided to make this *soirée* a periodic event. It was clear due to the nature of immigration, the male population was growing more rapidly than the female. Seeing this problem in their class of society, they had decided to recruit intelligent young ladies from the convent, many of whom had arrived as captives. Lizzie was surprised when Madame told her how many wives of skilled tradesmen and businessmen had come from this group over the past several years. To this end, Madame had also collected old eveningwear from her peers and donated it to the convent.

"Mademoiselle Hurst? Sister is waiting."

Sarah-Lynn looked to the young novice and answered with a lack of enthusiasm, "Yes, I'm coming." Then turning to Lizzie with less enthusiasm, "I'll see you there."

Before leaving, the novice said to Lizzie, "My, those are beautiful shoes."

Collecting her things, Lizzie started downstairs. Because she had an escort, she would arrive with him at the appointed time, while the unescorted ladies would march over with Sister Marie-Angélique to be in the receiving line early. Forbidden to wait in the entry for a male caller, Lizzie had to sit alone with her thoughts in a small anteroom awaiting the announcement of his arrival.

Eventually Sister Marie-Clare opened the door. "Elisabeth, your young man is here." When Lizzie stood, the nun whispered, "He's a handsome man, where did you find him?"

"We just met," Lizzie said bending to pick up her shawl.

"Well, I would hang on to him," chortled the Sister as she looked down and noted, "Oh my, what beautiful shoes!"

Entering the foyer, she found Jean waiting. He *was* a handsome man. In his dress suit, he could pass for a prince. When he saw her, he declared, "Madame, each time I see you, I think you could never be more beautiful, but then you prove me wrong." She merely smiled and he added, "Nice shoes."

"Do you like them?" she asked coyly.

He chuckled, "Ask me tomorrow." Not certain what he meant, she took his arm.

When they entered the street, she inquired, "Where did you get such a perfect suit?"

"At the guildhall, we have a few good tailors who will trade services."

It wasn't long before they were ascending the stairs to the Rue Saint-Paul mansion. "Elisabeth, how nice of you to come," Madame Roi, said, "and what elegant evening slippers—where did you get them?"

"Monsieur Fourneau made them, Madame."

Turning to Jean, Madame said, "Good evening, sir, I am Madame Roi, welcome."

Jean took her hand, "Thank you Madame. I am Jean Fourneau."

Looking back at Lizzie, she said, "I see. Well, you are obviously talented, Monsieur." Then in a stage whisper Lizzie could overhear, "And you have wonderful taste in women, Monsieur."

They made their way through the rest of the line of society women, only a few of whom were still with their spouses since most of the men had already abandoned the reception for the bar. Each asked Lizzie about her shoes.

The ladies from the convent were gathered at the entrance to the front room where some had already been approached by gentlemen. Father Meriel stepped out of the crowd to greet them and took Jean to show him the bar. Lizzie suppressed her giggles, trying to imagine Reverend Williams in that role.

When Jean returned with two glasses of wine, he told her, "Your friend LeMieux is tending the bar. He said they heard of his good work at the guildhall."

Starting to laugh, she choked on her wine when she heard a ruckus from behind. Turning, she was not surprised to see Pierre Roi along with the Tontys, Jacques de Noyon and Abby. Bringing up the rear were four very rough appearing men. It seemed someone had tried to make them look respectable, but had fallen well short of the mark. Pierre took Lizzie in his arms and gave her a long and passionate kiss, after which he introduced himself to Jean, joking, "I'm actually her brother." He whispered for a while in Jean's ear. She could only imagine what he was saying. He introduced the rest of his party, referring to the four new men by first names only before instructing Lizzie in a voice anyone in the room could hear, "If they ask you to go out to see something—don't go!"

Soon dinner was served. Lizzie was seated on Jean's left. To his right was a society lady who had noticed Lizzie's shoes and was already deep in conversation with Jean about her painful feet. To Lizzie's left was Pierre Roi, next came Father Meriel and then another society lady. Pierre occupied most of his time with Lizzie, but when the Father turned to the lady on his left, Pierre would mischievously refill the clergyman's wine glass. Across the table she noticed Sarah-Lynn seated next to one of Pierre's rugged associates from Détroit. She seemed enthralled with

369

the conversation, and he was equally interested in keeping her wine glass filled.

Once dinner was finished, the music began, drawing the guests to the ballroom. While Lizzie and Jean watched the dancers, three more ladies admired her shoes, and she in return told them they were the work of the talented Monsieur Fourneau. Soon he led her to the floor. As she had discovered at the guildhall party, he was a good dancer, in fact as the evening progressed, it appeared he was among the best.

Fortified by Pierre's wine pouring, Father Meriel took the floor, dancing with a society lady before moving on to the convent crowd. Seeing him snuggle close to Catherine, Lizzie tried to hide her giggles wondering if the Father was experiencing *impure thoughts*. She also noticed Sarah-Lynn dancing close with Pierre's friend. When the musicians took a break, she went to investigate.

Sarah-Lynn's attitude had changed dramatically, "His name is Antoine Tremblay," She reported. "He's a friend of Pierre's from Détroit. He is lots of fun." Then she whispered, "And he's a *real* voyageur."

It was apparent, Sarah-Lynn had a good deal to drink, and Lizzie warned her, "Be careful. You really don't know this man."

When the musicians returned, Pierre had convinced them to play some *folk music.* They complied but were not nearly as adept as the men with makeshift instruments at the guildhall. Nevertheless, the guests loved it. Soon Father Meriel was on the floor but gave up after his second fall. Sarah-Lynn was more successful with Monsieur Tremblay. Later, Lizzie noticed her dancing close to the voyageur who now had his hand far below the customary position on her back. She remembered Pierre's advice but thought Jean would counsel her to stay out of it.

People began to leave before midnight, and Jean suggested he see her home. When she saw the convent girls gathering to depart, she realized Sarah-Lynn was not with them. Surveying the room, she observed Tremblay, too, was missing. Panicked, she asked Jean, "What should we do?"

Thinking for a minute, he concluded, "I think it best you say nothing for the moment."

Lizzie agonized to Jean all the way home. When she went to the dormitory, there was no trace of her friend. Returning to the entry, she waited about an hour before returning, unrelieved, to bed.

* * *

The summer sunshine coming through the high dormitory windows woke her before the Angelus. Enjoying the sun and shadows, she reflected on what a good decision it had been not to drink so much. Suddenly she was shocked to reality—Sarah-Lynn! Jumping from her cot she was relieved to see her friend's cot occupied but, on closer inspection, noticed Sarah-Lynn was snoring and still wearing her gown. Moving stealthily across the room, she shook her friend, whispering, "Sarah-Lynn, wake up."

Opening bloodshot eyes, she groaned and Lizzie continued to whisper, "Get up, you must be ready for chapel soon. Go, take off your gown, put it in the wardrobe and put on your nightshirt." Sarah-Lynn nodded, tried to stand and promptly vomited on the floor. "Go, I'll clean up," Lizzie ordered. When her friend had left, she took a dustpan and managed to get most of the mess into a chamber pot.

When Sarah-Lynn finally returned, she looked more worried. "I don't have my bustier," she whined, sitting back next to Lizzie. "I don't know where it is."

Lizzie could scarcely believe it, "Where did you go?"

She thought, "Somewhere—maybe a tavern?"

Lizzie realized this was getting worse. "Fortin's?" she asked.

"Maybe. I remember standing on a table."

"Sarah-Lynn, did anything *happen*?"

"No, I don't think so. I'd feel it after my first time, wouldn't I?"

Lizzie hung her head, "Usually."

"I feel all right down there. It's my head and stomach killing me."

Just then the Angelus rang.

* * *

Late in the morning Lizzie was cleaning in the dormitory, taking the opportunity to remove any evidence of last night's indiscretion. "Madame Elisabeth?" Looking up, she saw her young novice friend, who continued, "You have a caller in the office."

Rising from her knees and the task at hand, she groaned, "I'll be right down." As she descended the stairs, she wondered if this could be more bad news.

In the office she found Pierre Roi, holding a package while looking the worse for wear.

"Pierre, what happened last night after the party?"

Pierre sat rubbing his head, "When I realized your friend had left with Tremblay, I decided I should look around town. I found them at Fortin's."

"What had happened?" she asked anxiously.

"She was dancing on a table. She wasn't wearing much."

Lizzie sat and rubbed her head, "What *was* she wearing?"

"Her shoes."

"What else?"

He shrugged, "Not much."

"Oh, Pierre," she moaned in her most unhappy tone.

"Well, it could have been worse, Liz. Nothing else happened."

"How can you be certain?"

"I'm sure. I put her clothes back on her and brought her home. My sister was back from the mission and watching the office. She put her in bed." He handed her the package. "I forgot this. I wasn't about to struggle with it last night."

Lizzie opened it and found the wayward bustier. She broke out laughing.

"You said you wanted her to loosen up," he added.

She stood. "Pierre, you are one of a kind—at least I hope you are."

"Well, we are headed back to Détroit tonight. So I suspect your friend is safe." He gave her a platonic kiss on the cheek and left.

That afternoon, she made her standard trip to Jean's shop. "Come in," he invited cheerfully as he opened the door. "We had a busy day today, and I *do* like your new shoes."

She looked at him as if he had two heads, before he explained, "Twelve ladies came today ordering evening slippers similar to yours. I suspect there are many more out there that will be in during the next few days."

Sitting at one of the counters, she asked curiously, "How does that benefit you if you already have all the work you can do?"

"Economics, my dear."

"Economics?"

"Yes," Sammy broke in, anxious to take part. "You see, an evening slipper sells for much more than a regular shoe. If we have a lot of orders, I can do the basic work, and Jean can finish the intricate art work, making each pair different."

She still appeared confused so Jean added, "You see, that way we can produce more shoes than each just doing our own work, and the evening slippers sell for three and four times as much."

The light went on. "Oh my, we—you will be rich."

Pulling her to her feet, "No, my dear, you are correct, *we* shall be rich."

Giving both a hug, she exclaimed, "I have here the two smartest men in North America." Turning, she told Sammy, "Why don't you head home?" Taking Jean's hand, she suggested, "Let's go for a walk, and I'll tell you about *my* day."

Chapter Seventeen

<u>Early October, 1705: Montréal</u>

Turning colors rapidly, the leaves were beginning to fall in earnest. The spectacle in the city could not compare to the cornucopia in the forests of western Massachusetts, but Lizzie loved it all the same, even if it signaled the approaching brutal winter. Holding Jean's arm, she was again content—as she had been in those glorious few weeks before the raid. The scars of the raid would never completely heal, but in her heart she knew life would go on and happiness remained attainable.

Jean's business was thriving. Sammy had become a valuable and, more importantly, a satisfied member of the enterprise. Even her sister-in-law, Mary, had achieved some sense of normalcy. The nuns had arranged for her to see her daughter twice when the girl was brought to town by the tribe. During those bittersweet encounters, they had talked, and Mary had come to grips with the fact her daughter preferred, at least at this point, her current situation.

Nearing the convent, she told Jean, "I think Mary is almost back to normal."

Turning the corner onto Rue Saint-Paul, Jean said, "Be careful what you say." Then pointing, "Isn't that her?"

Mary was pacing in front of the convent, speaking to one of the nuns while throwing her hands up in the air. Fearing the worst, Lizzie ran towards her, "Mary, Mary," she called out, "it's all right—calm down."

Her sister-in-law turned to face her, "No, it is not, Lizzie!"

Trying to remain calm, Lizzie said quietly, "Young Mary…"

Interrupting, Mary exclaimed, "Lizzie, this is not about me or little Mary—it's Mrs. Hurst!"

Still thinking her sister-and-law was raving, she tried to speak but was cut off as Mary shouted. "Sarah-Lynn is gone!"

Attempting to maintain some calm, Lizzie replied, "She can't have just gone. She probably just…"

"Lizzie, her things are gone!" Mary took her by the hand. "Come, talk to Sister."

Entering the office, she saw the nun behind her desk and Mrs. Hurst in a chair, clutching a handkerchief. "Oh, Lizzie," she sobbed, "Thank goodness you're here. Do you know where she is?" Lizzie only shook her head while Mrs. Hurst continued. "She has been so good since she went to that party with you this summer—cheerful, energetic and genuinely interested in her religion and French studies. Before that, all she did was sulk and cry—what could possibly have happened?"

Lizzie had some thoughts but considered it would be wise not to air them at this time. "Are you sure she's gone? Maybe she just took a long walk."

Drying her eyes, Mrs. Hurst responded. "That's what I thought when I awoke this morning, but when she was nowhere to be found, I looked through her things."

"What did you find?"

"Nothing—nothing at all! Everything is gone from her locker."

"Could she be trying to return home?" Lizzie questioned, doubting this was so.

"No," her mother sobbed, "She even took her catechism. She wouldn't take *that* back to New England."

Lizzie took Jean's hand, "Let's go talk to people in town and see if anyone knows anything." Putting her hand on Mrs. Hurst's shoulder, she assured her, "I'm sure she will turn up, don't worry." She walked out with Jean, realizing she now had another lie to confess.

Heading into town, he asked, "You're holding something back, aren't you?"

She actually smiled, remembering how Andrew could read what she was thinking. "You remember those friends of Pierre's at the *soirée*?"

"Yes—the voyageurs."

Nodding, she continued, "I think I'm the only one she talked to, but she was infatuated with them. She told me Antoine Tremblay said he would take her with him some day—but he's gone and no one has seen any of those men since."

They canvassed their friends to no avail. Abby and Madame Roi, along with all their other acquaintances, had heard nothing.

* * *

Three days later: Montréal

Setting her laundered clothes on her cot, Lizzie did a mental inventory for the evening. Jean had invited her to a dance at the guildhall, and she wanted everything to be just right. Before she went for her bath, she should put away the laundry and organize her dress for the evening. Opening her footlocker, she noticed one of her treasured evening slippers was out of place and in it sat a neatly rolled paper. She removed and unrolled it, the writing was English. She had anticipated this, but not expected it here. The dormitory was empty, so she sat on her cot to read.

Dearest Lizzie,

I placed this so you would not find it right away. By now, my mother must realize she cannot come after me. As you have likely surmised, I have gone off to Détroit with Antoine. That day of the party was the beginning of my life—in spite of my foolish actions and being sick in the dormitory. Every day since then has been wonderful as I can now look ahead to a life of adventure—as you have said, a life of fun. I may even go west trapping this year with Antoine. I will likely come visit next year when he comes to Montréal. Tell everyone I love them, especially my family, and tell Mama not to worry.

Love,

Sarah-Lynn

She showed the letter to Jean when he came calling. Once they were on the street, he asked, "What do you plan to do?"

"I must tell Mrs. Hurst, and I suppose Sister," she told him. "I don't know when and how. I think they'll both blame me. Taking her to the *soirée* was my idea."

Putting his arm on her shoulder, he counselled, "I would simply show them the letter. Really I don't think they will blame you. It was her idea—and she said she has never been happier."

"I suppose. But what kind of life will she have? My God, it must be hard."

He held her closer. "Did everyone think it was a good idea for you to marry Andrew?"

"Hardly."

"And was it?"

She put her arm around his waist, "You're so smart. How did I get so lucky?"

He laughed, "How did Sarah-Lynn get so lucky?"

By the time they reached the guildhall, night had fallen and the cold wind threatened the approach of winter, but inside it was warm. The collective members of the various confraternities were a tightly knit group regardless of profession. Many, like Jean, had come to Canada with a military unit and later taken up their trade. It seemed over the past year Lizzie had met almost all the various members and what few spouses there were. She was beginning to feel as much at home here as she did at the convent and in some ways more so than in Deerfield.

As soon as they entered, friends welcomed them to sit at their table. They joined two carpenters, a blacksmith, and a rifle-maker along with their spouses as drinks were poured and the buffet dinner opened. Conversation varied from predictions of winter to the war with the English. Lizzie was happy her new group of friends felt they could discuss this in front of her. She believed it showed their acceptance, and it pleased her. By the time the band assembled, they had concluded winter would be mild, and all politicians were scoundrels and thieves.

The band began, and they danced until the group began to leave. When they stepped out into the rapidly increasing chill, she announced, "I'm not ready to go back to the convent."

"Where would you like to go?" he asked.

Taking his hand, she whispered, "Follow me."

Fortin's Tavern had not changed since her visit with Pierre. In fact, the cliental looked the same and seemed to be wearing the same clothes. They took a table and soon Gervais Fortin arrived. "Two shots and beers," she said with total confidence. After the drinks arrived, she inquired sweetly, "Do you know how to drink this?"

He laughed. "I'm French—but you go first and show me."

She swallowed the shot in one fearless gulp. Shutting her eyes to stop the tears, she threw down the beer and slapped the mug on the table. "Not bad," he complimented and followed suit.

The band was playing when he took her hand, "Let's dance. That drink was more than enough."

They began to dance, and soon other patrons were inviting Lizzie to the floor, some more bold than others. Jean came to her rescue with her coat. "We should leave before you are dancing on the table." She realized it may not have been wise to share that piece of information from the Sarah-Lynn saga.

As they passed his shop, she said sweetly, "Let's go up for a minute and get warm."

"I don't think that's a good idea," he told her.

She pulled his hand and replied with her sexiest style, "I know it's not. Come with me." Once inside he started the fire and lit two candles. She was bold enough to get the wine in the kitchen and pour two glasses.

"Haven't we had enough?" he said in his voice of reason.

She sipped hers with a sly grin, "That depends."

She boldly embraced him with a long passionate kiss, while caressing his back. Then she began to unbutton his shirt. Jean knew this was a very bad idea, but was losing control. Soon they were down to their undergarments when she unbuttoned the front of her slip, guiding his hand to the top of her breast.

"Ouch!" he hollered, jerking his hand away. Examining it, he said, "I was burned!"

Opening her blouse, she looked down at the red mark on her chest, "So was I."

Trying to examine her burn without seeming to inspect her exposed breasts, he asked, "What in the world is that?"

She took the medallion in her hand. It had evidently spent its fury. Pulling a blanket from the bed, she went to a seat by the fire. Holding up the blanket, she said, "Come, I'll tell you." As she snuggled next to him, she told him about Makya and his story as a young boy. "He gave it to me for luck." Holding him, she added, "But now it has given me all the luck I need. It has brought me to you. I would stop wearing it, but it's not mine. It belongs to some man. I don't know who or where he is or if he is still alive or even still in Canada. But I feel I must return it to him."

Returning her embrace, he said, "Elisabeth, will you marry me?"

"You know I will."

"I asked Father Meriel, he thinks we should wait until after Christmas, otherwise…"

"I know, Sister told me. I think it's silly, but I suppose."

Jean continued, "He said we could read the banns after Christmas. We could be married early in February."

"If that's what you want, that is what we shall do." She took his hand and gently placed it on her breast. "See, now that is settled, the medallion is no longer angry."

Chapter Eighteen

<u>Christmas Day, 1705: Montréal</u>

W orking their way north, and away from the jubilant church bells, Lizzie hung tightly to Jean as they made their way through the paths and ruts in the snow. In spite of earlier predictions of a mild winter from the local weather-sages, today's depth was at least double that of last year when the couple made their virgin voyage to Jean-Paul's Café. In spite of being fitted with runners, the carts and carriages still had difficulty.

"What will we do if the snow gets much deeper?" she asked.

"Some of the farms close to town have teams of horses and they can pull a plow to maintain a path. Outside of town, however, sometimes everything stops. The country houses are usually two levels, like mine, so the lower level can shelter the stock and the living quarters are above the snow. Even so, I'm told sometimes they must go to the roof to shovel out the chimney. Canada is not for the faint of heart."

"I'm not faint of heart," she said softly, holding tighter to his arm.

Once they entered the café, she put her coat on the chair so her new boutonniere would show. "Have you heard anything about Sarah-Lynn?" he asked.

"No, Madame Roi wrote to Pierre, but probably won't hear back for a while longer—maybe spring if the winter stays hard."

"Your friend, Monsieur French, stopped by my shop yesterday. He asked if he could come over Wednesday night with a couple other Deerfield people," Jean had stopped calling them *captives,* "to discuss the future. I said he could. He asked if you might attend."

"I could."

"I just hope he is not going to persuade *you* to leave."

She put her hand on his, "He's not *that* persuasive."

* * *

Wednesday, Lizzie appeared at Jean's shop as usual. Deacon French was already there along with Benjamin Burt and Dame Beaman. French indicated he had called the meeting away from the seminary to keep their plans private. "My sources in Montréal tell me Sheldon and Wells are making plans as we speak for a second visit. Once they arrive, there are many issues, and this may take a long while—however, we must be ready to move quickly if necessary. I need each of you to canvass our people to find who is ready to return home. I realize some have indicated a desire to stay, which is their prerogative. They can change their mind, but there are no guarantees.

"One other matter of which you should be aware has come to my attention, and it grieves me greatly. Apparently there is a pirate called *Baptiste...*" French went on to explain things much as Pierre had, adding. "It seems that if *our own* Governor Dudley would release this man, the French are willing to release all captives in French hands. This includes not only our people but many others from previous raids—I always thought Dudley was a *bleeding sot*!" Lizzie almost laughed out loud. It was the closest she had ever heard the man come to profanity.

Following a few questions that revealed Deacon French had no other information, they disbanded. Once they were gone, Lizzie put her arm around Jean, "Can we go upstairs and have a glass of wine?" He gave her a skeptical look but she added coyly, "I'm wearing the medallion so I should be safe." Having met his match, he agreed.

Seated by the fire, he told her, "Benjamin said Sarah-Bee might be pregnant. He hopes it won't be a complication in leaving."

"It won't," she said, "They will be long gone by then." She rose to pour more wine. When he frowned, she asked innocently, "Have you spoken to Father Meriel?"

"Yes," he replied. "He said he'll read the first banns next week. He has set the wedding for February third."

"Wonderful! That's only four weeks." Standing, she took his hand, "Come, I'll take off the medallion. Even if I get pregnant, no one will ever know it wasn't from the night of our marriage."

"You'll have to confess it."

Still pulling on his hand, she said, "I have a system. I'll tell Father I have no more sins this week. Then, next week I confess to a lie. He never asks what they were any more. He thinks my lies are all silly."

Jean frowned, thinking, *must be Puritan logic.* Offering her coat, he said, "Come, I'll walk you home."

* * *

February 3, 1706: Montréal

The preparation for her baptism had taken on the appearance of a minor event as the entire convent was preparing for the wedding. Lizzie found it interesting that these women who had promised to avoid marriage themselves were so excited. But she was thrilled and loved them all.

"They say if you were previously married, you should not wear white," explained Sister Marie-Clare. "But this is your first time in *our church,*" she rationalized, "so it will be fine," adding with her chortle, "In addition, this is the only gown we have."

Marie-Clare accompanied her to the office as Lizzie recalled that fearful uncertain day two years ago. Who could have predicted she would be happy today. She knocked on Sister's door.

"My, don't you look nice?" the nun told her. Holding Lizzie by the shoulders she added, "Elisabeth, you are a beautiful young lady." Suddenly Lizzie was again facing her mother in the make-shift bath chamber of her house.

Choking back tears, she squeaked, "Thank you, Sister."

"Madame LeMoyen has allowed us her carriage," the nun said, as they exited. Lizzie had never been in a real carriage.

Sister Marie-Angélique and Catherine escorted her down the long aisle of Notre Dame where Jean awaited in his good suit. A far cry from her father's front room, the church had never seemed more beautiful than today. Her friends from Deerfield, Jean's friends from Montréal, and the residents of the convent made a sizeable group, although they occupied but a small section of the much larger church. Father Meriel's service was much longer than that of Deacon French in Deerfield.

They had convinced Sister to have a reception at the guildhall in place of the convent. Jean had told Lizzie, "Some of my friends get very nervous in a house filled with nuns."

At the end of the night, no one regretted the decision, everyone dined, drank, and danced. At first the nuns danced with each other, but as the evening wore on, Jean's friends overcame their nun-phobias and began to escort them to the floor, and some of the musically inclined *religieuse* took over from the band—they were surprisingly good.

At the end of the evening, the carriage whisked them back to the convent where Lizzie traded the gown for her own dress. Picking up her small bag containing all her worldly belongings, she kissed her many friends and headed with Jean through the snowy night into their new life.

As soon as they entered their new home, Jean set to building a fire after which he went to his sideboard and poured two glasses of wine. Turning, he was shocked to see his bride naked from the waist up. She came to him, took the glasses and set them on the table. Taking his hand, she put it gently on the medallion. "See," she said, "Nothing. I guess it's no longer angry," and with a sly grin added, "I suppose Sister is correct—it is a Catholic medallion."

Once their marital energies had been spent, they fell asleep. Her dreams were jagged and disconnected. However, when she awoke to see the sun touching the horizon and hearing her new husband snoring beside her, she knew life would go on and be good as she rose to make breakfast for the first time in two years.

As Jean stood to go to the shop, a knock came to the door. "Makya!" she exclaimed, opening the door. "Whatever…"

Entering, he explained, "I came to see your wedding yesterday. I remained in the back."

"But why?"

"I feared your friends from Massachusetts would not favor my presence." Lizzie considered he was likely correct as he added, "I must go back, my wife has had another child, a girl—we named her Elisabeth."

She kissed him on the cheek, "Thank you."

"Thank you," he responded, and was gone.

Chapter Nineteen

I always associate May with planting," Sarah-Bee said, while the two women were making their way south to the church square where they went twice weekly for the big market.

"I do, too," agreed Lizzie. "This year I'm going to have my own garden in back."

"Not me, we hope to be gone soon."

Lizzie gently brushed the head of Christopher who rode papoose-style on his mother's back. "How are you coming with the new one?"

Putting her hand on her prominent abdomen, Sarah-Bee answered, "Fine, I just hope this one isn't born on a voyage—hopefully we'll be home by then." Looking at her friend's flat belly, she asked, "Have you missed a *monthly* yet?"

Lizzie had been reluctant to say anything but could hold it in no longer. "I haven't had one since the wedding," she whispered as though the world was listening. "And now I'm a little sick in the mornings."

"Oh, Lizzie, how wonderful—but we'll miss it."

"I keep worrying, thinking about the last one."

She had finally shared the sad story with her friend who now reassured her, "Oh, Lizzie, that was because of—you know, this time it will be fine."

"How are you coming with the plans?" Lizzie asked. Once they had confirmed she and Sammy would not be returning to New England, the meetings had been moved to Sarah-Bee's house.

"Deacon French has received word from Ensign Sheldon who is in Québec," Sarah-Bee explained. "He said it could be any time—and we may have to move quickly."

"Is your passenger list complete?"

"I guess, Beamans, Mary and young John Field..." Sarah-Bee rattled off the list she had now committed to memory ending with, "What confuses me is some of those staying. Of course I understand you and Abby, but the Hursts are staying. Mr. and Mrs. Stebbins are coming with young John, but Thankful's staying. Deacon French is going with Mary and young Tom, but not Martha or Freedom. He thinks it is because those three young girls started staying with the rich families and had their heads turned." Lizzie remained silent. She was more conflicted than she let on but had made her decision.

The market was busier than ever. In addition to the growing population, spring produce was beginning to appear, and Lizzie now bought things she would have never previously considered purchasing. Sarah-Bee had been correct—wife of a tradesman was less work than wife of a farmer.

"Aunt Lizzie!" Turning, she saw young Mary Field with her *Indian mother*. Soon there was a crowd as they were joined by Abigail French and Eunice Williams. "Aunt Lizzie," Mary said in excellent French, "have you met *Kahn-Tineta*." She nodded at the Indian while Mary continued, "How are Mother and John?" Not prepared for this encounter, Lizzie resorted to the truth, explaining the plans to return home.

Mary thought for a moment and in very adult fashion, replied, "That will be better for *them*. Tell them, I said hello and that I love them."

Lizzie was able to control herself until they moved on before collapsing in waves of sobs. Sarah-Bee came to console her, and once she was composed, they headed home.

* * *

"How are my boys?" she asked, as she came into the shop giving each a peck on the cheek as they continued turning out shoes.

"Good, how was the market?" Jean asked.

She sat in the extra chair and poured out the story of Mary Field. As she finished, she sobbed softly, "Jean, why does life have to be so difficult?"

Her husband shrugged, "So it won't be boring?"

She stood and hit him with her scarf. He had made her smile as she realized he was adapting her sense of humor. "I'm going to work in my garden," she told them.

"Oh," Sammy said, "the milkmaid came by and filled your bucket." When she turned to leave, he added, "And, Liz? Don't tell Mary about the market." Now her little brother was giving her advice.

Lizzie retreated to her garden, marveling that she was *buying* milk and someone was *delivering* it. She had tilled most of the soil which had been lying fallow for a while, and had outlined plots for various vegetables. She had even purchased seeds, *who would believe one would buy garden seeds?* She finished planting the carrots, radishes, and other hardy spring crops, resisting the temptation to do more. She knew if there was a bad frost, it would draw an *I told you so* from her husband. Before she rose from her knees, she felt softness against her leg. It was a young black cat. "Hello, where are you from?" The cat continued to purr. Picking it up, she diagnosed, "You're a girl." She went to the house and returned with a small saucer of milk. She had a new friend. "I'll call you Midnight, maybe you will save my life one day—my last cat did."

* * *

May 30, 1706: Montréal

"Jean, someone is at the door!" Her husband barely stirred. *I suppose I have to get it.* Lizzie stood and put on the night shirt she had abandoned in a moment of passion. The sun was peeking on the horizon as she peered out the window. "Sarah-Bee!" she exclaimed, as she opened the door. "What..?"

With Christopher on her back, her friend said, "I only have a minute. Lizzie, we're going!"

"Now?"

"Right now! Benjamin is taking our things to the dock. I had to say goodbye."

"I'll come with you, let me get dressed."

"No!" Her friend said, "We are leaving immediately—Deacon French said no one else is to come, he wants no attention drawn. He came to the convent this morning with the news, then to our house." She kissed Lizzie, "So this is goodbye. Go over to our house and see if there is anything you want. Tell our landlord we have left, but wait a few days."

"I'll go to the convent and say…"

"Don't," her friend interrupted. "They've all gone to the boat already. I must run or we will miss it." Going down the stairs, she called up, "I'll try to contact you if I can, but I don't know how or when—I love you Lizzie!" And she faded into the dawn.

Lizzie sat on the porch chair wearing only the thin nightshirt. *She's gone. My oldest friend, I shall never see her again. They're all gone, Mary and John, Dame Beaman, Deacon French, all the others, gone…I never got to say goodbye.*

She told Jean and left for the convent, arriving at chapel time. Entering quietly, she sat in back. Father Meriel was saying mass. Everything looked unchanged. At the end of service she met Mrs. Hurst in the dining hall. "Sister is going to meet with us after the meal. Stay here." Lizzie nodded and went to get a bowl of Sister Marie-Clare's porridge.

"I am certain you have all heard the news," Sister told them once they were assembled. "I have a list of names of who has left and who has not. Monsieur French asks that you speak of this to no one but yourselves. He is afraid of

393

the government meddling. I don't know what they would do, but sometimes the government works in ways even more mysterious than the Lord.

"The plan is to sail this morning for Port Royal in Acadia. From there they sail to Boston. This will likely take two or more months. We shall pray for their safe passage daily at mass. Should you have questions or concerns, my door is open."

Chapter Twenty

<u>August 1706: Montréal</u>

The north wind had brought relief from the summer doldrums as Lizzie and Abby wandered through the market. "How's Gabi?" Lizzie asked, referring to Marie-Gabriel de Noyon born in March.

"Fat and sassy," Abby replied.

"It must be nice to have nannies," Lizzie observed. Madame Roi's staff often provided this service.

"How are you coming?" Abby asked looking at Lizzie's protruding abdomen.

"Good, so far," Lizzie told her, "especially since Monsieur LeMieux moved next door."

"Why?"

"His new wife is a midwife." Lizzie explained. "Has Madame Roi heard anything about our friends?"

"Oh, yes. Just yesterday she heard they had made it to Port Royal some time ago, but are stopped. Apparently there is some problem with Governor Dudley still not releasing this Baptiste fellow."

Alarmed, Lizzie asked, "What does that mean?"

"Well, no one knows, they may let them go, send them back or keep them there as prisoners."

"Oh, poor Sarah-Bee, with the baby on the way. I'll ask Sister to pray for them." It seemed that would be more effective than doing it herself.

Once home, Lizzie returned to her garden where she could discuss her concerns with Midnight who was a better listener.

* * *

November 1707: Montréal

In spite of her constant fretting and regular nightmares of crosses under spruce trees, Lizzie's pregnancy was as trouble-free as any. When she felt her time was at hand, she assured Jean she could handle it due to her experiences. Three hours later she changed her mind and sent Jean next door for their new neighbor, Madame Casandra LeMieux. An odd counterpoint to her leviathan husband, Casandra was just under five feet and ninety pounds.

Arriving with special potions and salves, she efficiently heated water and went to work. Two hours later, young Marie-Elisabeth Fourneau was screaming. When Lizzie objected to naming the howling soprano after herself, Jean assured her the girl would always be known as Louise, for his favorite aunt in Limoges.

Young Louise was perfect. Her green eyes were bright, her skin clear, her extremities intact, she had a full head of sandy-brown hair, and from the moment she encountered her mother's breast, she was a voracious eater.

* * *

January 1, 1707: Montréal

The annual guildhall party was becoming more popular as more tradesmen had discovered more women among Montréal's many New England females who had decided to remain in Canada and were looking for men with good jobs. On this night Lizzie was joined by Mrs. Hurst, her daughter, Elizabeth, Catherine, and Marie-Joseph, as well as Abby who felt the chronic absence of her man freed her from staying at home. Even Sammy came, escorting one of Pierre Roi's young cousins.

Lizzie had not expected to be able to attend this year, but Madame LeMieux, who had no children, was only too happy to watch young Louise. The only cloud over tonight's festivity was the continued worry about their friends at sea. They had heard rumors earlier that one boat with some refugees had landed in Boston, but the rest remained mired at Port Royal, and there was no information as to who might be with which group.

Following dinner, music and dancing commenced. Lizzie loved dancing with Jean who confessed he had learned a great deal about French social events while a boy in Limoges. "My older brothers," he told her, "played instruments and were hired to play at society events. I went to set up and stayed to watch the activity where I learned dancing and other social graces."

397

When Lizzie pleaded to take a break, she headed for a seat, but before sitting, saw two black-clad figures entering. Sister Marie-Angélique and Marie-Clare worked their way over to Mrs. Hurst. Lizzie and Jean went to investigate.

"We have just received word from people in Détroit." Sister said, as she pulled out a paper. "On November 21, the last of two boats from Port Royal sailed into Boston Harbor. All of *our* people are safely back in New England. It seems some people went in earlier, but the English finally released Baptiste and the rest were sent home." Jean stood and announced the news. Pandemonium soon reigned. Drinks were on the house.

While the dancing resumed, Lizzie sat quietly, pondering. Most of these people were French-Canadian. Many of the men had come to Canada as French soldiers. Someone may have even taken part in the raid. These two nuns who now danced with these men in jubilation and drank toasts to success, belonged to a cult that detested the New England Puritans who in turn, detested the Catholics. But once they had met, they became friends, and they began to care for each other. It was as if the two cultures outside were Montague and Capulet, but inside this room tonight, they were Romeo and Juliet, free from their fearful passage—at least for tonight.

"Why can't the world always be like this?" she asked her husband.

He stood, extending his hand, saying, "I don't know, but tonight, in our little corner of the world, it is—let's dance."

* * *

Spring had again rescued Canada from winter, as Lizzie strolled along the market with Louise on her back. At six months the girl was becoming more curious and active and today she had discovered the two leather cords hanging around her mother's neck. Suddenly she had a firm grasp as she began to choke her mother. "Louise... stop that!" Struggling in vain to release the strangle hold, she began to unfasten the back carrier she had bought from a native lady in the market a few weeks before, but the more she tried to undo the carrier, the more Louise pulled. Unable to solve her problem standing, she ducked into the nearest facility with seats—Fortin's Tavern. Happily the ambiance was more sedate than in the evening, but all tables were taken.

Still struggling, she asked two men at the nearest table "Excuse me, gentlemen, may I sit down?"

They both stood as the older asked with a smile, "Is that child attacking you, Madam?"

Sitting down while trying to remain calm, she sputtered, "No she's just..."

Now into the game, Louise pulled again. "Here," the older man said, "Let me assist you." Unfastening the pack, he held Louise who refused to unleash her mother. Finally he retrieved the straps from her tiny hands. Straightening out the straps, he stopped as though he had seen a ghost.

Lizzie took the baby as the man stared intently at her neck. His eyes were different colors. "Is something wrong?" she asked.

He continued to stare, "No... well, I had a medallion like that once."

399

She now realized Louise had pulled the medallion out from under her dress where it habitually lived. "Oh?" On impulse, she asked, "What happened to it?"

"It's a very old and long story."

"I like old stories."

He smiled. "If you insist." Then referring to his companion, "This is my son, Jean-Baptiste."

"This is my daughter, Louise, I'm Lizzie." She was rarely so bold but now was interested.

"You see my father had a medallion like this," he told her. "When I left France, many years ago, he gave it to me—for luck." She felt a chill. "When our ship reached the Bay of Saint-Laurent, we stopped for rest and water. I went hunting with some men but became lost. Then I encountered an Abenaki man and his young son who had…"

She was mesmerized. The story was that of Makya. When he finished, she told him Makya's story. Removing the medallion, she handed it to him. "This is yours."

As it hit his hand, he jumped, "It still tingles."

Her smile was uncontrollable. He politely tried to refuse, but she insisted. She could sense he was thrilled. When they stood, she inquired, "What is your name?"

"Allard—François Allard. We are here on business. We live in Charlesbourg—near Québec." Putting the medallion around his neck, he shook her hand, thanking her again.

When they left the tavern, she asked Louise, "You knew, didn't you? You knew he was in here and who he was so you pulled it out." Louise gave only a baby giggle as they headed for home. Suddenly Lizzie felt lighter, as if a great weight had been removed.

When they arrived, she was surprised to see Makya on her porch.

Before he could speak, she told him about the encounter in town. Listening carefully as always, he responded, "It is good. It was always his." He stood, pointing to an object covered by a blanket. "I have brought you something." She opened the door as he carried it in, setting it carefully on the table. He motioned for her to remove the blanket. When she did, she was speechless. Finally she whispered, "Where—where did you find it?"

"Market in Trois Rivieres," he responded.

"How much did you..?"

"Nothing. I told the man your story and he gave it." She was again speechless as he added, "Just as the medallion always belonged to this *Allard*, so this has always belonged to you. Sometimes in life there *is* justice." He kissed her gently on the forehead. He had never kissed her before. He turned and was gone.

Lizzie caressed it. In spite of the recent history, her mother's precious chest remained in excellent condition. Opening it carefully, she found it clean and empty. She suspected there would be nothing underneath, but holding her breath, she pushed the knob. Suddenly she was back in her mother's room in Deerfield.

"When I'm gone, these will be yours. I know you will appreciate them and, God-willing, perhaps you will live to a time and place where you can enjoy them publicly."

It was there! It was *all* there, untouched. She removed the pieces, slowly and carefully, inspecting each one. Finally she came to the book, caressing it to her bosom as Dame Beaman had many years before. Suddenly the Dame did not seem gone forever. She placed it carefully on the table and whispered to her daughter, "As long as I have this, I'll always have my mother, the Dame—and Andrew."

Then she put on the jewelry, piece by piece, examining it in the small mirror Jean had given her. Once it was all in place, she took her daughter down to Jean's shop. "Louise and I are going back to town," she announced.

"For what?" he asked, without looking up.

"I have an errand to run—for my mother."

THE END

AFTERWORD

Lizzie and Jean enjoyed a secure marriage, producing six living children. Their seventh, Marie-Josephe, died at birth in 1716 along with her mother. Elizabeth Price-Stevens-Fourneau was 33 years old. Two years later, Jean married Marie Lat, an older, twice-widowed woman with one adult son. They had no children but raised all six of Jean and Lizzie's. Marie died in 1748 and Jean in 1751, he was 72.

Lizzie's fourth daughter, Marguerite, born 1711, married the voyageur Pierre Saint-Aubin from one of the first families of Détroit. They settled a farm at the Grand Marais in Détroit which became the elegant suburb of Grosse Pointe. Their five children went on to help populate the new city with descendants of Elizabeth Price.

Not all redeemed captives returned to Deerfield. Johnny Field took his family to Connecticut to join his brother, as did the Burts with their new son named *Seaborn*, as he was indeed born during the voyage.

At the end of 1706, French-English relations deteriorated, and there were almost no additional captive exchanges or ransoms. In 1711, relations improved and with the Treaty of Utrecht in 1713 most captives remaining in Canada were given the freedom to return if they wished, and several more former captives returned including Sarah-Lynn Hurst, who eventually returned from her voyageur adventure, along with her mother and her mother's new husband. Sammy Price returned as well, joining his stepbrothers in Connecticut.

Abby moved back to Boucherville where she could manage her husband's holdings and continue to bear his children conceived during his occasional visits to Montréal.

Most of the captured children remained with the Iroquois. Mary Field, Eunice Williams, Mercy Carter, Abigail French, and Hannah Hurst married Indian men. Thankful Stebbins and Freedom French married Frenchmen. Martha French married the young stonemason, Jacques Roi. Their grandson became the first Archbishop of Québec.

Read more about the Allard Medallion in the *Allards Series*, books one to eight.

BIBLIOGRAPHY

Baker, C. Alice. *True Stories of New England Captives Carried to Canada during the Old French and Indian Wars.* 1897. Reprint, Bowie, Maryland: Heritage Books, 1990.

Charbonneau, Hubert, Bertrand Desjardins, Jacques Légaré. *Le Programme de recherche en démographie historique (PRDH).* Montréal, (Québec) Canada: Université de Montréal,
.

Colby, Susan Melanie. *With Sword, With Cross, With Plough.* Vancouver, Washington, 2000.

Coleman, Emma Lewis. *New England Captives Carried to Canada Between 1677 and 1760 During the French and Indian Wars.* 2 vols. Portland, Maine: Southwick Press, 1925.

Demos, John. *The Unredeemed Captive: A Family Story from Early America.* New York: First Vintage Books Edition, 1995.

Denissen, The Rev. Fr. Christian. *Genealogy of the French Families of the Detroit River Region.* 2 Vols. Detroit, MI: Burton Historical Collection, 1976, 1987.

Haefeli, Evan and Kevin Sweeny. *Captors and Captives The 1704 French and Indian Raid on Deerfield.* Boston: University of Massachusetts Press, 2003.

Jetté, René. *Dictionnaire Généalogique des Familles du Québec des origines à 1730.* Montréal (Québec), Canada : Les Presses de l'Université de Montréal, 1983.

Parkman, Francis. *Half Century of Conflict of France and England in North America.* New York: Library of America, 1984.

Sheldon, George. *A History of Deerfield, Massachusetts.* Vol. 1, Deerfield: privately printed, 1895.

Simpson, Patricia. *Marguerite Bourgeoys and Montreal, 1640-1665.* Montreal: McGill-Queen's University Press, 1997.

Williams, John. *The Redeemed Captive Returning to Zion.* Bedford, Ma: 1706-7, Reprinted, Applewood Books.

Lifelong resident and student of the Detroit River Region, orthopedic surgeon Wilmont R. Kreis has authored eight acclaimed historical novels along with three medical thrillers, The Corridor, The Pain Doc, and The Labyrinth. He and his wife, Susan, a healthcare attorney, live in Port Huron, Michigan.

www.wilmontkreis.com

40594630R10235

Made in the USA
Charleston, SC
09 April 2015